Piers's
Cadetship

by

J N Cleeve

Considering all developments, things are getting more complicated all the time — for instance, bombsights for bombing from great heights or in cloud and darkness, new navigational devices, new airborne interception devices, and, most recently, the most difficult problem of the lot, the problem of the guided missile.
The most obvious consequence of this increase in complexity is the need for very highly trained technical officers.

Extract from the Air Estimates, 1956–57
delivered by Secretary of State for Air (Mr. Nigel Birch):
Hansard 5 March 1956 → Commons Sitting → SUPPLY

Piers's Cadetship

*The front cover is a composite of a computer generated graphic
assembled by the author and described on page iii of this novel.*

Published & printed in Great Britain by

FastPrint
Publishing
www.fast-print.net/store.php

The moral right of the author has been asserted
A CIP catalogue record of this book is available from the
British Library

ISBN   9781780356907

First Edition

First published 2013 by
FASTPRINT PUBLISHING
Peterborough, England.

Acknowledgments

For the sixth time, I continue to be indebted to my rigorous editor, Deanna Freeman, for her sustained advice in converting my manuscript fable into a readable tale. She helped me strike a balance between history, high level politico-social pressures of the period — real or imagined, a measure of contemporary technology, revision of certain historical and geographical settings in the interest of literary pace, contemporary documentary and correspondence and a degree of gender interaction. The syntactical presentation is hers, any textual imbalance is mine. Equally important, the continuity within the fictional family across thirteen generations and three continents has been rigorously addressed with the aid of Deanna's unfailing memory, thereby allowing the saga's literary hooks to relate to episodes in the five previous *Warranted Land* novels. And, while still needing to be watchful for opportunities laid for future novels since this is could be the penultimate of the *Warranted Land* saga, she has ensured that *Piers's Cadetship* at least matches the style and pleasure of the other novels in the series.

Gladys Page, Jill Iredale and Jackie Renfrey each encouraged my continuance at the keyboard when the author's energy appeared to flag. As the eleven year cycle to construct the *Warranted Land* saga clocked away, these ladies showed interest and support when it was most needed — and discouraged me from laying down my pen. "Why stop now?" they asked. The answer lies in the author's note at the end of this book.

The cover graphic derives from a former Anglo-American signals' site in Berlin, Germany constructed in the 1960s upon an artificial mound of the WWII building rubble. An example cadet in uniform overlays one corner of the image, which also has a representation of the RAF ensign and a wing commander's command pennant. The site, Teuflesberg (Devil's Mountain), closed in 1994 and its signature 300 feet high antenna mast which was maintained by the RAF was removed; at the time of writing, in 2010, the complex had been heavily vandalised. Further detail is at page 288 of this novel.

I appreciate the service and support from my chosen in print on demand publisher: Fastprint Publishing of Peterborough, England. Their ever friendly advice has ensured that *Piers's Cadetship* may be available in hardcopy wherever interest in the *Warranted Land* saga may arise.

And to my ever-patient wife, Jean, who gives me the space and freedom — and not a little encouragement — to convert the first glimmer of '…there's got to be a story there…' to setting the whole thing down on paper.

J N Cleeve
29 March 2013

INTRODUCTION

The Warranted Land Saga, of which this is a part, tells a story of a fictional English-origin family determined to make a new life in the American colonies set against the intriguing characters, episodes and lifestyles of the period spanning the four centuries from the arrival of King James I in England, through the extended chapters of the Anglo-American Wars of Independence between 1771 to 1815, up to the war in Europe between 1943 to 1945 and on towards the 21st century.

The title Warranted Land derives from the inducement of promised wealth by the 17th century English Crown to persuade emigration from an over-populated England to the New World. In exchange for immigration, at the rate of 1 head per 50 acres, the Governor of Maryland was empowered to warrant undeveloped colonial land to any who could raise the funds for the hazardous Atlantic crossing. Later, when Australia replaced America for the exodus from overcrowding in England, the principle of land settlement for population displacement continued and touched on the trading area of the East India Co.

As this novel opens, the sixth within the saga, the tale of one example English family continues. They were not always harmonious, having faced many happy and a few tragic episodes under the umbrella of World War II, as the decades of the mid 20th century rolled by. But a career in the Royal Air Force, following in father's footsteps, was all but inevitable for eldest son Piers. Seeking the opportunity to fly in the era of 'through the sound barrier' held its own challenges. It was the air force way that career paths might deviate from the expected mainstream, but the requirements of specialised secret intelligence present difficulties and rewards of their own.

The Ploughman family is entirely a fictional creation of the author's imagination. Any resemblance between the fictional characters and any person, living or dead, is unintentional. The historical characters are portrayed for the purposes of this novel within fictitious settings and are not intended to be biographical. Many are mentioned in the historical notes at the conclusion of this work. Historical events shown with a full anglicised date: dd mm... yyyy are historically accurate according to public archives; any other date format implies fiction. Certain liberties have been taken with geography for the sake of fictional pace. Family names have retained the old English contemporary spelling; some of the fictitious documents and letters retain the style of the time. In some cases an element of dialect has been used to differentiate between speakers in dialogue sequences.

In this saga, the pivotal decision to emigrate is made in 1659 by a former naval surgeon with a successful London practice. When members of the Ploughman family decided to emigrate to the new American colonies, their lives intertwined with unstoppable forces driving their new communities towards conflict, independence and yet further travel. They could not have foreseen that, within three centuries, fate would place an American Ploughman back on the same land quit by his ancestor and once more handling the family heritage documents written in the 1600s. The saga tells of the proud heritage sustaining the family and its continuity, through 3 previous and 10 subsequent generations, in England, America, the East Indies and on the high seas. The full saga is planned to be presented in six novels, each designed to be free-standing. Any novel in the saga could be read individually, or the whole sequence could be taken in any order, although there is a chronological structure to the six titles:

Warranted Land	broadly 1605 to 1662
Bernard's Law	broadly 1662 to 1730
Rosetta's Rocks	broadly 1752 to 1799
Ada's Troth	broadly 1770 to 1840
Makepiece's Mission	broadly 1943 to 1965
Piers's Cadetship	broadly 1938 to 2001.

The Piers of this — the sixth — title is a son of an RAF technical officer who was born into a family with strong Royal Navy traditions founded in military service in and around the RN Dockyard, Chatham, Kent which stands on the estuary of the River Medway. Piers's RAF officer cadetship will launch him, with his life-long sweetheart, away from his Medway roots into a world that few would ever experience.

Piers's Cadetship

Part One

1937 - 1970

A Bachelor Gay Am I (lyric):

At seventeen he falls in love quite madly with eyes of tender blue
At twenty-four he gets it rather badly with eyes of a different hue
At thirty-five, you'll find him flirting sadly with two or three or more
When he fancies he is passed love
It is then he meets his last love
And he loves her as he's never loved before.

James William Tate 1916,
For the musical: *The Maid of the Mountains.*

Piers's Cadetship

Prologue

The good times of 1938 quickly turned into the worst time to be one and a half years old.

The first memory stayed with Piers for more than 68 years until he was required to write it down during an authors' training workshop. In 1939, his father, William Arthur Ploughman, was about to be commissioned into the embryonic Technical Branch of the RAF, having just failed pilot selection because of colour blindness, and would live through the war and for three decades of peace. Olive Marjorie Ploughman (always known as Marjorie) would wait another year before starting the sister who would be delivered, Piers would remember, in 1941 in the midwife's bag brought to their Stafford home on her bicycle carrier while he played in the street.

There is no doubt that it was Nana's lap in that first memory. A copious warm lap and Piers was wrapped in a sky-blue satin sleeping bag with a pink rabbit sewn on the outside. Father's mother had a special smell which was just like her kitchen on washday; out would come the tin bath and the copper would heat the water. On that 'first day' of his memories, they were in Father's Ford 8 on a family outing and perhaps their last if Father became busy with the looming war with Germany. Grandad Ploughman had been left at home in Gillingham; he was a victim of naval coal stoker's lungs, worsened by asthma, abetted by smoking and the onset of the throat cancer which would kill him in 1944. The outing was to the sea, near Leysdown on the Isle of Sheppey, where the River Medway joins the North Sea; someone was persuaded to take a precious photograph which survived. But Piers did not need the Kodak image for the memory. Family love locked an indelible special moment in his subconscious.

Some days later, it was Sunday 3 September 1939 at just after 11 o'clock, when Neville Chamberlain spoke to the nation. The house windows were open to the garden, somewhere in Kent, close to Father's fighter airfield, when the BBC radio announced that peace was shattered. There have been many reruns of those momentous words, on radio and TV, but there is no doubt that Piers remembered where he was on the day that war was declared. Whenever that broadcast was repeated, the trembling Prime Minister Chamberlain declaring, 'A state of war exists

1

...', Piers's memory cut back to the warm sunshine, to toys down three steps from the backdoor to the grass and the pleasure of a September lawn in the garden of England. If there has to be a justification for an 22 month old boy remembering the day, an explanation must surely lie in the reaction of the adults to the announcement, reinforced every time the air raid warning sounded in the four — of the WWII six — years the family spent in Kent. Under the Luftwaffe's blitz route to London, living close to Chatham dockyard, or near to RAF fighter bases such as West Malling, Tangmere or Manston, under the Kentish skies of condensation trails and searchlights and noise, how could any child forget the trigger for all those countless other memories of war?

As the broadcast was being made, the boy Piers was taking his first steps into infancy. 65 years later, his father's pencil drawing of the 22 months old boy came to light in his papers carefully safeguarded by his devoted mother. That memory of a momentous day would not fade as other remembrances dim with the passage of time. Perhaps, also, the roots were being sewn for a deep interest in the heritage of the Ploughman family which would engage Piers so deeply in the years to come.

Piers aged two years

Chapter 1
1940 ~ Three Candles

Junior technical officers of Royal Air Force Fighter Command spent much time with their squadrons' aircraft. William Ploughman was no exception; he arrived at RAF Tangmere, about three miles from Chichester on his first commissioned posting, at the height of the Battle for France. Simultaneous with his arrival on 10 May 1940, No 145 Squadron flew in their Hurricanes to begin to cover the evacuation of British troops from Dunkirk's beaches. The squadron took part in the Battle of Britain until withdrawn to Scotland in mid-August leaving their groundcrew to support replacement squadrons.

William took the opportunity of bad weather interrupting flying to rent a country cottage close to the airfield and there to install Marjorie and son Piers. The three resident squadrons of Hurricanes were operating to provide air defence for Portsmouth Naval Dockyard and Southampton docks in near constant air operations. Then, on 9 October 1940, No 145 Squadron returned with their 16 additional Hurricanes, to see the Battle of Britain officially end on 31 October 1940. The Luftwaffe had changed its tactics away from direct attack on Fighter Command's airfields.

Young Piers witnessed lots of air activity, the take offs and landings of the RAF fighters and the air-to-air combat in the high Sussex skies. Their cottage was just far enough away from the airfield to escape damage during bombers' attacks. He knew nothing of the occasion when a German Me-110 strafed the airfield or when six ineffective rounds were fired from an airfield bomb crater, by novice Pilot Officer Ploughman, using his revolver sidearm.

The night before 145 Squadron's return, William and Marjorie tucked Piers off to bed early and enjoyed a quiet evening to themselves. A sister for Piers was conceived that night.

Marjorie splashed some of her food coupons for a sponge cake to celebrate Piers's third birthday on November the fifth. Children under 5 had a daily pint of milk and a double supply of eggs; she was pretty sure that she would get her own green ration books when her suspected pregnancy was confirmed. The village store contributed three cake candles from their cherished stock for the occasion.

3

In February 1941, William was summoned to the office of the station's Senior Technical Officer, a hard-pressed Squadron Leader William Whitely. The STO was under continuous pressure to keep the station's aircraft and their support systems to the highest state of availability and readiness. Understandably, he wanted to satisfy the pilots' demands for ultimate performance of their machines, but they had a serious complaint about their otherwise superb Merlin engines cutting out in a dive. The strain showed in his eyes and he thought he ought to be sent for a recovery leave in the same way that the aircrews were having.

"Pilot Officer Ploughman. I have asked you come to see me to tell you that you're being promoted — to Acting Flying Officer paid — effective immediately. Congratulations."

William began to respond, politely, "It's very good of…"

"You've settled well, Ploughman. The Hurricanes are getting into the skies when Sector calls for them."

"Yes, sir. The airmen are pulling out the stops to…"

The STO did not have time to worry about whether the technical airmen were busy or not. "The squadron commanders have told the Station Commander that the battle readiness numbers are good — more kites than pilots." Squadron Leader Whitely was shaking his head to indicate there was more to come.

William knew better than to interrupt *the old man* who would impart whatever the bad news was in his own sweet time. It would have been nice if he'd been invited to sit.

"I've noticed that you pay a lot of attention to 145's aircraft…"

William breathed deeply; was this it? Surely all the station kites got the same treatment without favour.

"… and so you'll be interested to learn that 145 is going to re-equip with Spits."

"That's great, sir. Spitfires are said to have the edge at altitude. Their supercharged Merlins get them above the Me-109s and…"

"You know something about engines, Ploughman? Of course you do; weren't you an Engine Fitter before being commissioned."

"Instructor at the RAF Apprentice College, Halton, sir, and…"

"So you've heard about this problem when the aircraft dive. The Merlin suffers with fuel starvation because the carburettor float gets confused with what is horizontal and what isn't."

"The alternative, sir, direct fuel injection didn't seem so good because of freezing…" This was familiar territory and William was beginning to regain confidence. But something was troubling *the old man.*

"Quite." The STO had it so often; these young officers were forever enthusiastic about their specialist subjects. 'Later, they'll have to broaden their knowledge base, airframes, hydraulic, electrics, guns and, God forbid, radio.' Aloud, the squadron leader said, "It seems the Gerry fighters do not have this problem. Now it seems the Royal Aircraft Establishment has come up with a fix."

"It needs a system to pressurise the carburettor, sir, to maintain constant…"

"That would be a major modification, Ploughman. With 1200 fighters flying and goodness how many others about the world, including whatever we might be giving to the Americans, that will be a big job. We need a fix today. You're the man for the job at Tangmere."

"I can strip a carburettor as well the next man, sir, but I don't have …"

"Hush, young man, and listen." The STO was trying to calm, or at least silence, the young officer in front of him. "I don't expect you have heard of a female engineer, one Beatrice *Tilly* Shilling, once described by a fellow scientist as *a flaming pathfinder of women's lib*; she always rejected any suggestion that as a woman she might be inferior to a man in technical and scientific fields."

William was shaking his head and the STO continued.

"Well, up to now, *Tilly* Shilling's claim to fame was that, in the 1930s, she raced motorcycles around the Brooklands circuit and was awarded the Gold Star for lapping the track at over 100 mph on her Manx Norton[tm] 500. But, more recently, she's been working at Farnborough and has come up with a metal diaphragm with a hole in it to be fitted across the carburettor float chambers. It partly cures the problem of fuel starvation in a dive and has become known as 'Miss Shilling's orifice'. We've got 64 installed engines, 12 spare and 4 spare carbs. Your job…"

Unable to contain his airman's grin, "Blimey, sir, with a label like that the fitters are going to riot."

5

"Your job, Ploughman, if you'll let me finish, is to have them fitted with Miss Shilling's orifice diaphragm by the end of March — beginning with the Spits of 145."

"In 5 weeks, sir? That's a tall order, sir." The grin had vanished.

"You'd better get started then. I'll have a pint on your promotion, in the mess bar, at six tonight." Squadron Leader Whitely nodded a response to Flying Officer Ploughman's smart salute and watched him leave the office.

'He's up to the job' he thought. 'I only hope the Germans hold off long enough for us to complete it before Fighter Command starts jumping up and down.'

*   *   *

"Goodbye, Marjorie. I'll get there as quickly as I can. I've been saving the petrol ration for the car. You'll be safer in Stafford." William kissed his wife and ceremoniously shook hands with a 3½ years old son who didn't want to be kissed. At just after nine o'clock on May the fifth, seven months pregnant Marjorie with two suitcases and an active boy, rode the London bound train from Chichester, to arrive in an air raid. There were no porters and no assistance was offered. Marjorie had to make her own way to the taxi rank, doing her best to control Piers across the broad Waterloo concourse until they were able to climb aboard a black cab for Euston station. Their journey north was far from pleasant; a crowded train, many stops presumably because of enemy air activity so that it was after 6 pm when they arrived at Stafford where they had to wait for a taxi to the house. Fortunately, the warden had left the front door key with a neighbour who provided a cup of tea, and some beans on toast for Piers, before they retired to their new home.

On Majorie's due date, the 13th of July 1941, Piers was playing in the street in a pedal car. No through traffic in their cul-de-sac put the boy at risk. A black-caped midwife, riding a bicycle is an image that Piers would later associate with the *Witch of the West* character portrayed in *The Wizard of Oz* movie, is how Piers rationalised Gaenor being born at home. The midwife took the boy to see his sister and to give his mother a kiss until his father could get home. His father let him play outside, in the brightness of double summer time, until long past his normal bedtime and the boy did not stay awake for the bedtime story to finish.

The family would not remain at Stafford long; William's duties took him to the installation and trials unit for the development of airborne interception radar. Here his activities were secret and his responsibilities had the added burden of promotion and movement to several, albeit dispersed, fighter stations throughout Great Britain and Northern Ireland. Father was at home very little, Mother was having difficulty coping with the two children so it was decided they would take a house in Gillingham to be near Aunt Vie Chandler — the same place he'd heard war being declared.

It was in Gillingham that Piers began to appreciate the realities of war. Few nights passed without the air raid warning sounding; sometimes the heavy crump of anti-aircraft guns could be heard or the sickening thud of bombs falling on Chatham only two miles away. During the air raids, the family crouched under the stairs, it being thought to be the safest place. It was too cold and damp and spidery to go down the garden to the Anderson shelter. Sometimes at night, Marjorie or Vie would take him out to see the searchlights probing the skies and on one night they clearly illuminated nearby barrage balloons. They were watching one night when a balloon broke loose and the searchlights tracked it out over the Thames Estuary.

*   *   *

The family home had access, via a footpath cum back alley, to Aunt Vie and Uncle Ray's garden. Here the washing line was attached to a twenty foot high pole with a hoist akin to a flag pole. Piers risked the wrath of the authorities in the form of the local Air Raid Precaution warden resplendent with armband and tin hat denoting his status. Piers constructed a black flag adorned with cutout white skull and crossbones. Now the roof of the air aid shelter could be the deck of his pirate ship, while he defended his family's real estate against all comers.

Uncle Ray's garden had a pair of apple trees, and the neighbour's pears overhung the separating fence. Such lawn as there was could be made into a cricket pitch or simply somewhere to play chase. But Uncle's pride was his strawberry patch, lovingly tended and nourished with the aid of horse droppings collected from the main road. Milk delivery was by horse drawn float carrying milk bottles stowed in crates. Rationed orange juice for the children was also delivered this way. Gaynor and Piers would encourage Uncle Ray, with his shovel and bucket, at first sightings of the desirable fertilizer. The resulting fruit was delicious.

During one collection exercise, Piers asked his uncle what had happened to the steel fence which had run across the top of the garden wall facing the road.

"They come along and cut it off."

"Who cut it off?"

"They said they was from the dockyard. Navy wants the steel for the ships so they came and cut the fences off."

"Did they ask the ARP Warden if they could take your fence, Uncle?"

Uncle Ray pulled a scowling face and shook his head.

"Why do we have Air Raid Precaution wardens, Uncle?"

"Thems as checks our blackouts at night, Piers. We wouldn't want to show them German bombers where we live, would we? So the ARP checks when it gets dark. You sometime hear the wardens holler: 'Get that light out.' And if it's you what's showing a light, passed your blackout curtain, then he'll bang on your door to make sure you know it's you what's doing the showing."

"Are we going to win the war, Uncle?"

" 'course we are, my boy. Let's go and see if your aunt's got some of her strawberry jam for tea."

*   *   *

It was from Gillingham that Piers was taken, for a treat, through Rochester to Maidstone. He was given the front seat on the bus's top deck so that he could see the view as they climbed over Bluebell Hill. They took a different route home, through Snodland, where Piers could see what he thought were rows of tanks being assembled for the American General Patton and his invasion of France.

It was in Gillingham that Piers went to his third school, this lasting the unusual duration of two terms, with two further temporary schools near Nottingham before the family were able to come together again in north east Kent where acting Wing Commander William Ploughman was posted as STO, RAF Manston for the winter months of 1944. It was the closest English airfield to occupied Europe.

Air warfare, in daylight and throughout the night, was about to come much closer to the seven years old boy.

Chapter 2
1944 ~ Airfields and Doodlebugs and a Bicycle Made for One

On October 10th, 1944, William Ploughman loaded his family into his car and drove to the north Kent seaside resort of Birchington. He was posted to be the Senior Technical Officer, RAF Manston which was a busy, possibly the busiest, wartime airfield recovering damaged aircraft able to cross the English Channel from the continent. The airfield had a very long runway and a novel device for burning multiple kerosene flares to disperse fog.

There was plenty of family accommodation standing empty for renting; the German indiscriminate onslaught with their V-1 flying bombs had driven the sensible folk away. These *doodlebugs* had a pulse jet engine which powered the missile's 2000 lbs payload of the explosive Amatol over a nominal range of 200 miles. To the observer on the ground, its distinctive throbbing noise assured continued safety. But, if the engine cut out then they had 15 seconds to take shelter wherever they could. With practice, this was adequate to dive into an air raid shelter, beneath the stairs or under a sturdy table.

Piers, now one month short of seven years, was quickly found a place in his sixth school. Gaenor was too young for school, but there was a neighbour stay-behind mother who opened her doors for three days a week to children between three and five to play with her own family.

When, on the third of December, the Home Guard disbanded, there was widespread hope that England was somehow safe. The British blackout was lifted six days later, although many households kept using the curtains and blinds as protection against the penetrating winter chill. The Allies were driving across northern France and Paris had been liberated. But all this discounted the ongoing V-1 assault and Hitler's new V-2 ballistic missile bombardments.

This was the period when Piers felt closest to his father. Some weekends, William would take his son along the seafront, holding hands, playing *keep your feet dry* avoiding waves, watching the air activity including the hated V-1 passing overhead. When the tide allowed them onto the limited beach, the minefield being still in situ beyond a barbed fence, they had fun collecting shells or pretty pebbles or with a ball. When William was able to get home at children's bedtime, he would do stretching and other athletic exercises, sometimes tell them stories and tuck them into bed. The children would not be aware that their father was going back to the airfield until the small hours, directing recovery operations and moving crashed aircraft, to keep the airfield open — especially in bad weather.

From 15 December, the weather in southern England and the near continent became progressively worse for flying. Fog blanketed southern England and may have contributed to the loss of bandleader Glen Miller in the English Channel. Now the sun seldom burned through the overcast. The wind veered to the north east, off the North Sea, and snow was threatened. By saving rations points, and with a little help from the station's Officers' Mess, the family was able to enjoy a generous wartime Christmas fare: clear noodle soup, cold ham and beef, roast potatoes and vegetable salad, stewed apricots served with hot egg custard, local cheese & biscuits. Presents were few and were cherished the more for that. In the afternoon gloom, the family walked together to the beach promenade and noticed how disturbed the waves seemed to be; their white caps were stained green and the rolling surf looked muddy and somehow defiled. They were pleased to get home to a coal fire treat and the comfort of music on the radio. Outside it began to snow and, later, drift. There would be time enough to worry about that tomorrow. Now there were fresh apples wrapped in tissue paper to enjoy.

*   *   *

The war in Europe came to an abrupt end for the Ploughmans of Birchington. VE day celebrations were hardly over when a message was received warning William he was going to Burma. In many ways this was just one more move on top of so many and it was back to Gillingham again for the family. There was no knowing for how long William would be staying in the Far East. The car had to be sold, since Marjorie did not drive. Tropical uniform had to be procured and medical and dental preparations completed. Piers remembered a big, black, steel trunk with his father's uniforms in it, its top surface with his father's number rank and name in 2 inch high letters. Now Wing Commander W A

Ploughman, just once, let Piers hold his service revolver, then carefully took it to somewhere safe away from the boy. William left Marjorie to cope with childhood illnesses and early education in Prime Minister Clement Atlee's austere post-war Britain; whooping cough, measles, chicken pox and, most significant of all for Piers, asthma all struck in the year that father was abroad. When he returned, he was sent to Staff College, separated again from the family until, in 1947 and just after the fenland floods of earlier that year, William was posted to staff duties at RAF Mildenhall, in Suffolk's fenland, where he could have an on-base married quarter within walking distance of his office.

RAF children were conveyed the two miles to the village primary school in an RAF coach. The *garry* stopped outside *The Bird in Hand* pub for the journey. Both Piers and Gaenor travelled. Piers always fondly remembered Beck Row School. The headmaster was a kindly gentleman who had a private, leather bound collection of the complete diaries of Samuel Pepys. He taught Piers to write with pen and nib on unlined paper. He also encouraged Piers to learn to tell the time and to do arithmetic. Playtime was very active and the boys assisted in digging a deep hole to take the cinders from the coke stoves which heated the classrooms. The BBC's schools programmes had a fascination for the boy and it sowed the seeds of being a good listener for the rest of his life. But most of all Piers remembered his time at Beck Row as when he learned to read real books and newspapers. He would rise early and lie on the lounge floor with the newspaper trying to match the radio news with the newspapers' stories. He developed a fondness for *Just William* and any of Enid Blyton's adventure books and always enjoyed radio adaptations on BBC *Children's Hour*. He was taken to the local cinema to see the current releases which he would remember as being either war aeroplane movies or about *Dick Barton, Special Agent*.

There was little flying from Mildenhall airfield which seemed to accommodate every conceivable sports pitch. His father participated in the throwing events on Station Athletics Day and won prizes for the shot and discus. Slowly, but inexorably, Piers was being steeped in RAF life. When, in October 1948, William was posted to Air Ministry, in London, Piers took the move to his eighth primary school in his stride even if it did mean father spending less time at home.

Nevertheless, Piers did well at his final primary school and passed his 11+ Scholarship exam for admission into Hampton Grammar School. He was climbing the ladder towards a successful adult life.

*   *   *

In anticipation of his 14th birthday and on his own radio, on 25 October 1951, he lay in bed listening to the results as the Conservative Party won a general election and Winston Churchill was elected Prime Minister for his third term. He had to wait for his new bicycle until his actual birthday on the fifth of November. 'His' radio because the family now had a television set and didn't need two sets downstairs. A whole new world opened to the boy: popular music and the hit parade, world and domestic news, the learning opportunities from the features and lectures on the Home Service until late into the evening. He found the chase for the world's air speed record to be enthralling; also, the more adult astronomy lectures and anything to do with space, whilst more challenging, were adjuncts to his mathematics and science preferences at school. This listening complemented his testing popular adult literature by Dennis Wheatley, Agatha Christie and Mick Spillane; but he did not ignore the boys' comics such as *Eagle.*

Piers was indeed streamed into the science subjects at Hampton Grammar School. He participated in school sports, but found that sustained demands for stamina, such as cross country running or distance swimming, were demands his breathing would not support. Tennis or the variant of Fives Handball played at the school were pleasurable and he had a measure of success at both; sprinting and throwing were his disciplines during athletics. When he was permitted to pace himself, he was able to endure as long as any of his fellows. But breathing difficulties and the after effects of juvenile asthma continued to trouble the boy.

Although keeping up with schoolwork, Piers noticed what was going on around him, particularly in the military world. He devoured every detail of British and American pilots breaking the sound barrier and, of course, there were movies about the problems associated with this endeavour. New jet aircraft were engaged in aerial combat over Korea. He took note when Britain first tested a nuclear weapon; although he knew the device was tested off Monte Bello Island, Australia, he was amazed to hear a commentator describe the Royal Navy vessel carrying the device as being 'vapourised' in the explosion. He accepted the second and subsequent tests as routine, little expecting that his future would be so influenced by these weapons. The science and mathematics of these machines had greater relevance to the young mind trying to make sense of it all.

Hampton Grammar offered the opportunity to join the military Combined Cadet Force. Initially, he had to wear Army brown, but quickly he transferred into the RAF troop. He was issued with blue serge jacket and trousers, beret, boots and blue shirt which he was required to wear twice a week to school, through the day and during the after-school evenings. He took a pride in keeping his uniform smart and, in April 1953, Piers Ploughman was promoted to Corporal in the school's CCF(RAF) troop. Naturally, he took especial interest when two British test pilots set a new world's airspeed record: on 7 September 1953, Neville Duke flew at 727.6 mph in a Hawker Hunter F Mk3 at sea level off Littlehampton, UK and just 19 days later, this time at Castel Idris, Tripoli, Libya, Mike Lithgow flew at a new record of 735.7 mph in a Supermarine Swift F Mk4. These men were his heroes and he was sure that flying as a test pilot was what he wanted to do. His albeit short experience in flying a glider at RAF Hornchurch had persuaded him that there was no other option.

But first, CCF(RAF) Corporal Piers Ploughman had drawn the lucky ticket to attend the Coronation of the new Queen.

*   *   *

Father William took Piers to Bentalls[tm] store in Kingston to select the new bicycle. The choice was a Raleigh[tm] sports model with drop handle bars and fitted with a luggage rack and a pair of removable panniers. Father insisted the bicycle had battery lights and a serviceable reflector on the mudguard — Piers insisted that the parental purse purchase a pair of 'cycling shoes' whose only distinctive feature was a leather flap over the laces. Piers was allowed to ride the new bike home, through Bushey Park where the former wartime headquarters had not yet been demolished. Independence had arrived for the 14 year old youth and he took every opportunity to use it.

He enjoyed cycling, often pedalling long journeys of up to 100 miles on a Sunday. Journeys of this length he initially undertook with a school colleague, but later alone. He was learning to enjoy his own company; he saw no point in girls! The return journey from Hampton to the south coast was 105 miles. If a whole day was not available, on most other Sundays he would race the clock from Hampton to Box Hill which was about 26 miles each way — the round trip, if it included a climb to the Box Hill summit, was about 3 hours. The vogue youth activity at the time was the Youth Hostels' Association; Piers went on school organised bicycling holidays into Wales and Scotland — and to West Germany where their route took them into the Harz Mountains and within three miles of the Inner German Border with a strict warning to stay well away.

Piers enjoyed the opportunity to maintain his bicycle. Puncture repairs, cleaning and lubrication, minor modifications such as pedal toe clips all contributed to hands-on experience of basic engineering. He considered, but didn't join, a cycling club. When his parents moved house, late in 1953, he was able to stay at Hampton Grammar School; continuity of education was important. He willingly rode the 4½ miles to school; there was a roadside cycle track for some of the way. Sometimes he rode home for lunch, just because he could. He was developing speed and endurance in this sporting activity and yet there was no suitable outlet to demonstrate now accomplished he was. He was now 4 miles closer to the centre of London, an easy 12 miles along wide, well made roads. A familiarity with the London routes, byways and main sights were developed by close exposure; by mid-1955, Piers had begun to think of London as his home city.

He did not have to prove to anyone that he could ride a bike well. He knew it. In his independent mind that was enough. But in the summer months of 1953, a whole new perspective on life was about to appear.

Chapter 3
1953 ~ Growing Up is Also an Education

The long awaited 2 June 1953 arrived. Queen Elizabeth II's Coronation Day dawned drizzling. Coincidentally, so did news of the conquest of Mount Everest. The 03:30 London Transport route 667 trolleybus from Hampton to Twickenham, the Southern Region train to Richmond and the Underground to Sloane Square were conducted in that half light when day did not want to get out of bed. It was overcast with a hint of a light, penetrating rain showers in the air.

A million people were on the move towards central London, making their way to join 100,000 others camped overnight at procession route vantage points, to catch a fleeting sight of, and maybe a wave from, their Queen. She would be on her way to be crowned, they to be soaked. She would return, they would have mostly dried out.

'Be at the Victoria Memorial by 07:00. The roads will be closed after that. Nearest Underground station is Sloane Square.' The instructions on how to get there were brief. Piers could have cycled the 15 miles from home in under an hour; by public transport it actually took nearer three.

As a Combined Cadet Force(RAF) cadet, turned 15, going to London was still a special adventure. The circumstances don't come much more special than a coronation. 'Well, once in a lifetime special, hers at least,' thought Piers being not altogether sure that he wouldn't rather watch the whole thing on the new television. However, in Air Force uniform, a packed breakfast/lunch in one hand and a firm hold of the trench cape in the other, he made his way to the front of Buckingham Palace.

The Victoria Memorial steps began to fill. The television and long-lens press cameras had the uppermost whole step to themselves. Piers recognised the image makers, BBC TV cameras with rotating turrets and Pathe[tm] news cameras, behind a railing to keep the pressing crowds out. From 06:45 until 10:30, not much of any significance happened, but at least the drizzle stopped. There were lots of comings and goings, soldiers and police, horses and cars, workmen and officials. By the time the route was lined by armed guards and the road was a deserted aisle between crowds 20 deep lining the Mall, the rain soaked gritted surfaces had dried.

There was a cheer — 'she's coming' — a false alarm. It was the first of a dozen horse drawn carriages, conveying pretty, tiara-adorned ladies

15

and uniformed men, going ahead. From their coaches they waved; some in the crowd waved back. 'Who's that?' was whispered, sometimes not quietly. Somewhere in the distance, a military band was playing rousing music.

'She's coming.' This time it was no false alarm. The band struck up the National Anthem and out through the Palace gates came the Golden Coach drawn by 6 white horses. As she went past, she waved at Piers. 'I don't expect she'll remember me.' Those privileged to be crushed on the memorial did not know whether to stand to attention, to cheer, take photographs, salute, sing the National Anthem, or whatever. Piers did them all at once.

She was past his spot in 20 seconds, moving out of camera shot for his black and white film. A follow-up squadron of horse guards brought up the rear. Nearby, someone had a portable radio so the crowd could hear what was going on in the Abbey.

Then she came back. Photographs were impossible from Piers's angle, but he joined in the cheering of the coach anyway. Once the Palace gates were closed, the police allowed the throng to press forward against the railings. Behind those fortunates on the Memorial, the crowds lining the Mall were now advancing 40 abreast towards the Palace. The chant began.

'We want the Queen. We want the Queen.'

It was well into the afternoon, Piers thought she had her lunch while he ate sandwiches, when she did come out on her balcony. She was only small and a long way from where the young cadet had been pushed and shoved by the mêlée. But she waved, absolutely certainly at him this time, and he waved back to wish her a happy day. Later, his developed photographs were found to be not very good so he did not send her a copy.

The return home journey was easier because there was more public transport. Piers got home to find the family and the neighbours sitting in a curtains-drawn room, lights out, watching it all over again on BBC-TV. The pictures were quite clear and did not suffer from heads blocking the view. On the living-room screen, there was no sense of it having rained and the assembled group didn't want to be bothered with such details.

But she looked happy that day. "A radiant Queen," one commentator said.

Piers thought, 'It must have been the wave she got from the likes of me that made her day. Well, a million people can't be wrong, can they?'

          *   *   *

Just three weeks later, the steel launch hawser slithered over the airfield's grass. Half a mile ahead the cable winch inaudibly belched black exhaust. The taut hawser lifted clear. The white glider shivered in anticipation and began to move. Its young solo pilot checked the wings were level and eased the control column into his stomach. In just a few yards the glider was clear of the ground. Airborne! The glider had no radio. The rush of air and the vibration through the tow cable in the steep climb were the only sounds he could hear.

The closely cropped grass of Royal Air Force Hornchurch fell away from the climbing glider. Once home of Douglas Bader's fighter wing, and the scourge of the Luftwaffe, now the once proud Battle of Britain aerodrome was retired from powered aviation. It was 8 miles from the centre of the City of London and lacked concrete runways. The main role of the former wartime base, in 1953, was now to accommodate the RAF Officers' Selection Unit and aircrew aptitude test facilities for the Royal Air Force and Royal Navy aircrew. It also provided training camps for schools' Combined Cadet Forces (RAF). Cadet Corporal Piers Ploughman, aged 15 years, was undertaking one such 5 day course — glider pilot experience.

'600 feet on the altimeter,' thought the pilot. 'Pull the cable release and watch it fall clear.' The cable's small parachute helped keep the line in tension for efficient coiling on the winch's drum. His interest was, however, in the cockpit, in the flying sensation, in the view. RAF Hornchurch airfield was visible below with the dark River Thames to the south.

"You've shown me you're safe. Try taking it around the circuit. Anyway, I need a cigarette." The instructor had opened the Perspex hood and had climbed out before the student pilot had a chance to reply. "Bring it back in one piece, old lad, there's others want a go!"

'Nose on the horizon. Airspeed's OK. Wings level.' Thoughts make no noise. It was absolutely quiet. The nearest gilders were circling a mile away and much higher.

'Let's do it,' he thought. 'Check the airspace is clear for the turn, then gently to port. Heh! That's good. Check the instruments ... airspace still clear ... concentrate.'

Too young to drink, buy cigarettes, have sex, to vote, drive a car on the road, be hanged for murder, or to join the RAF, the pilot began to sing. He would not remember what he sang only that he shut up when just 15 feet from touchdown. 'Should I keep a watch outside ... or on the instruments ... both?' The resolution to the conundrum did not register in Piers's memory.

'Fly with the left wingtip moving along the runway line. Check airbrakes are in ... check airspeed ... wings level ... rate of descent.' Years later, the cadet pilot could not decide if the discordant singing resulted from pleasure or mounting fear of the approaching touchdown. No-one could have heard it anyway.

'No aircraft ahead.' One thing was certain: this was the most exhilarating moment of the young man's life so far. The die was being cast for a career in flying.

'400 feet, time to turn for landing. Gently does it. We're lined up now. Cross the boundary fence at 200 feet. A touch of airbrakes to knock off the surplus height.' Bump ... bump! The rumble of the single undercarriage wheel shuddered through the glider.

'My God! We're down. We're alive! Hold the wings off the grass as long as possible. We've stopped. Fantastic!' Without a sound the right wing gently settled on the grass. All was calm as the young pilot's heartbeat regained its normal rhythm.

An open Landrover drew up towing the cable for the next launch. Out stepped the smiling instructor.

"Well, young man, congratulations — your first solo. I suppose you'll want to do that again; you'll have to wait for tomorrow. Climb out now and we'll do the paperwork."

As they walked away from the glider the instructor said, "Have you heard about the RAF Flying Scholarship scheme?"

The elated young pilot was too hoarse to reply. His face said it all. The instructor suppressed a grin, knowing how the young man felt. 'Another recruit for the stairway to the stars!' the older man thought. 'Been there, done it and got the T-shirt.'

* * *

With the 4th Form summer exams behind him, Piers could relax. There was the school holiday excursion to Germany to look forward to. The Raleigh[tm] had to be in tip-top condition and Piers decided that a new bell for his handlebars was required. He chose Bentalls[tm] as being likely to have what he needed and he did indeed make the necessary purchase. But he met a school colleague, a tennis partner who was looking for a second boy so that he could take out a girl from the girls' college next to Hampton Grammar. She wanted to take her friend so Dennis Annis had to bring a balancing friend along. A reluctant Piers took some persuading but eventually agreed to support his friend.

The foursome rendezvoused at Molsey Lock on the River Thames. The sun shone and each bought their own choice of ice cream from a vendor. The riverbank provided the excuse to lock their bikes against a suitable railing and walk along the towpath. Presumably seeking some privacy, Dennis needed to steer his girl away from Piers and Sylvia Cuttle who talked about nothing memorable. Eventually, the four reassembled to sit on the riverbank watching ducks and making inconsequential chatter until someone remarked on the time and they made their way back to their bikes. Piers noticed that Dennis had his arm around his girl's waist, he felt no urge to copy the posture.

A phonecall during the following week and this time Dennis Annis and his girl wanted to play tennis. A second, different girl was available; would Piers make up the four? The foursome rendezvoused at the Hampton Wick gate to Bushey Park where the municipal tennis courts were sited. The sun shone and several sets were played: firstly, a boys' pair against the girls, then Dennis with his girl against Piers and Gloria Jackson. Piers had packed four bottles of Vimto[tm] in his cycle panniers so the foursome rode into Bushey Park, settled in some shade, made inconsequential chatter until someone remarked on the time and they collected their bikes to make their way home.

Piers invited Gloria to play tennis with him, without the others, on the next Saturday, but his tennis strength overwhelmed the girl and they parted without agreeing to meet again.

His mother was concerned that Piers was not making headway on the girls' front, but Piers was content. There had been females to chat with on the Dover ferry to Ostende, at the continental youth hostels. One German *mädchen* was particularly attractive, in a shapely girlish sort of way, but Piers did not know what to do with the shapely girlish parts being offered. There was no hurry to learn.

When, towards the end of the summer holiday, William announced he had rented a family caravan for a week, at Polzeath in Cornwall, then the opportunity for an extended cycle ride arose. The 250 miles would sensibly require two overnight stops each way, spare clothes were packed into the panniers. Equipped with four £5 notes, a puncture repair kit and an emergency telephone number, Piers was on the road again.

*   *   *

This was the first time that Piers had ridden alone to stay overnight. He knew there were plenty of 'Bed and Breakfast' places along his route so he could stop when and where he chose. This was an adventure, tiring and not overly hazardous to one who negotiated the streets of London. He was lucky with the weather. As he approached the Cornish coast, it seemed the seagulls cried their welcome as he passed. The undulating roads were quiet by his standard, his machine performed without a problem. But he was pleased when he rode into his terminating caravan park, found his parents' rental because the family car was parked outside and grateful for some home cooking.

Coming home, he left Polzeath at the same time as his parents. He expected to take three days to ride home. However, during the second day, he decided he would try for home. His front tyre decided otherwise. It blew out of the sidewall. No puncture repair kit would fix that rupture in the tube or the damage to the outer casing. Piers wrapped the damage in adhesive tape, finding that the inflation held for just a few minutes only. But the tape meant the front brakes had to be removed so that wheel could go round. This temporary fix was clearly not going to get him home. By good fortune, he passed over a major rail line feeding London; a phone call home to be collected from an agreed railway station and the bike was consigned to the freight car.

A very tired Piers was dunked in a bath. He resolved to better prepare for any future excursion he might be tempted to attempt.

*   *   *

It was Piers's fifth year at Hampton Grammar School. He had to do well this year to ensure selection for the Sixth Form and opportunities to advance to university. Cambridge was ruled out because he had not stayed with the essential qualifying Latin as a subject. But engineering courses at Southampton or Bristol looked to be distinct possibilities. He thought that entry into the Royal Air Force Halton Apprenticeship scheme was a possibility, but his father, having done joined the RAF that way, had his own views on that.

"Why start at the bottom of the ladder when you can start part way up?"

"Well, Dad. How do I do that?"

"First you read this," offering a booklet, "then we'll see about getting you on this scheme. And you'll note that you will be expected to work hard to get the right academics — Maths and Physics at 'Advanced' level."

The pamphlet was about the RAF Flying Scholarship scheme which Piers had first heard about from his gliding instructor at Hornchurch. He thought there might be more information in the CCF(RAF) folders at school and promised his father he would study the matter. It was, perhaps, fortunate that the boy's academic skills aligned with requirements of the scholarship scheme; his 4th and 5th years at school were streamed for science leading to O-level:

physics	English	applied mathematics
chemistry	French	pure mathematics.

The plan was that these would lead, for those who demonstrated the ability, to the 6th and 7th years streamed for science leading to A-level:

pure mathematics	applied mathematics	physics
world affairs	religious affairs.	

On the sports front, Piers gained half-colours for sprint breaststroke at swimming and qualified for a Life Saving Certificate. In athletics, he competed in sprint athletics and throwing. He played rugby for the school in every year, rising to the 2nd XV for the two years he was in the 6th form. He played house level cricket having the distinction of being hit on the head three times by a cricket ball, each time thrown by his own side and once knocking him unconscious for 30 seconds. The social game throughout his whole school life was a variant of fives, quite similar to squash but played without a racquet using a tennis ball and the bare hand. He also continued to play tennis, both doubles (occasionally mixed) and singles.

He was involved as a walk-on extra in three school stage productions: *Androcles and the Lion*, *The Merchant of Venice* and *Macbeth,* in 1954, making a particularly impressive witch. In the Combined Cadet Force, in the RAF section, the rank of Corporal brought responsibility for the Corps registry and its armoury of rifles; he attained the 'marksman' qualification for rifle shooting.

With the neighbouring Lady Eleanor Hollies Girls School, the two 6th forms combined to learn ballroom dancing. Piers never found out how many of the girls volunteered, but there usually enough partners. It was here that Gloria Jackson and Sylvia Cuttle crossed his path again. Close proximity to theirs and others' charms triggered whatever latent masculine juices lay dormant in the boy's teenage body. Quite suddenly girls had become interesting; he thought it was time to find out more about these strange creatures. But not at any price! An American named Frank K. Everest had flown a North American F-100 Super Sabre at 755.1 miles per hour, just five mph shy of the speed of sound and the British needed to get ahead.

'Girls? OK, but first, what was it that Father said about Flying Scholarships?'

Chapter 4
1954 ~ Sixth Formers Have to Dance

Shortly after the family move to Twickenham, Piers had to go to a newsagent for his mother's weekly magazine. He decided to stop for a cold drink in a lane which ran from the main High Street towards the River Thames. Mother's magazine held no interest for Piers — no sports, a few advertisements for lingerie, who cares about crockery, anyway?

The attractive blonde was seated in Henrico's Coffee Bar with her back to the wall, facing onto the main open area where Piers was seated. If she noticed Piers, it did not show in her body language. She was talking with a female teenage friend dressed in a dark cardigan. Piers noticed two things about the enthusiastic conversation: it was one-sided and the blonde receiving head, generally facing towards him, above a white cotton, open collar, blouse never stopped moving. Neither did her eyes; the chin turned to the left and the eyes surveyed to the right. And vice versa. All the while, whatever the couple were talking about, their topic engrossed the couple sufficient to generate an occasional chuckle, smile or, once, a girlish giggle. Piers concluded they were sixteen, attractive in a girl sort of way and probably from the local girls' school in Richmond — St Margaret's High School. Blondie's cropped hair seemed full of natural curls over a long soft throat.

Piers decided he liked girls' throats. He'd check mother's magazine, later... After all, he's got the real thing here.

Shy Piers lacked the confidence, or male support, to join the girls' table. They'd probably want refills for their coffee and he couldn't afford that. After all, he was going to the movie that afternoon and that had to take priority for his pocket money.

What was it that Father said, 'Take care when your penny bun costs two pence...'?

Blondie's eyes still engaged her still talking colleague, even through her Danish pastry. If those transiting eyes registered his presence they did not appear to dwell. Of Blondie's companion, Piers could see only her unribboned hair reaching below her collar. He didn't care. He tried to avoid goggling as Blondie's image registered for all his attention as she cupped her beaker on the tabletop with long fingers.

23

Piers decided he liked long delicate fingers. The magazine…? Perhaps there would be long fingers for comparison?

'I've got to get a ticket to their Autumn Dance,' he thought. 'Who do I know that can get me in?' He was trying not to stare. 'I wonder if Mum will sub me for the ticket.'

Blondie's head was now rested on the hand supported by the elbow leaning on the table. Her eyes listened to her companion, her smile responded showing perfect teeth. Piers couldn't hear anything of their conversation. He was unaware, at that moment, he was looking at the rest of his life.

Piers was tidying his table when Blondie rubbed an upper eyelid with a finger. Her sea-green eyes never faltered from her companion who glanced sideways for an instant, her profile square to Piers's observation.

Piers was convinced he had made the right choice.

*   *   *

It was Sylvia Cuttle who phoned. She wanted a partner to take her the Thames Ditton Barn Dance on Saturday. "Would Piers like to come? Dutch treat, of course."

The almost reluctant, decidedly shy, Piers agreed. Sylvia attended the wrong school for Piers's purposes. Appropriate arrangements were made, the couple would travel by trolley bus and, "Yes, it will be all right to leave your bike at my house." The couple went to the dance, danced some, won a spot prize and left to catch the last trolley bus home. Sylvia Cuttle made small talk while the couple stood in the shadows of her house porch, Piers said goodnight and Sylvia went indoors. Neither attempted a teenage kiss. There was no discussion about a further date.

Piers thought the evening was pleasant; Sylvia was quite good looking — in a girlish teenage sort of way — but nothing really special. He purged strange feelings (not yet being aware of the influence of testosterone) out of his blood with a vigorous bike transit to Twickenham. As he parked his machine in the garage, he thought about Blondie.

Piers decided there was no harm in looking at the menu, maybe even trying this kissing business that they did in the movies. He would keep his special attention for Blondie. Yes, he had made the right choice. 'I've got to find out her name.' But he did not get a ticket to the St Margaret's Autumn Dance.

*   *   *

It was approaching Christmas and the sixth formers were looking for ways of earning a pocket money boost. For some in Piers's sixth form class, that meant becoming a part-time postman with the GPO. The Twickenham sorting office was easily accessible from the bus and train routes for those that didn't want to use their bicycles. The tedious business of form filling put Piers off, but a classmate called Graham Hunter, who happened to share Piers's interests in rugby and tennis, had become friendly with a sixth form part-time postman called Joy Wakefield. Graham wanted to take her to a New Year's Eve dance and they decided that one of the community halls' events would do the trick within their limited budget.

But Joy Wakefield's father would not let her out, to such a late hour, without female company. No amount of pleading that Graham was a nice boy could carry the day. So Graham thought of a solution which he presented to Joy.

"Listen, you need a chaperone. What's wrong with Helen Blythe? She'll be discreet and push off if she's in the way. I'm sure I can find a date for her if she hasn't got someone already."

"Who?" Joy was sceptical.

"No names at the moment. I'll ask around. You ask Helen if she's up for it."

"He can dance, can't he?"

"I can guarantee it." Joy's conditional agreement limited the choice, but Graham would not be deflcted.

So a blind date was set for an initially reluctant Piers and Helen Blythe, meeting at Graham's home. But when Piers caught first sight of Graham's date, Joy, with companion, Piers could not believe his eyes. Standing there, in a cerise knee length dress was Blondie from the coffee bar. Her eyes seemed to search his, perhaps to weigh up if this was a good idea. But, meanwhile, Graham was making the introductions and doing his best to manoeuvre Joy for some boy-girl interplay.

Piers offered a hand. "Hello, I'm Piers." Their handshake was the gentlest of touches.

"Hello, I'm Helen. I work with Joy... and Graham... at the Post Office when I'm not at St Margaret's."

"Oh, yes. I didn't get a Xmas job. I keep pretty busy, though, making model aeroplanes out of balsa wood."

"That sounds interesting; do you...? Her enquiry was cut short.

"Come on you two," interrupted Graham. "We can leave our bikes here and walk round to the hall. It's only a couple of hundred yards. Come on; you can chat while we walk."

Three and a half hours later and the witching hour arrived. New Year's traditional exchanges of kisses all round, as the clock chimed twelve, took on a new dimension when Piers kissed Helen. The others were entirely platonic, but it did not feel that way to Piers when his partner reached for a second.

Helen said, "I shall have to go soon. I have to ride back to Hampton Wick, close to the Kingston Bridge. I don't want to be too late, my Dad will be worried."

"I'll ride you home. I mean, I'll ride my bike home with you... to see you get there safely... if you like." He was holding her waist even though she was not pulling away from him. He was trembling, what was he letting himself in for.?

"That's very kind of you. Are you sure it's not out of your way?" He noticed she was searching his eyes for his innermost thoughts. He was so confused in his shyness that he could not have described them if they even existed. He couldn't take his hands off her.

"It's not out of my way. I'd like to see you home. It's the least I can do for my date..." 'Did she notice the lie? I'll have to ride all the way back here to get home.'

"Oh," she breathed sweetly over his hopeful mouth.

"...my blind date," he repeated, "and I've got to find out where you live so that I can find you tomorrow when I come to take you out to the cinema. Today... yes, after midnight... later today... for the matinee."

"Oh!" Her eyes had closed as she waited for a kiss. She didn't notice her repeat.

"Have you seen *White Christmas*? Bing Crosby and Danny Kaye... would you like to see it, with me?" The kiss was sweet; the next date was a formality with only the details to be worked out.

Piers and Helen's courtship had begun. It would last for 7½ years, through their final school years and colleges, until their marriage in 1961. But before all that, Piers had to do something about the result of his attendance at the Officer and Aircrew Selection Centre, RAF Hornchurch which had not come out the way he wanted.

Chapter 5
1954 ~ Officer and Aircrew Selection Centre, RAF Hornchurch

Piers's second visit to RAF Hornchurch came twelve months after the glider course — this time to the Aircrew Selection Centre which doubled as the RAF Officer Selection Centre. He later learned the RAF had deployed the gliders to another airfield further from London. Piers's application for an RAF Flying Scholarship had the support from his headmaster and Piers duly applied. His father had warned him that he would be asked why he wanted to fly? He had better have a strong answer.

Irrespective of age, ethnicity or state of health, all candidates were processed through the same routine. Having travelled for two hours across London to arrive at 10:30, an hour's worth of form filling, mostly requiring answers to the same questions, was rather tedious. Piers thought of asking for a sheet of carbon paper to save having to write his name and address, sex and date of birth so many times. A cursory health check was followed by a rudimentary intelligence and arithmetic test using the 'tick the correct box of five choices' type. That weeded out the obvious no-hopers. There followed some dexterity and observational tests, loosely introduced as aptitude tests, which were marginally more interesting intended to be followed by food and a night's sleep before the promised leadership tests the next day.

"Before you go, we'll do the medical checks now." It became obvious to Piers that some candidates were too mature to be seeking scholarships, but were here on the same routine used to select potential aircrew or officer material.

There were fifteen candidates, including four candidates for the Fleet Air Arm, being herded through doors hiding dental, optical, genital, breathing and heart probing devices operated by bored National Service technicians. Piers had to repeat the answers to the arrival questionnaire about childhood asthma, but it seemed there was no issue with this aspect of his medical condition even if a second specialist came in to check his nose and breathing. His blood pressure was a touch high for his age, but these were trying conditions and everyone recorded high readings! The colour blindness check was no problem, but there was something that did not gel with his stereo perception.

27

"Did you come here by train?" questioned the RAF technician, looking away from his test instrument.

"Yes. I took the Underground from the Embankment."

"That's 29 stops to Elm Park."

"I counted them. The flashing sunlight was very tiring as we got beyond Whitechapel. I had to stop reading my book. Dennis Wheatley…"

"Your eyes look tired. Eye strain is a common complaint if you come here by train. You shouldn't read on the Underground. I'd say you are normal. Eyes 20/20. Next…"

"Does that mean fit aircrew?"

"That's for the doctors to decide." With a sideways nod, "Now, hop it. Next."

Blow here! Pee there! Are your bowels regular? Any scars, operations, muscular spasms? Cross your legs while I check your reflexes. Cough!

Then it was off to the dormitory barracks, for a freshen up, meal and "…use of the NAAFI bar if you wish. Remember you'll be quite active tomorrow morning, so don't over do it." Half the group, who had arrived with Piers for his initial paperwork, were presumably chopped and no longer with the group; there were now nine candidates, one being a serving airman although he wore civilian clothes throughout.

The following morning, immediately after breakfast, the surviving candidates divided into two groups and were marshalled into syndicate rooms. There were two assessing officers in Piers's room, one a WRAF flight officer wearing the same rank insignia as a male flight lieutenant, without wings brevet, noted Piers. The lead was taken by a male flight lieutenant who launched contentious ideas for discussion. It was obvious there was no correct answer to any of these topics; the aim was to get the candidates talking and expressing points of view. Piers would later remember such topics as: should the country be developing weapon systems capable of delivering nuclear weapons? Or, given only two lifejackets but three characters on a sinking boat, viz a pre- eminent musician, a politician, and a child, who would be allowed to drown? Or, should police women be permitted to carry firearms? To finish the syndicate discussion, the question was asked: what was the greatest invention of the 20th century? Piers thought they might agree on his choice, of atomic power, but the group settled for penicillin.

Piers was glad the discussion session was finished. It was, to his mind, a pointless period. What had it to do with flying? The group was transported to a hangar with lots of areas curtained off. This was to be the leadership assessment phase. A number of tasks were set which involved the use of apparatus and team work, to overcome a problem. The candidates were instructed to put on overalls and a yellow visibility vest carrying an identifying number.

"Ploughman, you go first." Four other candidates were selected to constitute Piers's team. "In this test, you have to cross a crocodile infested river. You have to get all your team across using only three oil drums, two lengths of rope and two short planks. You have ten minutes starting now." The mock 'river' was painted on the flat hangar floor and the planks were obviously too short to make a bridge.

With a combination of luck, balance, doing what they were told and sheer strength, the team crossed the river within the time limit. Piers experienced a form of debrief, mainly about how he had wasted time working out his plan and not having got all four oil drums over the river. He was not told if he had passed or failed the test — he did not mention he had started the test with only three oil drums. Why argue?

The candidates then moved to another curtained test area, were given a fresh leader and different set of apparatus to complete a similar task. And so on until everyone had completed their test challenge — some unsuccessfully. Expecting lunch, the candidates returned to the syndicate rooms to sit a second, this time rather more advanced, maths test. Then it really was time for lunch. The candidates were to remain in overalls and numbered vests until they had completed their interviews that afternoon when they would be free to depart.

There was some friendly chatter about the tests until it was assembly for the all important selection interview. The atmosphere in the reception area would have done justice to a dentist's waiting room, all nerves and no conversation. The clock was making a resounding click as the minute hand advanced one notch — the sort of

noise pattern where you wait until it happens; it is going to happen; you know it; then it does and the relief is palpable. On one wall was a painted loudspeaker with the fretwork logo 'Tannoy' clearly visible. The magazines were old copies of flying related publications and a couple of very ancient *Aircraft Recognition* journals marked *For Official Use Only*. There were four interview rooms and Piers had to wait for half an hour before it was his turn. His colleague candidate came out of the room shaking his head; evidently it had not gone well. Piers knocked on the door and entered in response to the invitation.

"Good afternoon, Ploughman. I am Squadron Leader Brazenove and this is Flight Officer Yates." It was the WRAF officer Piers had noticed earlier. "The purpose of this interview is for us to decide if you have what it takes to be an officer or non-commissioned aircrew in the Royal Air Force. Now relax. Just answer the questions and we'll see how we get on. There will be an opportunity for you to ask us about anything you don't understand at the end."

'Surely they can't see my hands sweating. Try deep breathes...' Piers tried to keep his hands still in his lap.

The two officers asked, and made written notes, about school, sport, the local community, books and newspapers, activities as a CCF cadet, any scouting experience, interests and hobbies. The interviewers were encouraging the interviewee to talk. Piers's ambitions began to surface with Sqn Ldr Brazenove asking, "I see you are applying for a Royal Air Force Flying Scholarship. Tell me about that."

So Piers explained that his RAF officer father had told him about the scheme and he appreciated that there were two ways to join the Technical Branch of the RAF. He knew about apprenticeships through Halton, etc, or from university, but he really wanted to fly and that meant becoming a commissioned officer and that, in turn, meant completing sixth form education. A scholarship would help him keep his eye on the ball while his parents were meeting the demands of service life.

"I don't want to do national service," said Piers. "I am hoping for a full time Royal Air Force career through to retirement. The opportunity to be in a University Air Squadron sounds very attractive."

"Very good," prompted the Flight Lieutenant. "But tell me, why do you want to fly?"

Father Ploughman had warned the now nervous candidate months ago. It wasn't a trick question, but the reply he chose to give could affect the outcome of the whole selection process. He had wanted to fly himself in 1940, during World War II but colour-blindness stopped his selection; he survived the war — 'many of my colleagues did not' he had said only once in Piers's hearing. When the interview question eventually was posed, Piers was far from clear how to respond convincingly.

"When I was young, flying seemed a glamorous pursuit. All through the war, and ever since, the RAF is inevitably to the fore in Father's footsteps. The cinema movies and stories about real pilots have made aircrew seem larger than life. From another perspective, flying represents the ultimate freedom; to be able to move in three dimensions is something I yearn for. Gliding taught me that. In swimming, I am offered a limited solution, but the chances of air-tank diving are pretty limited and has some problems of its own; I lost an uncle in a diving accident. My goal is to be a test pilot. The RAF has new aircraft such the Hunter and the Swift breaking the sound barrier, the Comet is showing the future for air transport, and surely man will reach the edge of space by the end of the century. I want to be part of it."

"That's very interesting, young man." Flight Officer Yates was speaking. There was no body language to help Piers know if he had answered satisfactorily. "Thank you. Now, do you have any questions for us?"

"Well, yes sir. What happens next?" His hands, still in his lap, visibly clenched.

'Thank heavens I was looking at him, not her, when I said that,' thought Piers.

Sqn Ldr Brazenove replied, "We need to think about what you have had to say and the result of the tests over the last two days. We'll make a recommendation and there will be a closure interview with the wing commander before you leave. You may take a breath of fresh air now; relax, walk round the airfield. You'll be able to get out of those overalls, too. But be back in the reception room at 16:30 from where you will be called forward and be told the wing commander's decision. Close the door on your way out."

As Piers rose, the squadron leader transferred his attention to the papers in front of him, indicating that the interview was over.

31

At the appointed time, Piers was back in the reception area. A flight sergeant, wearing a uniform blouse with RAF wings over a Distinguished Flying Medal ribbon, was sitting behind a desk shuffling papers. The clock was still making that resounding click as the minute hand advanced one notch. At precisely half past four the flight sergeant looked at his watch, stood, shuffled his papers, sat down again and held his hand waiting for the telephone to ring.

'Just like waiting for the fighters' 'Scramble' call,' thought Piers. The flight sergeant did not have to wait long. The shrill telephone rang just once before the handset was snatched off the carriage.

"Sir," was the all the senior non-commissioned officer said. He stood. He tidied the already tidy sheaf of papers on his desk and went out of the room. He returned within two minutes carrying a single sheet with very little writing on it.

"Right, gentlemen, listen up. In a little while I shall be calling your name and you will come forward to my desk. When I have finished with you, you will go forward to meet the wing commander who will tell you your fate. Now then, there is no rush, the underground trains run until 23:40 from Elm Park so you can easily get to London in time for the milk train from your chosen terminuses to your destinations where you will stop. When you meet the wing commander, you will address him as 'Sir', like what I does, and you does not offer to shake his hand until he does likewise."

The nine 'young gentlemen' were dumbfounded. Surely good English was a pre-requisite of being a pilot? Only, nine? There were more than forty of us yesterday morning.

"Right, when I call your name... you will approach... Mister Ploughman."

"Yes, Flight Sergeant. I'm coming."

"Right. Down the corridor until you comes to the fourth door on the left." The flight sergeant's right hand index finger was pointing vaguely over his shoulder, through a glazed double door labelled 'Fire Exit'. "You can't miss it. It says, 'Wing Commander Brocklebank, Officer Commanding, Officer and Aircrew Selection Centre,' in big bold letters on his door. You knocks confidently, like. And enter on the command: 'Enter'. Do you understand, Mister Ploughman?"

"Yes, Flight Sergeant."

32

"Right. Go on then, lad, and... err... good luck!"

*   *   *

It was getting gloomy as Piers rode the District Line underground train through London and beyond to Richmond. He would take a bus from Richmond station to his home in Twickenham. It was an opportunity to reflect on how his application had gone. It was not comfortable travelling sideways in the carriage; he regretted not buying an *Evening News,* but he'd pick up a discarded copy before the journey was finished.

The detail of the final interview was a bit of a haze. He had not known what to expect as he entered the wing commander's office and was not really sure of what it meant as he left. Surely, he was being given a second chance, it would be in the letter. It was not going to easy telling Father, but... 'Let's go over the whole thing as best I can remember it. One thing, this train is so slow it'll be tomorrow before I get home... well nearly anyway... well, at least it's going to be too late for a meal. I'll get some fish and chips and then phone to let the Mum know what time I'll be in. I'd like to phone Father too, but that's out of the question; I'll see him at the weekend. He'll be worried about me. I wonder how the school will take it?'

"Right, Ploughman." The wing commander had come straight to the point. "This is how we see it. You have shown aptitude for aircrew; your morse code and dexterity assessments are satisfactory. General fitness is good. Your eyesight and symbol recognition are below par for a pilot and the maths test result is only marginal for navigator. We will be writing to offer you training as an Air Signaller."

Piers reacted quickly, "I didn't come here looking to be an Air Signaller. I came here to get a Flying Scholarship for pilot training. I want to be a pilot." Then, as an afterthought, "Sir."

"Now listen, Ploughman. The standard is very high for commissioned service and higher still for pilot. You have not reached that standard although there may come a time when, with a great deal of effort on your part, you'll get there. There is, however, one other point. The ear, nose and throat assessment has identified an issue with your nasal sinus. I am not a medical expert, but to reach the full medical requirements for a modern pilot, your breathing system has to be... let me put it this way... unobstructed. When we write to you, we shall include a letter to your doctor so that you can discuss the situation with him."

33

'News to me... I can run and swim better than most at school... I ride my bike harder than anyone I know. There's nothing wrong with my breathing...' Piers knew he had not got what he was looking for. The rest was just words.

"The RAF needs Air Signallers and you could expect a full career in that branch."

"That means non-commissioned aircrew, sir?"

"Initially, yes, but some Air Signallers go on to demonstrate skills and other qualities required of commissioned officers."

"So that's it, then, sir?"

"I quite understand you are disappointed, Ploughman. We shall not be recommending you for a flying scholarship. That in no way precludes you from completing your time at school and I wish you luck in completing your A-levels. You may, of course, re-apply for commissioned service in a ground branch, for example the RAF Regiment or Supply, but I do recommend you have a word with your doctor before you come back to see us. You only have one second chance here at the OASC and you would not wish to miss out because of a nose problem. You should also speak with your school about whether you will make the grade at A-level for university, particularly if you want to specialise in engineering or the sciences."

"No, I wouldn't want to miss out. Thank you for your advice, sir."

"That's all for now, Ploughman. Speak to the Flight Sergeant on your way out. Goodbye and have a safe journey home."

'He did not even offer a handshake, the cold bastard,' thought Piers as he left the office.

The train rattled, Piers jerking left and right in his seat. The stations passed the dirty windows as the suburban countryside surrendered into London's East End grime. The carriage filled and become unpleasantly overcrowded through central London as the office workers made their way home. Piers was not going to give up his seat. He'd had a lousy day and this was a miserable ending to it. The future he had planned had coming crashing down.

'I did that piloting job OK in the glider. Well, I didn't kill myself or break anything. So I didn't get a scholarship... so what? I got one for Hampton Grammar so what's the problem?' The misery crunched Piers's gut, but there was no way he was going to show it to the pressing crowd around him.

'At least I've got the dance with Sylvia Cuttle to look forward to.' The 'so-what' shrug was obvious to any who bothered to watch the 16 year old. 'She's OK, I suppose... no great shakes. I can't wait to talk to the doctor about my nose... that letter they promised might help. I want to know what that's all about. At least she might have something helpful to say. Oh, sod it...'

The train had passed through tunnels to reach Earls Court interchange station. It seemed to hold for an eternity with the passengers becoming restless. Without warning, the doors slid to a close and onwards they went, rattling over rail forks and out into what passed for fresh air in west London. It was now fully autumn night beyond the carriage windows.

*   *   *

Father Ploughman arrived home after half past eight on the following Friday. He was obviously tired with his journey and was pleased to settle in front of the open coal fire.

"How did you get on at Hornchurch, Son?"

"Not so good, Dad. They said I wasn't a potential pilot and would be offering Air Signaller. I said that was no good to me."

Father's sigh said it all. "Tact was never your strong point, Piers. What else did they say? Colour blindness...?"

"No, that was OK. They said I had to work hard to get A-levels. But those old codgers wouldn't know an A-level from a new French frock. I mean..."

"I don't want your opinion." Father's countenance showed some anger. "I hope you didn't say that to them! I want to know if they are going to offer you a scholarship."

"No Dad. They said... the wing commander said... they would not be recommending me for one. They are going to write me a letter."

"And?" The grilling continued.

"And... Something about a nose job. They say I've got a problem with my... err... sinus and I should talk to the doctor about it? They are going to give me a letter when they write."

"And what do you think about that, Piers?" Perhaps it was a little calmer... just.

"I still want to fly, Dad. I really would like to make pilot. I can crack the school stuff, I know that. But the doctor's stuff, well I don't know."

"There is another way. I've been reading a pamphlet about technical officer cadetships, a sort of Cranwell for engineers. I've brought a copy home. You can have it to read tomorrow. But I've got news too."

"I'm sorry it didn't work out, Dad."

"Yes, I'm sorry too. But my news is that I am to be posted to the Far East. I am being sent to Singapore in March and there is the opportunity to take your mother and you children too. We have some pretty deep thinking to do because we shall be away for 2½ years, beyond when you finish 6th Form. That's not so much of a problem for Gaenor. But for you it's different. So if you are going to join up, cadetship or not, or even go to college, then we need to decide if you should come to Singapore with us."

With some anxiety, "I really don't want to go into boarding school, Dad."

"We'll talk about it, Son. Why don't you switch on the TV, the *Nine O'clock News* is about to start. In Paris, today, the Federal Republic of Germany is being invited to join NATO. That's sure to put the cat among the pigeons and affect all our futures."

Chapter 6
1955 ~ Supernumerary Crew

With a father who is a RAF wing commander on the staff at Headquarters Far East Air Force, an uncle who is a RAF wing commander on the staff at HQ Transport Command, an experienced retired RAF squadron leader who is the Commanding Officer of your school's Combined Cadet Force(RAF) contingent, and you run the contingent's Orderly Room wearing a RAF air cadet's uniform, there really was no excuse for not taking the opportunity to use RAF air transport from the UK to Singapore. The procedure was formally known as flying as an indulgence passenger. When your uncle goes one better and arranges for you to be supernumerary crew and therefore unlikely to be 'bumped off the manifest down route', Piers really had to do it.

Hampton Grammar School offered no objection to losing the last week of the Autumn Term; indeed the opportunity to fly to Singapore was viewed as a positive contribution to the experience of a would-be RAF officer. The paperwork, the RAF identity card and supporting passport just in case, and a couple of inoculations against the perils of smallpox and yellow fever — all was in order and Piers was set up to go. Even the return rail warrant between Twickenham and Swindon was provided — after all this was an 'air experience' duty journey attributable to the public purse.

"It will be our first Christmas apart," complained Helen.

"Absence makes the heart…" started Piers.

He did not finish. Her kisses were insistent and her tears did not want to stop. But a final cuddle and a prolonged kiss and Piers had to depart.

"I'll see you in the New Year. Take care of yourself, my love…" His final words were lost as the train pulled away.

The RAF Railway Transport Officer at Swindon told Piers to get on the RAF coach for Lyneham. The clerk at the Travel Desk at RAF Lyneham told Piers that he should get on the coach for RAF Cliff Pypard where he would be held, in transit, until the early call forward to board his aircraft tomorrow.

"I know 04:15 is early, corporal, especially in December, but you've got to get down here for breakfast with the crew." Piers was being addressed as 'corporal' because he was travelling in CCF(RAF) uniform, complete with greatcoat, and would be on the crew manifest as Corporal (Cadet) P P Ploughman with all expenses charged against the aircraft's account. "They start preparing two hours before take off."

"Oh!" replied Piers.

"I suppose you've got tropical KD," said the bored airwoman on the desk. She was thumbing through Piers's inoculation certificates.

"Yes, I was issued with tropical clothing…"

"You'll be wearing it from tomorrow. You wear long slacks and long sleeves in the aircraft. It's regulations. You'll be able to wear shorts when you're on the ground."

"Oh!" replied Piers. "But it's snowing outside."

"Yeah, I know. Bit of a chilly start to your trip, ain't it. You can wear your greatcoat over your tropical kit, we all do it." Sniff. That seemed to close the conversation off since she glanced over Piers's shoulder and called, "Next please? Can I help you?"

The wooden huts, dormitory style, offered only the barest protection against the penetrating cold. Piers arrived at RAF Cliff Pypard in the dark and departed three hours before December dawn. But the snow did not lie and the four engines Hastings aircraft rolled down Lyneham's runway, on time, at 07:45. The aircraft was configured in freight transport role, with just two pairs of seats at the rear of the fuselage cabin. Piers was surprised that the hold was filled with sorbo-rubber mattresses addressed to a hospital in Malaya. 'A bit like carrying coals to Newcastle,' thought Piers as he wondered if he could find a flat surface on which to lie. Ahead, he had five legs of nominally eight hours each spread across five days and four nights. And he'd had a lousy night's sleep at the hilltop, wooden hutted, transit camp, at one point getting up to write a letter to Helen. Worse… he'd left his framed photograph of Helen at the transit camp.

The aircraft staged through the USAF base at Idris in Tunisia where just-turned-18 years old Piers was introduced to cold beer. The second day was taken up with flying along the North African coast, across the Mediterranean into Syria and their second night at RAF Habbaniyah, a few miles from Baghdad. The crew seemed very keen to drink because, Piers was told, the next stop was dry. The crew was unaccustomedly quiet the following morning. They had been airborne only ten minutes when the navigator, a master aircrew wearing his 'Tate and Lyle' rank on a wristband, unhooked a rubber mattress laid it flat on the floor and went to sleep. A few minutes later and the aircraft captain did precisely the same thing except that he was a few feet closure to the cockpit.

Looking out of the windows, Piers could see why. The only feature of any significance, in the winter Iraqi landscape from 7000 feet altitude, was the Euphrates River and they were tracking southwards along it. Piers took the opportunity to go to the cockpit where the co-pilot, sitting in the right hand seat, pointed to the left hand (captain's) seat to sit down. He indicated the headset and motioned that Piers should put it on and do up the seat lap straps. The sun was beating in through the windscreen and from an indicated 7500 feet altitude, Piers could see the horizon through nearly 270 degrees. Here, up front, it was warm and pleasantly remote from the engine noise.

"Are they asleep?" The voice in the headset was crystal clear. The co-pilot's left thumb was being jerked over his left shoulder towards the prostrate figures in the aisle behind him.

Piers spoke, his words resonating in his ears, "Like lambs."

The co-pilot smiled with a nod. "We're on auto-pilot. Don't really need a navigator on this leg: we fly down the river, then down the gulf until we run out of land, turn left and run down the coast of Persia until we see Karachi. Piece of piss."

"What are those fires down there?"

"That's the oil wells flaring off their gas. It makes a useful navigation point at night. You can see them from a hundred miles. I'm surprised they don't find a way of capturing it and selling it as fuel. It's miserable looking place, isn't it?"

"My dad did three years down there, in Basra. He was an engine fitter on an RAF squadron."

"Would you like a go?" The co-pilot was pointing at the flying controls.

"I've only flown a glider before."

"Same principles. Treat her gently, so you don't wake them up back there. You make sure you can reach the pedals and I'll disengage the auto-pilot. Just so we don't got lost, just aim it at that column of cloud ahead, it's about 50 miles away. Just go straight for it. You have control…"

The four piston engines didn't murmur at the change of command. Piers held the aircraft at steady altitude without too much strain although he was reluctant to attempt to talk at the same time. The officer in the right hand seat seemed content to watch the world go by. The radio crackled incomprehensibly twice and once the co-pilot replied with his callsign, altitude and heading. The cloud column was approaching at 250 miles per hour.

"I have control." Piers lifted his hands clear and the co-pilot seemed to be concentrating on the approaching white column. He was flying directly at it. It was a solitary pillar of cloud, Piers guessed three miles across, perfectly white, reaching two miles above them and apparently solid. The bright chimney was dead in their track.

When the aircraft nose was all but touching the cloud, the co-pilot swung the controls to the left and the Hastings dropped its port wing. The aircraft flew around the cloud, appearing to Piers as though the top of the cockpit was running along the mist. It was the only time on the five day trip that he got a sensation of speed in the aircraft, more pronounced than take-off or landing. Then, on a prompt which Piers did not recognise, the co-pilot returned to his original heading, re-trimmed the aircraft controls and engaged the autopilot.

"It's a hard life in this man's Air Force," he feigned a yawn. But he was having difficulty concealing the pleasure the manoeuvre gave him on an otherwise normally staid transport aircraft. "Why don't you go and see if there's any coffee? I'll be waking the skipper in 30 minutes so I can have my lunch." What had seemed to Piers as a violent change of attitude had, in fact, been so smooth as not to disturb the sleepers.

Three hours later, the last two just off the Persian then Pakistani barren and almost featureless coast, RAF Murharraq (known to the aircrew as Karachi military) was shining buildings' and street lights in the dusk as they landed. The staging airfield was indeed dry in every sense. It was hot, sandy like a desert, no alcohol but plenty of stewed hot drinks with evaporated milk or cold, cola style bottles offered as the alternative. The crew suggested he didn't drink any water, or use the ice. "It is probably OK, but I wouldn't risk it if I were you!" It was here that Piers was grateful for his corporal's stripes; he had the use of the Corporals' Mess and the food and the environment appeared to be more comfortable than the facilities for the airmen.

The fourth leg demanded another early start and then south, along the western India coast, until Ceylon came into view. The aircraft did the work, the aircrew made the transit routine. With nothing but ocean to view through his porthole, Piers had time to reflect on his situation: he was missing Helen and wondering how she was coping with the cold — and being without him; he was flying — or at least experiencing passenger flying which was how he wanted to spend his working life; he was en-route to see his parents. His reflection from the porthole glazing caught his eye.

'Are you unhappy? Of course you're not. You got a week off school to do this trip and you may even go swimming on Christmas Day. That'll be a first. Why aren't you thinking more about Helen? I haven't got an answer to that one. She's my girl and I really would like to be with her, but I wouldn't miss this for all the water in the ocean down there. Narh, she'll be fine and we can have a good cuddle in the cinema when I get home.'

The pilot put the aircraft on the ground with a positive landing which drew a cheer from his crew. At the staging post of RAF Negumbo, the Indian Ocean tropical paradise conditions and coconut palms persuaded them to be in the pool before settling for a generous post-flight meal. Plenty of alcohol was available here which teenage Piers declined — fresh pineapple juice was more to his appetite. Then it was under mosquito nets in what the crew called a 'basher' — a palm frond roofed tropical shelter, on stilts, open to the balmy ocean breeze — for a good night's sleep.

"You don't need to worry about snakes here," was the reassuring message from the co-pilot. "The Barrack Warden has a couple mongooses to keep them down!" The unusual plural jarred with Piers, but he didn't comment. However, he did knock out his shoes in case a scorpion had taken a fancy to its shelter.

Judging by the aroma, the sorbo-rubber mattresses clearly didn't appreciate being left in the aircraft's hold overnight. Perhaps it contributed to Piers's lack of thoughts about his girl back home. It took at least two hours for the stink to be purged from the aircraft ventilation system, but soon it was time for the long descent over Malaya towards Singapore. From the air, the island looked to have three colours: all the visible greens were uniform lawn-like shades; the bare earth and much of the edges to the roads, where earthworks or building sites could be seen, were prominently arterial blood red; and the buildings seemed to have soft patterns of grey or sandstone reminiscent of Wiltshire stone under red tiled roofs. It all looked freshly washed from a recent downpour.

This time the Hastings was set down on Changi's runway with a smoothness as gentle as a lover's kiss and taxied to its parking space. Piers's mum and dad were waiting for him.

"Hello," Piers said, "I've just got to say thank you to the skipper. I shan't be a moment." Duty done, it was time to be re-united with his parents who had come overseas eight months previously. "Blimey, it's hot. Can we get something to drink? And is there somewhere I can post a letter to Helen? I wrote it before I left England. And I do need to get out of this uniform; I've been wearing it for five days..."

Corporal (Cadet) P P Ploughman was about to experience military overseas life, in the established, post-war colony of Singapore, for the first time.

Chapter 7
1955 ~ Swimming on Christmas Day

His parents, with Gaenor, were still living in the Grand Hotel[tm], Katong when Piers arrived. They had been waiting, in nominal transit accommodation, for seven months for married quarters at RAF Changi, but there still was none available. So his father had made his own arrangements for private rental, through the ever-resourceful grocer, and they would be moving before the New Year. The grocer had also identified a suitable servant, the amah, to be ready when they moved in.

The hotel was a substantial building possibly dating from the 1830s. The wartime Japanese occupation had left no obvious lasting scars. The tranquil square grounds were bounded by eight feet high walls each 40 fathoms, ie 720 feet, long. One wall had a gate directly onto the south-facing beach overlooking Singapore harbour; unfortunately, the sea was visibly contaminated with the effluent of three million city dwellers and the plentiful shipping which was Singapore's *raison d'être*. Across the hotel grounds, in the opposite north wall, there was a gate access to a 100 yard long drive to the East Coast Highway joining Singapore City with its easternmost Changi Point. The grounds were laid to lawn with tropical flowers and palms. A central bandstand cum fountain was overlooked by four, double storey, buildings where guests stayed; the upper floors had balconies and awnings, the lower floor windows were set back under cloister-like frontages.

Because of the season, and no doubt because of his father's senior rank, Piers was allocated the hotel's VIP room with its emperor size bed and, naturally, a mosquito net. He would only have the use of the room for four nights before the family moved away. 'I bet this cost Dad a packet,' he mused.

"First things first," insisted Dad. "You've got to get some proper clothes."

So, on his first evening, Piers became acquainted with Changi Market. Four lanes of back-to-back stalls in the road, each with two kerosene lamps to supplement their many electric lights, occasionally interspersed with a local cooking stall, some fresh peeled fruit 'chilled' stalls, at least three second-hand books stalls and countless fabric swathes in every colour imaginable. Changi taxis, all diesels, cut through the multicultural throng adding to the noise and smell of the alternative and cheaper transport, the local bus.

"Come on, Piers, keep up. We're going to the tailors. Your mother's doing the Xmas shopping…"

Behind the stalls there was, on each side of the road, a row of shops, many with glass fronts. These windows displayed a wide range of Japanese products, principally electronic goods and watches and many advanced cameras. There were Indian and Chinese tailors, and food stores, records and musical instruments, even restaurants. Piers was led into 'Khan the Tailor', his door closed to retain the merciful air conditioning and to reject the hubbub beyond. An Indian gentleman, standing straight to his full six feet height beneath an air force blue turban, with arms crossed across his chest, waited to greet them. He looked as though he had been positioned for the Ploughman customers to arrive — a character straight out of a Disney textbook.

"Ah, Wing Commander Ploughman. It is good to see you. This is obviously your son. A chip off the old block, if I may say so. Would you be so gracious as to be seated, Sahib? A cold drink, Sahib?"

"Hello, Khan. Piers has just got off the plane and he needs a pair of longs and a pair of shorts, …*jildeh hi*."

"No problem, wing commander." Turning to Piers he took the tape measure from around his neck and began his measurements.

"And a long sleeve shirt and a couple of short sleeves as well, Khan."

"No problem, wing commander." Kahn was snapping his fingers and already two turbaned assistants were conveying selections of cloth for the customers' choice while a sari-dressed woman was bringing over a tray with two glasses and two sealed orange fizzy drinks already misting with their chill.

"May I ask the honoured wing commander how *jildeh* is his need?" Khan was writing notes in a book. "If the need is truly urgent, my hands will get to work immediately…"

"One hour, Khan. If you have a suitable shirt, he…"

"These are the finest silk on the whole island, Sahib. For the honoured wing commander, I'll make it two for the price of one. Please take your pick, I'll just check your neck measurement, young master, and you can wear it straight away."

"I think Dacron^{tm} would be more suitable than silk, Khan. It will hold its shape better."

"As you desire, illustrious customer." Khan snapped his fingers and the silk shirts disappeared to be replaced as quickly by some smart male shirts in blended material. A selection was made. "Will there be anything else, wing commander? A pair of trousers and jacket for your New Year's party, perhaps?"

"Do the measurements while we're here, Khan. We'll call in tomorrow evening for a fitting. And the price...?"

There was a bartering of numbers, with multiple mental arithmetical conversions of fourteen Singapore Straits dollars to the pound sterling. The deal was done, no handshake offered or expected. Since Piers was wearing his new shirt, he was offered his UK shirt, now neatly folded, in a bag as they went out to look at the market.

"Dad, do you think I might have a new watch, one that shows the date?"

"Let's see what we can find, perhaps call it a Christmas present."

Piers selected a British Newmark^{tm} rather than an expensive Swiss or Japanese model. He preferred the clear, luminous face of the UK design. He found the Japanese market goods unsettling in this place where well-documented atrocities had been commonplace barely ten years ago.

One hour later, Piers was much more comfortably, and appropriately, dressed for whatever colonial Singapore might throw at him. They had missed hotel dinner so Piers was introduced to the local roadside food stall eaten within five feet of the passing fume belching traffic. The quiet of his room, and the tropical night time scent, carried the teenager into a deep, dreamless sleep.

With their impending moving into a house, Piers's parents had to make their household purchases before the possible effects of the Christmas season took effect on the shops. They need not have worried; the shops would be open throughout. There was the social life of the staff senior officer, and naturally the teenage son needed to be shown off especially for the benefit of the teenage daughters of other officers. There was to be a troop ship sailing to be clear of the port before the seasonal difficulties; one of Piers's first 'duty' visits was to say goodbye to someone he had never met. The excursion provided the excuse to be in Singapore City centre and to browse the immense arcades and cosmopolitan departmental stores and, for Piers, to observe the delights of the varieties of human female in town.

'No harm in looking at the menu,' thought Piers.

There were two swimming pools used by the family. British families were discouraged from swimming in the sea near the island. The Officers' Club pool at RAF Changi had a front straight onto the waters separating Singapore Island from the mainland of Malaya. Then there was the Singapore Club pool, the club being reserved for English military officers, officer status civilians such as teachers and expatriate civilians of the colonial or finance sectors. At both pools, it was more difficult to avoid having the 'menu' become the dominating feature of the 18 years old's landscape.

*   *   *

Christmas morning was spent in the Singapore Club pool where the water temperature was 93°F. The hotel put on a fine Xmas lunch spread of nearly fifty choices of European and Asiatic dishes with copious alcohol and juices to support their guests. The table was set with traditional, British, Christmas decorations. There were jugs of chilled fresh milk flown in from Australia for the ladies's tea. As the tropical night fell with equatorial rapidity, which always surprises visitors with its absence of dusk, the teenagers left the adults to do their thing while they settled in the bandstand and talked teenage talk. The hotel garden fragrance and the crickets' constant chatter provided a magical setting for youthful exchange well into the balmy evening.

One enterprising son had found a sprig of plastic mistletoe which became well used for its traditional purpose as the evening lengthened.

Two days later and the Ploughmans moved into their new home. Deep sea boxes were delivered and there was unpacking and the corresponding oohs and aahs as much loved treasures were rediscovered. A couple of excursions around the island bridged the gap until New Year's Eve was upon the family. Arrangements had been made for the Ploughmans to join with three other families in the Singapore Club for dancing and a traditional New Year's party.

As they drove about the island, the Ploughmans had seen streamers of firecrackers hanging on poles from high-rise blocks of flats where Singaporean laundry was usually hung out to dry. Some streamers were 20 feet long. With no concern about the accuracy of the timing of their celebration, beginning at about half past nine, the chains of firecrackers were variously ignited over the next four hours. The noise supplemented by echoes off the buildings was amazing; the aftermath was a litter of red dyed cracker cartridges which was swept into the monsoon drains to be purged out to sea. The water of Singapore Strait was turned bright pink and remained so for two days.

Three days into the new year and the family enjoyed a final evening excursion to Changi Market. It was time for Piers to prepare to return home to the English winter and school.

*   *   *

It was a different aircrew who flew the Hastings's return trip. He was flying on a regular trooper transit as an indulgence passenger this time; there was no need to have the status of supernumerary crew. First staging stop was RAF Negumbo and this time there would be an opportunity for Piers to look at the transit lounge souvenir stalls — all five of them — one selling Kodak^{tm}, one selling fruit and cartons of Ceylon tea, one selling sarongs and miscellaneous silks, one selling local carvings in hardwood or ivory and one selling gemstones especially sapphire and diamond. It was to this last that Piers gravitated.

Piers thought this would be an ideal opportunity to buy a diamond for the ring he knew he would eventually give to Helen. Little matter that he was just eighteen and she just a couple of months older.

"Show me a diamond," instructed Piers. "Make sure its good, now, I don't want rubbish."

"Here is a selection, Master." Twenty stones of various sizes and some with indistinct cutting or polish were laid out on a black satin cloth. "Perhaps Master would care to see our selection of sapphires; they are truly of oriental magnificence and your lady will greatly obdure her apparelling such gemstones around her abundant neck." A selection of blue stones appeared on a tray again covered in faded satin.

"Yes, well, I... err... I would like to concentrate on diamonds for the moment." Piers looked reasonably closely and he was offered and accepted a magnifying glass when offered.

"If Master cares to inspect this delightful stone in full light, he will be able to see the birth line which makes the stone so special." Piers did as he was bid. He had no idea what he was looking for or at.

"I can see a line in the crystal... actually I can see it with my naked eye. I would say that this crystal is cracked internally."

"Ah, kind master, you have exceptional foresight with your vision with the bare eyes. You are witnessing the place of origin of the gem in the ground when it was made before we mined it." Piers let the salesman keep talking his rubbish patter. If he was going to part with hard earned pocket money, really that meant hard saved pocket money, the goods had to be perfect. The salesman had stopped talking, reducing the impact of curry-stained breath.

"How much for this one?"

"For you, Master, we have a special price for the new year. Before the new year, during the old year, our price would have been thirty dollars American, but now we are able to dispatch our stock to our British friends in the Royal Air Force, servicing her most excellent majesty Queen Victoria and her heirs and dependencies, for twenty American dollars."

Piers was thinking, 'Doesn't this idiot prattle on — he's even got the wrong queen.'

"What's that in real money?"

Without hesitation, "For you, Master, seven pounds ten shillings."

"You can do better than that..."

"Ah, Master, I can tell you are going to drive a hard bargain. But I have to concern myself with the exchanging dollars and pounds for rupees. I could lower my price by ten shillings, Master."

"For a cracked stone? I don't think so. I think I'll buy her a length of silk!"

Helen would not receive a souvenir from Ceylon although her mother would get — and appreciate — a one pound box of genuine Ceylon tea leaves.

The second staging stop was RAF Bahrain on the Persian Gulf. There was neither opportunity nor desire to find a souvenir stall. The transit lounge was unbearable, the offered table-water unpleasant, and there was no escape from oppressive heat and draining humidity. Beyond the patio it seemed there was nothing but sand visible in the extraordinarily bright night when, from nowhere it seemed, a British Army officer of indeterminate rank appeared wearing sand-stained khaki and a bandolier of bullets over a shoulder. He was carrying an automatic weapon of a type that Piers did not recognise. He did not speak, went directly to the bar where he drained a pint of ice cold beer without pause, turned and left. The lounge was quiet through the whole minute the 'presence' was there and burst into hubbub with the soldier's departure. Only the most hardy slept well that night.

The relief to be at a cooler altitude, on the long third leg to Malta, was to be short lived. Once clear of Turkish airspace, over the Mediterranean north of Cyprus, the pilot announced that there was a severe weather system ahead and he could not get above or go round it. He was therefore going to fly beneath it to avoid the worst turbulence and all passengers and crew were to remain seated and securely strapped in. Children were to be directly supervised by an adult.

Piers later learned that the Hastings was forced down to 500 feet above the sea by the storms. In later years, Piers would reflect that this was an especially hazardous piece of flying and would be grateful never to have to repeat it in a passenger aircraft.

Adults were 'given' small children to look after in the exceptionally turbulent ride. Wearing corporal's stripes, 18 years old Piers happened to be sitting next to a PMRAFNS nurse, in uniform, who was being repatriated to demobilise from the service. She had a two year old girl who blessedly slept through most of violence. The five year old on Piers's lap wanted to know of the nurse why he was coughing into the brown paper (air sick) bag! Handley Page's aeroplane assembly technology was sorely tested that day and the crew received a round of applause when the Hastings reached RAF Luqa.

As the aircraft taxied through the Maltese rain to its hard-standing, 'Perhaps there's more to this piloting lark than I thought,' considered Piers.

Luqa's Transit Mess was justifiably known for the best John Collins cocktail in the Mediterranean — recipe: gin on ice, thinners, Cointreau^{tm}, lemon squash and soda water in a tall glass with a twist of lemon — cost price sixpence. It was here that Piers became educated in the hidden value of 'adult' drinks.

With the chilling January rain ceased, it was dry by the time the passengers had checked into their transit accommodation. A couple of passenger RAF junior NCOs asked Piers and the nurse if they would like to go into Valetta. It was a chance not to be missed. Pleased to be wearing their blue greatcoats over whatever uniform they chose, the

49

foursome rode a local bus into the capital city. A remarkable feature of this mode of public transport was the use of colour to denote the route, rather than numbers, and utterly confusing to the unwary under neon road lights. A cushion was placed beside the driver for the Holy Mother to keep the vehicle safe. In the complete absence of traffic discipline — 'much worse than Singapore,' thought Piers — and crossroads being acknowledged only by sounding the horn, it seems likely that the local drivers had selected their Guardian wisely.

Even on a cold January evening, Valetta itself was busy. Its densely packed buildings, surrounding a natural harbour, was still recovering from extensive war damage. The knowledgeable NCOs made directly for 'The Gut' as the downhill Strait Street is known. With every shop being a drinking and girlie bar supporting the naval requirement, it was a source of bewilderment to the novice Piers watching the comings and goings of the night. The nurse remained sensibly close to her male escort. The local beer was the lager called Cisk^{tm} which could be drunk in copious quantity without apparent hazard. Tonight, unfortunately, an USN carrier had put its crew ashore and the place was alive with USN Shore Patrol with night-sticks. That was like a red rag to the Royal Navy and some of the wise RAF quickly moved away.

As the foursome crested the summit for more savoury nightlife, their military uniforms in full display, a fat Maltese approached Piers with a semi-whispered offer.

"How much you wanta for the girl?"

Piers reaction to the proposition must have been disbelief because it was repeated.

"Eh, I say. How much you wanta for da girl?" Piers had difficulty shrugging off the man's grip on his forearm.

Still Piers did not know how to respond. More important, he did not understand what the Maltese was talking about.

"I'll give you twenty pounds." The grip had tightened.

"I don't, err…"

"OK, OK. I'll make it twenty five."

"What are you saying?" The innocent Piers was simply not understanding that anyone would expect to buy a woman wearing WRAF uniform. 'Anyway, what for?'

"I giva you da cash. Twenty five in sterling or you name da currency… dollars, lira? All OK."

"No thank you," was all that Piers could say as he used his free hand to remove the offending grip. The nurse Corporal watched and overheard this exchange with some amusement. But she did not say anything as the group moved on although she did remained noticeably closer to her male escorts as they ambled forward.

In one shopping alley, there seemed to be a gold something in every window. Lacking confidence in a clothing purchase for a female, Piers asked the nurse to assist in the purchase of a cardigan for Helen. A window display had a selection of garments with embroidered fronts and several appealed to Piers. Wisely, the nurse decided that Piers should make his own choice. As they made their way back to the bus station, the two NCOs decided they were going to do the traditional challenge. Travel between Luqa airfield and Valetta was not exclusively by motor bus. Horse drawn carriages were available and races back to the station were routine with the last home having to pay for drinks. Luqa was 350 feet above the town of Valetta on a two mile climb and it was not the tradition to have the horses race downhill — poor things!

Being lighter, the nurse and Piers won their free nightcap.

The last leg of the flight home was uneventful. It was snowing at RAF Lyneham. By five o'clock the passengers had cleared customs and were waiting for the coach to take them to Swindon railway station. Piers was grateful that the last leg of their journey had been made in UK blue uniform. Trains were being delayed and the coal fire in the platform waiting room had gone out.

Ahead were two and a half more hours of travel before a warm bath and clean sheets would embrace the young traveller back to normality. He was able to muster a few pennies for a telephone call to Helen from Swindon. He was learning that RAF life offers a variety of experiences and demands a great deal of patience.

Chapter 8
1956 ~ 'You have been selected...'

Daedalus House at RAF Cranwell, Lincolnshire, was the final selection centre for Royal Air Force Officer Cadetship, not exclusively aircrew. The letter from the Air Ministry, now re-titled Ministry of Defence (Air Force Department), instructed:

> *Mr Piers P. Ploughman ... be at Grantham Railway Station by 12:30 on August 26th for transportation to RAF Cranwell. Bring a pair of casual slacks for physical activity exercises.*
>   *A rail warrant from your postal address to Grantham is enclosed herewith...*

The building probably had something to do with the former Royal Naval Air Station on the site back in 1916. This was of no interest to Piers or any other candidate for RAF officer selection, not necessarily aircrew or cadetship. The selection process repeated the same techniques as the Aircrew Selection Centre Royal Air Force Hornchurch, without the medical component, and this time Piers was successful. A final pre-enlistment visit to Hornchurch during the summer of 1956, confirmed that all his medical bits were in the right place and that the nasal operation had been successful. An officer cadetship at the RAF Technical College would be offered where, subject to final confirmation of medical fitness, he would have up to 120 hours of flying plus the opportunity to go on to 'Wings'.

Piers's ambition was back on track! Pilot training, as an engineer, could lead to test pilot for the newest aircraft...

And the bonus: through the RAF Technical College, Piers would have an engineering officer's qualification so that he might follow in his father's footsteps when he was too old to fly.

*   *   *

The beach at Clacton-on-Sea was not an exciting stretch of East Anglia coastline. Piers had said to Helen that the most interesting feature of the whole place was the horizon when you could see it. From where they were sitting, on a bench 'In loving Memory of Harold the Scotch Terrier — passed away 23rd May 1938' according to the corroded plaque, the

52

pebble beach extended for nearly a mile to the pier adorned by the vertical ring of a big wheel amusement ride. Today, even the sea seemed reluctant to roll ashore against the dismal Essex coastline. The pier had somehow survived the war and the weather, but now definitely was in need of a coat of paint. From this bench, the distant amusements on the pier, even when illuminated in coloured night lights, was beyond hearing range. That suited both Piers and Helen who, anyway, had only ears for what each other said.

On their days off from school vacation work, they rode a bus or hired a tandem bicycle inland, away from the crowds at the coast, to the quiet fields where the sun was ripening the corn and where the birds sang enchanting songs. On workdays, there was only spare time sufficient to find solitude on a windy beachside bench.

Both teenagers had completed their schools' sixth form, sat exams and had been advised they had achieved the grades necessary for Helen to proceed to University, in Exeter, and for Piers to enter officer cadetship in the Royal Air Force. The requisite documentation had been mailed and written confirmation of a place was awaited. Now they were on work experience, with Butlin's^{tm} Holiday Camp, in the catering support areas. They had been at Butlin's^{tm} for six weeks when they each received their letter of offer; Helen's required a telephone call to confirm her wish to go ahead. Piers's letter was rather more formal; it had been forwarded from the River Medway town of Gillingham, Kent where his grandmother lived and which he used as a mailing address while his parents were on Royal Air Force duties in Singapore.

Telephone: Holborn 3434

Air Ministry
Adastral House
Theobalds Road
London   WC1

TC.1956/21/A.R.1a.   *30th August, 1956*

Sir,

1.	*I am commanded by the Air Council to inform you that you have been selected for me to offer you a Technical Cadetship (Henlow) at the Royal Air Force Technical College following which, upon your successful completion and graduation following the three years course, will qualify you for appointment to a permanent commission in the Technical Branch (General List) of the Royal Air Force.*

2.	*Subject to satisfying appropriate medical checks and your confirmation of willingness to undergo flying training, this letter includes the offer of additional training during and following your Technical Cadetship (Henlow).*

3.	*You will be required to attend the Aircrew Selection Centre located at Royal Air Force Biggin Hill, Kent for medical assessment of your continued fitness for service in the Royal Air Force.*

4.	*If you wish to accept this offer, please return a signed and dated copy acknowledging receipt of this offer. I enclose an envelope and second copy of this letter for the purpose. Please also enclose a short letter of acceptance and state from which railway station you wish the return rail warrant to be made. Our letter with the warrant will advise you of the date for your appointment at Royal Air Force Biggin Hill which will include an overnight stay in service accommodation.*

5.	*If you do wish not to accept this opportunity, please write a short letter advising me of your rejection of this offer.*

I am, Sir,
	Your obedient Servant

	L C Aubruy

Piers's reaction was to sit on the bench, close to Helen, reread the letter and enjoy the moment. He was oblivious to the sea breeze, the sun's glinting on the breaking waves and the background noise of the holiday camp behind them.

"You've gone quiet," said Helen. She could feel his excitement bridging the proximity of their position. "What does it say? Come on... don't keep it to yourself..."

With great difficulty, Piers controlled himself. Very quietly, he said, "I've got it."

"What?" She guessed his letter was official; she had to wait for him to tell her.

"I've got it. The RAF is going to let me fly. I've got it." Piers held his gaze out to sea — savouring the moment yet realising the cliff edge represented by the letter.

"Well done," whispered Helen and planted a kiss on his cheek. To her surprise, Piers did not react to the kiss. He re-read the letter, and then again.

"They've done it. They've offered me a cadetship and they are going to let me fly. It means pilot training." He breathed deeply, so deep that his shoulders hunched. His hands closed to loose fists, but his fingers kept moving.

"Can I see your letter? Henlow is quite a long way from Exeter, isn't it?"

"I'm going to fly. It's what I've wanted to do ever since... I don't remember when... all those cinema films... school... father... the war... the sound barrier... books. And all those medicals... and fixing my nose... I am going to fly." Helen clung more tightly to his arm, but Piers was not moving. She could feel the pent-up excitement coursing through his body. Helen had to take the letter out of his grasp to read and that provided Piers the excuse to move his head to read it again while she held it.

"Gosh that nose job was awful... but it was worth it... as a pilot." Their heads were now so close they could feel the others' warmth radiating and the lingering kiss became inevitable, their eyes wide open searching for each others' innermost thoughts.

"Do I say congratulations? Or what?" Helen's sea-blue eyes looked deeply into his, telling him of her shared joy at his good news. She did not know how the news would affect their lives; separation for a while maybe, but there was the phone... and letters... and the train... and holidays. For the moment, her man was happy and that made her happy too. The future would look after itself. She had his future… surely their future together… in her hands… in the letter.

Piers had to say something. "And for you, too… you're off to wear a mortar board and learn to count numbers bigger than 10 …I'm in love with a swot… What was it the man said? The future starts here."

"Sh!" Even her first attempt at a kiss could not silence him.

"And never again to have to go to that miserable Hornchurch…"

"Sh!" she mouthed with their lips just touching. "You'll wake up the gulls or even Butlin's^{tm} happy campers."

Piers received another kiss and the couple quietened, looking at the horizon, their heads joined at their temples. Each had private thoughts — thoughts to be shared at some later time.

Their teenage lives together had just become much more complicated.

Chapter 9
1956 ~ Cadet Wing, RAF Technical College, Henlow

After a long summer holiday, it was the first Monday of October 1956 that Helen was on the railway platform to see Piers off to join the RAF at the RAF Technical College in Bedfordshire. Wearing his first trilby hat, a kiss and a steam engine whistle saw the 14.10 depart from Kings Cross. It safely carried 22 Henlow and 23 University cadets in a train of three uncomfortable carriages, via Hitchin, to arrive at 15.45 at Henlow Camp railway station.

Shortly after departing Hitchin, a middle aged lady, eying the assembled youth in her carriage, gratuitously announced, "They don't run the trains on this route on Sundays." Then she volunteered, by way of explanation "It's church land, you see." The travellers couldn't see any difference in the ploughed fields until the RAF station buildings appeared. By that time, several cadets were smoking nervous cigarettes as arrival at their destination approached.

The joining instruction from the MOD(AFD) induction desk had been direct:

... to arrive at Henlow Camp railway station between noon and 17:30 on 1st October 1956... A railway warrant is enclosed for your use...

Piers's interest, as the train approached Henlow, was for the first sight of the airfield. 'How soon will it be before I can get to fly?' He would be unable to see the airfield from the rail station.

Two Royal Australian Air Force cadets arrived, two days late by boat via Southampton, having enjoyed the delights of the Suez Canal; one University cadet attempted to fly in by private aircraft and was diverted to Luton airport and arrived by hire car, to be told that 1st year cadets were not allowed cars (or motorcycles or aeroplanes) on the station and aren't late for appointments either!

" Bicycles?"

"Yes, but fill in this application form first." The pleasures of service life were about to begin.

The arrivals were greeted by members of the Senior Entry and were assisted to their rooms, individual bed-sitting-studies with sink, affectionately called bunks. Piers was allocated a ground floor room in what he learned was known as Block 57. It was made clear that the arrivals were expected to partake of welcoming tea in the Junior Cadets' Mess at 17:15 where the Commanding Officer would greet them. They were expected to be there, in the mess, five minutes early.

So it was that the 1956 entry assembled to join the service. Notionally, twenty-four officer cadets travelled to the Cadet Wing of the RAF Technical College Henlow on Monday 1st October 1956, destined to spend the next 2 years and 9 months as Henlow Cadets (Technical). Twenty male and two females graduated at noon on 30th July 1959, as Pilot Officers of the Technical Branch; the two Australians joining their equivalent branches in the Royal Australian Air Force — the RAAF. The register of the 1956 Technical Cadets (Henlow) Entry, assigned to the Cadet Wing's existing two squadrons, comprised 12 cadets each, to:

A Squadron:

Lionel Banks	Allen Davies	Robert Dewhurst
Bartlet Dunmow	Peter Fischer	Julius Henson
Ian J King RAAF	Oliver Knight	Basil Leitch
Denise Mercer WRAF	Richard Petts	Julius Shepherd.

B Squadron:

Martin Caine	Osma Drake	John Dawtry
Paul Ellis	Derek Hedley	Theo Kaggel
Kirk Knight	Claudette Leigh WRAF	Joe MacLion
Piers P Ploughman	Bridgenorth P Thackray	Drew Wilde RAAF.

In the mess anteroom, the Henlow cadets sat on one group of chairs divided from the similar group of University cadets separated by a central space. Those chairs were allocated to a further twenty three officer cadets who had travelled to the RAF Technical College on that same Monday, but were pre-selected to graduate at 12:00 on 30 July 1957 as Acting Pilot Officers of the Technical Branch; they were all destined for 3 years study at university before returning to Henlow for a final term on a Technical Officers' (Graduate) course.

The cadets of No 1956 Technical Cadets (University) 1956-57 were also equally divided into A and B Squadrons. Their names did not initially register with Piers or his fellows. They were of a different caste and the paths of the two academic streams would only cross in social or sport activities or on the Drill Square.

While they were waiting for their welcoming address, the arrivals learned that there were two cadets' messes at Henlow. First year cadets, including both Henlow and University cadets, were assigned to the Junior Cadets' Mess. At the end of their first year, the University entry were given acting-commissions and went their various ways. Second (middle) and Third (senior) year Henlow cadets had the use of the Senior Cadets' Mess. The Junior Mess was in an adapted secco hut, the Senior Mess was in the converted brick built station Sergeants' Mess. There were plans to erect a purpose built Cadets' Mess, but there was no sign of the building for the 3½ years that Piers was resident at Henlow. Nevertheless, there was a rumour that the rooms had been designed to be too large for SNCO occupants and too small for officers. Cadet occupation was therefore inevitable. But that was for the future.

The two Mess Committees were managed by the Cadet Wing instructors but had cadet members. In all other respects they functioned as normal officers' messes. In these days of national service, they each had assigned (airmen) staff, a bar, and full dining facilities. Both ran seasonal balls and less formal social events. The food was of good quality — it had to be because the active lifestyle of the cadets kept the members ever hungry. Junior cadets slept in either the three storey Block 57 for the Henlow Cadets or secco (temporary, fibre-board clad) accommodation for the University Cadets. Both groups ate in the Junior Mess.

Middle year cadets slept in Block 57 and ate in the Senior Mess. Senior year cadets ate and slept in the Senior Mess except when an individual was nominated to be Duty Under Officer, a week long duty rostered for the senior year, when he was required to eat in the Junior Mess and sleep in a designated room in Block 57. The new arrivals noted that the Duty Under Officer had responsibility to ensure lights-out at the correct hour (22:30 Sun to Fri and 23:15 on Sat) and not to check the cadet incumbent was actually in the room. It therefore became common practice to return after lights-out. Leaving a ground floor window unlocked had its perils. More than once Piers was disturbed by a second year cadet using his window rather than the Block 57 main door to escape detection after a night on the town. The timing of the Hitchin cinema or pub closure, and the bus service, was such that invariably an evening movie show resulted in being back to quarters after lights-out.

Despite the largely testosterone fuelled environment of Block 57, there was, during Piers's two years in Block 57, there was only one instance of there being an additional (female) body in a room after lights out and that contravention of Cadets' Standing Orders remained undetected by the authorities. No male cadet of the entry attempted to 'entertain' or 'be entertained by' either female cadet of the entry.

*   *   *

As part of the training to be officers, lovingly known as the knife fork and spoon phase, each mess had two formal dining nights per week. These Dining-In Nights required the wearing of the cadet version of Mess Dress which was best uniform, soft collar and bow tie. Once per month the occasion was designated a Guest Night when the principal guest would be expected to make a speech; in celebration the cadets were required their No 1 Uniform — a suit made by a bespoke tailor — the same uniform which had to be worn on formal parade, but with starched front shirt and wing collar with black bow tie. The Duty Under Officer took the role of Mess President for the Junior Mess, the Wing's Under Officers shared the task in the Senior Mess. These events always took place on Tuesday or Thursday evening, assembling at 19:30 for 20:00, and often lasted into the small hours. The lights-out rule was simply forgotten on such occasions. Cadets' Mess nights had all the features and procedures of officers' mess nights, including formal grace, full waiter silver service, the loyal toast with port or water, except that music was not usually played. Sometimes there was a guest speaker.

A full range of mess games were played, imported by the flying instructors who had all had operational flying experience, ie WWII or Korea. Piling armchairs seemed to occur in many. Hanging from impossible features on the ceiling was common. Tug of war (using a broomstick) and pushing a beer bottle furthest from a chalk-line were feats of strength. Climbing round dining chairs or, more difficult, over and under a dining room table was quite challenging especially when it had been recently polished. Piers learned the hard way never to play

'Moriarty' with a padre: both players started blindfold and kneeling, armed with a rolled newspaper. The object was to locate your opponent by his reply to the query, 'Are you there Moriarty?' A swipe was then made at the supposed sound. It usually happened that the padre had his blindfold removed resulting in a sore head for the other player.

Schooner races had some popularity with the beer drinkers. Teams of at least six would challenge other teams to drink pints of beer in sequence. Proof that the pint glass was indeed empty was given by placing the upturned glass on the head of the drinker.

Once a year, the whole Cadet Wing went to the Station Officers' Mess for a Dining In Night when music was played in the Dining Room Minstrels' Gallery. Two recent portraits, of the Queen and her consort, gazed down on the assembly as the cadets remained on their best behaviour — at least until the loyal toast.

Those cadets selected to fly in their first year quickly learned that oxygen, as supplied for pilots, made an excellent cure for a hangover; student pilots also learned that flying instructors, many of who might have been at the mess the previous night, were reluctant to teach aerobatics during their first flying period of the day.

On that first evening on arrival day, most newcomers were polite and respectful. Some colleagues were recognised from the Hornchurch or Deadulus House tests. Following a good evening meal, it was back to the bunk to unpack and prepare for an early start. Breakfast was to be served between 07:00 and 07:15 prompt and was compulsory.

*   *   *

Induction into the RAF on 2 October 1956, was a formal, individual, multiple form filling, oath taking process and extended throughout the morning. The afternoon was devoted to being kitted out — the process of been issued with, and signing for, kit bags full of uniform appropriate to recruit airmen. Two different patterns of boots became an instant topic of conversation — one for drill and one for regular daily use. (Shoes, airmen for the use of — came later;

comfortable shoes, officer pattern came much later.) The kit bags quickly filled with underwear, socks, shirts, trousers and jacket (blouse and jacket patterns), peak and forage hat plus a beret with a removable polishable brass RAF badge. Everyone elected to wear their greatcoat over their civvies for the one mile march from Clothing Stores to the bunk. All issued clothing had to be labelled. A similar process was repeated with the essential personal copies of mandatory reading volumes — the Manual of Air Force Law, Queen's Regulations, RAF Maintenance Procedures and, for the select fraternity, multiple flying regulations and manuals concerned with the Laws of the Air.

Individual's bunk space was rapidly filling. Just before tea on the third day, a Wednesday, it was announced that the Cadet Wing's Warrant Officer would undertake his routine bunk inspection at 10:00 on Thursday — the next day. Panic ensued. What was expected? What to do with all the packing waste associated with any military equipment including clothing? Fortunately, the Duty Under Officer was on hand to guide those prepared to listen. All the while, new uniforms were being labelled, ironed and aired because tomorrow was the first day of formal lectures — and the first punishment parades for the dishevelled state of the bunks! Anything that could be polished had to be, including buttons, badges, belt brasses and all footware including civilian pairs, bunk door handles, sink, taps and, not least, the mirror.

"All cadets shall assemble in the Cadet Wing briefing Room at 08:30 hours for a briefing on the daily routine and the regulations pertinent to smooth life and living amongst cadets. All cadets are informed that cadets are expected to be five minutes early for every appointment, including parades, lectures, meals, sports fixtures and medical appointment should they desire to see the quack or his dental colleague — the fang farrier. Church parades likewise..." Cadets rapidly learned the difference between the voluntary 'will' and the mandatory 'shall'. To a junior cadet they meant the same... do it!

The working day routine for first year cadet was consistent through the year:

06.00 rise — breakfast in the mess — deemed compulsory
07.15 drill parade
07.45 finish drill, change uniform, freshen for classes
08 15 march to lectures

08.30 — 10.30 lectures

10.30 refreshment break at own expense

10.45 — 12.30 lectures

12.45 lunch in the mess

13.50 march to lectures

14.00 — 15.00 lectures

15.00 refreshment break at own expense

15.20 — 16.45 lectures

17.00 tea in the mess (bread and butter with cakes)

17.30 — 19.00 activity, sport, hobby, homework, laundry, kit preparation

18.00 punishment parade taken by the Duty Under Officer

19.00 dinner in the mess (never less than 4 course meal)

evening; 90 minutes study homework, plus:

                    preparation of uniform,

                    cleaning room and preparation for inspection

                    occasional night out at pub or cinema.

22.30 lights out — relaxed to 23.15 for middle year cadets

Lights out was enforced by the Duty Under Officer. Of course the expectation was that cadets who had been off the station would be in their rooms by that time. Indeed, any who had been socialising in Block 57 would be expected to be in their own room by lights-out. There was no concession for last minute ablutions, either. But, favourite haunts included evenings out at public houses in Hitchin or Ickleford, or the cinema in Hitchin. Some went to Bedford, but needed a car or motor bike to get back from the cinema before lights out and these were not permitted on camp during the junior year. However, the pubs did not close until 22.30 and the Duty Under Officer would take pleasure in catching, and summarily punishing (that is instantaneous without redress three days extra parades — jankers) for anyone he discovered coming in late. Avoiding him became a sport; as the first year cadets were on the ground floor, their partially open windows provided the easy route indoors and more than once Piers was disturbed by a heavy second year cadet coming home that way. A broken bed-frame resulted from one such incursion and a disturbed night's sleep on the floor. Much to Piers's

63

surprise, he was never called to account for how or why the damage to Her Majesty's dormitory property had been occasioned.

*   *   *

Summary punishment was also given for poor turnout on parade — no excuses were admissible. A more formal punishment might be given by the Cadet Wing staff for something really heinous. Punishment parade comprised appearing in best uniform in good order, or else it accumulated further days, and up to 30 minutes drill on the adjacent parade square.

Wednesday and Saturday afternoon was devoted to sport, often competitive team games against local colleges and clubs. The needle matches against the RAF College Cranwell, where flying and non-engineering ground officers served their cadetships, was always compulsory attendance for home games and actively encouraged to travel as supporters for away games. Piers played rugby union in the winter, mainly for the 2nd XV, including sometimes being its captain. Athletics was the primary summer sport, where he followed his father as a sprinter and thrower, with no particular success in these events competing against others who achieved better standards courtesy of boarding school coaching. He continued with social tennis on the Cadets' Mess courts and the Wing had the use of the station squash court.

Sunday's routine started an hour later, and there was a formal, compulsory parade on Sunday at 09.45. Cadets dispersed to churches of their own faith at 10.15, receiving the order, 'Jews, Roman Catholics and Other Denominations: fall out!' The afternoon and evening of Sunday were usually left to their own devices; one popular feature of Sunday's evening meal was that a curry was served.

*   *   *

Missing Helen was going to be a problem for Piers. The busy daily routine numbed the separation which was defined in Cadets' Standing Orders. Boldly set out therein, Piers found:

> *Freedom to travel, ie 'bounds' is defined as:*
>
> *a. First year cadets are not allowed motor vehicles (on camp), and are restricted to 25 miles radius except on leave, but not at any public house within 3 miles of the Main Gate. Social contact with the airmen of the station is discouraged.*
>
> *b. Second year cadets are allowed one motor vehicle on camp and the use of the garages attached to the Cadets' Mess; use of said*

64

vehicle is restricted to a 50 miles radius, excluding Greater London, except on leave, but not at any public house within 3 miles of the Main Gate.

c.   Third year cadets are allowed motor vehicles without restriction and are permitted to visit London at any time.   The stipulation concerning public houses within 3 miles of the Main Gate remains.

The Birch^{tm} Bus Company had its garage close to the RAF station entrance and the adjacent railway station was known as Henlow Camp. A main road divided the station in two, the road crossing the railway lines at a level crossing. Birch^{tm} Bus ran its regular service 203 from Bedford to Kings Cross via Henlow, Hitchin and Hatfield.   The journey from Henlow to Kings Cross took 1 hour and 40 minutes. It departed for London, on Sunday, at 10.38 and there were two return buses from Kings Cross at 22.10 and 23.59.   Piers became a frequent passenger despite London being out-of-bounds to first and second year cadets except on transit for holidays.   That the buses arrived at Henlow Camp at midnight or at 01.15 respectively, somewhat after official lights out, compounded the felony.   But, during his first year, Piers always left his ground floor bedroom window unlocked and was able to climb in undetected.   During his second year, he used a corridor window on the ground floor and again was not caught.   His absence never drew remark on any Sunday afternoon, evening or at lights-out during his cadetship.

Chapter 10
1956 ~ Nicknames, Gravel and Chipmunks

Nicknames between cadets started during the first week. It was the influence of the ex-boarding school cadets that kept up the impetus. Some thought the habit silly, but that didn't stop it happening. Initially the names, sometimes highly offensive, flowed freely and were quite meaningless out of context. Then it was realised that there were two ladies in the entry and the worst genre examples were quietly retired.

It became obvious that the Cadet Wing instructors knew many of the names and their association. Piers never heard any instructor use a nickname even when the alcohol had flowed in the mess. In Block 57, it was completely different; given names were seldom if ever used and it was nicknames that were freely exchanged as the cadets went about their business of studying or spit and polish.

This was the time when Piers decided he ought to keep a diary. He had been impressed with what he had seen of Samuel Pepys's writing while at one of his primary schools. He had tried to keep a diary in the fifth form while he was swimming with school colours and girls were becoming noticeable. Neither attempt lasted long and he rightly expected that this diary would turn out to little more than notes which would be consigned to the waste bin when he could no longer read his own writing. But the issue of nicknames had a lasting interest. And so he produced a register of real verses nickname with an explanation of why a particular one stuck.

Piers's did not share with his list with his course, despite all the nicknames being in common use, and he thought it too silly to show to Helen:

Lionel Banks	*Shylock*	mean with money, perhaps Jewish
Allen Davies	*Shark*	proficient swimmer
Robert Dewhurst	*Bunk*	difficult to get out of bed
Bartlet Dunmow	*Nurse*	St John's Ambulance service, first aid kit
Peter Fischer	*Simon*	biblical Simon Peter the fisherman
Julius Henson	*Pimple*	shape of head, problem with acne
Ian J. King RAAF	*LMN*	extension of his initials 'IJK'
Oliver Knight	*Ollie*	corpulent figure after Laurel & Hardy
Basil Leitch	*U*	uranium, last digits of service number 235
Denise Mercer WRAF	*Aspirin*	rumoured to say 'no' due to headache

Richard Petts	*Rick*	suited him better than Dick, bowlegged
Julius Shepherd	*Ba*	as in sheep
Martin Caine	*Abel*	biblical association, also skinflint
Osma Drake	*Imam*	wrongly attributed religion, he's catholic
John Dawtry	*Ganglion*	ungainly
Paul Ellis	*Crab*	the way he walks, especially to public bar
Derek Hedley	*Uncle*	someone to talk too, confidant, wise owl
Theo Kaggel	*Neutron*	short fuse temper, as in fission bomb
Kirk Knight	*MacKay*	Scottish accent, especially when upset
Claudette Leigh WRAF	*Bumper*	well endowed chest
Joe MacLion	*Southpaw*	left hander, catholic (left footer)
Piers P Ploughman	*Peetot*	burned out aircraft's airspeed sensor (pitot)
B.P. Thackray	*Derv*	extension of BP fuels, also motor freak
Drew Wilde RAAF	*Fu*	smelly feet, corruption of phew!

*   *   *

"Right oh, Ladies and Gentlemen. Recognising this is your first day on this 'ere drill square, today it's Sergeant Johnson's *be-kind-to-cadets* day. Ter morrer, you're gonna have a *be-good-to-sergeant* day." The surprisingly loud voice, easily sufficient to carry the 150 yards diagonal of the parade square, emanated from an immaculately turned out 5 feet 4 inches of squat RAF sergeant sporting RAF Regiment badges on his uniform sweater encasing a ramrod straight back.

"Yes, sergeant." The cadets' reply was somewhat quiet.

At a separation of twenty yards in front of his drill squad, "Did I hear a mouse squeak? While you are on parade, you xercises yer voices from the pits of yer bellies. Nah then. You've got to *be-good-to-sergeant*."

"Yes, sergeant." This time the reply was rather louder.

"Better. You'll have to do better when the Warrant Officer comes along. He likes to hear what cadets is saying."

"Yes, sergeant." This time the reply was rather louder still.

"I sees you are learning quick, like. That's good. Now I'm going to teach horrible young officer cadets to stand still and at attention. I don't want none of yous to pass out, like. That gravel don't do no good for them of you as has a need for shaving."

Sergeant Johnson was standing stationary, only his head moving for emphasis as he surveyed his newly recruited charges, in front of the assembled 47 cadets divided into two flights of 8 frontage by 3 rows. If

67

his shaving remark was intended for the two WRAF cadets, it did not show. He knew that some of the fair-haired cadets would try to avoid the 'clean shaven rule' on morning drill parade, simply to get three more minutes in bed. It would only happen once; 3 days extra drill would deter repeats — 7 days from the Wing adjutant on the second offence. The girls' version of the same problem, rampant hair above the collar line, was to tuck their neck hair under their headdress. There were standards and this lot would comply!

"Now, on the command: 'Attention' you will come smartly to the attention position moving your left boot until it touches your right. There you will remain until you hears the command: 'Stand at ease', upon which you will move your left foot 15 inches to the left, smartly like, grinding the gravel down into the ground, like. Right?" Johnson's head moved from side to side assessing whether his instruction had been understood.

"I said, 'Right?'" The bellowed delivery was effective.

"Right, sergeant," almost in unison.

"Parade… parade… Attention!" 47 left boots moved sideways and a few backs straightened. The gravel under the hobnailed drill boots made 47 discernable crunches.

"As you were!" The left boots moved in their own time. "We'll try to do it together next time. Nah then… parade… Attention!"

"I suppose that was better. Stand still… those of you what's got chests, stick it out. Those of you what's got bums, stick it in. Arms straight down your sides… fists loosely clenched, thumbs in line with the seams of your trousers, thems what's got trousers… curb your giggles ladies… this is serious stuff." Sergeant Johnson had not moved one muscle (apart from his jaw) and yet he knew this novice collection would look like a rabble. "Stand tall now, you're proud to be serving Her Majesty… One day she'll write to you and let you know she's pleased to have you aboard, like. Stand very still. When I see you all standing to attention proper like, then I'll give you the order to 'Stand at ease'. Now then, my young ladies and gentlemen, stand still. Breathe if you've got to. I don't want to see you moving. Stand still! Parade… wait for it… parade… Stand still!… parade. Stand at ease!"

There was a discernable sigh of relief, but they had only just begun.

"Parade... parade... Attention! That's better. Chins in even if you've got more than one, I'm not counting. Heels together, feet at thirty degrees... hold it. Stand still! Parade... Stand at ease! Don't talk. You're on parade and I'll do all the talking that's necessary. Do we understand?"

"Yes, sergeant." This time the reply was scarcely louder than a whimper.

"Do we understand?" Johnson allowed his head to move as if to engage every one of the 47 pairs of eyes whose gaze was firmly fixed ahead of their body.

"Yes, sergeant."

"Nah then! I told you that today it's Sergeant *be-kind-to-cadets* day. Now I'm a man of my promises, so... as soon as yer cans stand to attention to my satisfaction, then... we'll all go home and we can do it again ter morrer."

"Yes, sergeant." There was a degree of enthusiasm about getting off this infernal drill square. And they hadn't started marching properly yet!

"Parade... parade...Attention!"

"Ter morrer is a momentous day. Ter morrer is the day you gets yer name badges then we can all address you by your names instead of just 'you'. Stand still! Ter morrer, the warrant officer will come and demonstrate how drill is done while you is cadets. Now that's something to really look forward to 'cos yous gonna be spending lots of time out here, come rain or shine. I ain't told yer to move... stand still. And... wait for it... ter morrer, yous is gonna look like RAF cadets not like sardines what's just got out of bed. What's you grinning at, miss?

For a moment Cadet Denise Mercer WRAF had let her face crease to a smile. She'd never experienced anything like this. The sergeant had not changed his posture, but some movement caught his eye.

"I said ... Stand still! You young gentlemen has got to learn to stand still and not to tremble like a belly dancer on heat." And he remained statue still, his face showing not a vestige of emotion.

"You'll wipe that grin off your face, miss. Parade's not a place for girlish grinning. As I was sayin'... you's gonna be wearing polished boots, you's gonna be wearing pressed trousers, you too ladies, and you's gonna have your hairs cut proper military like. No body's told yer ter move... Your Wing Adjutant has arranged for the barber to be in the mess for the purpose and you're all gonna have your hair made nice to look at, like. Ladies too; the Commanding Officer has invited a lady officer to come and make sure you ladies get treated fair, like. Stand still. Gawd 'elp me... Stand at ease! Wake up there... Attention!" Was there just a sign of colouration on his cheeks?

The reaction on the faces of the cadets was individual and fearfully silent. Unfamiliar muscles in legs and back were already complaining.

"Now we'll do a little practice marching, remember to swing your arms, keep your arms straight, swing your arms to shoulder height. This is the real air force not like them Yanks what's in the movies waving them about like Fred Astaire. Arms is for swinging. We'll go once round the drill square and if I'm satisfied, like, we'll practice attention and then go to get our hair cut and switch on the iron. A bit of spit and polish never done no-one no harm and could do you lot a lot of good."

There was a pause, then, "Stand at ease!" A longer pause, then, "Attention!"

Sergeant Johnson moved. His right foot crashed into the gravel like a gunshot. He had turned to his left.

"Parade... parade... Right turn!"

47 bodies were grateful for the movement.

"As you were... In this man's air force, like, there only one right... right? ...and only one left... right? In case you are in any doubt, raise your right arm, straight, out front, to shoulder height and hold it there. It'll ache after a minute... keep it up, straight, like... it hurt more after two minutes... but it gets bleeding painful after five. Now then. I remembers that I promised yous that today it's Sergeant *be-kind-to-cadets* day. So I shan't... keep your arms up there... I ain't told yous you can lower them... so... wait for it...so I'll save the five minutes experience for the next time you cock it up. Attention."

The attention position prevented anyone relaxing. Blood rushed to the closed fist making it tingle. No-one dared move.

"Let's try again. Remember which way's right... right? Parade... parade... Right turn!"

"Parade... parade... by the left... Quick march!"

Forty-five minutes later, the 1956 Entry was in the Junior Cadets' Mess, taking a cup of tea and freshly baked teacake, before the rigours of the forthcoming hairdressing, changing for evening meal and preparation of their uniform which would take them well beyond lights out to achieve. The first lesson of the next day was timetabled as:

'08:30 - Drill - Parade Square - Sgt Johnson'.

*   *   *

The notice in the mess instructed those Technical Cadets who were scheduled for flying training to report to the flight line at 08:30. Eleven cadets met the criteria and duly marched the mile to the airfield hut where flying instruction and operations took place. It was close to a servicing hangar and the hardstanding opened directly onto RAF Henlow's all grass airfield. About 600 yards away was the Air Traffic Control tower, painted in high visibility black and white squares. It looked as though it had been assembled out of packing crates. Beyond ATC stood the dark silhouette of a workshop-cum-store known as, for some reason, 'The Pickle Factory'. As the cadets broke from their marching formation, a four engines Hastings of the Parachute Test Unit flew overhead and released its load, under an enormous white canopy, onto the airfield. Presumably the test load was too heavy because it broke away from the parachute and plummeted into the grass while the white silk drifted away on the wind towards some distant cottages beyond the airfield boundary.

There were eight Chipmunks parked outside the hangar. They looked so small, fragile even, and yet here they were and waiting for their students. While the new arrivals watched, six student pilots of the senior entry came out of the flight line building, wearing flying overalls, each carrying a parachute over his shoulder and a leather flying helmet in one hand. Having deposited their parachutes, they began an external check of the aircraft before being joined by six flying instructors who began to climb into the rear seats of the tandem cockpit.

"OK, you lot. Stop gawping and come on in. We've got some paperwork to do before you can ride in one of those machines."

Paperwork was a loose description of an hour's form filling, confirmation and repetition of the information they had filled during last week at the induction.

"Right, that's that. Have a cuppa — help yourself to tea or coffee or chocolate. Leave the choccy biscuits for the CFI — sorry you sprogs won't know that's Chief Flying Instructor. He's 'sir' to you and his word is strictly for you to obey. You let him have the chocolate biscuits and we all have an easy time!"

71

The aircraft that had taken off as they arrived were now returning. The new students wanted to go outside and watch but that was not on the agenda.

"Right, the CFI will address you in 5 minutes. Stand up when he comes in and remain so until he tells you sit down. He'll be telling you about where and when you'll get kitted out and what the training routine will be. You'll also have a chance to meet your instructor. So, sit tight until the CFI comes in. Remember, this is a smoking area, you do not smoke outside this building. Anyone who does is for the highjump and won't get a soft landing. Right?"

There was a mumbled understanding. Piers wondered if anything was ever 'not right'. But this was the RAF and everything had to be just right! *Flying Officer Right* made sure of that! 'I suppose he's got a real name.'

The Chief Flying Instructor turned out to be a Flight Lieutenant still wearing flying overalls. Piers recognised him as one of the instructors who had gone out to fly as they arrived. Now he spoke for half an hour, without notes. He told them about the pattern of ground and air instruction, about day and night flying, about accurate records in the aircraft maintenance record and the pilot's personal log book. He told the students that he wanted them to fly safely and stay alive, "It saves on paperwork," he said. They were shown where their individual flying clothing lockers were and were issued with its key — as always against a signature.

The new students were told that the next time they were on the flight line they would receive their personal issue flying clothing and then the real business could begin.

"You only wear your flying kit on the flight line. It's not for general use or for polishing your car when you get one. And I shall expect you to wear gloves while you are flying to save getting your hands burned, and your flying boots too to stop your toes getting frostbite."

The instructors had filed into the briefing room while the CFI was talking. They mingled with the students and were introduced. Piers met *Flying Officer Right,* whose real name was Flying Officer Roy Board and who would be his first instructor, a wizened forty something standing five inches shorter than his student. He wore the Distinguished Flying Medal ribbon and the yellow and blue ribbon of the Queen's Korea Medal on his tunic. They did not have time to chat because it was time for the cadets to march back to the lecture halls on the other side of camp.

*   *   *

It took four weeks for Piers to summon the courage to ignore the 'London out-of-bounds' regulation. Reconnaissance had established three feasible public transport routes to Helen. It would be impossible to do the return journey to her university at Exeter in the available Sunday window; compulsory church parade on Sunday precluded being away on Saturday overnight. Therefore, when she wrote that she would be a having a weekend at home, from university, the chance of a few hours together could not be missed. Each practicable route depended on getting through central London, then out to Kingston on Thames near where her parents lived. Kingston happened to be beyond the '25 miles from the Main Gate' limit applied to the first year cadets, but that was a mere detail.

It did not occur to Piers that Helen's parents might object to having to share their daughter. Although they were still teenagers, they had been courting for twenty months and her parents always made Piers welcome... almost another son.

There was a direct London Transport *Greenline*[tm] coach service between Hitchin and Kingston. Although getting to the Hitchin terminus was possible, it was not in sufficient time to take the any departure before noon. The *Greenline*[tm] route passed through central London and went on to terminate close to Kingston at Hampton Court. But the journey took 2 hours and 40 minutes each way and was relatively the most expensive of any option. Worse was the last return through journey arrived in Hitchin before 22:00 so their time together would be very short. Piers used this route once only and then abandoned it.

Rail provided the fastest option. The train did not use the branch-line Henlow Camp station on Sunday (the church land problem!). But, it was only a 15 minutes bus ride to Hitchin railway station and then a mainline train into Kings Cross. The Sunday 22:40 Kings Cross to Bedford, via Hitchin where it held while church times ruled, was available; it went through Henlow Camp at 00:10 and was popular with airmen returning to camp. But this was the most risky route since any instructional staff or the senior entry, who were allowed into London and who ignored the concept of lights out, would use this return train as the most convenient means of transport. Another consideration, if Piers missed the train, there was the backup of the much later Birch^{tm} Bus route 203 — even if it did not depart Kings Cross until midnight. And, importantly, he could use his RAF identity card to get a discounted rail fare.

The extra time that this rail route gave Piers with his beloved Helen, living at home in Piers's second and third years, was worth the risk. In his second year, Piers used this route once per month to avoid the tedium of the 100 minute bus ride through the dark country lanes of Hertfordfordshire. In his third year, London bounds' limit was not an issue, but extending the time with his sweetheart was.

The third option was Birch^{tm} Bus. The Route 203 double-deck bus stopped outside the camp gate and with a great rush Piers was able to shed church parade uniform for civilian clothes and, by skipping church, he was on the bus at 10:38. He had to leave Kingston by 21:15 to be sure of the train or bus back to camp, but on several occasions parting was so difficult that he was lucky to catch the midnight bus out of Kings Cross. The first bus of the morning would not have got him back to Henlow until after drill parade or first lecture so he would be in real trouble. Piers came to dread the 100 minutes on the bus; it was uncomfortable, sleep was impossible and attempting to do lecture homework — reading, etc — could not be attempted in the lighting available.

'Roll on next year when I can have my own transport.' Of course that meant getting a driving licence, but a solo motor-cycle didn't require a qualified instructor. It was something to look forward to and, possibly, it was feasible to get down to Kingston midweek too.

Chapter 11
1956 ~ Uniforms Up to Standard For Church Parade

The first term passed quickly with every waking minute the cadets doing what he or she was told, being where he was told to be, sleeping from physical exhaustion. The demands of an extended day, marching, sport, mess life, academics including homework, spit and polish and, for some, flying were hard on the physique of even the fittest young men or women.

Piers dreaded Wednesday evenings. The weekly Thursday morning room inspection, once per month, became a full kit inspection involving the display of all items of uniform, not being worn, on the bunk bed. Out of bed promptly, no let up on daily morning drill. Then fold the sheets, blankets, towels and clothing — in an approved fashion and in accordance with the defined layout — was the order of the day. A cadet knew he had occasioned displeasure when, on his return from morning lectures, his carefully laid out worldly possessions were liberally strewn about the room. Civilian clothes, although not laid out, were expected to be smartly stored out of sight; every sock paired and folded, every shoe gleaming on top and clean underneath. Get this wrong and it could cost '*jankers*' with being confined to camp over the weekend.

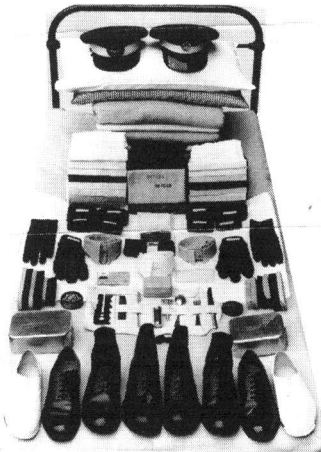

Cadets' uniform layout on bed for inspection

Of course, Piers compounded his difficulties in complying with the strict cadets' regime being made more difficult with his Sunday excursions into out-of-bounds territory. His colleagues didn't comment on his Sunday absence and Piers didn't volunteer what he was doing. If any of them noticed his absence, none remarked upon it — at least in his presence — such was the wide space available on the RAF camp and its surroundings. Perhaps they were all taking the opportunity of the day of rest to escape from the proximity of their fellows; perhaps they each had unauthorised escapes of their own.

Classroom lectures by experienced lecturers served to level the academics' maths and science knowledge baseline for the demands of the degree-level engineering subjects to come. Some of the lecturers were recent graduates from university who were doing their national service despite the knowledge that, within two years, the requirement would have been phased out in favour of regular officers. Nevertheless, this levelling of basic academic skills offered an opportunity of differentiating potential mechanical from electrical specialist engineering streams, not always to the cadets' preferences, required for the middle and senior years and thence into their commissioned service. The college had well equipped laboratories and workshops so there was plenty of opportunity for hands-on experience.

But each week there was Sunday's Church parade. And there was no compromise on standards of uniform on the alleged day of rest. The cadets had been warned!

*   *   *

It had been on the second Saturday of October, that the now twelve-day experienced 1956 Entry was joined on the Parade Square by the 1954 (Senior) and 1955(Middle) Entries. There to supervise the wing's preparedness for Church Parade was the wing's commanding officer, the Adjutant, the two squadron commanders, the helpful WRAF officer co-opted from somewhere on the camp unconnected with the Cadet Wing, the Wing Warrant Officer, whose name was Fetcham, and drill instructor Sergeant Johnson. There was a rumour that the Assistant Commandant (General Studies), renowned for watching the cadets' morning drill practice through high powered binoculars, was also observing the proceedings from a distance.

While the Middle and Senior Entries stood about, wearing the daily working uniform for what was for them a routine drill exercise, the Junior Entry wore its best dress uniform for the first time. While Piers's entry was waiting for their officer pattern suits, shoes and headdress to be tailored, they wore airman's pattern uniform and boots, uncomfortable in its newness and not designed for comfort in its woollen material. This contrasted with the officer pattern, worsted barathea material of the more senior entries; these early church parades of the college year would be the

76

only times the uniforms would be mixed on parade. That the Junior Entry was also novice at drill was recognised and hence the Wing executives were out in force to minimise potential damage to the Wing's image on a high visibility parade on the first 'real' Sunday of the term.

Piers was anxious that the Entry's inexperience was about to draw a great deal of practice between Saturday breakfast and the same meal on Sunday. Practise drill and spit and polish 'bull' was a tedious process interrupted only by meals.

Appointed from within the ranks of the senior entry, twenty years old Senior Under Officer Kingham, the SUO for A Squadron, took charge of the Junior Entry while his B Squadron colleague, SUO Bartles, took charge of the others at some distance from the juniors.

SUO Kingham called his 47 cadets to 'fall in by squadron', the manoeuvre that they had been practising with Sergeant Johnson all week. He stood before the two groups of eight by three.

"Entry... Attention!... Stand at ease... Stand easy... Listen up. This is a rehearsal for tomorrow. It's straightforward, but the CO wants it right because the Assistant Commandant is coming to take the salute. The sooner we get it right, the sooner we can get back to our bunks."

He let that message sink in, then continued, "When we get on the square, the CO will do a formal inspection. Just do as I tell you and all will be OK. For Christ's sake remember which way to turn on the command 'right turn' and that the first foot forward when you march is your left. Now, let's practice the inspection before you join the grown ups..." He was referring to his colleagues in the Senior Entry just two years older than the group he was addressing.

Kingham turned to Sergeant Johnson, who was watching his flock about to be tested for the first time, and received the nod to proceed.

"Entry... Attention! Remember to stand still, but don't strain because it upsets the blood flow and you'll pass out. If you feel yourself going, rock on the balls of your feet to take the weight off your heels. Practice that now, gently does it. Good! Stand at ease!" Forty seven right boots separated from forty seven left boots with varying rates of movement.

SUO Kingham looked at the Wing executives assembling near the saluting podium. The time for 'March On' was approaching. But first, "Today, we're going to practise marching past the Assistant Commandant in column of route; on the real day we'll only do it once. So it's got to be right, or else… The CO may want us to do it more than once today. This is quite easy, really, just do the eyes right when the command is issued and try to keep in step. Look the reviewing officer in the eyes as you march past him, but don't move your head while you're doing it. Now then, Entry… Attention! I am going to check your uniforms."

While each cadet was inspected, out of sight, but not out of hearing, the other entries were being marshalled by SUO Bartles. Warrant Officer Fetcham marched to the centre of the square and commanded, "Cadet Wing … march on!" His voice easily carried the one hundred yards to the parading cadets.

Bartles followed the accepted, well drilled route. The Wing did the same thing every Sunday expect during college leave. Once Bartles' cadets were in position, Kingham commanded, "Junior Entry… Attention!... Right turn… Listen for commands… Smartly now… Quick march." Kingham did his job well and the Junior Entry arrived at the correct area of the parade square reasonably tidily.

Kingham commanded, "Halt… Left turn."

Warrant Officer Fetcham now had 95 cadets drawn up in front of him. "Cadet Wing… Stand at ease!... Stand easy!" They could all relax for a moment.

The first march past the podium, with the eyes right salute, was a shambles because the experienced and novice cadets did not march at the same pace or stride length. However, at the fourth attempt, the CO declared himself satisfied, instructed Bartles to march off the Middle and Senior Entries while he set about a uniform inspection of the beginners. Accompanied by the squadron commanders and Warrant Officer Fetchham, while the cadets were held at attention for more than fifteen minutes, every brass button, cap badge, bootlace, collar, tie, trouser crease, haircut and shaved chin was inspected and discrepancies pointed out.

"Mister Fetcham," the CO addressed his principal non-commissioned officer according to RAF custom. "This is a motley turnout, don't you think?" He turned to one of the squadron commanders and asked him to request the WRAF officer to approach. "These uniforms need smartening up and those boots are not up to standard. I would be pleased to see the Wing's standard double Windsor knot on every tie, Mister Fetcham. They won't be wearing gloves so I shall expect clean hands, free of ink stains or dirty nails. And personal jewellery is to be consigned to the pocket or better still left in their bunks. I am pleased to see the haircut standard is good, long may it remain so — short, back and sides."

"Sir," uttered Fetcham, accepting his commanding officer's comments. His Saturday was being ruined, but it was only once a year — usually — unless someone important died and he had to go and organise a guard of honour.

Flight Officer Philippa Pendleton WRAF approached and saluted smartly.

"Ah, Miss Pendleton, I would be grateful for your advice about my girls' uniforms. They won't be getting their officer pattern kit for a couple of weeks. Those trousers are not right for parade use. They look too... err... World War Two like. OK for lectures and regular drill and climbing over aeroplanes in work, you know... The men are being smartened up. If I tell them to wear skirts, will their... stockings... bear muster? I mean... it's only two, maybe three, Church Parades until their best kit arrives and then... I guess you... err... have standard hosiery, officer women for the use of... on parades."

"I understand, sir. You want me to arrange something?"

"If you would be so kind, Miss Pendleton. Stores have arranged for each cadet to have an officer-style loan card. The women cadets can draw what they need on those."

"I understand, sir. You want me to arrange something this morning?"

"In time for tomorrow, if you can. I intend for a dress rehearsal at 18:00 outside Block 57."

"I understand, sir. Skirts and stockings, sir. They'll need shoes too, sir, the boots will look awkward, sir."

"Just fix it, Miss Pendleton. Do you require Warrant Officer Fetcham to accompany you?"

"No, sir. Just have the girls fall out of the parade and I'll do the rest."

"I'd be obliged, Miss Pendleton. Perhaps you'll join us later, my Adjutant will give you the details..."

"I understand, sir." Having stood absolutely still for 15 minutes, the two girls faltered in their first movements but were quickly marched away, under the care of the WRAF officer, to go and wake the duty store-man from his usual Saturday morning siesta.

"Mister Fetcham," the CO turned square onto his warrant officer as if to emphasise the serious nature of his requirement. "These cadets need smartening up to standard. I would be grateful if you, and Sergeant Johnson, would make the necessary arrangements for the Adjutant to inspect the Entry at 18:00 hours today. You may have such support of the Senior Under Officers as you see fit. I shall expect the Wing to pass muster with the Assistant Commandant tomorrow... What's wrong with that man?" Both men looked where the wing commander was pointing.

Cadet John Dawtry, already nicknamed *Ganglion*, had turned pale. The unaccustomed static strain on muscle and sinew was having its inevitable effect. Cadet Dawtry was about to faint. Piers sensed there was a problem, but there was nothing he could do about it. The Warrant Officer recognised the symptoms.

"With your permission, sir?" He received a nod. "Sergeant Johnson, stand the cadets at ease and then move them to circulate their fluids in the appropriate manner."

"Sir!" acknowledged the Drill Sergeant. "Entry, stand at ease! Stand easy!" The movement was welcome and Cadet Dawtry appeared to be recovering. Clenched fists, by the seams of their trousers, opened and closed, one or two shoulders rotated.

"Parade, Attention! On the spot... quick march... get those knees up... I said on the spot... double time, march... on the spot. Halt. I said halt. Stand still."

Sergeant Johnson announced to his warrant officer, "This here entry is now fully circulated, sir, and appropriately prepared for your purposes, sir."

"Very well, Sergeant Johnson. March the cadets to their barrack block and get them fell in to tidy up their uniforms for their commanding officer's inspection. I shall be in Block 57 immediately I am released from this here drill square."

"Sir. Entry, Attention! Officer on parade... let's get it together then... stand at ease! That's better... Entry, Attention! Right turn! By the left... Quick march!..." Then the salute on the march, "Eyes... left!... Eyes... front!... Halt! About turn! Quick march. Halt! Right turn. Stand at ease. Stand still, gentlemen. No body's given you permission to sway about like tree in a storm. Stand still!... That was bloody awful, young gentlemen. Thank heavens you wasn't showing your worst to your two of the fairer gender, like... downright bleeding awful. We'll have to do better than that."

It was time for Fetcham to assume control until the inspection at 18:00. "With your permission, sir?" He received a second nod from his CO. "Sergeant, march those cadets back to their block where I shall address the young gentlemen on the expectations of their officers."

Fetcham saluted his officer and received the customary dismissal, "Carry on, Mister Fetcham. We'll meet again at 18:00." The CO acknowledged Fetcham's salute. The warrant officer was being warned that the CO would probably not delegate responsibility for tomorrow's turnout to his adjutant. Miss Pendleton was likely to have disturbed arrangements for her Saturday evening also.

The time was 09:20. It was going to be a hard day's graft for the cadets of 1956 Entry and, for some, rather later into evening too.

Chapter 12
1957 ~ Checks Before Solo

Flying training, interlaced with engineering education was an extended process. Piers flew, with his instructor Flying Officer Roy Board in 40 minute flights, practising handling the Chipmunk in take-offs, aerobatics, navigation, emergency procedures and landings. Powered flight was very different from flying a glider and, to Piers, both more challenging and satisfying. The onset of winter interrupted the flying programme, much to the despair of the cadets. The short Christmas break came and went, with Piers spending much of the time with Helen. They went to the cinema a couple of times and celebrated the New Year at the Town Hall dance. Helen sensed that her man's thoughts were somewhere else.

RAF Chipmunk T Mk 10

Author's photo

'He will tell me in his own sweet time,' she thought. She tried to describe her life at university, but felt she did not really do it justice.

Instructor Board took Piers on three more 40 minute dual training flights during January. Fg Off Board was increasingly confident that his student was ready for his first solo and checked with the CFI that he could choose the moment. He got the necessary approval.

On February 18, 1957 the instructor and student climbed into their Chipmunk's cockpit. Board had briefed Piers that they would be staying close to the airfield today, doing circuits and bumps. There might be a practice 'engine failure on take-off' exercise, so just remember the procedure.

"Right! Let's get on with it."

'There it is again, *Mr Right*,' thought Piers. 'now he'll want me to do the cockpit checks...'

"Right, Ploughman. Cockpit checks before startup... aloud please."

Piers called out the 10 point checks of switches, instruments, throttle, trim, freedom of controls, carburettor heating and fuel indicators. "Checks completed and satisfactory," he said into the intercom microphone on his facemask.

"Very good. Start her up."

Thumbs up signal to the groundcrew, received a similar signal in reply, then aloud, "Fuel cock on, switches on, press starter cartridge." A small charge in the engine compartment fired and the propeller turned. The engine stuttered, caught and began to fire smoothly as it dissipated clouds of unburned exhaust smoke until it settled down. The flight instruments came to life, the engine instruments showed the Rolls Royce Gipsy engine was ready for business, the Chipmunk was set to do its master's bidding.

"Right, Ploughman. After startup checks... aloud please."

Around the cockpit once again, plus this time, "Wheel brakes on... cockpit closed and secure... radio channel selected... fuel cock on... straps tight. We're ready to go, sir."

"Right, Ploughman. Call the tower and taxi when you are ready." The instructor would hear the exchange with ATC through the intercom. With air traffic clearance to move on the airfield, Piers waved the groundcrew to clear the wheel chocks; he revved the engine sufficient to break the static inertia so as to move forward to check the brakes, and then followed the ground marshaller's signals until he was well clear of the parking area. He saluted the groundcrew with his left hand in acknowledgement of their help. The instructor was not going to speak unless he needed to; Piers knew it was the way that Flying Officer Board worked from the dual controls at the rear. He taxied the Chipmunk to the end of the runway.

Using his radio callsign, Piers spoke, "Henlow Tower... this is Fulmer Two Seven... request take off clearance for local circuits."

The headphones reacted almost immediately. "Fulmer Two Seven... Henlow Tower... you are clear to line up for take off... one other aircraft in circuit... remain on local frequency. Check your altimeter setting is 1005."

"Fulmer Two Seven... altimeter 1005... lining up." He would have to wait for clearance to accelerate for take off.

Piers adjusted the throttle to manoeuvre the Chipmunk along the grass strip which served as a runway at Henlow. He checked the engine oil temperature was within limits for take off. He said aloud, for personal confidence, "Engine oil temperature within limits... fuel sufficient for this exercise... showing full..." There was no verbal reaction from the instructor in the rear seat, his student was doing the proper checks.

"Fulmer Two Seven... Henlow Tower... you are clear to take off... circuit now clear... remain on local frequency."

"Fulmer Two Seven... take off." Piers pushed the throttle lever fully open, the engine purred in response and with the release of the brakes the Chipmunk began its bumpy acceleration down the runway. Soon the tail wheel was off the ground and with flying speed of 45 knots the aircraft lifted into the sky. It was gentle, steady, comfortable, 'A good take off,' thought the student.

Piers spoke, "Climbing away at 70 knots." No verbal reply from the instructor. It was not yet time to call the tower. The aircraft was passing through 600 feet when the throttle was pulled back and the engine lost power.

Piers reacted to the simulated emergency. He said, "Practice engine emergency. I would call the tower now. Altitude 600 feet." He pushed the aircraft nose forward to maintain airspeed with the loss of propeller traction. He weaved the nose to assess the opportunities for a crash landing. He spoke, "Clear area straight ahead. 400 feet. Check fuel cock off..." Piers moved as if to close the fuel supply control between his feet but this was a practice and he did not touch it. "Straps tight... 250 feet... lined up for landing... airspeed 50 knots... flaps now... "

"Climb straight ahead. Turn on to downwind heading and call the tower." The instructor's requirements were quite clear. There was no comment whether the emergency drill had gone satisfactorily. Air Traffic control did not comment on what they recognised was a routine student's test.

"Henlow Tower... this is Fulmer Two Seven downwind... request clearance for landing."

"Fulmer Two Seven... Henlow Tower... you are clear to land... Circuit clear. Check your altimeter setting is 1005."

"Fulmer Two Seven... altimeter 1005... turning finals for landing."

The instructor came on the radio, "Henlow Tower… Fulmer Two Seven… for touch and go?"

"Roger, Fulmer Two Seven… this is Henlow Tower… you are clear for touch and go."

The Chipmunk completed a further four circuits without actually stopping on the runway. Only once did Piers make a mess of his landing, but he made a good recovery, which drew from the rear, "I have control." The Chipmunk climbed at full power in a fairly tight turn around the ATC Building until it reached 1000 feet on the downwind heading. "You are downwind, call for landing, and this time put it down in one piece. You have control."

Piers recognised his instructor was none-too-happy. 'Do it properly next!'

"Fulmer Two Seven… turning finals for landing."

"This is Henlow Tower… you are clear to land, Fulmer Two Seven …Circuit clear. What are your intentions?"

From the instructor, "Fulmer Two Seven for touch and go."

Around they went again, then the instructor said, "Right, this time we'll land and go back to the line."

"Yes, sir," acknowledged Piers. His modified call to the tower was, "Henlow Tower… Fulmer Two Seven… for landing and return to the hangar?"

"Roger, you are clear to land. Taxi when you are ready."

The three point landing was as good as any that Piers had done. It was a satisfactory way to finish the day's training. The taxi over the grass went well and the marshalling crew were waiting on the apron in front of the hangar. The next instruction from the rear was totally unexpected.

"Right. I've had enough and I need a fag. You're ready. Go round by yourself and come back in one piece. Use the same callsign." The cockpit perspex cover was sliding back. "Check the brakes are on. Enjoy it." Flying Officer Board climbed out, dropped his parachute on the wing, reached in to secure the rear seat-straps, touched Piers on the shoulder, slid the perspex to the half-closed position and jumped off the wing. He slung his parachute over one shoulder, and moved away from the aircraft to where Piers could see he was clear. Piers slid the cockpit closed and called the tower.

He was being sent for his first solo. No time to be worried…

"Henlow Tower… this Fulmer Two Seven… request taxi clearance for take off."

"Fulmer Two Seven… this is Henlow Tower… you are clear to taxi and take off… circuit is clear… remain on local frequency. Confirm you altimeter is setting 1005."

"Fulmer Two Seven… altimeter 1005… take off."

The Gypsy engine wanted to give him the ride. The Chipmunk aircraft wanted him to gently adjust its control surfaces for a smooth flight. The sky beckoned its new aspirant. At 45 knots, tyres separated from earth and the magic of manned flight happened. Earth released its captive. At 70 knots, the aircraft climbed at 300 feet per minute. Three minutes later it was time for the downwind radio call and cockpit checks. Another two and the call, "Henlow Tower… this is Fulmer Two Seven… request landing clearance and return to the hangar?" Piers guessed there were a dozen pairs of binoculars focussed on him, looking for the mistake.

"Fulmer Two Seven… this is Henlow Tower… proceed."

Perhaps the landing was not his best. It shut up his singing, what song he never would remember although discordant it no doubt was. He'd done it — solo — the first of the entry. As he parked the aircraft, under marshaller's directions, and closed it down while repeating every check, twice with out-loud instructions just for confidence, Piers realised he was shaking. It wasn't fear. No, it had not been frightening. The aircraft had seen him right. He was never in any doubt that it would. It was released exhilaration — pent up hopes — through four years since gliding at Hornchurch. It was as if the bubble had burst. It was fantastic! Utterly, bloody, fantastic!

The airman at the wheel chocks smiled to himself. He'd seen it all before. 'Them lucky bastards what get to fly solo. I'd like to have a go myself… Don't he look pleased with himself.' Piers was oblivious to the airman's plight. He strode, head held high, to the Operations' Desk to sign the aircraft log and record 55 minutes flying, six landings. Much more important was the Pilots' Log; there he put 45 minutes dual and 10 minutes solo.

'Now let's go and find *Flying Officer Right* and find out what happens next.'

As Piers moved towards the dispersal hut, he glanced at the sky. He was on track to conquer that sky. There, all seeing, the white disk of the moon was visible in full daylight; the man in the moon seemed to approve of the day's events. 'One day... just one day... maybe I'll come visiting, Mister Moon. Just you wait and see.'

*   *   *

There was another five months of the first year training to complete. Their best uniforms had arrived and were individually tailored. Formal parade drill became an art form and the entry knew when they did it well — or was in no doubt when they didn't. No-one escaped jankers or the consequential extra square bashing it entailed. Many found it difficult keeping up with the demands of the advanced academics but co-operation among the cadets certainly helped.

The long breaks, Easter and Summer, held the opportunity of a sort of lengthy escape from the classroom, when the cadets were expected to go away, in self-selected groups, to something adventurous and challenging. Selecting something suitable was a welcome diversion from the routine.

And for Piers there was the company of Helen without the pressure of being out-of-bounds.

Chapter 13
1957 ~ The Junior Entry Relaxes

If anyone had asked a cadet how he passed his spare time, inevitably the reply would be that he did not have any. Every waking minute there was something to do, to clean, to swot, to tidy, to prepare, to square off. But that would not convey the complete story. Some cadets had the knack of closing their bunk door to the outside world to read, listen to music or the radio, to write to friends or loved ones, even just chat with a shoe brush in hand. The lunch break often afforded just a few such private moments – that is if exceptional additional disciplinary drill was not being meted out. In the evenings, some junior entry cadets mixed with the other entries in the cadets' garage where authorised motor vehicles were variously dissembled then reassembled with differing degrees of skill. The sportsmen practised, the wise studied, a kit was assembled into a model or working radio, some used the cadets' mess bar.

Money was always a problem. Some brought ready cash with them, from rich parents and the like. Four cadets had previous RAF service before joining the cadet programme and it was a fundamental principle that an airman's pay never fell except under disciplinary procedure. The Australian pair were rich with overseas allowances. However, for the majority of cadets earning just twelve shillings per day, before National Insurance deduction, with some receiving a supplement of 5 shillings for each day flying training happened, the pennies had to be watched. Cadets' finances were perpetually tight.

Cadets each had their own bank account, managed by Lloyds Bank[tm] of Hitchin. A form of cheque book encouraged account awareness and enabled payment of mess bills and similar minor charges — all practical training for the real officers' world which lay ahead. All the while, a cadet had to be aware of forthcoming expenditure, not least for the activities which were expected in the Easter and Summer leave breaks.

However, it was not all homework interspersed with spit and polish. There was a degree of socialising, even including the two girls. *Bumper* and *Aspirin* often came downstairs to share homework or just chat; on these occasions the bunk door was always left slightly ajar. There was plenty of male bonding, particularly the sharing of academic skills in the face of challenging mathematics. In exchange for sound education, the former airmen knew how to achieve to highest standard of spit and polish especially on footwear, of near permanent creases in trousers, how to minimise the perpetual tidiness problems associated with one cupboard, one chest of drawers, one shaving cabinet above the sink and one pre-planned weekly inspection. The cadets' bunks were also inspected out of sequence just to keep up the pressure. The ex-servicemen had been through the regimen before although perhaps not to the same exacting standards.

There were the mess nights: 19:30 for 20:00 was the routine, in uniform and bow tie, for a formal dinner of four or more courses with wine and full waiter service. It was rare that a mess evening would be over when the diners left the table at about 21:30; the mess bar was open and often impromptu mess games were begun. It was considered impolite for any cadet in a host mess to depart before the last guest had departed. It was one such night that the Senior Mess had a guest who was one of the Cadet Wing staff whose departure was inevitably quite late! Block 57 had been secured because it was unoccupied and in the absence of the middle entry and the Duty Under Officer who was with the junior cadets, the junior entry was therefore locked out. The entry trooped back to their mess and demanded that the bar be reopened until the Duty Under Officer could be found.

RAF Henlow had a NAFFI general purpose store and an Astra cinema available for use by cadets. The NAFFI was reasonably well stocked for toiletries and other essentials; the Astra showed movies and doubled as a theatre. Outside the camp gate there was a newsagent for the essential magazine. The nearest pub, *The Bird in Hand*, was one hundred yards from the Guardroom, but out-of-bounds to the cadets.

There was a circuitous Birch[tm] Bus journey to Luton, involving a change en-route. This was not a pleasant journey and even the most adventurous only did the journey once. The attractions of Luton were not that persuasive!

*   *   *

"What are we going to do about girls?"

"We've got some — well, at least two. Upstairs."

"I'm talking about real girls."

"They look pretty real to me — but I don't know too much about girls, except they cry some. Men don't cry. It's got to be the movies that make them cry — and books…"

"And fellows like you. When did you last go after a girl and … you know… snog?"

"Well I don't like to say."

"Exactly. Look, these hands have spent half the evening bulling up these toe caps so that Sergeant Johnston can say they're not up to scratch. And he knows I can't answer back. I want to use these hands to get a grip of some flesh… human, female, flesh.

"Is that how you diggers down under think of your women? Bits of flesh to grab by the fistful?"

"No way. But girls are good for holding on to, if you can. I'll go and get *Fu* Wilde," said *LMN* King, "and you get… err… *Crab* Ellis, he thinks he's God's answer to womankind. We'll sort out something. I'm getting withdrawal symptoms from an insufficiency of cleavage; Henlow is not exactly Bondi Beach."

Within five minutes the four had become six, standing in the corridor with the prospect of an interesting discussion about the other sex being magnetic. Heads were looking out of doors wanting to know what the noise was about. No-one was offering any solution to how 19 year old teenagers could access the fairer sex. Money was a major obstacle and there was no way the cadets could stage a mess function without agreement of the Cadet Wing staff; anyway, mess functions such as balls were already timetabled and half the cadets had long distance girls that were invited. No, whatever the plan, it had to be off-station, local and cheap … and soon.

"Look, fellows," chimed Basil *U* Leitch. He was the sort of character who liked to take the lead. "If we can't get the girls to come to us, then we'll have to take ourselves to them. After all, they don't know what they're missing."

"OK, *U*, where and how?" *MacKay* Knight was allowing his Scottish accent to surface, more in frustration than anger. He did not like insolvable problems and he was not sure he liked Leitch taking control.

"Hitchin, *Palais de Dance*, in Hermitage Road, Wednesdays, eight pm. It'll cost a quid plus bus fares. They'll already have paid to go in, the girls that is, so we don't have to stump up for that. We can catch the

22:10 bus from Hitchin and be back in the block by lights out." *Crab* Ellis was offering a plausible plan. "We could organise an early supper in the mess and catch the Birch^{tm} Bus into town at 19:38."

LMN King had adopted an uncharacteristic facial expression which slowly matured into a grin. "What did Henry Higgins say? *I think you've got it...* Sounds like a good plan to me. Say, has anyone finished the electronics homework yet?"

A match struck and a cigarette was lit.

"Stuff the homework," said *LMN* King in his Australian drawl, "we've got to rehearse how to be nice to women, to say what they want to hear before we get on with the important business. I say we get our own girls down here and get some tips. They ought to earn their keep after we saved them from a fate worse than death."

"Are you talking about the raid by our university oppos?" queried Piers.

"Yeh, *Peetot*, that's right. Them coming over from their seccos, attempting to kidnap our girls, the very cheek! Even *Pimple* Henson horned in to repel the boarders! It's not surprising that a couple of them got cold showers — to say nothing some loosing their trousers and *Bumper* rinsing them in cold water. She's got some muscle, when she gets the mood, has *Bumper*. I don't think *Aspirin* cottoned on to what was happening."

"Someone is going to get lucky when they land *Aspirin*." It was a mumbled comment from within the group, now nine strong.

"Go on, *Peetot*, you've got a girl of your own. You go on upstairs and ask them to come down here and have a cup of chocolate. They'd have to bring their own mugs to save us having to wash up."

"So you are sending me into forbidden territory?" What happens if I get caught? Or if one of the girls complains? That would be 14 days jankers if not instant dismissal. And who's paying for the chocolate?"

U Leitch responded flapping his wrist, "Go on. I'll look out for the Duty Under Officer. The girls won't complain if you bring them both down. Tell them strength in numbers. Ask nicely, though — you could always suggest that if they don't come down then we'll come up, *en masse*." The group was nodding approval at the plan.

So thirteen cadets, including both Australians and both WRAF not wishing to miss the fun, were aboard the 19:38 bus from Henlow Camp to Hitchin Market Square on the first possible Wednesday evening.

*   *   *

Sonia Warner agreed to leave the dance hall with Piers so that he could walk her home. His arm was around her waist, holding her hip to his, as she steered him towards her house. It was less than 10 minutes walk and Sonia had no interest in delaying getting to the alley beside her house. This was where she tried the boys out, not letting them go too far in whatever liberties they might take. She did not want an accident, after all.

Their conversation lacked depth. It was mostly about how good the music had been and would they both be there at the same time next week?

" 'ere," she said, "did you see Millie go off with one of your fellers?"

"There was a young lady left with one of the Aussies. I don't know if that was your Millie?" They were now in the alley, dark and damp with condensation. Very little street light percolated into this space. Just right for the exploration of Sonia's physique that Piers had in mind. He could not have cared less about what *LMN* King and Millie got up to — the Aussie was big enough and ugly enough to look after himself.

"Look, Sonia, I've got to catch the bus from the Market Square at 10 minutes past, so…"

"Shut up then. Are you going to kiss me?" She pulled Piers around so that she had her back against a wall and pulled his mouth on to her. He was amazed as her tongue explored the inside of his teeth. Helen did not kiss this way! So he responded in kind and Sonia seemed content. Her body somehow seemed to will him on.

Piers pulled away slightly and fumbled with the buttons on her top coat. Sonia did not resist. Inside the coat felt warm to his hand and the breast within her dance dress was nicely rounded. When she spoke, her lips brushed his.

"You can reach to the top buttons of my dress."

He glanced down, interrupting her ardent kisses, to see what this wondrous object looked like at close quarters. He saw the luminous face of his Newmark^{tm} watch glowing green against the not yet naked flesh. It showed one minute to ten.

"Oh, Christ, I've got to run… to catch the bus… I'm so sorry."

93

"You won't tell anyone what I let you done." She was trying to get a kiss as she gathered her clothing about her.

"No… I promise… I've got to run… perhaps I'll see you next week…" Piers was away as fast as he was able towards the bus stop in the Market Square. He wasn't the last to arrive, but the bus was two minutes late which saved Ian *LMN* King from trouble.

LMN and Piers sat next to each other. The chill March air had misted all the upstairs windows and the air was acrid with stale tobacco. *Bumper* was sitting alone at the front of the upper deck, smoking.

"What's the matter with her?" drawled *MacKay* Knight in a dejected tone. His problem was that the girl he had chosen had refused point blank to leave with a Scotsman.

"Dunno. She was getting into a ruckus with a local fella and *Aspirin* stepped in." *Fu* Wilde was describing the scene. "I never thought to see *Aspirin* separate two warring tribes, but that was how it looked like to me. So *Bumper* didn't get a fella and *Aspirin* got another notch on her reputation as a no-nonsense kinda girl. She's on the bus, downstairs."

Bumper Leigh could hear this exchange and ignored it with a shrug, a deep drag on her cigarette and studiously watching the Hertfordshire blackness pass the bus's window. She did not react if she heard the lowered conversation between Piers and the other Australian, *LMN* King.

"Well?" The Aussie's question was succinct.

It was obvious that all the cadets wanted to know what had happened; they could hardly have missed seeing the departure of two of their number each with a girl on the arm. There were seven cadets in the group on the upper deck. Four non-smokers had wisely chosen to stay below, where it was marginally warmer and the atmosphere made breathing rather less unpleasant.

"Well what?"

"Did you?" Someone gently punched Piers's shoulder.

"No… I didn't." Piers was indignant about being pressed for such intimate details. "Anyway, she made me promise I wouldn't tell."

"So you got inside her dress then?"

'This bloody Aussie is persistent,' thought Piers. "I told you…"

"You told me nothing. But it's obvious you did…" with a grin.

"Well if it's so obvious… Do you?" with his nose querulously raised.

"Millie made me promise not to tell..." The two men burst out laughing and would continue to laugh for the twelve minutes it took for the bus the reach Henlow Camp. Then it was a rush to get back to Block 57 for the lights out check at 22:30.

The lurid details would have to wait for another day.

The realisation dawned that tomorrow was Thursday, Warrant Officer Fetcham's inspection. Every light on the ground floor went on.

"Screw the Duty Under Officer! Somethings are more important than three days on the drill square!"

There was no doubt this was full scale, junior entry, mutiny, instantly punishable should the DUO poke his head out of his door. However, this DUO used his initative; he sensibly waited until it was time for the lights out call for the middle entry before venturing out to the corridor. At 23:15, the lights were all extinguished in Block 57, except for the DUO's bunk where the exploits of Doctor Sparrow, as described in the novel *Doctor in the House* by Richard Gordon, were diverting the senior cadet from his thermodynamics studies.

'Anyway,' he thought, 'they'll all be up at 06:00 for breakfast and drill. That'll teach them not to stay up late. Trouble is ... it's me that's got to knock them up!'

Chapter 14
1957 ~ Training Exercise: Get Yourself to Changi

Cadet procedures required that each Easter and summer leave period had to include a challenging, self-fulfilment activity for the cadet. It did not necessarily have to be course related. It was as much an exercise in initiative and organisation as it was a task performed or problem solved in order to develop skill or understanding. Assistance with travel and certain equipment loans was possible. Most cadets elected to get as far away from Bedfordshire as they could, many opting for sightseeing on the Continent. Piers, with the cooperation of his father in Singapore, set out to fly to Singapore by indulgence flight in the new RAF fleet of Comet Mk 2 aircraft. It was thought impractical to fit the journey into the relatively short Easter leave, so it was decided the timing would be arranged for the summer months at the end of Piers's first year. On completion of the exercise, and within a week of returning to college, each cadet had to submit a written report on the exercise and the lessons learned.

Separation from Helen was inevitable, but they agreed they could have a motor-cycle holiday, perhaps in Cornwall, when he returned.

Since he would be flying to the tropics, on duty, Piers needed to draw from the Clothing Stores a personal issue of tropical uniform. RAF inoculations were not negotiable, no matter how loathed they might be. Railway warrants were issued from Henlow, via Swindon, to the departure airfield which was RAF Lyneham, Wiltshire. He had been this way before. At the appointed time, Technical Cadet PP Ploughman reported, in uniform, for emplanement.

Piers was allocated a seat in the rearmost passenger cabin section of the recently introduced Comet Mk 2. The RAF Sergeant Loadmaster, the equivalent of the purser on a civilian aircraft, had his duty seat next to where Piers was seated. There was no conversation offered by this SNCO who was busy with his 100 passengers and piles of paperwork. There was a planned crew change at Bahrain; the aircraft would refuel and continue with least delay. The quick turn-round, less than two hours, with a midnight temperature of 104^0F and humidity knocking on 100%, was very welcome. The replacement loadmaster was as unpleasant as he could be to the young man seated next to him, but whose sweat saturated uniform did not bear any rank insignia. So here was someone to ease the sergeant's workload, issue drinks, convey meal boxes and generally tidy up. Seated on the other side of the central aisle was a warrant officer identified by the 'Tate & Lyle' rank insignia worn on his wrist. More precisely, the passenger was a master aircrew pilot who noticed what was going on between Officer Cadet Piers and the loadmaster.

"Where are you going?" he asked Piers. They were somewhere over the Indian Ocean and en-route for the RAF staging post in Ceylon.

"Changi. I've got folks out there and I've been given three weeks leave."

"You're not an airman, are you?" What triggered the question Piers found out when the master pilot asked, pointing, "Is that your hat up there?"

Piers had chosen to travel with his best peak cap, officer pattern with a

RAF Master Aircrew insignia

white circlet ribbon around the headgrip. 'Mum would like it and it was comfortable if a little inconvenient to pack.' The hat was standard insignia for officer cadets who, although legally and paid as an airman of the lowest grade, no-one in the real air force knew how to address or react to. It carried an officer pattern cap badge with the royal crown. In short, unless you knew, you didn't argue with an officer pattern hat.

"Yes, sir." Warrant officers always rate 'sir' and it helps to show respect. Master aircrew, and master technicians, had the status of warrant rank, hence the 'sir'.

"You put your hat on your seat and go visit the facilities. It will save you a lot of hassle."

Piers did as he was told. He returned five minutes later, having rinsed his face, to find the sergeant loadmaster standing by his own seat looking down at the object residing on Piers's seat.

"Is that your hat?" nodding at the offending item.

"Yes, sergeant, it must have dropped from the overhead stowage."

"Hmm!" The sergeant went about his business elsewhere in the cabin. The master pilot grinned at Piers and nodded his head.

"Have a good leave, son. I hope you survive whatever course you're on. It's a great life if you don't weaken!"

Piers nodded back. "I'm working on it, sir. Thanks for your help."

The master pilot smiled again, closed his eyes and let his head settle against his seat's headrest. There was another two hours of uninteresting ocean still to cross and he'd seen it a hundred times before.

**Singapore Island in 1956 showing RAF airfields and
Causeway to Jahore Baharu**

Map: Drawn by author

**The deHavilland Vampire T Mark 11 – the RAF's advanced trainer
during 1950s. Flown by No 1574 Target Facilities Flight, RAF Changi
in the 1950-60s.**

Chapter 15
1957 ~ A Privileged Tour Of Singapore Island

The groundcrew airman put the safety pin with its attached red metal disc 9 inches in front of Piers's face. His ejection seat was armed; he was sitting on a live seat which had sufficient explosive primed to eject the seat, its passenger and his parachute, through the perspex canopy and 50 feet clear of the RAF's Vampire of Target Facilities Flight. The airman placed the disc in the seat's canvas stowage above Piers's left ear, pulled the seat-straps tight, stuck a thumb up for the pilot to see that he had checked the passenger was securely fastened, then climbed down his ladder.

The pilot spoke, "OK. Here we go. Just remember that if I say 'Eject' put both hands above your head, pull the ejection seat blind in front of your face, and enjoy the ride. I shan't have time to tell you twice!"

The officer cadet murmured something like, "Roger." Well, it sounded professional to him. Anxiety is insufficient to describe his feelings. Chipmunk trainers at Henlow did not have ejection seats; this was a first for Piers. The pilot tried to put his passenger at ease.

"It will be cooler once we're airborne. I've got to close the canopy now so it could get a bit stickier while we take-off."

The RAF is renowned for understatement. While they were climbing aboard the RAF's advanced dual seat trainer at the Singapore airfield on that July 1957 morning, the air temperature on RAF Changi's white concrete hard-standing was 90°F with high tropical humidity. Metal was too hot for ungloved touch. The reflected glare was near blinding. The greenhouse effect of the domed perspex cockpit canopy pushed the temperature through blood heat; Piers's loaned flying overalls were soaked in sweat and the river flowing down his neck from the 'bone-dome' helmet would have floated a tanker.

"Changi tower. This is Neon 219," the pilot was using his radio callsign. "Request taxi clearance and take off for a right-hand climb out to 2000 feet". Piers tried to watch the pilot do his internal cockpit checks, while taxiing, and also watch the features of the airfield pass much faster than he was used to in his Chipmunk.

"Roger, Neon 219, you are clear to taxi for runway 240. Altimeter QFE 1009." Air traffic was using one of many RAF Q-codes that no-one could remember except those related to altitude; QFE is the cockpit barometric setting, in millibars, however high the airfield altitude above sea level and whatever the actual meteorological atmospheric pressure. With the given QFE the aneroid altimeter would indicate '0' feet when the aircraft's wheels touched the runway. As it happened, Changi runway was as near sea-level as made no difference.

The Changi controller continued, "Wind light and variable. Clear for right hand climb. What are your intentions?"

"Once round the island, Changi. We'll have a look at Tengah and the harbour and be back in time for lunch."

The female voice of Changi air traffic acknowledged, "Understood, 219. Be advised we are expecting a four engine transport in 25 minutes." The pilot had been adjusting the flying controls and instruments while they were taxiing to complete his cockpit checks for take-off. In this heat it was highly desirable to have the minimum time stationary. The Vampire was lined up on the centreline of the 9000 feet long runway.

Air traffic control tower announced, "Changi, Neon 219 clear for take-off and right hand climb to 2000 feet."

The Pilot spoke through the intercom. His words came through the headphones clearly. "Here we go." Full throttle, a powerful surge of acceleration and in no time they were off the ground. They were at 30 feet when the pilot pressed a selector switch button to retract the undercarriage. At about 75 feet, the pilot looked over his right shoulder and smoothly lowered the right wing to make a climbing turn away from the airfield. Piers believed he was looking into the glass of the tower's control room. Lady controllers! They had covered one mile from stationary in 40 seconds.

Once away from the airfield, the view was fantastic. It was panoramic. Fighter pilot unobstructed. So different from the impression gained from an airliner's passenger seat. The Vampire climbed over the water separating Singapore Island from the mainland, the Causeway Bridge to Johore Barahu clearly visible 20 miles to their left. The Malay jungle was green and shimmering beneath the aircraft's nose as they flew towards the Malay east coast of the South China Sea. The pilot settled the Vampire at 2000 feet at 260 mph airspeed. The coast was dotted with Malay settlements known as kampongs, some with a column of wood smoke rising vertically in the still air conditions. There were many over-water dwellings on bamboo stilts and a large number of sampans and canoes moving over the calm waters. The RAF aircraft, presumably a familiar sight to the locals, attracted no attention.

"You have a try of the controls. Be very gentle with the little lady, she is a bit sprightly. You have control. Just keep her straight and level." As an officer cadet, he was privileged to be able to take an air experience trip with an air gunnery instructor although, on this trip, this Vampire did not carry ammunition for its guns.

Piers was amazed how light it was to pilot this aircraft. The gentlest of pressure on the control column was sufficient to move the Vampire's nose above the horizon for a climb, or down for a descent or to rock the wings. There was engine noise, not a whine more an awareness of rotating metal 6 feet behind a bulkhead; the engine instruments gave confidence that all was well. It was the fuel gauge that most excited; Piers was sure he could detect the needle moving anti-clockwise from 'Full' towards 'Empty' as he watched it. The pilot sensed his passenger was keeping his vision inside the cockpit.

"When you fly one of these types you have to keep a good lookout," he said. "We have fuel for 30 minutes at low altitude, so we have to be on the ground when the clock says we have been in the sky for 27 minutes. That's why they put an Omega[tm] timepiece on my wrist and a Smiths[tm] clock on the panel... RAF likes to work with a safety margin." They had taxied for 2 minutes and had been flying for 5 minutes — 7 minutes fuel gone.

"I have control. Let's go and have a look at some trees." He turned the aircraft west, away from the coast and dropped the nose. Soon they were rising and falling with the tree contours of the forest canopy.

"You have a go." The pilot offered Piers control again, but this time he did not fold his arms; his hands remained loosely resting on his knees.

Piers said, "My instructor at home would have a fit if he could see me doing this. He once said I was not to do this sort of flying, even around soft clouds. 'I'll meet the crazy idiot doing the same thing the other way — sure as candles have wicks' he'd say." Piers was being very gentle with the control column.

"There's rules and there's rules," said the pilot. "This is Singapore and there's different rules. You're doing OK." The pilot allowed himself an extended survey of the horizon ahead, but his hands didn't stray from his knees.

This was exciting flying, 260 mph at 50 feet above the jungle trees. Seat of the pants stuff! A mistake would put them in serious — possibly mortal — danger. But the Rolls Royce Gnome engine ran sweetly, air turbulence was non-existent. Below, the jungle had its people, beasts, snakes; it was dense and unwelcoming. The Vampire and its precious occupants had the sky to themselves.

The pilot said, pointing across Piers's chest in this side-by-side dual trainer, "Beyond the water you can see Seletar airfield and as we get abeam of the Causeway you'll be able to pick out the Royal Navy base at Sembawang. Take the aircraft up to 2000 feet and we'll go and see who's at Tengah today. Nicely done." Piers breathed a sigh of relief with the partial relaxation of safe altitude, but rivulets of sweat were pouring into his flying boots. The parachute on which he was sitting must have been drenched.

The pilot's right hand moved to the radio transmit button on the control column. He let his passenger do the flying while he used the radio.

"Tengah tower, Tengah tower. This is Neon 219. Request joining instructions for a visual approach, touch and go."

"Good morning, Neon 219. We've been expecting your call. Our D/F is showing you on bearing 015 degrees. Can you see our blacktop?" The tarmac runway was obvious against the verdant airfield. Time now to fly by the rules!

"Affirmative, Tengah. Blacktop ahead, no sign of snow at your location. I'm at 1750 feet indicated and approaching for a straight in." Blacktop was RAF code for 'runway free of snow or ice'.

Tengah air traffic now passed the vital safety data: "You are clear to continue for Runway 230, Neon 219." A slight pause then the radio continued: "The temperature is 93°F, runway dry. The wind is light and variable from the south west. Check your altimeter QFE is 1009."

The pilot pressed the undercarriage selector button on the cockpit panel; there was a little air turbulence as the wheels lowered until their safe landing position was indicated by three green lights near the button he had selected. He radioed, "QFE 1009 it is, Tengah. Three greens for a roller. I would like to turn away to starboard to clear the circuit pattern."

Tengah air traffic replied, "You have a negative on that request, 219. We have two two-jets doing mutual out that way. You are clear to continue along the runway line and climb to 1500 feet until you reach the Strait Waters."

"Straight down the middle, Tengah." The pilot removed his finger from the transmit button and spoke as he took a firm grip on the control column. His line of sight continued to sweep the airspace ahead as they approached the Tengah runway.

"I have control." The clock indicated they had been airborne for 17 minutes and the fuel gauge showed just above half full. "There's a couple of fighters practising air-to-air combat out west." The sun beat into the cockpit, the polarized visor on their helmets working overtime to counter the glare.

The Vampire seemed to rush towards the runway, its touchdown point shown by prominent black and white bands. The numerals '230' in white confirmed they were at the correct end of the 9000 feet long strip. Beyond the matt black anti-reflective Vampire nose, in front of the hangars, were parked rows of Javelin and Hunter fighter aircraft. At about 160 mph, the pilot flew the aircraft's main wheels onto the runway surface, closed the throttle to allow the nose wheel to make contact, then opened the throttle to full power and lifted the aircraft back into its element. The undercarriage was retracted with a reassuring thump. On Piers's side of the Vampire there was the white shape of a single Valiant bomber parked near four Canberras. The pilot adjusted the throttle so as not to climb above 1000 feet, but he did keep the direction straight as instructed. A glance at the fuel gauge, the needle was now showing under half full.

"Thank you, Tengah," the pilot radioed. "Neon 219 departing your circuit to view the shipping in the Straits."

"219, acknowledged. Good morning!"

The pilot used the intercom, "Did you notice the Valiant? New aircraft, out here on hot weather trials, I guess." Piers nodded; he was enjoying this too much to speak.

The nose was dipping below the horizon; the airspeed was rising to 300 mph. The Vampire descended to 50 feet above the calm smooth blue shimmering waters of the busy Singapore Harbour. For five minutes the Vampire weaved between the boats, some large freighters, an oil tanker, and some small ferryboats servicing the islands. The pilot steered the aircraft so that it never actually flew over any boat, such was the agility of the aircraft designed primarily as a combat fighter. They were progressing generally south and westwards back towards Changi and home.

At some point the pilot said, "Down there is Indonesia. That island marks the spot." He pointed a wing at a tree covered outcrop below. "We'll head north now. Don't want to upset the natives."

With a 60° bank of the wings, the aircraft turned left. The pilot changed radio frequency to monitor Changi's air traffic. As the radio retuned they heard, "Roger, RAFAIR 1356, we have you on radar for an instrument approach. Looks good. We estimate you'll be on the ground in seven minutes. Your altimeter QFE is 1009, wind light."

And the aircraft reply, "1356 acknowledge QFE 1009. I have three greens for finals." The aircraft's captain was confirming his undercarriage was indicating it was safely lowered.

Changi radioed, "1356 continue. The circuit is clear at this time."

The pilot spoke on the intercom, "There's a Hastings transport coming in. I hope he does not get in our way. Let's go and see what that Chinaman is up to." He was referring to a rust covered freighter, relatively larger than the majority of shipping in the Singapore Harbour waters. The Chinaman was approaching at what appeared to be a good pace judging by his wake, his speed was sufficient to blow the red national flag out at his stern.

As they turned, the pilot positioning the Vampire on the ship's starboard so that his passenger was closest to the ship. He gave the Gnome engine a little more throttle, he adjusted the flight control trim and settled at 300 mph at the freighter's railing height, say 25 feet above the water. Piers could clearly read the vessel's name — Tre Wun Fif — in English script alongside Chinese hieroglyphs — and the registration port 'Shanghai' on the stern above the screw which was churning up the water. The ship's Plimsoll line was 5 feet above the level of the sea. She was sailing light or empty.

"I would like to have a closer look. Up we go!" He selected full throttle, completed a half vertical loop. They were now flying 1000 feet above the Tre Wun Fif, upside down, and going in the opposite direction. When they were beyond the ship's stern, the pilot rolled the Vampire upright, closed the throttle and made a steep descending curve to position once again on the ship's starboard side. They were flying at 315 mph indicated airspeed, their wingtip about 30 feet from the ship's side and so low that Piers had to look up at the Chinese crew who lined their railing to see what the noisy RAF was doing. Only one man waved, perhaps they were all as anxious as Piers was. Later, judging by the vessel's plimsoll, he reckoned they must have been at 15 feet above the sea. There was some air turbulence at the ship's bow-wave as they passed above it and went through the roll off the top manoeuvre again.

The radio spoke, "1356 finals."

Changi air traffic acknowledged, "RAFAIR 1356 proceed."

The pilot pressed the transmit button. "Changi tower, this is Neon 219. I would appreciate a short approach. I'm showing three minutes' fuel." The Vampire's throttle was half closed and the nose was down for a gentle descent. Ahead the runway was in sight as the white walls of Changi Gaol slipped under the port wing. In the distance, 3 miles ahead, the white and silver reflective shape of a polished Hastings transport just crossing the runway threshold was visible.

"Welcome home, Neon 219. You are clear to land on Runway 240 behind the four engines ahead. Your QFE is 1009 and the wind is light and variable." The pilot's left hand was reaching for the undercarriage controls.

"Neon 219, three greens finals." The Vampire was already banking to port.

Changi radio commanded, "219 land. Turn off at the 4000 marker. 1356 hold your position until 219 is clear."

The pilot put the Vampire on Changi's runway with a smoothness which hid any anxiety he might have felt. A severe touch of the brakes, but they did not stop in their turn onto the taxiway. He allowed the momentum to fall away as they rolled towards the airman already waving his marshalling bats at their return. The only concession the pilot made to being on the ground was to taxi onto the hard-standing with the cockpit canopy open. He closed down the engine and radioed, "Neon 219 finished, out!" The fuel gauge was reading 'Empty'. The pilot turned off the aircraft electrics. The engine was still running down as two airmen climbed their ladders to relocate the safety pins for the aircraft's ejection seats. The pilot removed his face mask and indicated that Piers should do the same. The mask left a red line across his nose, across his cheeks and around the curve of his jaw. His mask's inner lining was drenched in sweat.

The cockpit clock recorded they had been airborne for just 25 minutes, but with the extreme manoeuvres of the final five minutes they had probably used all the fuel safety margin. The little Vampire had taxied on kerosene vapour. It had been an exhausting yet exhilarating ride. And he did it most days!

"Thank you for a super ride," Piers said to the pilot as he was undoing his parachute harness.

"Piece of cake ..." said the pilot. "Glad you enjoyed it. I must get away, got to see a man about a Chinese rust bucket. What was that boat called?... Tre Wun Fif."

'About right,' Piers thought. 'Three one five at fifteen feet. Yes, about right!'

*   *   *

The return flight to England, in an RAF Comet Mk 2, via Negumbo, Bahrain and Akrotiri in Cyprus, was uneventful except for Piers witnessing the circumstance for fellow cadet Osma *Imam* Drake being removed from the passenger manifest. *Imam* had used the passenger indulgence procedure out to India and thence to Ceylon for the journey home. But his weight would have taken the weight of the Comet above takeoff limits and so he was offloaded. No amount of 'I've got to get back for the college start date' carried any sway with the RAF Movements Staff. As the chums shook hands, Piers wished *Imam* well in the unknown territory of reporting back to Cadet College late for term.

As the Comet had accelerated down Negumbo's runway, Piers watched the coconut palms of the RAF's main airfield in Ceylon pass beyond the porthole. The heavy aircraft did not want to leave Mother Earth. Piers sensed the pilot feel for takeoff, but separation did not happen. The 5000 foot marker, then 6000 foot, then 7000 slipped through the vision. There was a rumble through the cabin as the runway extension surface of perforated steel plate rushed past as the machine reached for the sky. Suddenly, there was no more land and, in these circumstances, the Indian Ocean did not look at all inviting. But the combination of airmanship and de Havilland's design overcame the elements as course was set for the Persian Gulf.

'How many other passengers felt as I did? That take-off was about as hairy as it gets,' he thought.

As the RAF coach took Piers from RAF Lyneham to Swindon rail station, now changed into civilian clothes, he reflected on three weeks in tropical climes and flying across half the globe in the latest jets. This was the career he wanted and surely this experience would see him in good stead for the challenges ahead.

Soon it would be back to Henlow and more flying. 'One year down, two to go and this year I can have my own vehicle. Things are looking up. And there's my Helen waiting too…'

*　　　*　　　*

Having completed their first years training, the entry would now be divided – half to Mechanical Engineering and half to Electrical Engineering discipline. Two years training was to qualify for Higher National Diploma standard acedimically monitored by the University of London.

1956 (Henlow) Cadets' Register

Real name	Nick Name	Notes and academic origin	Elec/ Mech	Posting ex Cadet
Lionel Banks	Shylock	Faith school to age 18	Elec	Flying school chopped
Martin Caine	Abel	Grammar school to age 18	Elec	Ground communications
Allen Davies	Shark	Grammar school to age 18	Mech	Bomber Command Development Unit
John Dawtry	Ganglion	State boarding school	Mech	Flying school Operational tour
Robert Dewhurst	Bunk	Multiple junior and senior schools	Elec	Flying school then operational tour
Osma Drake	Imam	Indian Grammar & RAF apprenticeship	Mech	Flying school chopped
Bartlet Dunmow	Nurse	Grammar school & St John's Ambulance	Mech	Bloodhound SAM
Paul Ellis	Crab	Grammar school & RAF apprenticeship	Mech	Aircraft serving

Peter Fischer	Simon	Grammar school to age 18	Elec	Camera servicing Later flying training
Derek Hedley	Uncle	Fee paying 6th form college	Mech	Flying school chopped
Julius Henson	Pimple	Educated at home by mother	Elec	Ground communication
Theo Kaggel	Neutron	Grammar school & apprenticeship	Elec	Flying school chopped
Kirk Knight	MacKay	Scottish senior college	Mech	Flying school then operational tour
Ian J. King	LMN	Aus: Melbourne	Elec	Duties in RAAF
Oliver Knight	Ollie	Boys only private boarding school	Mech	Armament
Claudette Leigh	Bumper ♀	Mixed grammar school & WRAF	Mech	Parachute packing
Basil Leitch	U	Boys boarding school to age 19	Elec	Aircraft servicing
Joe MacLion	Southpaw	Boys only boarding school	Mech	Flying school then operational tour
Denise Mercer	Asprin ♀	Fee paying 6th form college	Elec	Medical Equipment
Richard Petts	Rick	Fee paying public school	Elec	Air-sea rescue servicing
Piers P. Ploughman	PeeTot	Grammar school	Elec	Flying school chopped
Julius Shepherd	Ba	Secondary modern then apprenticeship	Elec	Flying school chopped
B.P. Thackray	Derv	Grammar school then apprenticeship	Mech	Flying school then operational tour
Drew Wilde	Fu	Aus: Perth, WA	Mech	Duties in RAAF

Chapter 16
1957 to 1959 ~ Cadetship Middle and Senior Entries

Summary punishment was given for poor turnout on parade — no excuses were admissible. A more formal punishment might be given by the Cadet Wing staff for something really heinous, but the result was more of the same. Punishment parade comprised appearing in best uniform in good order at 18:00, or else it accumulated further days and up to 30 minutes drill on the adjacent parade square; Sundays were not excepted. Only once in Piers's three years was the drill square declared too icy for safe drill; heavy rain — or fog — was no excuse. It was the responsibility of the Duty Under Officer, rostered for a seven days' duty from the senior entry, to administer the punishment. He could award up to seven days also, It was rare for a middle entry man to draw summary punishment and unknown that a senior cadet would attract such a penalty.

Wednesday and Saturday afternoon was devoted to sport, often competitive team games against local colleges and clubs. The needle matches against RAF College Cranwell was always compulsory attendance for home games and active encouragement to travel as supporters for away games. Piers played rugby union in the winter, usually for the 2nd XV including sometimes being its captain. Athletics saw Piers following his father as a sprinter and thrower without particularly success competing against others who achieved better standards. Piers continued his social tennis on the Cadets' Mess court and the wing had the use of the station squash court. WRAF Cadets Leigh and Mercer made a balanced coxless pair in the rowing club on the River Ouse at Bedford.

Sunday's routine started an hour later, and there was a formal, compulsory parade on Sunday at 09:45. Cadets dispersed to churches of their own belief at 10:15 while Piers usually caught the Birch[tm] Bus to 'out-of-bounds' London to see Helen. During the afternoon and evening of Sundays, Piers was told, cadets were usually left to their own devices, the ever popular evening curry was served although he was rarely there to enjoy it.

Freedom to travel, ie 'bounds' was defined in Cadets Standing Orders: advancement to Middle Entry had few perks. Central London remained out-of-bounds. The most significant new circumstance was the allocation of a bunk on the upper floor of Block 57. These rooms were typically quieter, than their ground floor equivalent, and enjoyed better daylight and ventilation. A typical room had the same dimensions and was furnished the same as for the first year; it was still subject to the Warrant Officer's inspection each Thursday.

*   *   *

It was six weeks after the all male new entry's for 1957 had arrived; in early October. The annual cadet intake had duly followed the schools' summer exam results and the various selection processes. Entry to the Cadet Wing had become a routine. Piers's entry, which to everyone's surprise had survived intact without any cadet being chopped from training, had been elevated to 'Middle Entry' status and had moved to the upper floor of Block 57 to occupy the vacated rooms by the now Senior Entry. The Senior Entry had their own mess which also provided the dining facilities for the now Middle Entry. Only the two women cadets of 1956 Entry remained in their specially adapted accommodation in Block 57 although, of course, the two women ate with the other members of their entry.

The 1957, all British, junior entry had had time to settle into the Cadet Wing routine, suffered their first lockout by the Middle Entry and had already taken their rightful places in the Wing's sports' teams when the practice fire alarm sounded.

The Middle Entry raised the alarm at 23:00 one cool November moonless night and just 15 minutes before their scheduled lights-out. Everyone was expected to quickly vacate Block 57 and assemble at a muster point on the Parade Square. Those cadets that knew the form wore slippers and dressing gown, beginners were not so prepared and the gravel of the square was not comfortable on the feet. When nothing happened after 15 minutes it was clear that the alarm was a spoof. The Middle Entry had

Block 57,
RAF Technical College, Henlow

secured all the doors and windows, turned off all the lights and effectively staged a Junior Entry lockout. All attempts to re-enter were repelled with bags of flour and water hoses. The Duty Under Officer intervened after half an hour and the dishevelled young gentlemen were allowed back into bed. But the prank was not yet over; the spoof practice had been mounted on a Wednesday evening, the Cadet Wing Warrant Officer's inspection was on Thursday morning and a big clear up cost the rookie entry most of the residue of the night. It would be fair comment to record that their clattering and bucket banging did not overly disturb those on the upper storeys of the block from a good night's sleep.

*   *   *

Second year Technical Cadets (WRAF) Claudette *Bumper* Leigh and Denis *Aspirin* Mercer needed to hatch a plot. The only topic of conversation, apart from sport and the forthcoming rugby derby against rivals Cranwell, was the need for a masculine spectacular. Their entry's male cadets' favourite was a panty-raid, but reconnaissance against the local teachers' colleges and nurses' homes was proving difficult to undertake. So *Bumper* and *Aspirin* sought to defend the honour of their sex.

"Look, *Aspirin*. They can't have it all their way. Let's show them we've got bottle too."

"Don't you mean… err… balls?"

"I didn't want to give offence, you being a virg…"

"Who says?"

"The whole entry knows you haven't…"

"They're entitled to their opinion!" Denise's truculent tone brought a smiled reaction from *Bumper* Leigh. But she wanted to return to her plot.

"We're girls, right?" Denise nodded at the obvious accuracy.

Claudette continued, "We know a few hairy girls, in the Physical Education College, who can look after themselves. Right?"

'Where is this leading?' wondered Denise.

"So why don't you and I recruit them for the job?"

Denise looked surprised. "What job?"

"How about a JSH?"

"Why can't the air force talk in English? What's JSH?"

"Jock strap heist."

"They don't all wear jock straps," commented Denise. She instantly regretted her comment.

"How do you know that? You being a v…"

"You mind yours and I'll mind mine!" came the indignant reply.

"Come on, Aspirin," encouraged *Bumper*. "Spill the beans… Have you done it?"

Aspirin's head shook, "I'm not telling…"

Bumper's shoulders rose in apparent indifference while secretly waiting for the other to tell more.

"They don't call it ballroom dancing for nothing." *Aspirin's* cheeks blushed a little. "The partners got a mite proximate during bronze medal dancing classes."

This inadequate explanation did not satisfy the experienced *Bumper*, whose assets had been appreciated by many Mancunian males outside her Manchester home town dance halls before being researched by ripe airmen behind the NAAFI club while she was a serving airwoman. She had never knowingly come across the garment in use although there was that guy at Debden… But… modern dancing could wait!

"Well, have you? Rumour has it that you denied *Southpaw* MacLion on account of a headache. It's where you got your nickname."

"That's rubbish and you know it!" *Aspirin's* countenance now really did look cross at the wholly unjustified invasion of her privacy. The blush was turning purple. "Joe's from a boys' public school and they prefer their own sort… or so I was told. Anyway, he's got body odour so I wouldn't if he tried… which he hasn't! Not with me, anyway."

"All right. Let's change the subject." The grateful Denise nodded her agreement.

Claudette Leigh outlined her plan and Denise enthusiastically agreed. Leaving any ground floor window unlocked had its perils. It was well known that the junior entry, on the ground floor, seeking to avoid stuffiness in their small rooms were often disturbed by a second year cadet using his window rather than the never locked Block 57 main door to escape detection after a night on the town. Naturally, on the fateful Friday night, the girls would have to be well away with verifiable alibis. So the girls timed their plan to coincide with a concert, in Welwyn Garden City, by the Chamber Ensemble from Denise's sixth form college such that they needed late passes so as to travel on the return Birch[tm] Bus arriving at 00:45. That would be well clear of the trouble and Saturday mornings did not include a drill square bashing for the Middle Entry meaning that the first call on the 'stayouts' was compulsory breakfast in the Senior Cadets' Mess before the 08:30 lesson.

Later, the girls found out that the raid had been conducted in a female strength ratio of two to one. Every cadet's room on the ground floor of Block 57 — the junior (1957) entry — had been raided, rifled and relieved of at least one pair of the offending garment. All junior Henlow cadets and six middle entry cadets suffered, that is less one; for some inexplicable reason, *Pimple* Hensen admitted under threat of grievous masochistic torture, that he did not use the garment and a pair of Y-front^{tm} had been liberated in lieu. Since he was not in the target entry that had been 'attacked', there was no reason why he should have lost anything! The attackers, having ventured above the ground floor to reach *Pimple's* bunk, had made off before a sensible alarm could be called; at least two junior entry cadets had been notionally bathed. The ease with which the visitors had bypassed the RAF Guardroom surprised no-one. But it was the lower floor of Block 57 that remained awake well into the night; the rooms had to be ready in case the Cadet Wing Warrant Officer pulled a 'surprise' Saturday inspection at 10:00 and the cadets had breakfast, drill parade and first lecture at 08:30.

"When the light went on, I thought it was a wet dream…"

"It took four of them to hold me down."

"Bloody hell! I thought I was having a nightmare — invasion of the body-snatchers and all."

"I got a good handful of her…"

"Sat on my face while the other one…"

"She got both of them then?"

"There'll be hell to pay…"

"Oh my Gawd! What happens when Cranwell hears about this?"

"I'm running tomorrow, how will I manage without…?"

"My jimjams are in the laundry and she saw my todger."

The indignant banter was still in full flow, the normally dark building with every light on, when *Bumper* and *Aspirin* returned to the block They could scarcely conceal their amusement at the success of their plan but, wisely, neither offered anything but sympathy for the outrageous assault on male pride. There were loud bawdy remarks being thrown down the central stairwell from the upper floor where the Middle Entry did not relish having the night disturbed. As two girls settled in the comfort of their undisturbed beds, Denise reflected on the pleasant familiar music she had just witnessed. On the other hand, Claudette had difficulty in settling to sleep; she was delighted that her plan had come together so successfully and that she was going to get away with it.

'This leadership training looks like it could be a lot of fun,' she thought, 'and another eighteen months to go.'

Three senior mistresses wrote letters of complaint to the cadet college's Commandant regretting the imposition of testosterone-fuelled high jinks on their innocent girls. The Commandant's reply assured the honourable ladies that there was no evidence of injury to either gender, the short duration of the visitation effectively precluded any opportunity for unsavoury abuse and he promised an enquiry and punishment of the guilty.

Apart from *Bumper* and *Aspirin* enjoying obvious masculine discomfort at a particularly long haranguing during the next Sunday's Church Parade, the only beneficiary was the sportswear dealer, in the local town of Hitchin, who did a roaring trade in male attire.

During the following week, a parcel arrived addressed to Oliver Knight. When he opened it he found a laundered jock strap, definitely not his since the upper floor Middle Entry had escaped invasion, but it had the unmistakable imprint of a lipstick kiss prominent on the non-elastic fabric. There was nothing to indicate of the identity of the sender or why he or she had chosen a member of the wrong entry to receive the gift.

Ollie Knight was particularly proud of his untraditional 1958 Valentine's Day card. But he sensibly put it away for the Warrant Officer's room inspections each Thursday.

*   *   *

It was in May, 1958, that reliance on public transport got the better of Piers. He was halfway between birthday 1957 and birthday 1958. On May 5th, 1958, Piers purchased a 125 cc, single cylinder, two-stroke motor-cycle. He knew little about practical motorbikes, his experience of two wheels was confined to pedal bikes. However, he did not need a qualified instructor to ride with him; as a middle year cadet he was permitted to keep the bike on camp and he could just afford to fill the fuel tank once per week for the journey to Kingston. With a learner's licence and insurance, he was free and access to Helen was more to their convenience. She purchased a crash helmet and some warm gloves and now they were able to take Sunday excursions deep into Surrey and beyond.

This was the era of repeated world record flying achievements in the USA; Piers watched the news with growing envy as Major H.C. Johnson, flying a Lockheed F104A Starfighter, set three new world altitude records in less than 3 weeks, attaining a height of 91,243 feet.

With July's course exams behind him, Piers could look forward to the longer summer leave. The issue for the couple was that he had to go on a college approved educational exercise; he chose France believing that his passenger seat would be occupied, undeclared to the college authorities, by his love. But Helen's father thought differently: two teenagers, on a single motorcycle, in France, was too much liberty for his daughter.

"Of course I trust you. No!" It seemed to be an absolute decision.

"But, Dad…" moaned Helen who was unaccustomed to her father taking such a firm line.

"I said 'No!' I mean, No!" Addressing Piers, "What do you know about motoring in France?"

"Well, Mister Blythe, I know they drive on the wrong side of the road, and… err… I speak French reasonably well, and… err… there's plenty of places to stay… and there are at least four other cadet groups motoring somewhere in northern France at the same time."

"No."

"And *Shylock* Banks is taking his girl on his scooter." Piers knew it was not a persuasive point.

"Absolutely, no. Forget it. It isn't going to happen. No!"

Sensible Helen took Piers's hand and led him out of the house. "Don't worry about it. He hasn't said we can't go on holiday together. I always fancied Wales, you can take me there. And when you come back, you can tell me all about France."

So Piers followed his planned route. He took the Air Ferry[tm], operating Bristol Freighters from Lydd Ferryfield airport to Le Touquet and had ten lonely days in northern France. He did not enjoy the Paris Perifique (ring road), the fast straight autoroute to Le Mans via Chartres, the cathedrals at Rhiems and Rouen, or the coast hugging route back to

Le Touquet. After 500 miles, his machine was tired; indeed it survived just 15 miles back in England when the drive chain snapped. A courteous Automobile Association^{tm} patrol assisted and he crawled to his grandmother's house near Chatham Dockyard where he could rest and recuperate.

Piers knew his post-exercise report might contain an element of fiction, but that did not concern him now. His most urgent need was to get close to Helen and get away on a real holiday.

The motor cycle did not let them down. Her parents offered no objection and his were still in Singapore. Piers and Helen were able to explore the highways and byways of the west country, right down to the Pembrokeshire coast. The Atlantic rollers were too cool for comfortable swimming, but they found plenty to do. They experienced no difficulty in finding single accommodation along the way although more than once their hostess looked a little surprised at their insistence in the sleeping arrangements. It was an altogether enjoyable phase of their courtship. All too soon it was time for Piers to return to Henlow leaving Helen to wait for his weekly visit.

*   *   *

During Piers's third year, and soon after the Senior Cadets' Mess bar had been decorated, there was after dinner discussion about Fighter Command's pilots' reported habit of walking on the ceiling. Proof of genuine contact with the ceiling was difficult to demonstrate when stacked on three storeys of shoulders. Reportedly Fighter Command officers used chimney soot or paint daubed on the bare feet of the unfortunate soul at the top of a human pyramid and a footprint was deemed proof positive. Now senior cadets did not have access to paint, but someone found a tin of pitch being used as a roof sealer. Piers was selected to do the walk, with both feet suitably covered in pitch and, sure enough, proof positive was deposited tastefully in a conspicuous position on the bar ceiling. The Cadet Wing officer responsible for the building did not share the cadets' enthusiasm for the new artform and, following a short, one-sided interview, Piers had to pay for the ceiling to be redecorated. However, the pitch did not easily leave the soles of his feet and, for several weeks, he found the compulsory drill parades or chasing buses after a cadets' pub crawl a most painful experience.

Evenings out at public houses in Hitchin or Ickleford became a regular feature of their cadets' lives. The Australians certainly seemed to enjoy the experience. There were cinemas in Hitchin and Bedford and the dancehall, on Wednesday, in Hitchin. Piers preferred the movies, particularly when there were films about flying. Some cadets went to Bedford, but needed a car or motor bike to get back from cinema before lights out. The entry's cadet ladies often went with their male colleagues and Piers watched with amusement as the entry horde massed protectively around 'their' women at the first sign of trouble.

The heady mix of maturing interests and academia towards their final exams for Higher National Diploma in Engineering with, for some, the additional overtones of flying kept the cadets busy. Just occasionally someone would have a bright idea. In March 1959, it was suggested that the Tiger Moth on the airfield ought to be protected from the rain and somehow the aeroplane was manoeuvred into the foyer of mess where it remained for two hours until common sense prevailed. A meeting of the Cadet Debating Society got out of hand and the senior mess learned why debating houses usually have a dividing gap between opposing sides; the entry ladies had sensibly retired before Aussie Drew *Fu* Wilde, proposing the motion: 'Cricket should become an Olympic sport', was debagged by the majority opposition.

Not to be outdone, and while Piers was Duty Under Officer, the 1958 Entry managed to get an Austin 7 motor car into the foyer of Block 57. It attracted buckets of bathwater from the upper two floors, now devoid of WRAF cadets, before being mercifully returned to the cadets' car park.

Christmas and Easter dances, in the mess were formal affairs with the cadets in mess uniform and their guest ladies in flattering dresses. Spring turned into summer and it was time to prepare for final exams and the graduation parade. The end of officer cadet training was nigh; soon, the real work could begin.

Chapter 17
1959 ~ Gazetted

Senior Under Officer Basil Leitch had received the sword of honour from the 1956 Entry graduation parade's air vice marshal reviewing officer. He now stood in front of twenty three other technical cadets of his entry. It was the moment for which they had striven for thirty three months. As parade commander, it was Leitch's responsibility to march the entry off the parade square at which time they formally ceased to be airmen and became commissioned officers. The next sixty seconds were as important in the lives of these twenty four cadets as any before or after.

"Number 1956 Entry will retire. About turn!" SUO Leitch moved around to the now front of the entry. The Central Band of the RAF waited for the cue from the parade commander. In unfaltering voice, SUO Leitch's voice carried across the open parade square. Even the gloom of Block 57 seemed to brighten as the sun tried to burn through the July overcast.

"Number 1956 Entry will advance. By the left, slow... march!"

Twenty four mirror-shine left shoes shot forward and with a precision which made Warrant Officer Fetcham's heart flutter; these young cadets, well honed and drilled as befitting their future responsibilities, his cadets, were graduating. Their gloved hands were rigid at their uniforms' seams except for the three armed under officers carrying swords. Twenty four cadets moved forward towards the hedge gap at the rear of the parade ground. It was just sufficient, not accidentally of course, for a twenty four man flight, with a frontage of seven cadets to march through.

Leitch knew it was forty paces; every cadet knew it was forty paces. The band knew it was forty paces. The rear rank cleared the gap and marched three paces further. Forty paces completed. The echo of the march-off music faded quickly.

"Entry... halt! Entry, stand at... ease. Gentlemen and ladies, attention. Officer on parade... to your left... dismiss!" Every ex-cadet turned half left, saluted and reached for someone's hand to shake.

Royal Air Force commissioned service in the Technical Branch, soon to be renamed the Engineer Branch, had begun for twenty two British officers and for two others in the equivalent Royal Australian Air Force.

On the day of the Graduation Parade, in Piers's bunk, in the Senior Cadets' Mess which he would be vacating the next day, was a sealed envelope addressed to him. In it was the confirmation that the graft and energy over the past thirty three months had not been in vain.

Air Ministry   *Telephone:*   *Holborn 3434*
Adastral House
Theobalds Road
London WC2

OP. 789456/A.R.1.   *30th July, 1959*

Sir,

1.   I am commanded by the Air Council to inform you that approval has been given for your appointment to a permanent commission in the Technical Branch (General List) of the Royal Air Force on graduation from the Royal Air Force Technical College, with effect from 30th July, 1959. You will be discharged concurrently from airman service. The appointment will be in the rank of pilot officer and an announcement will appear in The London Gazette in due course.

2.   A copy of Air Ministry Pamphlet 106 is enclosed. This pamphlet includes an authority to purchase uniform which must be produced to your tailor. It will be necessary for you to provide yourself with uniform and other outfit as set out in Appendix B to Air Ministry Order A.11/1958.

3.   You will retain your present personal number, 789456, which should be quoted in all official communications.

I am, sir,
    Your obedient servant

        L C Aubruy

Pilot Officer P. P. Ploughman,
    Royal Air Force.

Piers's reaction was to sit on his bed and enjoy the moment. There could never, by definition, be another moment like this. From along the corridor Piers could hear the occasional whoop, cheer, expletive as the combined relief set in.

'The future begins here,' he thought. 'Roll on flying school.'

*   *   *

Moscow daylight did not extend into the sixth floor of the Headquarters on Lubyanka Square, an inwards facing office of the Soviet Union's Committee for State Security (KGB). Olga Brovorno sat hunched over a tidy desk, ready to set about her latest task. This had become routine; since the former military intelligence departments of the NKVD had been re-organised; her office had responsibility for tracking key, or future possible key, civilian or military British personalities. The March 1954 re-organisation had placed her group within The First Chief Directorate (Foreign Operations) — responsible for foreign operations and intelligence-gathering. This chief directorate had many sub-directorates of its own.

Political, religious, medical, industrial and military officers, and non-commissioned officers deemed to have intelligence or other skills or indiscretions, likely to be of use to the USSR, were registered in files maintained for the purpose of background briefings at all levels up to the Politburo. Of particular interest to Olga's customers was any evidence of susceptibility to recruitment as agents, with potential for penetration of intelligence and defence services, and as sources of nuclear or novel weapons systems' design information. Tendency towards political, sexual or criminal activity was of particular interest as opportunities to apply pressure in later years.

Into her office flowed many sources of names, dates and qualifications with some more reliable than others. It was accepted that the military college graduation lists, published in the London Gazette and repeated in the broadsheets, together with

Representation of the London Gazette Published by the Stationery Office price 9d

promotion lists and appointment notifications, were 100% reliable and also served to verify the accuracy of less overt agents passing similar data through clandestine channels.

Olga liked to work on the principle that two unrelated sources are better than one, but for this present batch the Gazette was deemed authoritative.

Twenty one new files were opened, and one extant was in the pile, as the Henlow commissioning results were processed. Slips were attached to loose copies of the Gazette sheet for the two Australians — King and Wilde — for their case files to be processed by the Australian desk. In one case, the woman Leigh, already had a file with a single sheet and a poor quality photograph cross referencing a possible connection with a folder concerning a suspect lesbian in Bedford; the folio was marked as 'probably unreliable'. With the details duly filed, and the material tidy to Olga's satisfaction, the files were put away for future events or purposes yet unknown. Photographs would be added later. Her UK department had 800,000 such folders; overall the KGB tracked 7½ million individuals worldwide.

Olga Brovorno wondered where the file on her was held, but then, she had nothing to hide.

*   *   *

RAF Aston Rowant, near Market Drayton, in Shropshire was where No 16 Flying Training School was based using Provost T1 aircraft as basic pilot trainers. These aircraft were more powerful than the Chipmunk. The instructor sat beside his student in the cockpit. There was a five week interval between closure of the four month Henlow, post graduate, training and beginning the flying course at 16 FTS. The gap included the New Year's break which enabled Piers and Helen to spend many happy hours together, including their engagement to marry when he had completed his wings course, next year.

The 26th January, 1960, eventually arrived. Following his 120 hours flying at Henlow, Piers was one of eleven ex-Technical Cadets required to report one sunny Monday for further training with 16 FTS. He was to live there, for the next five months, in a secco hut with a real batman.

Piers agreed to travel with Robert *Bunk* Dewhurst in his Hillman^{tm} California car; they were to rendezvous in London and be in good time to arrive by the required 16:00. The recently opened motorway M1 —

which at that date reached 60 miles north from the A41 junction near Watford to the A5 near Daventry — was thought to save 90 minutes on the road from London to Shropshire. The car was 8 miles north of Luton, near Woburn Sands, when *Bunk*, for some reason with his car in third gear at 60 mph, blew its engine. With all their uniform being transported, including some items of flying clothing which had benefited from a sample of mothers' tender loving care, they were sorely placed.

The car was ignominiously towed off the motorway to a garage where heavy maintenance was diagnosed. The two qualified technical officers had to take a taxi to Bletchley Station for a train in the correct general direction. It was 18:00 when they arrived at Crewe; Piers thought this miserable railway junction was the most depressing place he had ever visited — worse even than Swindon in the snow! And they were already late.

His telephone call to the Station Duty Officer at RAF Aston Rowant, later found to be an officer of equal rank to his bottom-of-the-rung pilot officer, but with the unchallengeable status of 'flying instructor', refused to organise RAF Mechanical Transport to come and get them. A second phone call to the Officers' Mess raised fellow ex-cadet Kirk *MacKay* Knight who agreed to collect them. Two hours later, the two weary students had arrived courtesy of Kirk's pre-war Singer[tm] Drophead Coupe to find an unsympathetic Duty Officer ready to dish out to standard, 'you're late...' and 'you will do what you are told....' and not prepared to listen to reason. And the mess dining room was closed!

Piers was off to a bad start.

*   *   *

With women not eligible for pilot training, the eleven ex-1956 Henlow graduates posted to 16 FTS RAF Aston Rowant in January 1960 were:

Lionel Banks	John Dawtry	Piers P. Ploughman
Robert Dewhurst	Osma Drake	Julius Shepherd
Derek Hedley	Theo Kaggel	Joe MacLion
Kirk Knight	Bridgenorth P. Thackray	

Only five were to complete the eighteen months course to the jet aircraft phase and 'Wings' at RAF Swinderby. They were: Dawtry, Dewhurst, Knight, Shepherd and Thackray. Two were destined to fly in V-bombers as co-pilots and all would return to ground engineering duties after completing a flying tour.

All that was for the future; in January 1960, the eleven pilot officers, now with six months commissioned service under their belts, collided with the RAF pilot training machine and, some, lost. It transpired that none of the instructors had undergone three years of pilot's cadetship and officer training at Cranwell. To Piers's mind, it showed.

Having survived 3 years of strict cadetship, returning to the training machine was neither easy nor welcome. Many years later, when Piers was sending SNCOs to officer training, he warned them to keep their mouths closed and their ideas firmly bottled up. Such training was one occasion when the end justified the means. However, he did not have this foresight in 1960 and it was to cost him his 'wings'. He was not warned to have to learn again the (different) values of commissioned life and certainly not from officers whose personal qualities did not merit his respect except for their 'wings'. One such example was that Station Commander had banned the (pro-Labour party) *Daily Herald* ^{tm} newspaper from the Officers' Mess because it had once criticised King George VI (who had died nine years previously in 1951).

Having experienced a 'real' station's officers' mess at post-graduate Henlow, Piers and the other students felt their freedom to judge others' ideas was cut off at source.

*   *   *

Piers's first flying instructor at 16 FTS was non-commissioned Flight Sergeant Geoff Cooper. His unfriendly welcome consisted of, "Good morning. My name is Flight Sergeant Cooper and when we are in the air you will call me sir. In the air, I am in charge. On the ground, I am still your instructor and you do as I tell you. Is that clear?" This was delivered without the courtesy of a salute such as would be delivered by any non-commissioned person to a commissioned officer. Having been recognised as a commissioned pilot officer for 6 months, and clearly displaying the rank insignia on his

Provost T1 – the RAF's basic trainer, with side-by-side seats

epaulettes, Piers did not expect to be addressed in quite that manner by a SNCO.

Piers's reaction must have showed because Flt Sgt Cooper said it all again. The initial impact registered because Piers was able to quote, verbatim, the very words while he was at his 'leaving the service' lunch in London some 31 years later. But Flt Sgt Cooper was a good flying instructor; he recognised Piers's innate ability as a pilot and, in return, Piers learned a great deal from him in the 3 months of their time together before being progressed on to another instructor.

*   *   *

Central London, which meant somewhere convenient for London Bridge Underground station, was a 3½ hours road journey from RAF Aston Rowant. Most weekends, *Bunk* Dewhurst would collect Piers, often with John *Ganglion* Dawtry and sometimes a fourth passenger and, as soon as possible after lectures on Friday, they would be off southbound for the weekend. A shared car reduced the travel costs. They would disperse from London Bridge on Friday nights and rendezvous at Archway or Kings Cross Underground station on Sunday nights. In 1960, the A5 road from Daventry to the A41 road junction for Aston Rowant was an easy uncongested, if tedious, drive with 60 mph being a comfortable cruising speed. Similarly, the 60 mile length of the M1 from Rugby to Watford took one hour because the motorway speed was 60 mph and would not change until Minister for Transport Barbara Castle introduced a 70 mph limit in the 1973 oil crisis whereupon everything including the lorries speeded up to the new limit.

Chapter 18
1960 ~ Flying Training School, Aston Rowant

Piers was assigned, with five other ex-cadets, including *Bunk* Dewhurst, to F-flight for flying the Provost trainer. Flight line accommodation was a secco hut with the students' crewroom having a coke burning stove at its centre. They were expected to keep it stoked and, during excessively cold days, they undertook this duty with some verve.

Among other student pilots assigned to F-flight was a Sudanese prince to whom concepts of discipline were non-existent and money was no object. But he had a keen sense of humour. When the stove had its periodic dull glow of heat, he would beat out tribal rhythms with his bare hands and with a grin that would do a Maclean's™ toothpaste advertisement proud; the students never learned to pronounce his name correctly and he fully understood why the Englishmen did not join his bongo performance.

It was not all flying although, for Piers, that was the best part of being at 16 FTS in remote Shropshire. He particularly enjoyed the smooth, no turbulence, air while flying at night. There were some rigorous components in the course, including a session in the de-compression chamber where lack of oxygen at altitude was simulated. There was a two day escape and evasion exercise which involved walking out of the Welsh foothills back to base. There was also the ground school where much of the taught lessons were duplicates of the ex-cadets' engineering training at Henlow.

In addition to the London excursions in *Bunk* Dewhurst's repaired car, there were opportunities to explore. Piers accepted a February sunshine ride in an ex-cadet's open MG-TC™ to Lake Verwnwy in late February, where the Welsh mountains were capped with snow, but the waters behind the dam were calm and shimmering. A group went to a local strip club in Crewe; it turned out to be a working man's drinking club with a stage act. Piers joined with the search for a local to the station hostelry with a good selection of ale, but generally there was disappointment on that front. But as the weather improved into spring, the sports field was marked out and Piers began to take advantage of the RAF training facilities for athletics.

And so nearly four months passed and, it seemed to Piers, progress sustained. At home, Helen had agreed to plan their marriage with a view to being his June bride in 1961. By that date Piers ought to have qualified for his wings. A second, then third cadet of his entry, also under training at Aston Rowant, had married although there was no married accommodation for student pilots or indeed any officer under the age of 25 years. A rented caravan was the only option. All the ex-cadets now owned a car.

Even when the first ex-Henlow student pilot was chopped from training, Piers sensed no risk to himself of a similar fate. The details of what went wrong for *Pimple* Henson never came out. In the real RAF, former cadets were now doing the engineering tasks they had been trained to do. Flying students were studying flying. The ex-cadets were maturing into real officers, but it was in the nature of RAF careers that there was minimal contact between the flying and non-flying streams.

*   *   *

"Climb to 7000 feet, heading 145°. Do your checks for aerobatics. Loop and then, when you are ready, roll to the right." The flying instructor's requirements were understood.

"You have control."

"I have control. Checks for aerobatics," replied Piers

The Provost trainer was climbing as if she owned the skies. They were flying using Piers's callsign: India Sierra. The instructor, a check-flight pilot who did not usually fly with student Piers, was seated to the right in this side-by-side RAF aircraft with his arms folded. He was looking around the horizon. On this May day, at nearly noon, visibility was better than 30 miles. There was little cloud, no air turbulence. It was an excellent day for flying with very good visibility of the ground nearly 1½ miles below. This flight, briefed before take-off as a course progress-and-check flight, ought to be busy but routine.

Piers levelled out at just above 7000 feet, throttled back to cruise, allowed the airspeed to stabilise using the loss of the excess of 50 feet altitude to bring the Provost into straight and level flight. 'Check the flight controls and trim for steady flight. Perfect.' He repeated his thoughts aloud; it was the routine procedure when flying dual training.

The aircraft was 25 miles east of the airfield, well clear of all other trainers from the Flying Training School. Piers scanned the horizon for other aircraft, rocking the wings to satisfy himself there was no one underneath.

"All clear," he said into the intercom. He checked the instruments: airspeed, attitude gyro, compass, fuel sufficient for mission, oil pressure good and engine temperature within limits. The altimeter had been set to the area's radioed atmospheric pressure to ensure all aircraft had uniform height reference above mean sea level. No loose articles in the cockpit. Wing flaps up. One final visual scan of the horizon, all clear. They were alone in the skies.

The VHF radio crackled in his headphones as a distant student exchanged messages with the airfield tower. 'No problem for me in their crisp words,' thought Piers. As instructed, he put the aircraft into a dive for the loop, nose down to gather airspeed, full throttle and eased the control-stick into his tummy allowing the Provost's nose to climb above the horizon. Head back as the aircraft passed vertical climb, airspeed falling off needing a little compensation on the rudder to keep the aircraft straight, through the horizon upside down hanging on the seat straps, speed increasing, throttle back through the bottom of the loop, maximum g-force, nose back to the horizon with throttle adjustment to settle at 6850 feet on the altimeter.

"Check your altitude." The instructor was as meticulously curt as the entire genre at the flying school.

The loop had not been as smooth as some previously done. Piers thought he must have exercised the manoeuvre 100 times before. It certainly was not his worst effort. But... now they were once again flying straight and level at 7000 feet, heading on bearing '090°' — due east away from the airfield. A significant built-up area was coming into view, 30 to 35 miles away.

"I'll turn north for the roll. I don't want to stray too far from the base," Piers said to the instructor.

If he spoke, the instructor's words were lost in the radio crackle. It was standard practice for a student to repeat an instructor's directions. That simple procedure ensured nothing was missed. But the instructor did not necessarily repeat the student's words. He was banking the Provost at 30 degrees left wing down, with a little right foot pressure on the rudder bar to hold the nose on the horizon, and rolled the aircraft smoothly out of the turn. The gyro compass indicated '350°'.

A minor correction was required. Straight and level, gyro compass on the instrument panel indicating '000°' — due north.

Piers set the aircraft up for the roll. This was not his favourite manoeuvre, too many adjustments in this underpowered aircraft. However, this was a progress check flight and so nose down, full throttle, correct airspeed, nose on the horizon, control column to the left. Piers held the aircraft's nose on the featureless horizon, with a strong forward pressure on the control column while upside-down, until the aeroplane had rotated through 360 degrees. It overshot its roll and Piers had to react quickly to drop the right wing to return to the horizontal. The gyro compass had toppled but was recovering to indicate '345°'. The aircraft had completed a left hand roll.

'Oh, shit!' thought Piers. 'I've rolled the wrong way!'

"You said North."

With a muted curse, Piers used the rudder to kick off the 15 degrees in an uncomfortable yaw manoeuvre. Knowing he had made a mess of the manoeuvre, he knew what would come next.

"You roll off your mistakes. Boots are made for walking and minor rudder trim. When I want to roll to the left, I'll let you know. Head west and let's do our roll to the right this time."

Piers visually scanned the horizon before turning.

"A Provost at 10 o'clock, low, is heading away. At least two miles."

The instructor acknowledged with, "Got him. Keep an eye on him."

The otherwise clear sky meant he could safely turn through 90 degrees to the left. Piers undershot this time and took three attempts before settling on bearing 270°.

"Settle down," the instructor commanded. "I said 7000 feet."

Piers eased the control column into his stomach to recover the lost 300 feet. This was not getting any easier. The roll to the right was a little more polished than his previous attempt.

Straight and level flight for two minutes, the opportunity to settle down again. 'Relax, Piers.' The student's eyes were doing a routine cockpit instrument check with an exaggerated head movement for the instructor's benefit: airspeed 145, altitude 7000, heading 270°, fuel over half a tank — an hour's flying, oil temperature 75°C. Good. Check air space for other aircraft, the other trainer was out of sight.

"I have control!" The instructor moved his right hand to the control column, rocked the wings violently and pushed the throttle lever for maximum power. The Provost began to climb. The instructor's head was locked to his right to observe an oncoming threat. He pushed the control column violently forward, the nose dropped and the Provost descended 3000 feet in 15 seconds.

"Jesus!" The instructor swore. "Where did he come from?" The instructor had seen another aircraft to their starboard and masked, invisible, to Piers from his position in the cockpit.

A twin-engine, light transport aircraft passed overhead, its course at right-angles to the Provost, about 1000 feet above them. His underbelly was clearly visible through our perspex canopy. His undeviating course suggested that he had not seen the Provost despite the instructor's manoeuvres.

"He's flying into the sun," said the instructor, as if that was an excuse, while he was recovering the Provost from its near-vertical dive. The acceleration pull out of the dive was recorded as nearly '4.5 g' on the cockpit meter, within limits for this type of aircraft, but very uncomfortable even when expected.

"We'll transit to the Kershaw Hill relief landing airfield at 3000 feet. You have control."

"I have control," Piers repeated. His stomach was somewhere above his shoulder straps. He was shaken by the near-miss.

His thoughts were racing, 'Concentrate on flying. Reduce altitude in a positive manner — as if you mean it. We didn't hit that other guy. Do it properly and think about the drinking chocolate waiting in the crewroom. That's better. Closing on 3000 feet altitude. Trim for level flight. Check instruments. Air space clear. We will soon be joining Kershaw Hill airfield circuit pattern. I suppose he'll want to do a practice forced landing. Relax. Breathe!'

"OK," said the instructor. "While we are transiting, let's make use of the time. Demonstrate a spin. You have control."

"A spin," Piers repeated aloud. This manoeuvre required reducing airspeed until the Provost stalled — the airflow over its wings unable to support the aircraft's weight. It would then fall, nose down until recovered. However, if the stall was induced with a rudder or aileron or both off-centre, the unstable Provost would rotate about it vertical and roll axes. This uncomfortable manoeuvre is the spin. The student pilot checked the surrounding air space. He'd done dozens of spin recoveries.

Piers said, "We are 1000 ft above minimum safe altitude. Air space is clear. Cockpit instruments check okay. Clear for spin. Throttle off, nose up, airspeed reducing to 45 knots. There's the stall. Nose dropping, right rudder. Spinning now." The sun went past; the Earth was rotating unrecognisably under the nose. The sun went past the second time, then a third. The aircraft's rotation was slow to recover. The altimeter indicated 2100 feet.

Piers said, "Recovering now." He moved the control column fully forward, rudders to neutral. 'Wait for the airspeed to read 75 knots,' he thought, 'throttle fully open, pull control column into tummy, altimeter now 1900, positive rate of climb, the altitude climbing through 2000 feet. Climb at 90 knots to 3000 ft and level out. Restore heading into '270°' on the gyro. Settle down.'

The instructor said, "You delayed recovery too long. You went below your minimum altitude. Insufficient left rudder to stop rotation. Call the tower and tell them we're going to Kershaw Hill." He was right again, of course.

This time Piers did not acknowledge the instructions. He pressed the radio transmit button on the control column and said, "India Sierra to Aston Rowant. I am en route to Kershaw Hill. Request Quebec Foxtrot Echo update."

The radio replied, "India Sierra en route for Kershaw Hill. Be advised your QFE is 1006."

"India Sierra, acknowledge QFE is One Zero Zero Six. Out." Air traffic was advising the barometric setting so that the cockpit altimeter would read '0' when the wheels touched the ground.

The instructor said, "Continue until you can see Kershaw Hill. Then change direction to pass directly overhead. Lookout for other aircraft in Kershaw's circuit."

There was no opportunity to relax. Check the cockpit instruments. Keep a good look out. The radio was quiet. The engine sounded good and the instruments read normal indications.

Kershaw Hill airfield came into view. The edges of its lightly used concrete runway were losing a battle with nature. Farmers had sown wheat on either side of the strip. The runway was used by student pilots to practise dead-engine landings away from the congestion of the parent airfield. Near the airfield fence stood a lone Provost presumably the result of some minor emergency, a caravan painted red and white and a Land Rover^{tm} fire engine. At two miles from Kershaw Hill's runway, at 2000 feet altitude, the instructor closed the engine throttle simulating engine failure.

"You have simulated engine failure. Practise landing, break off at 250 feet. Talk me through it." The flying emergency exercise was underway.

Piers described his actions aloud, "We have simulated engine failure. In a real situation I would radio: 'Mayday, Mayday, Mayday. This is India Sierra with engine failure landing at a Kershaw Hill. Mayday, Mayday, Mayday. India Sierra landing.' I can see a suitable landing area ahead at 11 o'clock, one mile range. The wind sock shows a light wind blowing down the runway strip, marginal crosswind expected. The strip is unobstructed. Altitude now indicating 1100 feet, airspeed 70 knots, emergency landing checks: altimeter 1000 feet and working, airspeed 70 knots and working. Fuel cock selected. Flaps up. Undercarriage is fixed down. No other aircraft in sight. Check straps are tight."

The instructor made no comment.

The Provost passed over the runway and continued its circular descent. The engine propeller was creating no thrust. Piers banked the port wing down so that the wing-tip appeared to point continuously at the spot on the concrete where he wanted the wheels to touch down. The aircraft was descending, in a gentle turn through a full 360 degrees, going down a shade fast at 315 feet per minute. Lift the nose, rate of descent now corrected to 300 feet per minute. Looks good.

Piers said, "I would repeat my 'Mayday' message now. We are at 400 feet, half-a-mile from touchdown. We are lined up into wind for landing. Nose up gently to reduce the rate of descent and airspeed. Indicated 60 knots, 375 feet. 50 knots, 200 feet. The ground looks closer than that. Half flaps now."

"I have control." The instructor selected full throttle; the airspeed increased as the Provost held its altitude above the concrete runway. The aircraft's attitude was nose high above the horizon. With the engine screaming in protest, they were no more than 5 feet above the runway. 20 seconds later the instructor spoke.

"This is where you should have been aiming. You were too close to the runway threshold. You could easily have landed short if you had selected full flaps." There was no point in arguing. Flying instructors are always right. "Add to that — you went through the briefed safety altitude, I said break-off at 250 feet." Piers knew they would have landed safely, on the concrete and straight, but the instructor was making a point.

The instructor pushed the nose forward, holding down to his chosen altitude of five vital feet clearance from the ground, raised the flaps and, when the full power engine had pulled the airspeed to a normal 'climb-out' 90 knots, raised the nose above the horizon. He said, "You have control. Take us home at 2000 indicated. Join the circuit on the downwind leg at 1000 feet. Tell the air traffic control tower that you want to make a final landing and take us back to the hangar."

"I have control," Piers acknowledged.

They made the familiar 15 mile transit at 120 mph airspeed on bearing '045°'. The landmarks were familiar, visibility was excellent; Piers needed no map. At two miles out, while beginning a gentle descent to 1000 feet, he radioed the tower.

"Aston Rowant, India Sierra. Request permission to join direct to the downwind leg for final landing"

"India Sierra. You are clear to join. Be advised there is one single-engine ahead, now turning finals for runway 275. Wind is 265 degrees at 9 knots. Check your altimeter for QFE 1006." The tower was giving the essential air traffic safety and weather details to set up approach and landing. The instructor's head was searching the skies for other aircraft, but he watched his student go through the motions of setting the altimeter on the instrument panel to the value passed by the tower's Q-code.

One more radio call, "India Sierra turning finals," drew the tower's reply, "Wind is 265 steady 9 knots, clear to land." Piers made uneventful landing with, he thought, just two small bounces due to trying to land 3 knots too fast, followed by a routine taxi to the marshaller in front of the hangar.

As a progress check flight, Piers felt it could have gone better!

"Close it down," said the instructor. "Then go to the Flight Line and sign the aircraft log Form 700 'satisfactory'. Mention to the Flight Sergeant that the tyres need to be checked for your possible heavy landing. We will talk later." The instructor made his way to the instructors' crew room while the student went to complete the aircraft documentation.

He was drinking hot chocolate and munching a packet of ready-salted crisps — it was too late for lunch in the Officers' Mess — when the flight commander appeared with instructions for Piers to deliver Flight Lieutenant Wigginstowe to Kershaw Hill to recover a problem aircraft from the relief landing ground. That explained the Provost on the ground. On his solo return flight, Piers did a barrel roll, his favourite aerobatic, smooth and unhurried. When he made his final landing, he greased his machine on a perfect three-point landing onto Mother Earth as though the Provost was grateful to be home.

"Aston Rowant tower. India Sierra finished for the day," he radioed.

"Thank-you India Sierra. Welcome home. Good evening."

He briefly pressed the transmit button on the control column in acknowledgement. Further words were unnecessary. The crackle on the tower's radio was sufficient acknowledgement. In the Flight Line office, he learned that he had an appointment with the Chief instructor at 16:45 in his office. At flying school, it was normal practice for the instructor to debrief all student dual flights, not just check flights, but rare to be summoned to the Chief Instructor. There was just time to freshen up for the interview. He was on time as he knocked on the wing commander's door.

"Come in."

Piers entered and saluted. He was not invited to sit.

"I have been reviewing your progress, Ploughman. Four months here with 47 flying hours: ground school reports are satisfactory. Airmanship — let's speak about that."

The student cleared his throat, but was not invited to speak.

"Your flight's senior instructor flew a check flight today, I see. His report makes interesting reading. He says you handle the controls gently and are sensitive to their response. That's good. However, I note that you chose to demonstrate your marginal prowess at aerobatics in controlled airspace — an airway — thereby potentially hazarding commercial airliners and their passengers. Not content with that, you narrowly avoided colliding with a military transport which had right of way. Then you risked a short landing at a practice emergency. Finally, your instructor says you completely cocked up your final check landing

135

here. Frankly I'm disappointed that you have not attained the necessary competence to continue training at this school. I am recommending to the Station Commander that you be withdrawn from pilot training."

Piers was astonished. Struck dumb. Grounded. Chopped!

"You will proceed from here directly to the Officers' Mess, collect your things and go on leave from the station by 18:00 hours today. You will return on Tuesday morning next and report in Number One uniform to the Officer Commanding Personal Services Flight where you will receive further instructions."

No invitation to comment; he hardly paused for breath. He'd done it before. No argument.

"Now get out." He was already closing the single folder on his desk. Finished!

Piers saluted, instinctively, because he was a senior officer. He turned, went through the door, walked across the hangar floor where the ground-crew were parking the Provosts under cover for the night. He made for the student crew room to store his flying equipment in his locker. There was no-one about to share his sadness. Outside, he noted the check-flight instructor's distinctive Triumph TR3A was gone from the instructor's car park.

The former student pilot drove his car through the RAF Aston Rowant main gate by 18:00 hours.

Just like that, with no debate. Pilot Officer Piers Ploughman had been chopped from flying. The RAF had lost a future test pilot.

Chapter 19
1960 ~ Hold Them, Store Them and Bury Them

When the RAF could not decide what to do with its men, or women, they were administratively posted to a Personnel Holding Unit. No 1 PHU, RAF Innsworth was where Piers was instructed to report. He was not the first or last ex-student pilot to be sent there, but he was the first permanently commissioned engineering officer to be so treated. Other cadets who were chopped flying went straight to engineering appointments, usually so-called supernumerary posts while proper vacancies were identified. Without explanation, Piers did not know of his unique status in the grand order of things, neither was he prepared for what would happen over the next months of his, to him, ruined career.

No 1 PHU had no instructions on what to do with this unfortunate officer either. The group captain Station Commander was sympathetic to the young man's situation, but he could not permit an officer to appear to be idle on his unit. So he decided that Pilot Officer Piers Ploughman should become Assistant Adjutant, reside in his outer office where he could watch the man himself, and let some of the difficulties of being an officer in the Administrative Branch rub off on this Technical Branch officer.

At Piers's arrival interview with Station Commander, the role of No 1 PHU was summarised as, "Hold them, store them and bury them — preferably in the correct order, but in any case make sure the paperwork is correct. In a nutshell, it means that when the RAF doesn't know what to do with its men or women, they get sent here." Not surprisingly, here was an officer confident in what he was doing and confident he could handle anything the RAF could throw at him.

"We hold the papers for long term prisoners and some who are waiting to be court martialled and would be an embarrassment to keep on operational stations, for long term hospital cases, the criminally insane, a few chaps lost in the weird world of intelligence, some fellows who really are lost in nasty places like the jungle or Commonwealth Defence Colleges, and now it seems for a grounded student pilot of the Technical Branch. Welcome to RAF Innsworth; do you play cricket?"

'So,' thought Piers, 'it all comes down to sport again. Typical bloody air force... He seems to be a pleasant enough guy...'

'It is all to the benefit of the RAF if there is mutual understanding between the ground branches,' thought the Station Commander. 'Take every opportunity offered. Give this young whipper-snapper some inkling of how difficult it is to be an administrator in this man's air force.'

A measure of cross fertilisation did indeed occur in the ensuing four months. Flight Lieutenant Neil Oliver, the real adjutant, taught Piers about filing systems and security classification of documents. Then, as a minor task, he had him complete the annual audit of all the classified documents on the station, including the top secret books in the Station Commander's safe. It took four weeks! It was interspersed with paying the troops, which involved the unescorted weekly collection of £160,565 (or there abouts) from a local bank, in cash, and arranging for its disbursement into 234 (give or take a few) pairs of airmen's hands on a pay parade.

Piers was only too aware of a similar bank run, from Bedford city centre to RAF Henlow, when the unfortunate courier officer was waylaid by four truncheon wielding robbers.

"Why don't the airmen use banks, Neil?"

"Airmen like cash in hand. Weekly, too! I know, and you know, the first thing they'll do is take the money to their bank so their mates won't pinch it. They'll keep ten quid in their pocket which they'll piss against a wall and consider they've had a good time. It's the air force way." He shrugged; such predictable circumstances produced a regular flow of routine paperwork — the lifeblood of No 1 PHU.

"Three of them will wind up pissed on Friday night; they'll get picked up by the bobbies, so we'll send the RAF Police along — snowdrops because of their white caps — who'll bring them back to our guardroom, drag them in front of the Orderly Officer who has been called out of his pit, where they'll sober up, be charged, go before their officer and get 14 days jankers. Same every weekend, it's the air force way."

"Neil, can I ask you a question?"

"Ask away, old lad. I may not answer though!"

"Why are you pacing up and down the carpet in front of your desk? You seem to do it a lot."

"It's my secret, old lad. Perhaps one day I'll tell you. Look, why don't you pop along to P2, they're looking for an effects officer."

"What's an effects officer? And what's P2 again?" Piers queried. He sensed there was no escape from this chore.

"P2 is 'Personnel No 2' where they do officers; P3 is where they do airmen and airwomen. You pop down to P2 and get the brief. I'll look out the manual."

Thirty minutes later, Piers was back. "They've got a group captain to bury and they want me to do it. I didn't join the RAF to dig graves, err... old lad... I'm a bleeding engineer."

"And a failed pilot, old lad. Sorry, I shouldn't have... Don't worry, Piers," with an encouraging smile, "it's all in the book. They've got a spare copy in the Air Publications library; you could sign it out. That would save my having to ask you for mine back if I need it. Read it from cover to cover and you'll know how to bury a group captain and anybody else, you know, the..."

"The air force way?"

"Right! Station Commander's instruction to me, before he went on leave, was to give you the broadest experience in what we Administrative Branch pen-pushers do so that you Technical Branch plumbers get an inkling of what hard work really is in Station Headquarters. Burying a group captain is a bit of a challenge, but I am sure you'll rise to the job. Feel privileged, old lad, it doesn't happen every day and rarely to plumbers. Don't be afraid to ask. Think of it as generous Neil keeping poor Piers out of having to run the Mechanical Transport section."

Piers did not appear persuaded, even when Neil added, "Don't worry, old lad. There's not a spade in sight."

Over the next four days, a number of tactical decisions had to be made by the inexperienced effects officer. There were a series of formal and sympathy letters to be written, closing accounts, paying the tailors, disposing of flying clothing, organising a coffin and a plot, gravestone and similar. The family had to be consulted and helped to decide what was best for their relative who had not recovered when his Meteor fighter met the ground at three times normal landing speed in a field six miles from its airfield.

A funeral, with full military honours, has certain immutable dimensions. Apart from arranging for an appropriate hole in consecrated ground of the correct denomination, the principal impediment to smooth progress concerns the quantity and rank of the pall bearers; the specified six available group captains (all supposedly of the same physical height) were impossible to identify so six student navigators from the local flying school were nominated and rehearsed. The next was an armed firing party to fire three 'devil frightening' volleys over the grave; the 'Effects' manual specified this party as 44 airmen for a group captain. Piers had to get by with 27 and lots of blank ammunition consumption paperwork to account for the rehearsals so that the volley didn't sound like machine guns on an army test range. An RAF padre from the local RAF hospital at Wroughton agreed to do the necessary holy stuff. To Piers's delight, the station's Mechanical Transport section agreed to polish the staff cars that were to be sent to collect the family although he was expected to make his own way there and claim expenses later.

At some point, Piers asked, "Neil, can I ask you a question?"

"Ask away, old lad. I may…"

"I know, you may not answer. But I was wondering, if this is No 1 PHU, are there any more PHU madhouses like this? Like number two?"

"I can't tell you, old lad, it's secret." Neil looked like he had been summoned to the dentist. "But I'll tell you where you can find out for yourself." Having to disclose a state secret was really serious stuff. "In the old man's safe there is a little book called Secret Document 98, SD98 to you and me. Have a look in there."

"How can I do that when the Station Commander keeps the safe locked?"

"I know, it's a puzzlement, it's the…"

"The air force way."

"Right! A useful source is SD98. You should read it some time! It tells you where everything is, air force wise, globally; quite useful when you've got to move someone somewhere… or bring his remains back to Blighty." Neil's face creased from worry to self-content since he'd avoided actual disclosure of actual secrets.

The graveside committal went as planned except that no-one had warned the deceased group captain's 85 years old mother about the firing party. On the command: "Present" twenty seven .303 rifles were raised and on the command: "Fire!" they all went off. The said group captain's 85 year old mother nearly passed out with shock. On the second volley, Piers had to support her arm and turn her away so that she had her back to the third volley as her knees buckled under her. Fortunately, said group captain's brother realised something was amiss with his mother and came to her rescue.

The discharge of guns at a military graveside is a very emotional moment — a sort of release, it's the air force way. Very few attendees are not moved by the experience with some being reduced to tears. Piers was no exception and had great difficulty choking his feeling to retain his RAF bearing. Neil hadn't warned him; this was well beyond the cadetship training at Henlow.

With the coffin lowered to its resting place, the RAF supporting act departed in their RAF transport and the family retired to a local pub where Piers had arranged for a buffet before their journey home. He hoped he would be able to claim the cost on his expenses!

*   *   *

"How did it go, Piers?" Neil was as consistent as administrators go.

"Oh, he's planted in… err… the air force way. It didn't rain on my parade either. A couple more letters and a signature on my claim form will wrap it up. Will you oblige?"

"Sorry, old lad, no can do. It's not the air force's way… Claims that size need a squadron leader's signature to approve payment. We've got a squadron leader dentist visiting sick quarters on Friday. You could go and ask him to do it."

"Neil, why are you pacing up and down the carpet in front of your desk? You look worried."

"Well, I don't know how to tell you. It's delicate and you might not have the worldly experience…"

"Out with it or you'll need the dentist before Friday."

"Look, we've got a court martial next week and you really need to do a stint as 'Officer Under Instruction'. It's how you find out what really happens when the court finds the rotter guilty and decides he needs to be put out of harm's way. When you have done three 'Officer Under Instruction' stints, then you can sit on the court bench and do the sentencing bit."

"And just what has this rotter done — or rather, what has he been charged with?"

"Not he, old lad, she… and not she… them." Neil looked self-satisfied with the correction and a problem was about to be solved —

141

what next to do with Piers? He could sit down now the issue was being 'put to bed.'

"They're being charged with lesbianism contrary to good order and discipline. Look, before we get into this too deeply, read the green file in the top drawer of my filing cabinet. You can read the RAF Police report because you won't be allowed to say anything in the court until they've been found guilty and the punishment decided. Of course, if they plead 'Not Guilty' all the juicy bits will come out in court. When the appointed board has deliberated, then the chairman of the court will ask you, and any other officers under instruction, for your opinion. If you speak before that you'll be in contempt of court and will probably be castrated or given to the wrongdoers for the duration."

"I know… I know… It's the air force way. For heavens sake, pass me the file and sit down. You'll wear out the carpet."

*   *   *

"How did it go, Piers? We missed you."

"56 days each and dismissed the service. It took two days, but they were guilty as charged… Oh, I'm not supposed to talk about it."

"56 days seems about right. I was thinking about what you could do next."

"I'll take some leave. My love life is suffering here in Gloucestershire and cricket never was my favourite sport. I'll take a couple of weeks out of my entitlement, take Helen down to Cornwall. We always enjoy Newquay. Perhaps, when we get back, they'll have decided how I might return to properly earning my living by then."

"Right! It's…"

"If you say …the 'air force way' I'll brain you. Where do you keep the leave application forms?"

*   *   *

"How did it go, Piers? We missed you."

"I do look forward to your greeting, when I get back to your mentoring, even if it is a bit repetitive for an adjutant. In the time honoured way, I asked her and she said, 'Yes'. So we're setting a date for late spring next year. And a honeymoon in Eire."

"Heh, that's great news. You can buy me a pint to celebrate. I thought I might teach you how to sail… in the air force way… on the River Severn. It's a tad narrow, but you can avoid ramming the river banks — with care. The station has got a dingy on the river and I could book it."

"Look Neil, I need an answer to my question?"

"Ask away, old lad. I may not answer though!" Piers frowned; he'd heard it before. "Actually, if I blow any secrets, I might have to shoot you. Well...?"

"Why do you pace up and down the carpet in front of your desk?"

"Hornblower!"

"What are you talking about?" Pier's head was shaking in disbelief despite his colleague's serious face.

"This desk is about the same as size Hornblower's quarter deck. When the wind is blowing outside and the RAF ensign is abeam the mainstay — whatever — and I need to think a problem through, I pace my quarter deck. A lubricating tot of rum and cola would do it, but alcohol is *verboten* in the office. So, when I've decided what Hornblower would have done, I do the opposite. He was always wrong so doing the opposite is always right. See? It's the air force way."

"You're kidding!" The adjutant was once more pacing his desk.

"No way, old lad. Look, you said you wanted to go on leave. So Neil *Hornblower* Oliver here had to make a decision — shall I let him go or shall I deny him. What would Hornblower have done?" Forefinger to cheek with mock thoughtfulness, "Chummy Horatio would decide that No 1 PHU could not survive without poor Piers so he should stay. The contrary view was to let you go, which is what happened, and look at the consequential damage — you've gone and got engaged and to a woman no less."

"That's utter bull..." Piers was still shaking his head in exasperation."

But experienced Neil was nodding and smiling. He had his protégé on a baited line. "It's the air force way, old lad. And while you've been swanning on the golden sands, their airships in London have sent you a letter. It says come and see us, in Adastral House, for a career interview." Neil was offering the younger officer a sealed letter retrieved from his desk. "So you're off on your travels again."

Checking the envelope was still sealed, "How do you know what it says? Oh, I nearly forgot, it's the air force way."

"Don't forget to press your suit trousers, old lad." Neil's head was nodding by way of reassurance while he was manoeuvring towards the chair behind his desk. "It's civvies for interviews in London; best get a haircut too, it might help. One other thing…"

"Go on…" As his eyes rolled upwards under his eyelids, 'What could possibly come next?'

"Don't forget to write a letter to the Station Commander asking for permission to marry. He'll write 'approved' on it and send it back for you to treasure and persuade your wife she needs to pay attention to your nuptial demands." Piers looked incredulous. "I'm serious, old lad, it's the air force way… and it does help ensure you get the meagre extra pay and allowances which go with marital bliss."

*   *   *

On the return drive along the A40 towards Innsworth, Piers reflected on the interview. There had been an emphatic denial of any opportunity to resume flying training, "You've had your chance and you blew it."

Piers's mute reaction was, 'I don't want to hear this…' He couldn't move on his chair with no opportunity given for him to speak.

And, delivered with a stern voice, "Put the last year down to experience, Pilot Officer Ploughman, and now go out and earn your keep as an engineer."

'Well, OK, but…'

And, the fingers on the group captain's right hand had clenched into a loose fist, "We expect our young officers to lead our airmen in the challenges ahead and to be under no illusion the new aeroplanes are a challenge to everyone."

'OK…'

And, with glowering eyes engaging Piers's, "Security on the V-force is paramount; I can't tell you why, it's classified; you'll find out when you need to know. Collect the security vetting forms on your way out. I don't expect to see you here again." It was dismissal, without a handshake, by an officer whose name Piers had immediately forgotten.

Somewhere midway between Oxford and Cheltenham, Piers pulled off the road for a coffee break. Quite suddenly, the impact of the 20 minutes interview in Adastral House hit home. It was made no easier by the fact that both men had been in civilian clothes yet subject to good order and discipline. It wasn't the two and half hours of form filling for his security clearance or the duplication it required of all the certificates and references that he supplied during the induction to Henlow four years

144

ago. It was not the repeat of the 'you're grounded' message delivered so abruptly. He concluded it was the unknown future, beyond his control. What did he actually know about the RAF? Sure, he could bury someone and safeguard his effects; the procedures of a court martial surely would not be relevant to his career. 'What do you say to an airman? What's all this fuss about V-bombers being painted in anti-flash white? How do you get the bloody bombs to stay on and, more important, how do you get them to come off when you want to? Talk about being dropped in the deep end! It's the air force way! I'm doing it now! Oh my Gawd!'

Piers did not sing his way over the remainder of his journey back to Innsworth. Somehow, the future was no singing matter.

*   *   *

Piers's and Helen's wedding was an RAF affair. Piers and his best man, ex-cadet Allen *Shark* Davis, were wearing their best uniforms with swords borrowed from the RAF central repository. The June sky was overcast, but dry, holding the noon warmth to a comfortable temperature. Four other ex-cadets, two proudly sporting RAF wings on their chests, provided a bridge of swords guard of honour as the couple left the church.

Helen was radiant. Her white dress complimented the RAF blues and gold in the air force uniforms. Her bouquet had a tinge of salmon pink to match the bridesmaids' dresses. One hundred family and friends celebrated the culmination of 7½ years of courtship — the longest of any of the cadet entry. At a Thames-side hotel there were speeches, champagne, photographs, the inevitable searching out the couple's honeymoon luggage, the dash to the airport, all passed without problem.

As the Aer Lingus^{tm} Viscount aircraft lifted off Heathrow's runway, Helen held — gripped — her husband's hand. This was her first flight and Piers had ensured she had a window seat. Helen just talked for the 95 minutes flight to Dublin. At one point she started to giggle.

"You know that *Bunk* Dewhurst stuffed confetti down my back?" she queried, looking at her husband with bright eyes. It was the first time her gaze had shifted from Mother Earth to within the passenger cabin.

Piers nodded his reply and raised his eyebrows to invite his lovely wife to tell him more while secretly praying the Irish pilot knew his professional stuff. "*Bunk*'s flying helicopters out of Odiham, you know. I got some — confetti — in my pockets too." He decided he liked sea-

145

green eyes — never any doubt about it! And cheeks that need no rouge, too. And those lips moved when she talked...

"When I went to spend a penny, it all came out." Her face mocked surprise, but her eyes showed happiness. He wanted to kiss those lips... "When I stood up, the floor was around the whatsit was covered in confetti. There was nothing I could do about it."

If she stopped talking to listen to the stewardess ask her to select her wine, Piers did not notice. His wife — what a nice thought! — was happy. This, surely, was no different to his singing during his first solo flights. It was his wife's way — his air force wife's way.

'Don't interrupt. She's happy therefore I am too. Fantastic!' Her mouth was close to his ear, her breath enchanting.

"I love you, Mrs Ploughman."

"I already know that, Mister Ploughman. And I love you back. At least those so-called chums of yours didn't get at the luggage. My Dad made sure of that."

In that respect, she was utterly wrong. The guests had found the luggage and the newly-wed couple were finding confetti through their whole two weeks in Eire and for some weeks beyond.

*   *   *

Piers had put Helen in the window seat again. The couple were silent as the Viscount airliner headed east taking them home from their honeymoon. Piers's head was back against the headrest with his eyes closed. Helen was looking out of the window at the passing cloud tops. She could appreciate, now, what Piers's fascination with flight was all about. She was holding his hand, its warmth passing into her smaller palm and into her very essence. Her body might be at rest, but her mind was racing.

'Here is the man I have promised to be with for the rest of my life, to have his children, wherever he takes me and whatever troubles lie ahead. I wonder: will we have enough money to buy a house, to have a new car, to enjoy clothes and fashions and films and stage shows? And what do I know about being an officer's wife — and RAF officer's wife, too? And his children — our children. His mother makes it look so easy, but I'll guess it's not really like that.'

She turned to look at Piers. 'That final drive, in the hire car to the airport, was not easy. I'm not surprised he needs a rest." She smiled at a

146

wicked private thought, 'I suppose his honeymoon was a bit tiring for the poor man, but what is it his chums keep saying? *Can't take a joke — you shouldn't have joined.* I love you Piers Peter Ploughman.'

Green fields appeared through the cloud breaks. England was beckoning. '7½ years and my fellow has grown from a shy six-former to an upright commissioned RAF officer, well built, almost handsome, smart, tactful... well usually... gentle, considerate, lover and mine." She reached to touch his hand holding the armrest. Maybe there was discernable change in the way Piers was breathing. He'd have to wake up, in a moment, for the landing.

Outside the cabin window, the clouds seemed a little closer and then the landing announcement came over the public address. 'I am glad that Dad will be there to meet us and take us home. Perhaps there will be a letter for Piers telling him where he — we — will be going. How exciting! A new home, a delicious husband, our new life together. Can you sense what I am thinking, Piers, my love?' There was no reaction from the hand she was holding.

Quite suddenly the white clouds seemed to be rushing past the windows. It was an impenetrable mist yet the descent was smooth. Equally suddenly, the urban sprawl of west London came into view. The magic of flight was about to end, the reality of 1960s Britain was about to begin.

*   *   *

The telegram was waiting for them when they got home.

> *Pilot Officer Ploughman report for duty at RAF Waddington Lincolnshire on July 1ˢᵗ 1961 for duties in Electrical Engineering Squadron.*

The honeymoon was over. Now it was time to earn a living. But first...

"Where is Waddington?" asked Helen.

"Lincolnshire," Piers answered helpfully. "Up the Great North Road for one hundred miles and turn right. The Romans went there first. If you get to Lincoln Cathedral, you've gone too far."

"Oh. Where will we live?"

"That's a good question. We won't get a married quarter until I'm 25. Three years."

"Oh. Where will we live? And where will we put our things?" Helen was raising obvious problems.

"We can hire a flat." The practicalities of setting up home in a place, never even visited, were beginning to become an issue.

"Oh. Where? And where will we put our things? And what will we sleep on?" Helen was nothing if not persistent — drop dead, utterly gorgeous, persistent.

"We'll go up early tomorrow and get a place through an agent."

"Oh. Which agent? And how will we move our things? Wedding presents and such. And what will we sleep on?"

"I do love you when you ask me questions. Give me a few minutes to think. It'll be alright, I promise." Piers made to try to kiss his bride. She was having none of it.

"Not before you've checked the bank, and filled the car, and... that can wait... and got on the phone to this Waddington place... and... ooh..." Piers did get his kiss and then the panic started.

Early the following morning, in a densely packed car, filled with driver, wife and all their worldly goods, Piers and Helen drove north for three hours, to Lincolnshire and the unknown, to find a roof for the night and to address the realities of their future life together. Their only preparation for domestic life ahead was a deep pastry steak and kidney pie prepared by Helen's mother for tonight's meal.

The kettle was in its box, a wedding gift not yet tried.

Chapter 20
1962 ~ 'You'll Take the City of Lincoln With You!'

The first estate agency Piers and Helen tried, in Lincoln, had a newly converted flat to let which was partially furnished and built on the Lincolnshire Edge. It had a cooker, two furnished bedrooms and two armchairs. It had a view to the Newark-on-Trent coal burning power station 20 miles away — if you climbed out of a window onto a flat roof. The local bus passed close to either end of the journey. The flat was two miles from Waddington guardroom and three from Piers's place of duty. The price was right and the couple had somewhere to sleep. Naturally, they had nothing for their larder, except for Helen's mother's pie, to cook or eat; there had not been room in the car even for a bottle of milk. Funds just stretched to a meal in a basket in a local pub and it was early to bed in the curtainless bedroom.

"Our first home," snuggled Helen.

A little unconfident, "I know it's the top floor, but it's not exactly a palace for a...." He tried to manoeuvre within Helen's embrace to see something good about the place.

"It's ours. Maybe this is not where we would want to raise a family, but we can always move." Her head pressed against his just not ready to kiss him for this first almost mistake.

"I know all that. It's just that... I wanted..."

Practical Helen interrupted, "We'll go around the place with a duster... tomorrow... and soon it will be spick and span. Right now, I want somewhere to put my cold feet. Hurry off and hang one of our wedding present blankets over the window so the man in the moon can't see us." Piers did as he was bid.

The age of the bedstead, its spring, the provided under-blankets and its kapok mattress really did not bear thinking about. The spring settled into a more pronounced bow than a ship's hammock and urgent application of Piers's car's toolkit was necessary before another night could be attempted. Although it was the end of June, the old adage about love keeping the heart warm was put to the test that first night. Piers resolved to find some fire wood, maybe even a sack of coal at a petrol garage, on the follow day — a Sunday. The living room had a fireplace. As usual, the kitchen was the warmest place in the flat which was what would later be known as a loft conversion. Purchasing anything substantial in the way of a heater would have to wait until the shops opened on Monday morning.

Six months passed and it was well into the 1961/62 winter that an opportunity arose to relocate to a flat set in a converted country house. It was further for daily travel, but the setting was the deciding factor. Piers and Helen occupied one of twenty such developments in a single property set in twenty acres of mainly grazing land surrounded by trees which needed progressive management; the owner felled unwanted timber and his tenants were welcome to consume whatever they chose. The converted former gentry's house was far from draft proof and free fuel was always welcome especially with the onset of the extreme, penetratingly cold, following winter of 1963. With no sign of family enlargement, Helen took a clerical job in Lincoln, usefully served by public transport since Piers's duties at Waddington were very demanding in time on base.

While he was waiting for his new squadron to form, Piers was assigned to supernumerary duties in Electronic Engineering Squadron at RAF Waddington. This gave him the chance to understand the workings of maintenance of the full range of advanced aircraft electrical and avionics systems way beyond anything he had learned about at Henlow. Time was available to attend specialist courses in techniques and design. Piers's squadron was to be equipped with the Vulcan B Mk 1A which was being fitted with a range of electronic countermeasures in a complex electronic warfare suite. With his security clearance now confirmed, Piers was attached to a specialist Electronic Warfare course at RAF Yatesbury in Wiltshire which, although he didn't know it at the time, was to provide him with the foundation for later responsibilities for the next thirty years of RAF service. Close interest in electronic warfare matters was also to have possible repercussions on his family life. But first, Headquarters No 1 Group had organised a presentation at an adjacent station; the RAF equivalent of a three line whip went out for attendance by all junior technical engineering officers from the stations in the group.

A morning presentation, security classified secret, was to be given by two representatives from an organisation called GCHQ. In 1961, this organisation which was to feature so prominently in Piers's later life, was hardly known and only spoken about in the most guarded terms. It was therefore a privilege to attend such a talk. The speakers took as their starting point an awareness that the 'nasty' Russians, like all enemies, had a high capability to listen to our communications and radar and derive our battle plans from it. There had been a series of security films on the subject which were of dubious accuracy, although Piers did not know that at the time. The speakers used as an example of the type of precautions necessary against the 'marauding bear' the need to turn off our radars if he came near. The example cited was the visit to UK by the Soviet premier on the cruiser *Ordzhonikidze* in the late 1950s — when Buster Crabb was lost in the harbour where it was docked. It appears that our east coast air defence radar chain was progressively switched off just before the *Ordzhonikidze* came to the horizon and was switched on after the Soviets had passed. Evidently these were assessed to be excellent precautions despite the radar chain having been operating continuously for 5 years and whose every mode would have been thoroughly documented by the Russian spy trawler fleet located in the North Sea for just that purpose. However, no one told the Royal Radar Establishment at Malvern that their hilltop test site for the next generation of defence radar permitted its signal to be detected at ground level on the other side of England on the coast. The new radar continued to radiate all through the *Ordzhonikidze's* transit through the North Sea and while it remained moored in Portsmouth.

*   *   *

"Darling? Piers, can I ask you something?"

"Go on; I'll try to answer."

"This Berlin Wall — I know it's a long way away, but..." East German forces had begun raising the apparently threatening wall seven weeks after Piers and Helen had arrived in Lincolnshire.

"But what? What is troubling those golden curls?" Piers was studying his adorable wife over a steaming cup of coffee.

"You... your work... Waddington... V-bombers and all that. They are such young men... the men on your squadron... you?" Even across the kitchen, Helen's frown indicated that he could not take this issue without saying something.

"Not all of them, Helen. Don't look so worried. Some of them flew with Bomber Harris."

"No. I mean… What's going to happen with this wall in Berlin? The newspaper pictures make it look so frightening and people are being killed trying to climb it. Are we going to have to fight about it?"

Shaking his head, "I don't think so. It's the Russian's way of keeping people in rather than keeping us out. I think we've got enough worries of our own without having to worry about a few East Berliners. It's a bit like the 'iron curtain' except it's concrete not wire. No, I shouldn't worry about it. We'll probably never even see it."

*   *   *

When Piers's Vulcan squadron formed, the most significant feature of their aircraft was an upgrade of the engines and modification to its internal electrical power system. The Mk 1 aircraft was designed around a 115 volt dc system, from a generator on each of the four engines, and there was no way that the modified Mk 1A could have that changed. But the electronic warfare (EW) suite required a 215 volt 400 Hz ac supply. So a device called a Bleed Air Turbine was installed in the Mk 1A variant to drive a suitable alternator for the EW suite. It used surplus air from the No 3 and 4 port side engines, which needed to be run above 40% power to provide sufficient bleed air from their compressors for the turbine. (Take off power is 100%, ground idle was about 18%.) Therefore running the EW suite on aircraft internal power, rather than a ground test trolley, was a noisy process.

Although every squadron had test equipment to confirm the EW equipment was doing what it was designed to do, it was necessary to prove that the devices still worked in flight. It was thought the high altitude, despite being in pressurized canisters, might have allowed electric arcing within the EW transmitters. Accordingly, Bomber Command set up an EW Test Range at RAF Stornaway in the Hebrides Islands. Aircraft on practice bombing or navigation exercises could route through the range and their performance be passed back to Bomber Command and Group Headquarters to direct the necessary maintenance. This well thought through plan forgot that the biggest fishing fleet in the world was operated by Russia. They had converted about 55 'trawlers' to be mobile signals intelligence collectors and one was invariably sited in the EW range whenever our aircraft were scheduled to make a test run. A decision was made that the only unmonitorable place to test our EW was in the middle of the Atlantic Ocean, but neither the RAF nor the boffins were able to get their surface performance assessment gear anywhere near this improvised proving range. Later, when the V-bomber force adopted its low altitude attack profile, the presence of the Russian trawler was ignored because, wrongly, it was thought possible to keep the now smaller EW footprint away from the trawlers.

It was known that the radio energy put out by one radar jammer, codenamed *RED SHRIMP*, was a possible biological hazard. In later years, the domestic microwave cooker used a similar transmitter valve to those in the jammer. In 1961, however, the cooking potential was not well understood; ground maintenance staff were normally cautious about going too close to the antenna when the transmitter was being tested. It became too hot to handle. They knew they were safe when a dummy load was substituted for the radiating antenna; it got hot even on the coldest nights proving that it was keeping the radio energy inside.

Each Vulcan was fitted with three *RED SHRIMP* systems and were considered essential for aircraft operational status.

But there was always a need to ensure that the transmitter cable to the antenna had been correctly refitted after ground test. One night, because it was late and the aircraft was required quite soon for a sortie, safety and security precautions went by the way. Rather than use a ground power trolley, Piers was on hand to supervise the use of the aero-engines and he stood in the relatively quiet zone under the port wing where the three *RED SHRIMP* antennae were fitted. The test took five minutes while he stood just four metres from the radiation source which he could not sense.

Years later, whenever Helen and Piers's apparent inability to conceive between 1962 and 1973 was discussed, as often happened during what they later called the adoption years, Piers remembered that cold night on F-dispersal at Waddington. "Fried gonads are not good in the offspring game," he would joke. He wondered if some permanent damage had been done. Their daughter Philippa's arrival, in July 1974, conclusively demonstrated that it was not a long term effect.

*   *   *

The *raison d'être* for the V-force was deterrence based around demonstrable nuclear readiness. This was interpreted as exercising the preparation of armed aircraft configured and crewed, ready to fly, within specified no-notice timeframes. No notice was interpreted as meaning weekend, or night-times, or both. Group Headquarters would exercise its stations at least once per month, requiring one or more weapons system per squadron to be declared within typically two hours on a Sunday afternoon. Ground crew, standby aircrews and appropriate specialist officers were called in to base for the purpose, only to put all the components back to safe, secure store when stood down by the Group.

Marital harmony, in the face of frequent weekend interruption, was not easy to sustain.

Sometimes, Headquarters Bomber Command insisted on exercising the whole command when all one hundred and fifty bombers were prepared, including those stripped in hangar servicing. In practice this might take 24 hours, sometimes more, before the last of the eight aircraft per squadron was ready for its weapon. Coordination of men, meals, security, time dependant pre-flight readiness maintenance, safety, fuel and a host of administrative details kept everyone busy. Occasionally, a so-called 'generation exercise' would specify inert training weapons; on others, the real thing would come out of their revetted storage bunkers thereby exercising the armourers and a very large number of security staff. On the flight line, the procedures were the same in both situations and no-one assumed any weapon was a dummy round.

On one such occasion, the exercise having begun on a pre-dawn Monday morning, but still ongoing during Wednesday, the final aircraft of Piers's squadron was declared serviceable for war-only operational flying, a rare but considered judgement in discussion with senior flying staff. But the 'generation' of armed aircraft had occupied all the station's available dispersed hardstandings so a decision was made to load the nuclear weapon while the aircraft remained close to the hangar. In the selected location its engines could have been started safely in an emergency.

OC Administrative Wing was in his office. It had been a long 56 hours, keeping the cookhouse open, the RAF Police alert, the paperwork properly constituted for the inevitable post-exercise financial audit. He happened to stand up, to look out of his window and saw a Vulcan with an approaching towed bomb trolley and armed police escort. The actual weapon was always moved shrouded by a tarpaulin cover — even its shape was classified. It was obvious to the wing commander that someone was going to hang a nuclear weapon on a Vulcan within two hundred yards of his office. He reached for his telephone.

The short, commonly used, telephone number sheet under the Perspex cover on his desk was inappropriate for Waddington in a major exercise configuration. Everyone was somewhere different! It was not until his third attempt that he connected with the squadron's engineering coordination desk. He did not wait to hear to whom he was talking.

"What the hell are you doing? What happens if the bloody thing goes off? Stop what you are doing now... This is OC Admin... Wing Commander..."

"I can't do that," replied the tired but still calm warrant officer. His primary interest was the squadron's aircraft status wall display on his wall. 'Officers! They'd try the patience of a saint.'

"I'm giving you a direct order. Stop what you are doing now... or else... What happens if the bloody thing goes off? It'll take the hanger and half the station with it!"

"Oh, I shouldn't worry, sir. If it goes off, it'll take the City of Lincoln and half the county with it, sir. So much less paperwork then, sir."

"Are you trying to be funny with me, warrant officer?"

"Oh no, sir. May I suggest you have a word with the Station Commander if you are uncomfortable about what we're doing, sir. I think you'll find that he will be able to reassure you that you won't feel a thing, sir. Now if you'll excuse me, sir, I just have to pop out to see that everything is hunky-dory with my Vulcan, sir, in a manner of speaking, sir. I've got to find somewhere to plug its electric blanket in. Good morning!"

Chapter 21
1962 ~ SUNSPOT and TYPHOON

The squadron was in Malta, on an exercise called SUNSPOT, while Khrushchev's missile laden freighters were moving towards Cuba. The exercise was a routine practice of the air navigation, loading and related target practice including live dropping, of the aircraft's conventional high explosive bombs on a desert range in Libya. On Friday October 26th, 1962, the squadron was returning the hospitality of the RAF Luqa Officers' Mess when a message arrived from HQ Bomber Command with notice of a possible early recall to the UK. Piers, in common with most V-force officers that evening, was under the impression that the Russian freighters, with obvious missiles as deck cargo, had turned away from Cuba to avoid a confrontation with the US Navy. It was assumed that the situation had been defused and that the reported USAF and Russian Air force's alert were nothing but mutual posturing after the event. Otherwise, surely their eight nuclear-capable V-aircraft would have been recalled earlier.

A decision was made that the squadron should fly its pre-planned training sorties on Saturday. Eight aircraft loads of twenty one 1000 lb bombs were prepared, fused and prepositioned on transport trolleys ready to load. The bombing range at RAF El Adem, in the Libyan desert, was pre-booked. The squadron could then pack up to be ready to travel if required. They were due to return to UK on Monday the 29th anyway.

Piers was the officer to oversee the Monday launch of the aircraft for the homeward journey with a minimum set of groundcrew. This duty meant he had to be on the flightline at 06:45. Their RAF transport, a Britannia, landed on Waddington runway at 01:00 on Tuesday morning with Piers having caught just 90 minutes sleep in the standard RAF non-reclining, plastic trimmed seat. After the warmth of autumn in Malta, the shock of Lincolnshire cold on Waddington airfield was numbing. HM Customs and Excise were not relaxed towards the arrivals so that the formalities took until after 03:00 when a coach departed Waddington to deliver the late home-comers back to their quarters. The squadron's commanding officer had passed the word that all personnel were to be 'on parade', in the hangar, at 08:00 for a briefing.

Helen was not amused to be woken at four in the morning by her shivering, smelly husband only to be told that she had to deliver him at Waddington by 07:45 and preferably with a breakfast inside him.

The briefing turned out to be an excuse to assemble the strength of the servicing tradesmen to service and rectify any accumulated faults on the squadron's fleet of eight aircraft. Conventional weapons carrying systems were to be removed and the Vulcans prepared in nuclear capable configuration, but without the weapons being loaded. Then it was announced that one was to be loaded with a live weapon and prepared for the Quick Reaction Alert posture, close to the end of the take off runway. The squadron was required, like its colleagues throughout the command, to maintain one aircraft per squadron serviceable, crewed and armed ready for launch at any time within 15 minutes notice. The QRA task had been imposed since 1 February 1962, and there would be no concessions from the task until the Royal Navy adopted the nation's nuclear deterrent role in 1969.

It would be two days after the return from Exercise SUNSPOT that the alert status was reduced from nuclear configured preparedness to normal role and the new month's flying training schedule could be picked up. There never was an audit of how many short cuts were taken by over tired airmen during those 48 hours.

*   *   *

Seven weeks passed and it was the time for the 1962 Christmas parties. All of Waddington's aircraft were either on or prepared for QRA, were in hangars to protect their weather-sensitive electronics, or chocked, locked, bunged and protected if they had to be left outside. All desks had been cleared, cabinets and safes locked, keys stowed in their secure stowage, windows double checked and non-essential power sockets switched off. The weather forecast was for an extended cold snap through the 1962 Christmas holiday period, with the possibility of snow after the 25th. The station had been told it could cease flying training from Friday 21st December until the New Year. So every squadron, section, department and office throughout the station settled to begin their festivities at about 11:15. The expectation was that most people would be off the station shortly after noon leaving just essential duty staff and the QRA teams to 'mind the show' and keep the runway 'blacktop' black.

The Station Commander was doing the rounds of saying thank you to his officers and airmen for their hard work during the challenging year past. At 11:35 the station public address tannoy system announced, "Would the Station Commander please report to Operations immediately."

Station commanders are busy people and no-one anticipated what would happen next. "Probably the AOC-in-C wanted to wish him 'Happy Xmas'", offered one observer.

After a short interval, the tannoy announced, "All squadron commanders are to report to Operations immediately." Staff cars drew away quickly; announcements like that demanded no delay.

But the office parties continued. Leave passes were not valid until the nominal cease work which had been promulgated in Station Routine Orders as 12:30. And it wasn't every day that alcohol was available in an RAF office — especially at a front line bomber station.

At 12:08, the tannoy announced, "All personnel report to their place of duty. All Christmas leave is cancelled. I repeat: all personnel report to their place of duty. All Christmas leave is cancelled."

More than a few rushed for their cars to attempt to get away before being trapped, but they found the RAF Police had secured the road exits and were turning cars back to their work places.

"What the hell is going on?" Everyone wanted to know the answer to the question, but none was forthcoming.

"All personnel report to their place of duty. All Christmas leave is cancelled. I repeat: all personnel report to their place of duty. All Christmas leave is cancelled."

The drinks were finished, the snacks consumed and many cigarettes smoked while waiting for the next order. It was impossible to communicate off-base; the telephone exchange had pulled the plug and only authorised calls were being accepted — in or out. Even those personnel with station married quarters, across the road but beyond the gate, were not permitted to go home. The mature SNCOs, who had never experienced anything quite like this, resigned themselves to their fate of working in the mysterious V-force and therefore to waiting for what their officers would tell them. The inexperienced began to complain at the lack of news. The wise settled on a chair and waited. This, after all, was Bomber Command and *if you can't a joke you shouldn't have joined.*

At 13:00, the officers of squadron leader rank were assembled in the squadron commander's office. "We're warned for OPERATION TYPHOON. Two Waddington squadrons, sixteen aircraft overall. We're one on the squadrons. We can borrow other squadron's airframes if we need to and make up tradesmen shortages from with the Engineering Wing pool. Vulcan crew chiefs are to stay with their aircraft no matter to which flying squadron their Vulcans are assigned. All aircraft to be brought to flying condition in the conventional role, each with racks for twenty one 1000 lb bombs but without the weapons, 100% fuel load, ready to fly at twenty fours notice. QRA is not being relaxed."

"Where to, and what's OPERATION TYPHOON?"

"I have not been told. Navigation leaders are being called for a briefing at 14:30 when we know where we are going. It may be a follow up to SUNSPOT training, but no-one should make any assumptions. The Station Commander has been called to Bomber Command, at High Wycombe, and they're doing the same thing with two squadrons of Victors in 3 Group."

"Is there an Operation Order?"

"Yes, two copies on the station. One is locked in the Station Commander's safe and he's got the key in his pocket. The other is locked in a squadron commander's safe, behind a manifoil combination lock, and he's skiing somewhere in France. He left last night. They're trying to contact him now."

"Sound like the usual cock-up."

"That's not very helpful. I want all the groundcrew fed and watered and back here at 13:45 to start work. No exceptions. Everyone involved in OPERATION TYPHOON is to be jabbed for yellow fever and TABT; the doctors have already contacted RAF Hospital Nocton Hall who are sending out a team to be here at 16:00."

"Leave arrangements, sir? What about those that have booked?"

"Cancelled. All Xmas leave is cancelled. We work until 20:00 tonight. I'll make an announcement when I know what the sleeping and mess arrangements are going to be. Well, gentlemen, it seems we may be going somewhere to spoil someone's Christmas."

"To say nothing of our own. There's going to be hell to pay for this…"

When husbands did not come home, anxious wives began to try to make contact only to find the telephone lines blocked. By 14:30 there was a small crowd gathered outside the closed Main Gate. By 15:15, the local press was making its presence known, to be joined at 15:30 by a newshound claiming to represent the *Daily Mirror*^{tm}. But still nothing was known about what the men and women were doing inside the gate around the station. The RAF police on the gate knew nothing except that leave had been cancelled.

While waiting in the inoculation queue, always a melting pot for military rumour, the sad case of Senior Aircraftsman Parsons of Engineering Wing's Wheel and Tyre Bay was the topic. It seemed that SAC Parsons had taken leave to marry his girl in London on Wednesday. The newly wed couple had returned to Lincoln railway station, that Friday morning, so that he could collect his things before they went off for a romantic Xmas honeymoon at Skegness before setting up home. According to rumour control, Parsons had kissed his beloved farewell at 11:20 and had ridden the bus to RAF Waddington, had stopped for a Xmas drink with his mates and was now caught inside the station gate. Meanwhile the distraught new bride, apparently deserted by an airman who had his way with her, had now abandoned her. What was she to do? She had given him all her money for the train ticket!

"No concession," was edict from on high. "He stays put while we sort it all out. If he can't take a joke, he shouldn't have joined. No he can't use the phone. If I can't, he can't. Tough!" SAC Parsons contributed nothing to the work in his servicing bay until his plight was sorted out. Rumour control never did circulate the closure of this story.

By eight o'clock, it had been decided that all but essential work would cease to be resumed on a 'normal' working day on Saturday. Everyone could go home but was to be at work at 08:00 tomorrow. "Pack a kit bag and be prepared for a recall. Be prepared to stay on-base overnight."

Piers went through his front door at 20:20. Helen was not best pleased with her errant man. Their plans involved driving to Kingston tomorrow for Christmas with her family; he had left her to do all the present wrapping and packing...

"I'm afraid I shan't be going to Mum and Dad's. There's something going on and we're on alert." She was not in the mood for anything physical and Piers's priority was to get a pint of beer inside him.

"There's been nothing on the news," remarked Helen. This *'air force way'* of doing things could very trying at times.

Piers shrugged. "The newspapers don't know everything. They've probably not told the BBC either. Anyway, they're all running down for Christmas, I suppose. The 'papers have got to get their holidays in before the 25th so that they can work on Christmas Day and earn triple pay so we can all enjoy their rubbish on Boxing Day."

"Well what's it all about? I don't want to spend Christmas away without you."

"I dunno." He shrugged, but what could he tell her? "They've jabbed us up to the eyeballs. We could be going anywhere. The saving grace, I suppose, is that we're leaving our buckets of sunshine in their garages." Helen had heard Piers's friends refer to nuclear weapons in that way; Piers did not normally mention nuclear weapons. The beer had been downed, Helen kept her distance.

"Oh. I suppose that's good news."

"Helen, look, it could come to being on your own anyway. Even if you stay here, and if they put us in an aeroplane for God knows where, you'll be alone then. I mean, I don't know if I shall be able to get home each night. The old man is talking about this thing going on through Christmas."

"Oh. I've got no makings for Christmas lunch. Mum was getting it all in. Oh…"

"I'm sorry. Tell you what… when I go in tomorrow, why don't you go on down to London, drive down, so you've got company. I can stay in the mess." Piers was trying to decided if he should try to cuddle some support into his wife. But, at that moment, cuddling was off the menu. The ever practical Helen suggested a plan.

"Why don't I go down by train? I like travelling on the train. Then, if you can get away you can come down and join us. The trains won't be running on Christmas Day so you'd need the car." She was already looking more cheerful.

"I love you when you make a good plan, my…" Piers didn't have a chance to finish his sentence. His mouth was otherwise occupied. Previous menus were superceded. Objections to physical contact were set aside; preparations for the exigencies of the following day were put on hold while more pressing issues were addressed.

"It's freezing outside." Piers was holding his wife very close in the afterglow.

"The weather man says it's going to be a white Christmas." Helen was enjoying her man. She had no concern for the weather snuggled under three layers of blankets.

"That would be nice. I hope we have a chance to enjoy it." Piers felt relaxed after the strains of the day; even the antiquity of their bed was forgotten in the warmth of her caress. "Hey, look out for my jabs... my arm is quite sore, you know. Gosh, there may even be a decent movie on the TV."

"I know a part that isn't sore and I want some more... gently does it... Oh!"

*   *   *

By 20:00 on Saturday, the situation and tasking for the bomber base was much clearer. Bomber Command's requirements had been stated as one aircraft per squadron was to be maintained at two hours readiness to fly, to Malta, to be followed by the remainder of the force within 24 hours. All non-essential personnel were to be allowed off base provided they could be recalled, by telephone or some other direct means, to be back on station within 12 hours of recall. The runway and all airframes declared for OPERATION TYPHOON were to be maintained frost and snow free throughout. The situation would be reviewed daily and the arrangements were to be continued through the New Year unless otherwise notified.

The station's three QRA aircraft were to remain at 15 minutes readiness throughout.

Piers arrived at the in-laws' Kingston home just before midnight on Saturday the 22nd. The Singer's heater was ineffective against the cold, dark December night. BBC news broadcasts carried no indication of a world problem which might call for 16 loads of 21000 lbs of high explosive — twice if you included the sixteen Victors from Number 3 Group, 'If they could get them started,' grinned Piers. There was no visible sign of activity at RAF Wittering as he drove past along the Great North Road for London.

It did snow on Christmas night. The following morning, England awoke to a white blanket, muting every sound. It continued to fall through the evening of Boxing Day. Piers went out once to clear the snow away from the Singer[tm] wheels so that he could start back if called.

There was no telephone recall, but the tension was always there. And still there was no public information about what was the issue. Helen's parents sensed the tension, but didn't understand that their son-in-law did not know what the problem was.

Piers and Helen had arranged that they would go back to Lincolnshire on the 29th and, in the twelve inches deep snow, they departed. Helen was grateful for her brother's present of a car blanket to ward off the cold. It was not a pleasant journey; they passed several road accidents. But soon after they had crossed the Lincolnshire border, the roads cleared and the last forty miles were not uncomfortable. They stopped, in Ancaster village, for essential fresh milk and eggs and ventured the last 15 miles to see what the cold had done to their home. The old building was still intact, but it was too large, needing open wood fires and a new paraffin burner to get the chill out of the place.

"Piers." She was sitting on his lap in front of a log fire with the car blanket tucked in under the cushions for additional warmth.

"Yes, my love."

"Did they tell you it would be like this... while you were a cadet?"

"No. They didn't tell us anything useful, especially what to do about a wife's cold... Ok... put them somewhere warm... Oh!"

In a very short time, their new electric blanket on their bed, a gift from one set of parents, was a real treat.

On New Year's Eve, while Helen prepared their evening meal, Piers went into the squadron aiming to check everything was OK. The powdered snow had a tendency to drift in the wind of which there was plenty along the Lincolnshire Edge. There were few technical people about and the squadron Vulcans appeared well clear of snow so that they could launch if so ordered. The duty groundcrews were doing a good job. The usual Officers' Mess party had been cancelled. Piers thought he would try Operations to see if there was any news.

At the entrance to the Operations Building, he met one of the aircrew flight commanders of his squadron. They exchanged seasonal pleasantries and then Piers asked the searching question.

"Is there any word what this TYPHOON thing is all about?"

"Hasn't anyone told you, Piers? There was a big scare about Kuwait." The squadron leader was reaching for his cigarette lighter.

"What... oil, I suppose?"

"Pretty much. You know that Kuwait was given its independence last year, and the Iraqis promptly made it plain they wanted Kuwait under their umbrella. The sheik didn't want any such thing and called on the Brits to help. Well, the Iraqis massed all sorts of armour down on the Kuwaiti border so we flew a Canberra photo recce over and took a couple of pictures. So the Iraqis backed off. This year, the intelligence guys thought they were up to their tricks again, but this time we couldn't get a Canberra near enough so Bomber Command thought it would be a good idea to show the flag."

"Thirty two V-aircraft is one hell of a big flag, sir." Piers's comment allowed time for the squadron leader to light his cigarette and inhale deeply.

"I guess… The story as I understand is that they, the Iraqi, were not answering our telephone calls and we thought that was a bit rude. So we were going to bomb Habbaniyah runway and let it be known that next time it would be Baghdad High Street or something like that."

"So what was different about this year than last year?" Piers was persistent.

"Buried under the Cuba news, and all that fuss, there was an insignificant item which broadly amounts to Kuwait has promulgated its own constitution effectively confirming its independence from Britain and every other odd and sod. Chummy in Baghdad didn't like the idea so he rattled his sabre. For him there was the secondary advantage that he would be diverting attention from the fact that he is round the twist — without a paddle — to mix my metaphors. The Caliph is two cans short of a six pack, but no-one has got the gumption to shut him up."

"So it's all over bar the shouting?"

The squadron leader shook his head. "I'm afraid not. We've got a defence treaty with Kuwait and, if the Iraqi tanks roll, we're honour-bound to leap to their rescue. That means we stay on TYPHOON alert until we are sure our mates are safe"

The two men parted, Piers giving the customary salute.

Piers thought, 'I took a joke and joined. There's no going back now…'

*   *   *

Piers and Helen stayed at home, in their flat, for New Year. The dreadful weather discouraged them from venturing along to the Waddington Mess for the residual party and it would probably be a bit muted anyway because of the weather and the alert status. The local pub held no particular attraction for the young couple.

"I wonder what the New Year will mean for us?" Piers was holding his wife under a sprig of mistletoe. Helen's neck was craned back, just slightly but sufficiently, as her husband caressed her back. Their eyes were engaged in a lovers' mutual search.

"Do you think you will be a little less busy? Your hours are so long under those noisy things."

"Those noisy things are the queens of the sky. They don't come any better and our squadron is second to none when it comes to all the exercises. Why..."

"Shhh... Helen wants the undivided attention of her own Father Christmas."

"I think that Father Christmas is going to tell us that we're going to be posted next year. The word on the streets from the other ex-cadets is that we rarely do more than two years on our first tours. They want to cram as much experience into us as they can so that they..."

"I know an experience that you would like, my love."

"Come, Woman. With an offer like that I will leave Frosty the Snowman to shiver outside. I've got all the warmth those twinkle toes could..."

"Oh..."

Chapter 22
1963 ~ Ground Radio Servicing and Secure Communications

Not a lot happened in West Suffolk. Situated approximately equidistant from Bury St Edmunds and Thetford, which is across the border in Norfolk and 'don't you forget it!', nestles the remote Suffolk village of Honington. Nearby is the swath of RAF Honington. When Piers arrived in June 1963, RAF Honington was base to one Valiant (air-to-air refuelling tankers) and two Victor (bomber) squadrons each of eight aircraft. The Victors were nuclear weapon capable, had five man aircrews each and the overall force required 1000 technical tradesmen and another 1000 'cooks, clerks and bottle washers' to keep them at readiness and to look after the 200 officers.

The community within the station boundaries included 75 officers' and 220 other ranks' families in married quarters and up to 300 rented houses in the district for those who could not get quarters on the station or did not own their own house. There was single accommodation capacity for about 50 officers and 600 other ranks.

Piers was appointed to manage the maintenance of the station's air-to-ground radio and radar facilities associated with Air Traffic Control, the mobile radios used by station's emergency services and the RAF Police; he also managed the station's networks of 450 telephones and the station's telegraph communications centre. His responsibility was known as Ground Radio Servicing Flight; Piers was assisted by two specialist warrant officers, 40 technicians and 25 telephone/telegraphy operators. All the facilities, including four air-navigation radar aids, were expected to be fully functional 365 days of the year and were the subject of weekly, monthly and tri-monthly availability reports to Group and Command Headquarters. Periodic on-site inspections, some at no notice, were conducted by headquarters' staff specialists to ensure that no short cuts were being taken. Allied with Piers's main task, that of being officer commanding of the serving flight, was the operation of the station's cryptographic documents and V-bomber communications codes' distribution facility: this had its own auditing and reporting system demanding very high security with zero tolerance of error.

By any measure, Piers was busy. V-force readiness required daily practice of the aircrews, their aircraft and the plethora of support services throughout the station to provide the much vaunted 15 minute reaction capability to the supposed 'bolt from the blue' threat — the QRA philosophy he had contributed to at Waddington. It would not be until twenty years later that Piers became aware that the whole premise was founded on myth: the Warsaw Pact did not have the capability to launch a no notice pre-emptive strike without western intelligence being aware of their preparations in just the same way that they knew about our rehearsals. It was conceivable that there might have been nuclear deterrent accidents, and the Cuba missile crisis had shown how far the politicians were prepared to risk mutual destruction, but junior officers on V-bomber stations were not given the time to reflect on such issues. So, just in case, Piers and his flight had to keep their equipment and services on top line or risk being replaced by someone who could.

*   *   *

Piers's experience at Waddington had prepared him for the pressures of his new post. He talked with Helen about the negligible likelihood that they would get a married quarter on station, even when he had crossed the 25 years old eligibility threshold. Rented accommodation in a local town, known to the RAF as a hiring, was the most likely option of setting up home together. Buying a house was out of their financial league. Lacking for any form of assistance in finding somewhere to rent, Piers and Helen searched the villages close to Honington and found a Norfolk farming community called Methwold. This former WWII bomber airfield was now a sleepy farming community which enjoyed a farmers' market once per week, with the searching odour of cabbage, and a weekly bus service to somewhere that they didn't want to go. But there was a bungalow, it was furnished with the rudiments and was cheap while they looked for something better.

Methwold was twenty miles from Honington. Sometimes Piers drove the return journey twice a day because of duties on the station. There was also weekend and Wednesday sport, '…essential for leadership, old man — team spirit — keeps you fit, but don't get injured — good for morale…'. Such were the unpersuasive arguments when time at home should have had priority, but didn't. Nevertheless, Helen was supportive; she had a disused wartime airfield, Piers thought it echoed to the American B-17s long since gone, if she chose to walk and the weather was kind. The excitement of the weekly farmers' market provided fresh fare for the table — the cabbages were loathed, but the homemade sausages were a real treat. Since Piers needed the car to get to Honington, she resolved she would have her own transport as soon as they could afford it. 'And when the children come along, I'll need my own wheels then if I'm going to avoid being stuck out in the cabbage patches like here!'

When the opportunity to move into a hiring in Thetford, a sizable town just six miles from Honington arose, the couple were pleased to make the move.

*   *   *

"You wanted to see me, sir?" Piers saluted before he closed the door. He was looking for somewhere to sit.

"Err, yes… Ploughman." The salute was acknowledged by a cursory nod. "Don't bother to sit… this won't take a moment."

Piers waited while the papers on the crowded desk were shuffled. Out of the pile came a copy of a signal message. Piers did not make a practice of reading many of the messages that came into his communications centre. Some were formatted and were, to him, gobbledegook. Others were routine administration. Occasionally there was something interesting and then his communication warrant officer would encourage him to glance at it. Some were actually addressed for his personal attention, but the registries and distribution system guaranteed that a formal copy would get to his desk. After all, that was what he was paid to do, to ensure every signal reached its authorised addressed desk throughout the station. And, incidentally, to ensure that any originated anywhere on the station was duly processed and its text transmitted in a timely and accurate manner. This particular signal message, of the average daily throughput of 350 messages, had not been brought to his attention, yet.

"You've been selected to go on a course." Holding the familiar message paper in both hands, the squadron leader did not look up as he spoke.

"Oh… somewhere nice, I hope, sir?"

"Don't be flippant, lad." The interviewing squadron leader was four years older than Piers! Wearing a pilot's brevet, the squadron leader was on an experiential, administrative ground tour. He was still reading.

"I'm sorry, sir. A course you said?"

"Bomber Command Armament School — at RAF Wittering. Next Monday — for a week — five days. Reporting at 09:45 in the Officers' Mess and take it from there. Only working dress required. Any questions?"

"Mmm. Wittering, sir? BCAS? Has this course got a name? I mean... I don't have anything to do with aeroplanes — or bombs come to that."

"What's that got to do with anything, Ploughman? You junior officers are always whingeing about something. Err... it's called, err..." searching the message's text "...'Principles of Airborne Nuclear Weapons'. It sounds interesting."

"But, sir. I'm pretty busy. There's a Board of Enquiry about some lost Bomber Code, and I am captaining the Station Second XV on Wednesday..." The face now lifted from the signal message to look Piers straight in the eyes.

"No buts about it. The wing commander has said you're to go and your squadron leader has been informed. Monday, at Wittering. Now, get..." The speaking head was waving in the dismissal mode.

"Can I have a copy of the signal, for transport, etc." Piers was reaching.

"... out. You'll be getting your own copy through the mail. This one is for the file. Now... I'm busy. Buzz off... and close the door behind you. There's a hell of a draft..."

*   *   *

"You wanted to see me, sir?" Piers saluted the wing commander before he closed the door. He was looking for somewhere to sit. There was a chair positioned for him opposite the wing commander, across a clear desk.

"Yes, Piers. Piers Ploughman? Did your parents have a sense of humour? Umm? Sit..."

"I guess they did, sir. Ploughman is my family name..." Piers removed his headdress and sat. 'What now? That last remark was a bit unnecessary...'

"I got a signal to say you passed your BCAS course. So now you know what makes them go off and how we stop them falling off the Victors when we don't want them to, eh?"

169

"Those nukes are not very nice things to have about, sir. I mean, we wouldn't want the aircrew to go dropping them any old place would we, sir?"

"You're being flippant young man. There's no call for that at Honington. So, now you are qualified, it's up to you to check that the control electrics on the aircraft are working and that the release mechanism will fire when the aircraft captain wants it to."

"Yes, sir. But the training rigs at Wittering are not the same as the Victors'. They've only got superseded Valiant bombing kit and..."

Across a frown, "Are you complaining again, Ploughman? You've got a reputation..."

With a wagging of the head, "Oh no, sir! I was just pointing out that I am not familiar with the electrics on a Victor — nuclear weapon wise."

"Well, now you've done the course, you'd better get familiar with the electrics on a Victor — nuclear weapon wise. You've got the fleet of 16 Victors to certify as being ready, electrics wise, to deliver nuclear weapons... safely!"

"It would be helpful if a crew chief could talk me through the systems and show me where the boxes are."

Across a deeper frown indicating a degree of exasperation, "Use your initiative, Ploughman. It's what you're paid to do. And don't forget to sign the aircraft records that you've done the checks — better, raise aircraft job cards to be sure."

"Yes, sir. Thank you, sir, will that be all, sir?"

With the loss of the frown, there was an instantaneous change of subject, "Don't see much of you in the mess, Piers. Or Helen come to that. It's a good opportunity to meet the aircrews..."

"We live six miles off base, sir. I don't like to mix beer and driving, sir."

"You've got to get the balance right, Piers. You must remember there's more to being an officer than fixing aeroplanes, Piers. Wives have responsibilities too."

"Yes, sir. Thank you, sir, for the advice. Will that be all, sir?"

In response to the nod, Piers stood, replaced his hat, saluted and departed. He kept his thoughts to himself. There was no-one to share them with anyway. It was not the sort interview he shared with Helen. This wing commander was all aeroplanes' hardware and little else in the spread of technical specialisations in his wing — especially telecommunications. It was not the type of interview for which cadet training had equipped him. 'If they want wives to do things, whatever, they bloody well ought to train them. Not that most wives I know will take kindly to being told what to do! It's not the air force way...'

As he climbed into his car for the mile drive to his office, Piers thought, 'The bloke is a complete idiot. He hasn't got the vaguest idea of what I do, or the pressures I am under. Now he expects me to look after his sodding aeroplanes too. No, perhaps that's unfair. I couldn't do his job; he couldn't do mine. I'm just one of his team. But I'd much rather be left to get on with what I have to do and leave those nukes to someone else.'

Piers did not tell Helen about his interview, or about the remark about the mess. He did, however, exchange his views with the friendly armament officer in charge of storage and maintaining the nukes. Piers got the impression that he was left to his own devices — nuclear weapon wise — without too close oversight by the wing commander.

*   *   *

On the up-line to London Kings Cross platform, at Peterborough railway station, the resting bench seat provided uncomfortable, drafty seating for waiting passengers. Mrs Janice Harpur had arrived in plenty of time for the mid morning express to town. She was not intending to ride on that service when it stopped; she had other business on the platform. She would be crossing the line to take the next service to Oakham although she was in no hurry.

She removed a small package, wrapped in weatherproof oilskin, from her handbag and worked it between the iron frame and the bench seat. When she was satisfied that it was flush and therefore not observable to anyone who do not know it was there, she stood, walked to the passenger footbridge and settled to await her train. Within five minutes she was on her way.

Janice Harpur did not see the gentleman collect the package from the dead letter box and secret it into a deep pocket. She did not know its initial destination was a shop off Harley Street in London where the contents would be checked for legibility before being passed to the Russian embassy for transmission to Moscow.

171

The names of ten engineers, including two Royal Navy and eight Royal Air Force were on the Bomber Command Armament School completion register for the 'Principles of Airborne Nuclear Weapons' course. Appropriate annotations would be made on personal files maintained by the KGB First Chief Directorate (Foreign Operations). Olga Brovorno was retained for just this purpose and it was gratifying to see new entries now being made to files she had opened four years previously.

'Ah... there's a photograph of the Ploughman fellow. It's good to see his file fill...'

*   *   *

"You wanted to see me, sir?" Piers saluted before he closed the door. He was looking for somewhere to sit. This time the squadron leader had positioned a chair in front of the busy desk. A hand gestured towards it. A cigarette had just been extinguished in the ash tray on the desk.

"Err, yes... Ploughman. You'd better sit... this will take a moment."

Piers waited while the papers on the crowded desk were shuffled. Out came a green file, emblazoned 'Confidential' and a title bar he could not read upside down.

"You are court martial trained, I suppose? Henlow and all that?"

"Since you are asking, sir, not really. I've have a couple..."

"Yes, yes, I know. It's on your record. 'Officer Under Instruction' counts, you know. That's why the wing commander is content to let you do it."

"...of periods under tuition, sir. Once at Henlow, but we didn't understand then what was going on. The instructors had obviously not been to a real court martial. Then, while I was at Innsworth, there were a couple of WRAFs charged for lesbian activities in the..."

"Good, so you know all about it. Well, Senior Aircraftman Goodman has selected you to be his defending officer."

"I don't know any airman called Goodman, sir."

"That's good then. You'll be unbiased." The squadron leader seemed to be deliberately keeping his focus on the papers in the file. "He'll get a fair trial before he gets hung out to dry. All you've got to do is read the Manual of Air Force Law and Queen's Regulations and then be his defending officer. Prepare a short plea of mitigation — good parents, volunteer airman, good at soccer, kind to animals — to read to the court.

172

Piece of cake, really. The guys in Personnel Services Flight will give you a copy of his file and the police reports. They'll give you all the advice you need short of actual help. Goodman is in the Guardroom awaiting your pleasure and the trial is set for next Thursday week. That gives you ten days. You can delegate your other duties until it's done. Any questions?"

"Why me, sir?"

"Goodman picked you. That's all I know. Pretty straight forward. I'll see you in the mess when it's all over. Now... I'm busy. Buzz off... and close the door behind you."

"I know, sir, there's a hell of a draft."

*　　　*　　　*

"How did it go, Darling? Mother rang, she's coming for lunch on Sunday." Helen was clutching a drying towel from the kitchen.

"OK, I suppose. I persuaded him to plead guilty and then I put in a plea of mitigation. On Sunday? I thought we might..."

"What's mitigation? Apparently her cat's got piles and Mum's upset so she says she needs some comforting chat."

"Goodman had been adrift for four months and got picked up by the military police — that's Royal Military Police, as in army — when the stupid ass walked into Colchester Barracks. So he loses four months pay and whatever the court gave him... Why can't she go to her sister's?"

"So what did you do to mitigate him? She got toothache and Mum doesn't like talking about dentists."

"I told them that his Mum's gone into a nursing home and his Dad's run off with the neighbour's daughter and his brother has just been put away for a two year stretch for arson and their mobile home was stolen from the park at Mablethorpe. That tale of woe had them reaching for their hankies. Then, I said, poor chided Goodman had a nervous twitch everytime he had to fill a Victor bomber with fuel when it had got a special weapon on it on account of his uncle having been under a ten thousand pounder when it dropped off a Halifax he was servicing. The senior officer of the court, they call him Chairman, had been appointed by Training Command and didn't know one end of a nuke from the other. So I could see I..."

"Do you know one end of a nuke from the other? Aren't you clever, husband mine?"

"Yes, not really. One end is pointed and sharp. The other is sort off… err… messy and not sharp. Are we going to eat in or go to pub? I like their scampi and chips in a basket. Your mum could eat chicken…"

"Mother doesn't like all that cigarette smoking in the pub. I thought I'd cook a stew and a lemon meringue pie. That's your favourite. Here, what are you doing?"

"You're my favourite pie and I want to taste you all over." The obstructing dish cloth was being expertly removed.

"Just because you did a Perry Mason bit…"

"Who told you?" Piers's hands were now holding her shoulders in a 'come closer' hold.

"Who told me what?"

"About my nickname. All the guys on the squadron are calling me Perry Mason, because I did the lawyer bit and got Goodman slung out — dismissed the service with disgrace — rather than having to do time. They were betting he'd get 12 months."

"You are a clever flight lieutenant and I love you… ooh… very much… especially when you nibble the pie… ooh… just there."

*   *   *

Piers was in the Air traffic Control Tower when the Bomber Command 'QRA Alert' at RAF Honington was triggered. There had been some tedious fault with one of the radio channels and Piers had been in to check the fault had been repaired. It was another one of those evenings when Helen was left alone at home. By way of relaxation, he was discussing how strange it was that everyone seemed to remember where they had been when the news broke that President J F Kennedy had been shot. For Piers, he had been in the ATC Tower at RAF Honington on 22 November 1963, when the news came through. He remembered saying to one of the ATC controllers, 'I hope to hell that they have got the hot line working between Washington and Moscow. Everyone is going to blame Nikita Khrushchev, but he wouldn't have been so stupid. Anyway, Bomber Command hasn't called us up to alert, yet, so perhaps they know something!'

It was a quiet autumnal evening at RAF Honington when the station klaxon sounded. In itself, this was an unusual occurrence; testing was usually at the same time, 10:00, every Tuesday when all the other alarms were tested. It also gave station personnel experience of each of the five optional sounds over the klaxon and what they were intended to mean. This time, in 1964, the Ballistic Missile Early Warning System radar at RAF Fylingdales had detected a 'threat' on its radar. An actual alert involving armed V-bombers was quite an event. RAF Honington, and seven other stations similarly, maintained two Victors armed on Quick Reaction Alert. Although practised virtually every day, the aircrew expected this to be just another exercise.

But on this occasion, at 20:30, the Tannoy announced, "Operation EDOM — readiness 05." The two crews had to proceed to cockpit readiness, ready to be airborne before the 'bolt-from-the-blue' nuclear attack arrived. They were connected to the Bomber Controller at Headquarters Strike Command by landline; the next command would relay directly into their headsets in the cockpits.

A few minutes later the Tannoy announced, "Operation EDOM — readiness 02" which meant start engines and taxi to the runway takeoff threshold. Inside the closed cockpits, the crews were breaking their sealed orders and preparing to takeoff for nuclear war. Only once previously had the QRA armed aircraft taxied for this exercise; recovering the weapon systems to its 15 minutes readiness status had proved to be difficult process — safety wise.

Not Exercise EDOM, this time; the man had said quite clearly, 'OPERATION EDOM'. The aircraft taxied to the end of the runway and waited. Their takeoff instruction would come via a coded radio message. No-one flew over England with a loaded, cocked, ready to drop, nuke!

They were held for 15 minutes before being relaxed to their normal 15 minutes readiness. The aircrew had to taxi their aircraft back to their hardstandings away from the runway, check the safety of their weapon and custody of the codes and orders before returning to their accommodation in the Officers' Mess. This was the only occasion that Piers saw aircrew on alert consume alcohol as the anxiety receded.

All the issued codes had to be replaced since the unsealed edition was deemed to be comprised – security wise.

It would be some hours later that the word was passed around that the BWEWS Radar at RAF Fylingdales, Yorkshire had not been programmed with the position of the Moon! The radar sensors had interpreted the radar response as a Soviet ballistic missile launch and issued automatic alarms to all military deterrent headquarters around the globe.

Piers decided that he did not need to worry Helen about this latest cock-up. Nevertheless, she sensed his tension and guessed he would tell her all about it when the time was right. Being the wife of someone who could not bring home his work — even the nature of his work — was a cross she had to carry. What was it he used to say, 'if you can't take a joke, you shouldn't have joined'?

Chapter 23
1965 ~ 'Go East, Young Man'

The last meaningful career interview of 1964 was typically one-sided with Piers in receive-only mode.

"Flight Lieutenant Ploughman. It seems that you and the cold of East Anglia are not a sensible mix. Their Airships in London, in their career planning wisdom, have decided to put you where you can do least harm. You are hearby warned that you are on the list for posting overseas. Sign here — they call it the Personnel Occurrence Report and you sign it to show you've been told. It seems they have a need for electrical technical officers at Changi, Singapore. You'll be going in May so you've got plenty of time to get your khaki and jabs… and have your teeth pulled, so you've enough time to pack your deep-sea boxes. You'll be taking Helen, of course. There's an envelope on the adjutant's desk telling you what's what — allowances, quarters, anti-malaria, snakes and the like. You're supposed to look happy at the news!"

"I don't know about that. Aren't they having a war with Indonesia or someone?"

"Confrontation, old lad, not war! It says here you've got to re-qualify on your personal weapon, so that's re-assuring."

"Thank you, sir."

"Someone is sure to know the answers to all your questions. Never been there myself. Too bleeding hot for me! Congratulations. Close the door on your way out…"

As Piers looked across the grass airfield that had been 'home' for twenty months, the only thought which came to mind was out of the mire into the tropical cooking wok. 'Make the best of your last cold winter, Piers. I don't know if I'm happy or upset — *saying goodbye is such sweet sorrow* as the bard might have said. This time next year you'll be dreaming of shivering and putting on a sweater. There's good news too; no more cold feet for three years. I remember it well. Changi again, it's the air force way! I wonder what Helen will think of moving again?'

Helen kept her reaction to herself. She had already consulted the family doctor about the lack of pregnancy and would talk with him about it when the time was right. She hoped that this new situation would not interfere with their plans to extend the family. 'I wonder what it would be like carrying a junior in the tropics… pretty awful I guess? It's not the sort of thing I want to talk with Piers's Mum about…'

*   *   *

"So you're off to the Far East, Piers?" The squadron leader was a pleasant boss and a stabilising influence in the madness of everyday V-bomber life. "How are you doing with your check-ups… or is it checks-up? I never can remember."

Piers had not been referred to a hospital again until early 1965, when Helen and he were becoming concerned that they were not producing children. Fertility tests were required and several trips to the RAF Hospital at Ely were made. On one occasion, he was required to provide a specimen; at the appointed hour he arrived at the clinic expecting a long wait. After all, such hospital waiting is par for the course. Accordingly, he had his current book — Field Marshal Montgomery's autobiography — with him. But he was not required to loiter and the receptionist could not avoid a questioning glance at the volume under his arm.

"Do you know what to do?" she questioned as she waved her latest clinic client into the men's toilets with one hand and offering a sample bottle with the other. Piers assured her that he did and thence performed as required. He often wondered if she searched Monty's book looking for voyeuristic prose!

The final fertility check involved an inspection as quickly as possible after Piers and Helen and had made love. Naturally, Piers had to clear his absence from work with his squadron leader whose wife happened to be a family counsellor. He burst out laughing at the explanation, remarking that he could imagine, "…your little white bum going up and down in your new sports car in a layby *en-route* to Ely hospital".

After a short, one sided, debate with Helen, Piers was pleased to be able to record in his diary that they had found a more appropriate location for their passion.

*   *   *

Every Tuesday afternoon, the internal mail would bring into Clothing Stores the weekly editions of Station Routine Orders and Personnel Occurrence Reports. Every Tuesday, a clerk would clip the routine orders and the personnel notices on a notice board, in front of the previous edition, so that everyone in the section could see what was going on and who was on the move — both onto and away from RAF

Honington. Every Wednesday morning, Albert Brewster would remove the Personnel Occurrence Reports from their wall clip and take the Roneo[tm] duplicated copies to his desk to update his records. He only ever replaced the current personnel sheets to the notice board; the superseded record went into the bag he used to convey his packed lunch.

The Personnel Occurrence Reports were unclassified and routinely would have been put into the waste by the 45 copy recipients of the routine notice around the RAF station. Albert Brewster's clothing records were well maintained and there were few observations during annual formal accounting audits. But Albert Brewster had a wish to do his small deed for the cause; if someone was prepared to pay him to save this material from the rubbish pit then so be it. He wasn't spying, no-one could accuse him of that. It was unclassified, notice board, stuff. They might have thought differently if they had known the use the material would be put to by its ultimate user.

Once a month a buff envelope was mailed to an address in Hampstead, North London. Within days, the material was on a desk in The First Chief Directorate (Foreign Operations) of the KGB. Olga Brovorno and her colleagues liked handling this material; it was typed, accurate and reliable. Useful correlation with service identification numbers avoided errors. No-one stationed at RAF Honington, from the station commanding group captain to the lowliest airman or airwoman, escaped mention of any significant training, course, attachment or promotion event which might affect his or her conditions of service or pay.

Olga's files absorbed the gratuitous information. Sooner or later someone from the corridors upstairs would ask for one or more of these files that she and her team maintained and Olga would know that she had helped the system even if she was not privileged to know what for.

Chapter 24
1965 ~ Married/Accompanied in Singapore and Commercial Broadcasting

The chartered British Eagle[tm] Airways transport Britannia aircraft landed at Paya Lebar airport, Singapore at 02:25 on Sunday 6th June 1965, having flown a 29 hours flight from Luton Airport, England via Ankara and Bombay. Piers was appointed to a station engineering post at RAF Changi. As they landed, it was obvious through the aircraft portholes that the city was still awake. When the aircraft doors were opened, there was an overwhelming combination of stench and moist heat. The airport building offered little protection and even at this hour was a heaving mass of humanity. The British Army's conducted arrival formalities took two hours for the 119 passengers and the sky was just beginning to grey as the coach dropped the exhausted Piers and Helen at The Grand Hotel[tm], Katong, which was their planned transit accommodation while permanent quarters were sorted out. It appeared unaltered, or decorated, since Piers was last there ten years previously.

'Fortunately,' thought Helen, 'there are no children having to endure this. What is that smell?'

"What is that smell?" asked Piers guessing his wife's concern.

"Ah, Massah, you no likee our durian... very good fruit, our durian. Very good for missy. Lots of street stalls selling durian. Very fresh. I get some for your room?"

"No thank you," replied Piers. "Mrs Ploughman and I just want to shower and go to bed. Can someone help with our luggage?"

"Ah, Massah, you want to go to your room now. We serving breakfast in 25 minutes... lots of fresh durian if you wantee..."

"Just our room please. We'll let you know about lunch. I expect we shall want dinner tonight." Piers was signing the hotel register while Helen was flopped onto a rattan chair. The air was being circulated by a slowly rotating ceiling fan making a warrah-warrah-warrah noise as the slow moving blades passed overhead.

"Ah so, Massah, you go to your room now and have a rest. England is long way away, yes?"

"Our room, please. Mrs Ploughman needs our room. Now."

"Our lunch is a buffet table with curries and sambals. Is Sunday, veree popular with our guests, Massah."

"Our room… now!" Piers's insistence had a touch of anger now.

"Ah so, Massah, yes, Massah… you follow the boy, Massah… he'll carry your luggage. Missee walk with you, please…"

The 'boy' turned out to be a 60 years old, probable Indian judging by his turban. His loins were girded in a folded cloth resembling an oversize nappy and his feet were protected by well used flipflops. He did not speak as he led the way across a 50 metres square walled garden to one of four two storey terraced blocks overlooking a central fountain. The 'boy' was carrying four suitcases possibly weighting 110 pounds total — more than his body weight. He opened the unlocked door and switched on the ceiling fan. He showed Piers where the door key had been placed and left without a word.

Helen collapsed onto the double bed and burst into tears. "I want to go home. This place stinks and it's unbearably hot. I'm tired and I want you to organise me on the first available seat out of here. It's awful."

"Have a shower and try and get a little rest. You feel better when we've had something to eat."

"I don't want to feel better." Her crying had made her tired eyes more sore.

Piers was adjusting the window shutters for maximum shade and maximum breeze.

Helen screamed. "What's that… that thing up there… on the ceiling. It's moving…"

"Oh he's friendly. He's a lizard… a chitchat. He's only three inches long, for heavens sake. He eats mosquitoes and flies. He's no trouble. Slip your things off, have a shower while I sort out the mosquito net and we'll have a couple of hours shuteye. There're fresh towels in the bathroom."

"Oh my God. It moved…"

It took a little while for the couple to settle. They did not bother to unpack although they did open their cases for the immediate essentials. It was too hot even to cuddle. While they were asleep, a Chinese maid — an amah — having kicked off her shoes in the corridor silently entered their room, placed a jug of iced water on the sideboard next to two

181

upturned glasses, removed the clothes they had dropped on the floor and took them away to be laundered.

Piers was woken by a distraught Helen. "We've been robbed. You didn't lock the door. All my clothes are gone, my underwear, everything. Someone has broken into our room and…"

"Have a drink of water, out of the bottle not the jug, just in case, and get dressed. Then we'll go and sort it out. I think I'll have another shower." The cold tap water was warm and there was no hot water. Piers's shave was not comfortable.

They had just made themselves decent when there was a knock on the door. The officer whose post Piers was to fill had appeared. They had never previously met although it transpired that he was an ex-cadet four years ahead of Piers. He had a bag of goodies: sliced pineapple, two oranges, a bottle of water, a bottle of cordial, an aerosol flyspray with a box of mosquito repellent coils and bite cream, some English biscuits and four cans of Tiger^{tm} beer.

"Come on," he bade them. "Grab your swimming cosies, and I'll run you up to the Changi Officers' Club were you can get in the water. The worst of the day's heat is over. It hasn't rained today so it's a bit sweltering. Never mind. Bring a couple of hotel towels. We can get a snack up there, round the pool. Dead cheap. You've missed today's hotel food anyway, it's Sunday. You can leave the room to the amah."

'Is he ever going to stop talking,' thought Helen. 'He's very much older than Piers.'

"You can meet my little woman and lots of others. You might even get invited to a party, but I don't advise it on your first night. You'll want to sleep. I expect. You can easily get a taxi from the club back to the hotel. Sher Kahn has a good line in Mercedes^{tm} and they're quite safe so long as it doesn't rain."

While they were away from their room, the still unseen amah had remade the bed through the locked door, tidied the mosquito net into its functional position tucked under the mattress edges and laid the washed, pressed and folded clothes on top of a chest of drawers. The window shutters had been opened for ventilation and the roof fan turned off. The box of mosquito coils had been opened, one mounted on its burning frame and placed in a saucer. A box of matches had been placed nearby.

Piers said to Helen as they tried to manage the mosquito net for the double bed, "Welcome to Singapore. Perhaps it's not going to be so bad after all." But the three second, goodnight cuddle suggested there was a lot of settling in to do.

*   *   *

Before the end of their first week, a ground floor flat with an air-conditioned bedroom had become available in the hotel grounds. After another month, Helen was much more comfortable with the environment; the durian season had passed and the replacement succulent, brightly-coloured rambutan fruit on the road stalls had no odour. It was also delicious, and when peeled, safe to eat. Piers had bought a car, so a rented flat seemed to make good sense while they waited for a house nearer the airfield. The nine miles commute from Katong to Changi was welcome to Piers; it gave a degree of separation from the RAF community and allowed them to get to know the Lion City much better, especially the air-conditioned cinemas where it was luxurious to put on a sweater to sit in the cool.

Helen found a pamphlet describing the history of The Grand Hotel. It seemed that the original buildings had been erected in the 1820s or '30s by an East India Company trader named Benjamin Ploughman — what a strange coincidence — who had retired to the site with his daughter. The construction had been so sound that the original structures were still standing and the carvings on the fountain were originals from that date. The daughter had returned home, to England, on her parents' deaths having sold the building to a local merchant. It had become a colonial hotel before the Japanese occupation. Between 1943 and '45, the Japs used it as a brothel before it reverted to its owner and was restored as a hotel. The majority of users were the British military in transit although there were a couple of wealthy oriental couples occupying flats but keeping themselves unto themselves.

Piers and Helen had six happy months in their flat. They employed their own amah who relished the name 'Ah-Lois' although it was unlikely that was her true name. The rooms were big enough to entertain large parties of engineering officers from the station. The advantage of being so close to the hotel within its walled garden, apart from the feeling of protection the ten foot high walls gave, was the option of an excellent

Sunday buffet and any other meal they desired including the occasional full English breakfast.

'Ah-Lois' kept the cockroaches out of kitchen and the empty beer cans which attracted them in a distant rubbish bin. Piers did not discourage the hotel cat since it kept the rats and snakes away. 'Boy' swept the monsoon drains which kept the bugs down and allowed the tropical rain to run off into the sea. It was an idyllic lifestyle until one day, about six months into the thirty month tour, Piers was summoned to his wing commander's office. The interview was one-sided.

"You've got to earn your keep round here. You need a secondary duty. Find one or I'll find one for you."

*   *   *

Life at Changi for a junior non-flying officer was not all work, or secondary duties. Among the attractions there was Malaya and holidaying up country. Piers knew of the causeway linking the island of Singapore and the peninsular of Malaya. They were a single country until Singapore unilaterally declared independence ('Merdeka' or freedom) in 1966. Lee Kwan Yu, the Prime Minister of Singapore, led a harsh regime to clean the Singapore tongs out of society with his brand of socialism. An interesting experience was that the banks, quite unprompted, declared the previous currency invalid for a day and then charged for handling old money while everyone was waiting for the new currency to circulate. This caused an effective devaluation of the straits dollar in the bank by 8% which it never recovered. The exchange rate at that time was £1=S$11.00.

There were negligible border formalities for the British to move across The Causeway northwards through Johore Bahru. One very pleasant trip was when Helen and Piers, accompanied by an ex-cadet from 1957 Entry and his new wife, in their two seat Triumph^{tm} TR2, drove 60 miles up the east coast to a lonely beach called Kampong Tuanseh. With the two ladies sitting across the rumble back seats, they all got heavily sun burnt and not a little bruised in a car not designed for 4 adults.

Routinely, Helen and Piers found it normally too hot to travel on the long Malaysian roads in their sports tourer with its roof off, along black ribbons of tarmac edged in loose sand, through the set-back unshading rubber plantations and rice paddies. They covered up well with solar protection which was a wise precaution as they climbed the central mountains, north of Kuala Lumpur, towards the holiday resort of Frazer's Hill at altitude 5000 feet. Certainly it was cooler as an escape from the heat and humidity at near sea-level, but the chance of sunburn was greater.

The attraction of Frazer's Hill was golf, bungalow lodges with corner baths and log fires away from the bustle and hurry of Singapore. Its clientele were overwhelmingly European. Some people walked the jungle paths, but that did not appeal to the Ploughmans. Piers learned to play golf and would, under pressure, in later years admit to enjoying it. He even completed 5 rounds of the 9 holes course in a day. The bungalows were comfortable and more akin to hotels. But most exciting was the single track access road open each way for only 15 minutes in each hour. With precipitous fall on one side and rock face on the other, the drive in or out was an experience. The childless Ploughmans experienced three holidays at Frazer's Hill and promised themselves to return there some day.

Another three day excursion up the Malaya west coast, through Ipoh, would also register in their memories. They stayed overnight, ordering a steak for dinner at their 3-star hotel. The sun had tanned their faces and bleached Helen's hair. She looked radiant in her man's eyes.

"There aren't many others staying here, despite proximity to the sea." Helen was being observant as usual. When the meal was served to their table on the patio overlooking the straits' water, the couple could not decide from what animal the steak came, or indeed if it was dead when delivered, but it was the coarsest and strongest flavour piece of meat they ever wished to encounter. Fortunately, there was a copious supply of Tiger[tm] Beer with which he could wash it down and sufficient tea for Helen even though it was served with tinned evaporated milk.

Their evening stroll along the promenade, with its palm trees adorned in electric fairy-lights, was but foreplay to a tropical night of enduring and romantic love, serenaded by a choir of crickets and bull frogs.

*   *   *

Piers was impressed by the Malaysian jungle although he firmly resisted any attempt to do the 'One Week Officer Familiarisation Course' at the RAF Jungle Survival School at Changi. He was first excited by the jungle during his first trip, to the Far East, from the safety of a seat in an RAF air transport Hastings for the Xmas 1955 holiday. The aircraft's long descent into Singapore seemed to start 200 miles north at Kuala Lumpur with an almost straight flight south towards Changi. The green undulating jungle seemed impenetrable from altitude, even then still harbouring anti-communist fighting, with very few clearings, rivers or roads.

A few months later and Piers was taking a much closer interest in jungle treetops, this time from the ejection seat of an RAF Vampire jet trainer flying at 300 mph.

Eleven years would pass before Piers was able to trundle at 140 mph over the jungle in an RNZAF Bristol Freighter of 41(NZ) Squadron from Changi to Butterworth opposite Penang Island. This time, he could lie on the glass windowed freight doors at the front of the aircraft and watch the jungle pass by at a few hundred feet vertical clearance. At Butterworth, which was now a Royal Australian Air Force fighter base used by the RAF V-force during the 'Confrontation' with Indonesia, he met an ex-cadet of 1954 Entry who was the resident RAF liaison officer at the base. These Henlow cadets certainly got about! He took Piers to Penang island, to his married quarter, for a farewell party to someone Piers had never met. 'It was the air force way', Piers thought. He loaned Piers a pair of dark trousers and a white shirt (the 'Planters Rig') for the event. Piers finished the evening by jumping off the high board into a swimming pool in the borrowed clothes. After a pleasant meal, it was into uniform for the ferry to the mainland and a rapid taxi trip to catch the return flight to Changi departing at 23.30. On the same flight was a squadron leader, then stationed at Tengah in Singapore, who was to become Piers's boss and neighbour four years later at High Wycombe.

Again Piers perched on the freight doors and watched the coastal lights and the utter darkness of the jungle pass under the aircraft until the glare of Singapore came into view. Once again, the first impression of Singapore, even at 01:30, was of a town that did not know how to go to sleep; the traffic appeared as dense at that hour as at any time during daylight.

*   *   *

"I see you have chosen to look after the Changi Broadcasting System as your secondary duty. Well, I suppose that it as good a secondary duty as some. A sport would have been better. I'll be watching how you get on."

186

The wing commander's confidence in Piers's choice did little to enthuse his young officer. He had to reply.

"Yes, sir. Well, I do run the Small Bore Rifle Club and Helen is the Far East Marksman Champion against all comers including locals and some competitors from up country. Shooting is an Olympic sport, sir. And Helen has been in three amateur dramatic productions; she was one of the leads in *Oliver*... and in a pantomime; I got roped in for the stage electrics..."

"OK. I get the picture. You are involved in station activities."

"Well, yes sir. CBS, as we call Changi Broadcasting, operates from studios in the camp. We use wire-relay broadcasting throughout the station because HQFEAF could not negotiate a VHF/FM radio broadcasting licence with the local government. It seems that Singapore Radio and British Forces Broadcasting Service (Far East), were both worried that we would steal their audience. Our system has 200 outlets, switchable between A or B channel, loudspeakers in all the messes, barrack blocks, the hospital wards, the air transit lounge, all the clubs and to a selection of married quarters. CBS is manned by volunteers drawn from all walks of life on the station, sir, who themselves compile and produce the bulk of the programmes which are broadcast. We cater for a broad interest by relaying selected programmes from the BBC World Service, the BFBS(FE), Singapore Radio and Singapore Rediffusion."

The wing commander was content, for the moment, for the young officer to continue with his animated description.

"You seem to be quite enthusiastic about this CBS thing, young man. You are not going to let it get in the way of preparing for the new transport aircraft coming through Changi?"

"Oh yes, sir, I mean no sir. The aircraft stuff will be OK, sir. CBS is operated by wives on Monday to Friday mornings, a sort of two hour's *Woman's Hour* but in the evenings, seven nights a week, the full team of volunteers, on a rota basis, combine to operate the station, five hours every night including Sundays. My own record request programme goes out at 23:00 every Sunday. We've about 60 producers and presenters; there's no problem compiling a schedule; we have a monthly CBS Magazine just like the *Radio Times*[tm] at home, but smaller you understand. I have a copy in my briefcase, sir."

Piers began to reach for his copy, but a wave of the head by his senior failed to stop him until he recognised his senior's unspoken instruction.

"A special team scripts a daily news broadcast based on a direct teleprinter feed from the Reuters[tm] office in Singapore who gear their feed to us for our 22:00 transmission. We beat the BBC with the news about the Aberfan disaster by a whole hour. You recall, sir, when 144 people, 116 of them children, were killed when a tip of coal waste slid onto the village of Aberfan in South Wales. Our newsreader that night was one of the wives; I was the editor. That was a tough call, sir."

"You are competing with the BBC?" The wing commander thought young Piers was over egging it. "You do understand that the VC-10 is quite a complex machine, electronically. The American Hercules will bring its own problems, too."

The ☰
CHANGI BROADCASTING SERVICE . . .

AUGUST
SEPTEMBER
OCTOBER
1967

MAGAZINE
AND PROGRAMME

VOICE OF THE COMMONWEALTH FORCES FROM CHANGI

CBS Magazine October 1967
The lion of Lion City

Piers did not want to be diverted. "Yes, sir, and our audience figures suggest we are getting a bigger slice of the pie." But it did make sense to concede ground to his wing commander.

"There are some good tradesmen coming in for the new aircraft, sir, with a good mix across the ranks and trades. And, to allow for postings home, *et cetera*, I need a steady stream of helpers for CBS too. I think we're bigger than any other RAF station network. We are fully independent of station funds being wholly dependent on advertising to pay for permanent staff, equipment and maintenance. We make a net profit of about S$1000 per month after all costs. I have no problem recruiting announcers, engineers, controllers, librarians or production assistants. Why don't you come along and see for yourself, sir, any evening after 7 pm? If I'm not there, the Duty Programme Supervisor or Duty Announcer will be only too pleased to show you around."

"Perhaps, I should, Piers, perhaps I should." Then he reverted to his primary concern, "And don't forget, Piers, we are also introducing the Belfast aircraft to our long haul fleet."

*   *   *

"Right, young Piers Ploughman. Did your parents have a sense of humour with a name like that? Your posting means a final confidential report." The wing commander was sitting at a desk, not cleared for the purpose. This failure to set the stage in the traditional way, Piers interpreted, was a good sign implying that the interviewer did not expect his interviewee to pick up something and throw it.

"Yes, sir." After all, the report on posting was the only reason he was there.

"Well, you have done alright. Your squadron leader writes you up well, your assessment numbers are good and you are leaving here with a 'Special Recommendation' for promotion. Well done, Piers, a good report and thoroughly merited. I am particularly pleased with the way you and Helen have joined in the social life of the station."

"Thank you, sir." Was he going to say anything about being up to the mark for the new VC-10s, the Belfasts, the Hercules, the updated Shackeltons, the new VIP-role Andovers, the new kit in the hospital? 'It was what I was put out here to do and I reckon I did alright,' Piers judged.

"Even this Changi Broadcasting thing seems to have been acceptable. The Station Commander remarked to me that he was satisfied both with your performance as officer in charge and the financial contribution it has made to the non-public funds for the airmen. A good all round report, well done."

"Thank you, sir." What else could he say? He'd earned it.

"Now, about your future postings preference. I think you are right for intelligence duties. What do you know about them?"

"Nothing, sir." Now this was unexpected.

"Always a good start, being honest, young man. I did a tour in intelligence, in the Ministry of Defence. Very interesting, it was. I didn't know anything about what was required when I went to… oh, I can't tell you where, either; it was in London. I can't tell you about what I did or I'd have to shoot you." Was he being serious?

"What do you suggest I do, sir? I'd be very grateful for your advice."

189

'Does he know I'm bullshitting. I want to stay near aeroplanes. It's what I joined up for. It's what my cadetship was all about. I don't want to drive some mahogany desk in London, shooting the breeze with civilian spooks. James Bond is strictly for the birds...'

"Fill in the box on your confidential report, the *Future Postings* box, with 'Intelligence duties' and where it says *Location* fill in 'As required'. It's good to see you accept advice, Piers. I'll recommend you as suitable after your Cranwell course and you'll have a good time being very interested."

"Can I tell Helen?" At this moment she was in the married quarter, packing deep sea transport boxes with their linen and china.

"Better not to, you don't want to give her false ideas; it might take some time to come through. Good luck on your course; they say it's snowing at home... maybe even a White Chistmas. Think of us around the swimming pool while you're listening to the Queen."

Chapter 25
1968 ~ 'This Length of String Represents Twelve Airmen'

Piers had to depart not later than 09:45 to be sure to arrive before the training machine's time of 14:00 prompt. Ashton Morley, he knew it well, was 147 miles north of Kingston with only 60 miles of motorway to help, snow covered motorway at that. A contact telephone number and a cursory kiss was all the farewell there was time for. 'Royal Air Force sodding Ashton Morley, who would believe it? Returning there after the unpleasantness of terminating flying training!' To cap it all, he had arrived too late for lunch.

'Junior Command and Staff School; it's Xmas and it's humbug!' Actually, it was after the New Year, but that was an insignificant detail in his general mood.

The weather depressed Piers. The place depressed Piers. The course curriculum depressed Piers. The endless repetition of RAF forms depressed him. The 45 other student RAF officers, with two foreign visitors and two Princess Mary's Royal Air Force Nursing Service (affectionately dubbed PMRAFNS pronounced 'parafins') were also depressed and it took a generous amount of alcohol in the well-stocked mess bar for the course to shake off the blues. One by one, each student trooped to the telephone kiosk to call a loved one and reassure that all was well. The RAF training machine melancholy had struck in the Shropshire January gloom.

Naturally, Piers remembered the RAF Flying Training School at RAF Aston Rowant when he was flying in 1960. That flying school had been relocated during the summer of 1961 and had become a helicopter training establishment. Now, on return to UK from Singapore in time for Xmas, in January 1968, he was to be attached to Aston Rowant. During the festive season, Piers looked for and found a Sunbeam^{tm} Alpine. Helen's and his enjoyment of two-seater motoring had not yet been satisfied. The car became theirs just before the New Year and on 5th January 1968, in the snow especially memorable after 2½ years in the tropics, Piers followed the familiar route up the M1 and A5 to the station last seen some 6½ years before.

Helen was to embark on her own adventure. A married quarter at RAF Cranwell beckoned. She had to go there and make it home for the planned next seven months before they were posted somewhere, somewhere as yet unknown, else.

Piers first impression was that nothing had changed until he drove into the Aston Rowant Officers' Mess car park to see a notice that 'All cars are parked on Ministry of Defence property at the Owner's Risk.' Apparently, at another station while he was abroad, a careless pilot had parked his aircraft in the Officers' Mess car park in slots which were already occupied. Since the helicopter was manoeuvring vertically at the time there was not much left of either aeroplane or motor car(s). But now the Aston Rowant mess was recovering from the Xmas festivities enjoyed by few instructional staff and zero students which had reputedly been launched by some enthusiastic Royal Navy student officers who had sought to manoeuvre a 40 foot long telegraph pole through a closed plate glass door. Once again, this being a training station, he was told that his Junior Command Staff School mess accommodation was to be outside the brick structure which was reserved for instructors and station staff. Piers was directed to the same secco hut from which he had departed many years ago. To cap it all, he was allocated the same bedroom. But at least the heating pipes worked.

On his first evening, Piers found the BBC-TV room which was equipped with the new colour television set; when he walked in it was showing the George Mitchell production titled '*The Black & White Ministrel Show*'. Piers could not avoid remarking that this was the first time anyone had seen black and white in colour. A few days later, on that same TV screen, Piers watched the Secretary of State for Defence Dennis Healey announce the government's policy to withdraw from east of Suez. This made him particularly sad because of the happy memories of Changi and the Far East.

Since they had just been repatriated from Singapore, Piers was eligible and had applied for an Officers' Married Quarter for the duration of his forthcoming 20 week course at Cranwell beginning in March. The allocation made provision for the prior eight weeks, ie January and February, to be quartered at Cranwell while Piers was detached to Aston Rowant. The plan was for Helen to travel from Surrey to Cranwell by train and Piers would drive across country on the first Wednesday afternoon of the Aston Rowant course to 'March In' to a detached house in the bleak, wintry Lincolnshire countryside. Piers would take the car back to Aston Rowant leaving Helen to cope until the weekend. Snow or not, she would survive; there was a NAAFI grocery store somewhere on the camp.

At least, that was the plan soon to be discarded by deep accumulation of snow in the Midlands preventing Piers's cross country journey.

Nevertheless, between Aston Rowant and Cranwell, Piers would commute across country (with the car every week bar one) each weekend for the remainder of the Aston Rowant course. He found a colleague who was going part of the way to share the cost.

Eight weeks of Junior Command and Staff School training involved the student in practical and theoretical schooling in the basics of military leadership, management, discipline and drill. For those students with station experience at junior officer, non-flying, level such training was a relearning of principles long forgotten under hard experience. These 'experienced' student officers knew more about how to motivate their subordinates and to achieve results than did their instructors. Piers found the concepts, or the examples chosen, to be unrealistic and mind-numbingly boring. So called 'homework' provided an excuse to delay excursion to the mess bar. Inevitably, 48 athletically fit officers would congregate to the benefit of bar profits and a steady deterioration of their health.

For ex-cadet Piers, the most memorable events of the eight weeks had little to do with managing a fighting air force. Years later, he would recount how the Station Commanding group captain came into the bar the night a gaming machine was installed; he inserted a sixpenny piece, won the jackpot of several pounds, remarked 'what a good thing these are', and never played again.

Each student was required to deliver a 15 minute talk on the subject of his choice: one officer demonstrated how to cook a sausage wrapped in a single sheet of newspaper — it worked best with the *Financial Times*[tm] — ignited by a match and then eat it; a doctor placed a cube of fresh raw liver in a sealed cola bottle wherein the offal turned green in, he said, 24 hours proving the vulnerability of animal organs to modern soft drinks.

Piers chose to speak about the planned automation of the military telephone networks. He knew something of the subject since his duties at Honington had involved managing the 450 line station manual telephone exchange on a front line station. The RAF intended the conversion to be completed within three years. His talk was judged by his unqualified 'instructors' to be utter rubbish, impractical, unaffordable and unworthy of the intelligence of the audience. By 1971, the RAF's telephones in the UK had converted totally to automatic dialled service within the 36 months described.

The gravest depth was reached while attempting to refresh drill instruction. There was no spare space inside the hangars formerly storing aircraft so the students were committed to exterior practice. The snow may have melted, but the slope on the requisitioned car park was never dry and overnight ice was reluctant to clear. With insufficient students, the representation of a twelve airman frontage with three ranks was achieved in a less than convincing manner using stretched rope. And wooden swords would never replace the real thing with their carefully designed balance. To those who had spent three years on a drill square at cadet college — Cranwell or Henlow — the entire episode was a farce.

Piers was glad when the whole business was over. The final drive to Cranwell for the Advanced Maintenance Engineering Course was cheered by the thought that it could not be worse than that.

Could it...?

Chapter 26
1968 ~ Sleaford Secondary Modern

In 1915, the Royal Naval Air Service needed a single unit at which officers and ratings could be trained to fly aeroplanes, observer kite balloons and airships. Tradition has it that a young naval pilot was briefed to fly around Lincolnshire until he found a piece of land that was both large enough and flat enough for the purpose. It is said that he flew over Cranwell and thought it quite admirable. The Royal Naval Air Service Central Training Establishment Cranwell was commissioned on 1 April 1916. Cranwell later became informally known as HMS Daedalus, not strictly correctly since the officers and ratings of the Central Training Establishment at Cranwell were borne on the books of *HMS Daedalus*, which was a hulk in the Medway.

With the amalgamation of the RNAS and the Royal Flying Corps on 1 April 1918, the unit became Royal Air Force Cranwell. The RAF College, which was the first military air academy in the world, opened on 2 February 1920. Thirteen years later, residing behind a new build frontage of 800 feet of Portland stone, the college building was opened. It is reputed that Marshal of the Royal Air Force the Viscount Hugh Montague Trenchard, who was Chief of the Air Staff during World War I, and was instrumental in establishing the Royal Air Force, said of the place:

> *"Marooned in the wilderness, cut off from pastimes they could not organise for themselves, the cadets would find life cheaper..."*

After World War II, the RAF College re-opened in 1946 and, in 1948, it became the first Royal Air Force unit to receive a King's Colour. In the years that followed, the college broadened its officer training to training for a range of air and non-engineering ground specialisations. RAF College Cranwell, the womb of the RAF's self proclaimed master race of pilots, became known to the cadets of the RAF Technical College Henlow by the disparaging name of Sleaford Secondary Modern. Not to be outdone, the said Cranwell cadets coined the name Shefford Tech for their Bedfordshire counterparts. Rivalry did not stop with name-calling; every possible sporting excuse was taken to engender competition between the two cadet colleges. Then, in 1965, to make room at Henlow for centralisation of RAF officers' (non-cadetship) initial training, the

RAF Technical College with its Cadet Wing was moved from Henlow to Cranwell, where it became the Department of Engineering wherein it would host advanced specialised training for the former technical, now much more correctly known as engineering, officers.

Henlow cadetships were a thing of the past.

*   *   *

The RAF VC-10 staging from Changi through Akrotiri, Cyprus had landed at RAF Brize Norton at 02:00 on December 18th 1967. Piers thought that all troopers from the Far East landed in UK at two in the morning, probably so that passengers couldn't see or photograph the west coast of Italy. It was cold, the baggage unloading slow, customs their usual tiresome selves. There to meet them was Helen's father, with a big warm car to convey the tired travellers from mid-Oxfordshire to Kingston-on-Thames and recovery. By the time they stopped, Helen and Piers had been in motion for 43 hours continuously.

Family Christmas was busy and noisy. But pressing was the need to buy wheels for Piers's use between a two month course, at Ashton Morley, and Cranwell where a married quarter stood vacant awaiting them.

"No, sir, I'm afraid the station is closed for Xmas and will not open until January the fifth." The Duty Storeman at RAF Cranwell was never going to be the right man to contact in this situation. He was really only there to issue road transport fuel if and when required. British industry was unlikely to wish to deliver anything during the Xmas/New Year shutdown. There certainly would be no call for aviation fuel; snow covered runways on public holidays and RAF training flying simply do not mix. In their wisdom, the 'College of Knowledge' enjoyed an airfield runway too short for V-bombers and therefore not suitable of V-force operational dispersal. In Piers's way of thinking, this was one further example of how RAF College Cranwell was too far removed from the real RAF.

"I am joining the Advanced Maintenance Engineering Course which begins in March and the Air Ministry says I have been allocated a married quarter at Cranwell."

"Yes, sir, I have found your name on the furnishing list, sir, but I can't give you the keys. Only the Barrack Warden can do that and he's not in until the fifth, sir. I suggest you give him a call then, sir."

'Heaven help me,' thought Piers. 'I'm back in the training machine again.'

"But I have to go 100 miles away, on a course, on the fifth." Piers had expected Xmas seasonal closure but not actual obstruction. He'd just come from an operational environment where time or day did not matter.

"I suggest, sir, that you telephone on the fifth and arrange for your wife to take the quarter over. It's only a question of checking the inventory and reading the meters. Then, when your course is finished, you can pop in and sign the documents to regularise the paperwork. We have this problem with officers doing short courses here, sir."

On Monday the fifth and before departing for his drive north, Piers rang the Barrack Warden and made arrangements for Helen to take over the keys for their allocated married quarter on Wednesday afternoon.

"Yes, flight lieutenant, the house is fully furnished and will be prepared for Mrs Ploughman. If she would telephone me when she gets to Grantham Station, I'll have transport pick her up. It's only a 45 minutes drive from here. I appreciate it's snowing, but the railways tend to keep running on the mainline. The house will soon warm up…"

*   *   *

Helen rode the 11:30 fast train Kings Cross to Grantham which took 85 minutes. She had tried to call in advance, to lessen a long wait at Grantham, but had been instructed, 'To call when you get there and transport will be sent.' The snow did not seem to cause too much trouble for British Rail, on this occasion, and the train arrived on time. Problem number one: find a telephone that works! A taxi driver showed her the nearest.

"Hello, this is Mrs Ploughman. I've been told to ring for transport from Grantham."

"Just one minute, ma'am. I'm the Duty Driver, you need the Duty Controller and he's off for lunch."

"I was told it had been arranged for me. Mrs Ploughman to Cranwell for a married quarter."

"Just one minute, ma'am, I'll check… I'll have to put the phone down… shan't be a moment…"

"I'm in a public phone box…" Helen was talking into an open line.

The demand for more money sounded. Helen complied; then a second time. "Oh, God, I hope I don't run out of coins."

" 'allo, Mrs Ploughman… are you there? … Everything is in order… the driver's just finishing his lunch… he'll be there in one hour… shame about the snow… at the ticket office at 2 o'clock."

"Please don't hang about, I'm freezing…" Helen was talking into a closed line.

At a quarter past two by the church clock, a 52 seater coach arrived in the fading January gloom. It manoeuvred precariously between the taxis towards the unaccompanied lone woman standing in the doorway of the station's ticket hall.

Sniff. "You'm be Mrs Ploughman? To go to Trenchard Drive?" Sniff. "Put your luggage on and we'll be off, then. I'll just phone in to see there's no more passengers, like. Don't fancy coming back in the dark… roads is icy now so they's gonna get grim tonight, like."

The telephone call duly made and they were off for the twenty mile drive through the darkening roads of central Lincolnshire. 52 seats for one passenger seemed to offer a great deal of spare capacity and the heater couldn't cope. There would have been nothing to see through the coach windows if they had been clear, but they were all misted up and such heated ventilation as was available was totally ineffective.

The journey took 70 minutes and the noise in the military coach was unpleasant; that version of the Bedford coach, designed for compatibility with the desert environment, drew its engine air through a filter in the cabin next to the driver's left leg. The functional plastic seats were never intended for comfort. But the driver knew where he was going and drove straight to the married quarter in Trenchard Drive. Helen, trying to see something of the environment in the inadequate street lights, thought the place was bleak beyond description. She had been driven across an out of use grass runway so there would have been nothing to see anyway…

"You'm here," announced the driver. The house door opened and against the backlight of the entrance hallway was silhouetted a man in buttoned overcoat, trilby hat and scarf, obviously wearing gloves and footwear that resembled Wellington boots.

"Come in, Mrs Ploughman, make yourself at home. It is rather cold to be travelling isn't it? I'm the Assistant Barrack Warden; look, I know it's dark and this is not a good time to check the inventory. I'll come back tomorrow, about nine o'clock. But I have to read the meters with you, for the paperwork. I've had the phone connected, if that's all right. The water and electricity is on and there's just enough coke for tonight until you can get a delivery in the morning. The useful telephone numbers are in the Station Magazine on the kitchen counter. Linen is in the airing cupboard and beds have been aired."

"How long has the place been empty, Mister err? It feels so chilly."

"Yarrup. I'll check..." barely coping with his paperwork in gloved hands, "oh, yes... I marched the flight lieutenant out myself in August... six months... it's been empty six months."

"We'll, Mr Yarrup, that would account for why it's so cold and damp. Are there any fireplaces for some heat?"

"Oh, yes, Mrs Ploughman, and the living room fireplace has a back boiler to heat a radiator in the bedroom. There are electric fires where there is no fire place." Helen was not persuaded. "You'll be nice and cosy. Sign here..."

As Mr Yarrup departed, there was a knock on the front door, which opened, and without ceremony, in came a beaming woman with a small grocery box. She was wrapped in a fur coat, wore a fur hat with integral ear muffs and her mouth just protruded above a thick woollen scarf. The ensemble was set off by sensible gloves.

"Hallo, I'm Janice Goodison. I'm the Trenchard Road welcoming committee. I couldn't hear the removal van so I thought I'd pop in to save you having to search for your tea in your boxes. I shan't stop now. I'll knock you up at 08:50 and take you to the NAFFI. Bye-ee."

"Wait... do you happen to have a match with you... to light the stove? Apparently there's coke out the back and there's an old newspaper to make the kindling... if I'm lucky."

Self sufficiency, Cranwell style, had crossed Helen Ploughman's threshold.

As the kettle boiled, Helen fought back the emotions of loneliness. "Oh Piers, I miss you so much. It's so perishing cold. You'd know how to get this coke boiler to work... I'll make a cuppa and phone Mum; she'll cheer me up." She was sitting, in the kitchen, with the oven on, trying to heat the room. She hoped she could get a coal delivery in the morning, otherwise the living room was going to remain a very lonely spot.

*   *   *

Nineteen weeks of the timetabled twenty had passed. The first eight had been designed to be a technology update for those deemed unable to take advantage of a master's level, 13 month, highly academic course. The remaining twelve weeks were devoted to management techniques, particularly optimised for RAF senior engineering posts. Only time would tell if the investment was worthwhile. The students were assembled in a classroom set out as a 'U' shape so that everyone could see everyone else. On this occasion which was the final period of the 19th week, the course's eight ex-cadets who all happened to be from the 1956 Entry had clustered for a catchup chat about colleagues when an instructor made an announcement.

"I know it's getting late for you chaps that haven't been told where you are posted. The RAF likes to prepare its minds and bodies for the exigencies of the service and would hate to put a square peg in a round hole. So, I am advised, by 14:45 today we shall have the definitive list of where you are posted to. Until then you have to be patient because we are doing our best."

There was a general murmur of disbelief at this promise… it was the air force way.

"Frankly," said Piers, in a not so silent whisper, "This lot couldn't organise a beer-up in a brewery. The instructors don't influence where we are going; it's down to the men in suits in some ministry hidey-hole. They've known since the first of March the precise day they are going to kick us out of Cranwell, because the course closes on 26 July, and we all lose our entitlement to housing — those of us that's got it, I mean."

The 14 course students sat around, lounged would be a better description, waiting in the largest lecture room. In came the Chief Instructor. They all stood as a courtesy.

"Right, the good news is that the postings are here. The bad news is you are going to have to wait while…" Whatever it was he said was drowned by derisory comments. Four of the course were smoking, two had cups of coffee. Everybody wanted to get on with it.

"OK, OK. I get the message." He was waving his hands trying to calm the reaction to his statement.

"First time in twenty weeks," was the comment from somewhere in the room.

"Five more minutes, then I'll see you individually, in alphabetical order. I don't want to be accused of favouritism." His attempt at cheerfulness was greeted with silence. Sensibly, he retired to his office.

"Have you guys looked at the course's statistics? All but one of us is married — and still on our first wife… well that's true for the ex-Henlow chaps anyway. What do you think that shows?" The speaker was Bartlett Dunmow, nicknamed *Nurse*.

"You're all unadventurous," volunteered Allen *Shark* Davies. He was the unmarried one and drew a guffaw from the assembly. The cadre of ex-Henlow cadets had grouped for mutual support; thirty three months of cheek by jowl training ten years ago could not easily be set aside.

"I quite like being on my wife, actually. Or under her come to that." The hoot from his fellows was not silenced by, "In fact, flying in any formation does it for me." Joe *Southpaw* MacLion had achieved his wings in flying school and had a flying tour on fighter aircraft under his belt. Shortly after being married, he was posted to RAE Farnborough to work on conventional armament. The technology phase of the course was a waste for him but the management procedures phase was, he thought, likely to be very useful. Left handed *Southpaw* was one of the smokers and was anxious about where they would send him next. He certainly did not want to be separated from his wife.

"Well I'm glad I've got my wife here," offered Piers.

"That was a bad business about Helen losing your chicko." Yeah, yeah was the sympathetic banter.

"She's all right now?" asked *Nurse* Dunmow.

Helen had miscarried at about week 8 of her pregnancy, 'after trying so hard', and the couple had to face the news that she was unlikely to be able to conceive again.

"We think so," nodded Piers. "Of course it means there's a great saving on not having to pop down to the chemist in Sleaford every week." Another guffaw of laughter.

"I get mine at the barbers. 'Something for the weekend, sir?' I always say it's not my *weak end* that worries me, it's worrying about the bloody calendar. Joan's regular as a pulse generator in a radar." *Nurse* Dunmow's input was calculated to ease the tension. He had been working on the UK's missile programme, particularly the Bloodhound air defence system. He was another student who knew more about the RAF's advanced technology than the instructors.

Addressing Piers, "Hey, *PeeTot*, I've been wanting to ask you." Trouble-starter Paul *Crab* Ellis had been posted from Henlow directly to flight line servicing, very much hands-on aircraft engineering. This Cranwell course was the first time he had been removed from the smell of kerosene and engine noise. Now pointing at Piers, he continued, "When you nearly set light to that Chipmunk, at Henlow, how did you talk your way out of a board of inquiry?"

"He sweet talked the Chief Flying Instructor's wife, the smarmy bastard." Julius *Ba* Shepherd's unlikely contribution to the debate was thought not to advance the ex-cadets' pool of knowledge. Again the background noise rose, but insufficiently to mask the next put down.

"Narh! He spent all his sweet talk with his beloved Helen, while he was out of bounds. He wouldn't know how to sweet talk anyone else." Derek *Uncle* Hedley, the confidant of the 1956 Cadet Entry, someone to talk to when the chips were stacked against, stood for *PeeTot*'s defence. "No, he intelligently threw himself on the mercy of his own flying instructor and got off scot-free. A brilliant, career saving manoeuvre if ever I witnessed one."

The rejoinder never came. *Uncle* had noticed the way his colleagues had grouped together, obviously apprehensive about their futures. This was one occasion when the non-cadets were being left out.

"Right. We're ready." An instructor had entered the room while speaking. "It'll be in alphabetical order. First in is Flight Lieutenant Caine. You don't need your hats." In they trooped, received the news, and returned to pass the news to any who would listen. Somewhere down the list, an instructor made an announcement.

"When you've all been through I'll post a consolidated list on the notice board."

"Have you found someone who can type?" drew a laugh.

While the process was going continuing, the business of catching up on colleague ex-cadets continued.

"Anyone hear anything about the Aussies?"

Piers offered, "I heard about Drew Wilde. I didn't have the chance to see *Fu* when I went through Butterworth about two years ago. I heard Drew the *Fu* was with an outfit called 78 Wing RAAF; he was up country on the Thai border on a detachment. I reckon he's still a smoker and playing rugby or golf at any opportunity. I wonder if he's changed his socks yet."

"I met up with *Derv* Thackray at a flight safety briefing last year." It was *Shark* Davies speaking. His audience wanted to know where he was going, he'd already had his interview, but he was not letting on. "*Derv* apparently met *LMN* King on a radar tracking station in the Australian desert. Something to do with making sure our A-bombs fall on the right bit of South Australia. They'd have a job to miss, I reckon. Anyway, *LMN* hadn't married yet; he was having too good a time with all the sheilas."

"Do you get the feeling that this waiting is like waiting at the dentist's?" *Ba* Shepherd's intervention was ignored; he was waiting for his future too.

"He always fancied himself as a lady's man, the tall athletic so and so." Paul *Crab* Ellis was feigning anger but not very convincingly. "*LMN* muscled in on one of mine at a Hitchin dance and..."

"Was that when you were dancing sideways, *Crab*?"

Before *Crab* could react, an instructor announced, "Flight Lieutenant Ellis, it's your turn." Cheers. There was no relaxation to the tension in the room; there were still some waiting to be called. As *Crab* Ellis approached the door, he was followed by, "She was lucky to escape your pincers..." He left the tense laughter behind to collect his fate.

Uncle Hedley, always sensitive to the mood of the moment, "The word has gone around that *Imam* Drake has got married, had a couple of sprogs and shoved off leaving her to manage. He's rumoured to have settled in Burma, according to my source. There's no news of how Japonica Drake is making out. They were catholic, you know. Lovely girl, Japonica... shame about the name." There was little reaction to this weak comment.

"Listen to *Uncle* 'according to my source'. Rumour control has spoken again. Word was that *Imam* Drake only made Acting Flying Officer paid and was invited to quit. He'd put a burst of 50mm cannon through a fuel dump during an engine test run. Anymore rumours, *Uncle*?" Laughter.

"Well since you ask, old chap," pause for effect, "*Bunk* Dewhurst still has difficulty getting out of bed. He got hurried out to an undisclosed

Maintenance Unit overseas, 'married unaccompanied' they say, about as far abroad as you can go before you start coming back." Yeah...yeah. "It seems he liked to have company... under the bed sheets... found by the batwoman who got jealous 'cos she wanted *Bunk* for herself, they say..." There were some catwhistles until:

"Flight Lieutenant Hedley," the instructor summoned.

"Good luck, *Uncle*." He waved goodbye as he passed through the door.

He had only been out of the room for 90 seconds when he returned, looking glum. "They want me to stay here... to teach this damned course... why me? I hate teaching. I hate teachers. I'll appeal. I'll petition the Queen. I'll apply to be an MP; they have to kick you out for that."

"Flight Lieutenant Ploughman please." *Southpaw* MacLion was already stubbing out his cigarette in anticipation of it being his turn.

"It's not my turn. Hey *Southpaw*, you're next. It's Flight Lieutenant MacLion's turn."

"Flight Lieutenant Ploughman, please!" There was no denying the call.

Around the corner, through the door. There was the Chief Instructor with a single sheet on his desk. Piers knew enough about RAF paperwork to recognise a teleprinted signal message.

"Have a seat, Piers. We have some news for you."

"Yes, sir." Piers breathed deeply expecting something pretty dreadful. An aircraft storage depot, perhaps. Some radar station in the Outer Hebrides; yes, they're out there too. How bad could it be?

The Chief Instructor was speaking. "You know that, three months ago, Bomber and Fighter Commands unified to become Strike Command. Well, they want some high calibre engineers to make the merger work and you are going to be one of them. You are being promoted to fill an Engineering Coordination and Plans appointment. You will report displaying the squadron leader rank on 29 July at Headquarters Strike Command High Wycombe. The signal says you will be acting unpaid for the first two weeks and will receive full acting squadron leader pay from August 11th. You will be entitled to married accommodation at High Wycombe. Congratulations."

"Yes, sir. Thank you, sir. Is that all? Blimey." Promotion? What have I done right? Coo, acting paid squadron leader... new car... maybe even a house? Gosh... 'They must have mislaid the Aston Rowant report...'

"Yes, Piers. You will be given a copy of this signal before the end of the day. You'll need it as authority to have your uniform amended and to claim your accommodation and disturbance allowances. Now, off you go. I have others to interview."

Piers stood, expecting a handshake of congratulations. This place could not get even that morale booster right. He turned to leave, then turned back remembering not to salute without his hat, turning again to exit closing the door behind him.

'Well, that's a turn up for the books.' He stood in the corridor, aghast at the news, thinking about the brevity of its delivery, the world changing message on that piece of paper. 'I reckon that will make me the youngest squadron leader in the branch. What a fantastic way to end a miserable seven months. I wonder what Helen will say about this...'

His glowing smile when he entered the lecture room was what the fellows call 'a dead giveaway'. This was going to be an expensive evening in the mess bar.

*   *   *

The flow of officers' data stemming from Cranwell onto the desk of KGB operative Olga Brovorno was always appreciated. There was so much of it! She felt she was being reunited with some old friends. All useful snippets contributed to the files as careers developed in the enemy's air force. Olga's files grew thicker as she compiled and waited. Already there had been three calls, from the fifth floor, about the students due to graduate from the Advanced Maintenance Engineering Course in July. She chuckled as she knew where they were going before they did. And those course photographs, some with names too, so helpful. Yes, Cranwell was a goldmine for her business.

As the requests for her files came in, Olga knew she was helping the system even if she was not privileged to know how.

Chapter 27
1968 ~ We'll Have Those Aeroplanes Too

Acting Squadron Leader Piers P Ploughman went through the new arrivals' procedure in Station Headquarters, RAF High Wycombe. This was located in No 1 Site; No 2 was the Officers' Mess and some married quarters. No 3 Site contained the headquarters buildings which had been deliberately laid out in disorderly higgledy-piggledy fashion to resemble, from the air, an untidy farmyard on the edge of National Trust greenbelt land. Piers drove the mile between Nos 1 and 3 sites to find that a temporary office building had been erected on the car park, '…dangerously under the emergency water tank,' thought Piers as he parked the Sunbeam[tm] Alpine.

'Here we go; brace up squadron leader,' thought Piers. 'The flight lieutenants will be saluting you now!' Piers climbed the three steps into the office Portakabin[tm] and knocked on the open first door on the left. The office contained his new boss.

Piers was waved in and motioned to the front of the desk. A single visitor's chair was placed under the closed window. The room, despite its newness, smelled of tobacco and the plastic venetian blinds were ineffective in keeping out the morning sunshine. The wing commander looked well worn to Piers; he wore a WWII medal ribbon and an Air Gunner half brevet. Piers judged him to be 50 years old, perhaps more. In five years, perhaps less, the RAF would compulsorily retire him. 'His problem,' thought Piers. 'I wonder what he knows about engineering. There are so many of these aircrew retreads…'

"Nice to see you. You are the last of my staff to arrive. Get settled in, read the orders and we'll all go up to the mess for a drink. Have they said anything about a married quarter for you? I expect you are in the mess while you wait. Quite comfortable?" Piers remained politely still while this uninterrupted monologue progressed. If the wing commander moved, other than his lower jaw, Piers did not notice although he did wonder if the 'great man' would deign to offer a greeting handshake.

"There's some turbulence with the new organisation… and more to come when Coastal Command joins. Our role is to make it work with the new aircraft coming in. I'm a radar man, myself… Fighter Command… air defence radar chain. Getting these bomber types to understand heavy radar is going to be a challenge. Bit like trying to teach the Pope about condoms... first line of defence... can't live without it. My report on the future of the *UK Radar Chain in the NATO Context* will be in the runner's file delivery for you the afternoon."

"Where's my desk, sir?"

"Along the corridor, at the end. You'll find three other airfield people in there. The radar and communications team are next door... in a separate office. Is this your first staff appointment?"

Before Piers could reply, "Oh yes, I remember. Fresh out of Cranwell."

'He even got my training wrong! Not a word on congratulations on my youthful promotion...'

"Well, forget all that rubbish. Here it's real front line stuff. We keep the reds from under the bed and our secrets buttoned under our lip. I have a secret library in another room; you can run that for me."

"Yes, sir. Should I sit down?"

"No. Work to get on with. Your brief will be to get the Phantoms into Leuchars by the First of August. That gives you precisely 357 days so you'd better get started. I'll review progress next week before I go on leave; we're taking three weeks in a villa in Austria. Your interview with Group Captain Frobisher is at 14:30; bone up on hockey... he likes to talk hockey... he's the officer in charge of command hockey. Do you play hockey?"

With a concealed deep breath, Piers shook his head. He was going to volunteer that he did play golf, had his own clubs, when...

"My door is always open to any good ideas. The future starts here... in Engineering Plans. Welcome aboard."

"Just one question, sir. Why do I need to read a paper about radar, sir, when I have to worry about Phantoms and new aircraft?"

"The future, my boy. Radar is the future. Without radar your Phantom fighters won't know where to wack it to the reds. So it's all about projecting air power, my boy, and this is where it's at. Strike Command. We're implementing the future here. I'm at a meeting, in Whitehall, tomorrow, where we'll be sorting out the manpower for the new radars. I wrote the staff paper so I know it is good. Check with Willie... make sure he has got your security ticket. Now, you've got some reading to get on with... I shan't keep you..."

Piers saluted, exited the wing commander's office and walked along a carpeted corridor into his new office. The deep breath escaped as he opened the door to find his new desk. Who the hell was Willie? Four new grey metal desks, laid out in two pairs back to back each with two filing trays and a telephone, were separated by a bank of six, four drawer, steel filing cabinets. The uncarpeted room echoed as one officer spoke on the telephone while waving a greeting towards Piers towards a clear desk by an open window. An indication of being expected, Piers surmised. Venetian blinds had been lowered to minimise the glare. As Piers moved in another officer, wearing squadron leader's braid, rose and approached him with outstretched hand in greeting. No brevet! A real engineer!

"Hello. I'm Greg Barnes. Welcome to the madhouse. We're doing Phantoms together. I'm mechanical; they say I know something about missiles. I suppose these Phantom thingees are going have missiles. The guy on the phone, there, is James Leadbetter. He's OK even though he is a sparks man." Leadbetter thumbed his nose at the compliment. "Our backstop is Julius Hastings, flew in last week from Seattle where he became the RAF expert on all matters F111 — which the government in its wisdom had decided to buy with US dollars when we could have had a better machine called the TSR2 made with English pounds." Leadbetter nodded over a closed fist with a protruding erect thumb. "They've just cancelled the F111 and sent James home with his tail between his legs. He'll bore you with the details. What do we call you?"

"Hi. I'm Piers Ploughman, electrical, just arrived this morning."

"Those rank tabs look a bit new."

" 'fraid so. I only got them on Friday. I'm fresh out of training — Cranwell college of knowledge — advanced training! What gives here? What gives with the wing commander? Is he actually an engineer? Seems he runs a madhouse and its still only half past ten. And who's Willie?" Piers had removed his hat and placed it on the vacant desk. The furniture looked to be all new.

"Oh don't worry about him. He's ex-Fighter Command, believes the world revolves around radar, ground radar. He probably did a one day Debden conversion course from flying in '45 and is now an expert! I've come here from London. They pulled me out of the Defence Intelligence Staff to work here. Naturally, the world revolves around intelligence."

He beamed at Piers who was wondering if this really was a madhouse or just a bad dream.

"Do you know anything about McDonald Douglas F4 Phantoms? We've got to put a squadron of them, No 43 (Fighting Cocks) Squadron, into Leuchars by 1 August. They're ex-Navy Phantoms, with folding wings; that'll make for a few short landings!"

"Where's Leuchars?"

"Good start! Leuchars, dear boy, is in Fyfeshire, Scotland. About as close to Moscow as we get. That's not so important. Much more so is St Andrews Golf Course, just 3 miles across the mud flats, complete with a university when the putting get rough. We are going to be siting the noisiest aircraft in the RAF on the first green, give or take a VC-10 on max chat. Haven't you met Willie yet?"

"With missiles?" Piers had now sat down; the new chair was surprisingly comfortable.

"Hole in one, dear boy. Eight per aircraft. A gatling gun too—thousand rounds a minute! A great leveller is the Phantom. Tell me about Piers. My missus will want all the details... weight at birth, how many kids, which schools… all the gory stuff."

Piers summarised his eight years experience, married quarter situation, omitting the details of his flying training and minimising his cadetship. He concluded by aping the wing commander's statement, "The future's here, the future is Engineering Plans, and I'm in the deep end…"

It was nearly twelve noon when the wing commander came into the big room. He approached Greg and Piers's desks. Both shuffled to their chairs as if to rise to their feet, but he shook his head.

"I've just got the word that Coastal's date is set for 28th November. We'll be getting two more squadron leaders in here for the Nimrods and Shackleton upgrade. And, hot off the press, we're taking on Signals Command in the new year; it will be called No 90(Signals) Group. The details have yet to be worked out, but provisionally, the aircraft will fall on your desks. Can't talk about them, much… they're too secret. You'd better get those Phantoms sorted out quickly. Now, the bar's open so we've got some new rank braid to christen. The first round is on Piers. Don't forget the group captain's office at 14:30."

Piers's Cadetship

Part Two

1970 - 2008

There is no link to bind them…

Chapter 28
1970 ~ The Heritage Trail Starts Here

It was the family weddings that started it. Then there were the family funerals — always occasions for '...have you heard?' and '...did you know?' and '...well I never!' although of course Helen had heard it all before. So the search for the long forgotten began; the great, great ... great grandparents and their siblings... and all the cousins and any other valid member of the growing family tree. Piers and Helen started notebooks, drew family trees, visited libraries and graveyards and interviewed relatives. That this activity required lots of travel appealed to the couple since they enjoyed the comparison of English countryside and stately homes with their experiences in other parts of the world. And so their lists of the Ploughmans and Helen's family, the Blythes, grew.

Piers had problems finding the time to thoroughly research and document his genealogical findings. His career depended on passing a two-year correspondence course run by the RAF Staff College. As with most courses, Piers was in no position to judge what value, if at all, any aspect of the course would be relevant to his engineering career in the increasingly complex organisation which was Strike Command. He found it particularly irksome to be worrying about rescuing some unfortunate downed pilot, off a Japanese occupied Malayan beach, back to the safety of Ceylon; the artificiality of the setting already 25 years stale, hardly compared with the latest NASA Apollo moon-shot or Soviet air-launched guided bomb or the noise problem for St Andrews University from the ground testing of the Phantoms' engines. But satisfactory course pass, which included a formal written exam, was a pre-requisite in the competition for next promotion and Piers reluctantly complied.

So it was Helen who devoted her energies to the assembly of family history facts.

"I was thinking..." she opened.

"Always a dangerous activity when there's a 'r' in the month..."

Piers's comment was adroitly disregarded, "...that we ought to ask the folks to tell their stories before it's too late."

"Before they kick the bucket..."

She shrugged off the RAF slang for dying. "When they've gone… well… you know…"

"You want to use the tape recorder? That's a bit difficult when they've… well… you know…" He knew his wife was hedging the direct question about using 'his' toy; actually Piers would not object; it was the latest electronic gadget to be gathering dust, in its box, in the cupboard under the stairs.

"It would be nice to have their words in their own… err…"

"Words?"

"Words… as they would speak them… you know!" Her touch on his cheek was increasingly persuasive.

With the slightest of nods, "I know. Of course you can use the recorder. There are a couple of spare tapes in its box and your Dad will have some more. I think it's a great idea. When do we start?"

"I thought I would take the car over to Mum's while you are doing some studying. Let you have some peace and quiet…" Helen's delivery was deadpan; it was her way of saying that Mum Blythe would be more forthcoming if son-in-law was not there.

Research into the Ploughman genealogy had begun and would continue as a lifelong hobby. It was contagious. Parents and in-laws enthused in telling their tales and, very quickly, Helen had exhausted all the living memory and gravestones in the greater geographical footprint of the Ploughmans and the Blythes.

Later, "Piers?"

'Here it comes,' thought Piers. 'She wants something and it's bound to cost… money!' She was in the kitchen, doing kitchen things; he was at the dining room table with the latest course material spread over its surface, pen in hand.

"Yes, my love." In the hope of diverting the subject… trying to sound positive, "The RAF wants me to study the interaction of the coal industry with the post-colonial rainforest. I'm finding it a bit tedious. There is a two day related course at Dundee University they could send me on…"

"I saw this programme, on TV, about the Genealogical Society — in London — and I though we might join…"

"Go ahead… if you think it would help. I never trust these societies with long names… they are full of cranks and folks with strange agendas. But, I suppose it's what we're in the military for — freedom of thought

and expression. Grandma Blythe says *there's now't so queer a folk*, so…
Not much difference between the 'Ban the Bomb' cronies and long haired
professors or stretched cardigans rifling through archives in dusty
archives looking for archived… err… stuff."

"It's got royal patronage." She was ignoring his comment. "The
Genealogical Society; I've filled in the form and I thought," she had
entered the room, "I could do the cheque and… you could post it in the
morning — on your way to the office." Helen knew there would be no
objection, especially as her left hand was smoothing the short hair on her
lover's neck and her lips were within striking range. "And I don't have a
cardigan!" The discarded pen joined the notebooks on the table.

"Right! Did you know it takes 12 million years to convert a tree into
coal?"

"So 15 minutes — more or less — won't make any difference — in
the bigger picture — promotion wise?" She was winning…

"Is that my ration, 15 minutes?"

"You could tell me about the rainforest…" She didn't finish her
sentence and Piers didn't finish his course assignment that evening. It
seems that laying down coal seams can wait for no woman!

*   *   *

"Oh, darling, it's so exciting. They've got thousands of books and miles
of shelves of papers — and you can get a cup of tea… and eat your
sandwiches in the sitting room… and get advice… and buy things from
their bookshop… and go as often as you want…"

"Hey, hey. Not so fast. You like the place, then?" Piers was
delighted to see the sheer pleasure radiating from his wife's face. She
was clutching a notebook as though it was the crown jewels.

"I took lots of notes and I'll tell you all about it. You pop down the
road for fish and chips from the van while I wash the London dirt off my
face. Then I'll tell you what I've found. It may be there is another way
to spell your — our — name. I've asked for a copy of a will and three
birth certificates…"

With raised eyebrows, "I didn't know they do birth certificates." Had
Piers scored a point?

Shaking her head with a smile, "They don't." He hadn't scored a
point, damn. "But all the necessary data is there to identify who you want

215

a certificate about and then you do a form to the archives of the appropriate place and it comes in 10 days."

"You make it sound so simple. Frederick Forsyth found out how to get a birth certificate… in his book…"

Her enthusiasm was unabated. "These folks were real. They were born or died a hundred years ago. And there's the census records too. It's so exciting. You'll have to come next time I go. They are open on Saturdays…"

"Why don't we go down to the Medway and see what we can find in the churches there?" He moved to sit next to Helen on the settee. "Some of these places have records going back to before Cromwell — Thomas not Oliver! If we go down on a Friday, we could make a long weekend of it and maybe eat some shrimps." He reached to clasp her hands with his. "I used to enjoy eating shrimps when I was a boy."

"We'll do it. This Friday — before Mother says she wants to visit."

"Now that is a promise I can't refuse." Perhaps his nod was too emphatic, but Helen didn't appear to notice.

* * *

St Mary's Church was Chatham's original parish church standing on the eastern bank of the Medway above the town centre and Chatham Hard. It was unmistakable at the crest of Dock Road leading to the Royal Navy Dockyard entrance with its well-known ship's figurehead framed by the entrance arch. Helen knew exactly what she was looking for, in a vintage church at the entrance to a naval dockyard.

The church door was open. There was a descriptive sheet recording that the site is believed to have been used as a place of worship since pagan times. It also said that the oldest thing in the Medway Towns, a stone tablet 39 inches high and 19 inches wide depicting the goddess Euphrosyne, is built into the porch. It was thought to be of Greek trader origins having been built into the present porch by the Normans.

"So much history," whispered Helen. "Let's see if we can find the vicar. Perhaps he'll let us see the original records. This is where the microfiche in London said some Ploughmans and some Plowmans were baptised and married. Perhaps we can see the originals." With no hesitation, Piers led his wife to enter the old church. He enjoyed the interiors of such historic buildings.

The vicar was indeed pleased to show the young couple the church records. He took them to the vestry and opened a large wooden chest that showed its well used age in its battered unpolished surfaces. Sure enough, the record of marriages from 1750 to 1810 was the first available volume and, in there, Helen quickly turned to Ploughman marriages recorded in copperplate writing. "It's so exciting. To think that they actually wrote on these pages two hundred years ago. Look," pointing, but not quite touching the sheet, "here is your ever-so-many greats grandfather and Edith in 1775; it even says who their parents were and what jobs they had. See… dredgerman and scullery maid."

The vicar caught their enthusiasm. Each month someone came in wanting to research his or her antecedents in his precious documents, sometimes with success. There was an occasional American, even a family from Australia were here a year ago. But now this couple, extending their research into the baptisms, were being so careful with this cherished archive. He warned them that they needed to take care about verbatim spelling because the writers did not have the skill or education that we now enjoy. But there was no doubt that 'Ploughman' meant 'Ploughman' in any hand. The vicar suggested they visit the library in Rochester Cathedral where many other heritage volumes were stored.

However, this weekend, Piers wanted to take his wife to see where he lived during the Luftwaffe air raids, where he had played with his cousins on the Darland Banks while the soldiers practised their bayonets drills, where he saw the *Wizard of Oz* movie and east to the Isle of Sheppey and on to Birchington, where he watched the doodlebugs fly over.

It was standing above the beach at Birchington, with his arm around her waist that Piers said to Helen, "This must be where it all started — me and the RAF. Dad was out at Manston in '44 and '45, before he went to Burma. He showed me our fighters shooting down the flying bombs and our bombers going out to Germany. I was six, and we had a hard winter down here; the snow was so deep that the men had to cut through the drifts so we could get to school and the snow was over my head."

Ever practical, Helen suggested they stay in a coastal bed and breakfast so as to get a good start for Canterbury. "We could see if we can get into the Cathedral Library while we're here. I just have a feeling there are going to be some ancient Ploughmans tending their fields and paying their taxes and we are going to search them out."

Piers was pointing out over the North Sea. "That was where the Dambusters' bomb was tested… you know… those movies with a thing looking like a dustbin bouncing and coming straight at the camera…"

Helen was not interested in bouncing bombs. Piers detected the need to switch his line of topic.

"OK, OK! We'll stay!" Piers was in no way dismayed. Tightening his hold around his wife, "Now, have I told you about Uncle Ray and estuary winkles… or jellied eels? They were real Chatham Dockyard folk…"

*   *   *

The Officers' Mess Summer Ball at RAF High Wycombe had been a crowded success. The men had talked 'shop', the women had talked and sometime couples danced. A rock and roll marquee had been set up for the young bloods to exercise the latest fad. By the time 03:00 showed on the entrance wall, weary couples were taking their leave. Piers and Helen did not have far to walk to their married quarter.

"Piers, I don't want mulligatawny soup. Why don't we ask a couple of friends back to the quarter for a cup of tea?"

"Or something a bit stronger?"

"If you like. It would be nice to have a chat, we see so little of those who live off-base. Anyone else?"

"I thought I recognised Philippa Pendleton; she was a WRAF officer while we were going through Henlow. She had a smart Army medic in tow, in uniform complete with spurs — a captain I think. But I missed them to talk to. I don't know if she recognised me; I didn't have much to do with her."

"We'll manage with the six of us. You go and ask your Henlow cronies along while I get my bag." They unlinked hands and went to collect their outer garments from their respective cloakrooms

In their married quarter, just a few hundred yards from the mess, the conversation centred about what the three ex-cadets had done in the ten years gap between graduating and the present. Scotsman *Kirk* Knight said that his first wife, Louise, had gone off with a sailor while he was flying with the V-force out of Wittering.

"No accounting for taste…" was *MacKay*'s dismissal of his marriage disaster. "Lulu didn't have any kids so…" He shrugged. "When I completed my flying tour, they sent me out to Australia for the weapons trials and that's where Wyn found me. I asked her and she said, 'Fair dinkum…' and we got hitched and here she is. There…" pointing. "And a right raver she is too, pretty hard to keep up with." Wyn's eyes rolled upwards at the mantalk.

John *Ganglion* Dawtry, still with his nervous twitch looked a little uncomfortable at the direct masculine tone adopted by *MacKay* Knight. His childless wife Millie was unaccustomed to the RAF ways of conversing, not least about wives, and was looking forward to her bed. Helen could sense that men were going to delve deep in shop talk, what they called 'opening the hangar doors'. It was time for the wives to move to a quiet corner for a gossipy chinwag.

Piers remarked, "Hey, *Ganglion,* I see you're sporting a navigator's brevet. I thought you'd gone pilot after Aston Rowant. I bet they didn't like you transferring branches after all that stuff at Henlow."

"I didn't give them much choice, *PeeTot,"* responded John Dawtry. They were using cadets' nicknames in the absence of their womenfolk. "I laid it on the line — either you let me go General Duties (Navigator) or I quit!"

"That's telling them!" *MacKay* Knight was not impressed. There was no way that the RAF would kowtow to a threat like that. "So how did you pull it off, *Ganglion,* twitch your coffee into the instructor's lap?"

"There's no need to be personal," interjected the host Piers.

"I'm telling you straight," insisted *Ganglion* Dawtry, his nervous twitch a little more exaggerated.

Hostess Helen, ever mindful that the men's exchange could be getting heated, "Who fancies an egg and bacon breakfast? Come on, ladies, give me hand while these old cronies reminisce about their misspent youth."

The sun was well up, on a fine July morning, when the visitors eventually departed. A good lie in was just the ticket until…

"Will you answer it, Piers?" The clock showed 08:15 next to the telephone on the bedside locker. Piers did not speak; Helen could hear it was her mother wanting to speak to her and reached for the handset.

"Oh… really… when… are they all right, both of them… what weight… and Kitty, no problems with her labour… oh, twenty minutes… congratulations, Mother, and Piers is nodding the same too… you're a grandmother now… we're in bed… no, no, we just came in from the

Summer Ball… yes it is good news, I'm very pleased for them… speak to you later… yes… bye bye."

"Helen?" Piers's unspoken 'what was that all about' question was understood.

"It's my sister, Kitty. She's had her baby, in Hereford General. It's a girl, 6 pounds. They're both OK."

"You didn't get your cuddle last night. Come here and let's celebrate your sister's news." Piers's amorous reach was firmly rejected.

"Not now, Piers. I'm too excited about Kitty's news. Wasn't that the postman? I'll go and make us a cup of tea. What time is it? Does that say a quarter past eight? Post is always early on Saturdays. You stay there and we'll see what happens when I…" Helen moved to the safety of downstairs.

There were typical kitchen noises in the normally quiet house. Then, "Piers! There's a letter from Oxford, addressed to both of us. I'll bring it up." The tea tray was forgotten. She was offering the still sealed envelope to a reluctant hand.

"Go on, you open it. Perhaps it's news…" Helen handed the envelope to her husband who was still bleary eyed from lack of sleep. He ran his finger under the sealed flap and withdrew the contents.

'Letters usually have news', he thought better of saying the words aloud.

He read the typed page. It was from the Oxfordshire County Social Services Department. His quick scan was sufficient. Without a word, he handed the letter to Helen who had to read the text twice to absorb its single paragraph contents.

"They've got a baby for us." She looked at the letter again. "They've got a baby for us!"

Please telephone this office on Monday to discuss the way ahead.

"They've got a baby for us! How can you be so calm?"

Piers smiled as his wife bounced up and down on the mattress. "Hey," he said, "we're pregnant." He pulled the excited, blushing, near tears Helen down for a lingering kiss.

When she withdrew, she repeated, "They've got a baby for us!"

"You'd better tell your mother, dearest." He passed her the handset. "And breathe deeply before you start... you look like you're going to burst."

Her first dialling attempt did not work. "How can you be so calm?" The second time she made the connection.

"Mother, it's Helen... yes, it is good news about Kitty... but I had to tell you... yes, I can telephone the hospital later... no no, there hasn't been an accident... Mother... Mother, we're expecting... no... no, not that way... we've had a letter, from the adoption people... yes... no... they don't say if it's a boy... they don't say if it's a girl... they don't say when... we've got to telephone them on Monday... they don't say... Mother, I've told you all I know, you've got to be patient... you're going to be a grandmother twice on the same day... yes, Mother, Piers is here and he is delighted too."

Helen's eyes engaged Piers's as she waved her head as her mother kept talking.

"Mother, dear Mother. We can't give it a name until we know what it is. Well, we've have discussed names... Mother... Mother, dearest Mother... Mother I'm too excited to talk anymore. I'll call you later. No, please don't spread it around the family... let's wait until Monday when we'll know dates and things... yes, Mother, I love you too... speak to you later... yes... bye bye."

Piers reached for his wife and pulled her across him. An urgency was bubbling inside him; he desperately want to make love to his gorgeous wife. She lay outside the single blanket, her form pressing into his chest as he caressed her through her cotton nightdress. He kissed her passionately.

"Not now, beloved, not now. I'm just too excited with the news. Be patient. I'll go and get the tea if it's not too stewed. Later, my love. I love you very much."

"I know... and I love you heaps too. Don't be long with that tea... you've got to allow your husband to have another go... at friendly persuasion... and if there's going to be the patter of tiny feet, we may not have so many opportunities in the months to come."

*   *   *

The pregnancy phase of a wanted adoption can be perilously short. The couple could hardly contain themselves before the phone call to Oxford on Monday morning.

"Yes, Mrs Ploughman, it is real… we have a little boy born six weeks ago."

Piers had his head pressed against the telephone headset so that he could hear what the adoption society lady was saying.

"No, no… he's very well, nothing wrong I assure you… we'll tell you the details when we meet… of course you can see him, we thought Wednesday afternoon if you can make it."

Piers said, "Tell her we can make it, just give us an address and a time."

Helen said into the telephone, "Oh yes we can make it; just give us an address and a time. On Wednesday you said?"

There was a moment's delay and the rendezvous was passed.

"Right, I've got that… I know it, just outside Wallingford, at three o'clock on Wednesday the 23rd. We'll meet outside the house and go in together. Right… Wednesday… at three in the afternoon… outside the house… we'll be there… goodbye, and… err… thank you so much."

The distant voice was talking again.

Helen repeated the essence, "Yes, we quite understand that he can't come home with us immediately. There are some formalities. Friday did you say? We could have him on Friday? Yes, yes. That will be fine, we could make Friday morning. Yes, of course, and thank you so much…"

Piers moved away so that Helen could put the phone down. She was blushed, almost crying with happiness. She threw her arms round Piers's neck and held him close.

"It's a boy… I knew it would be a boy or a girl… we'll have to choose a name. I've always wanted one of the baby names books. We'll get one while we are shopping. And all the baby things we'll need — nappies, bottles, clothes, a pram. Oh I can't wait. There's a good Mothercare[tm] in Aylesbury. Blue for a little boy… Mother will be so pleased… She, Mrs Whatsit at Oxford, said we'll have to see him first… to see if we like him… of course we'll like him… and go shopping on Thursday…"

The formal adoption process went through the court on 5th November 1970.

Michael Ploughman was just nine months old when the news came through that Piers was posted to an appointment in the Ministry of Defence, London. Piers would be working in Whitehall. They would have to vacate their convenient quarter at High Wycombe, where he could walk to work, and select one which would be within 1½ hours commuting distance, each way, from his new office.

Chapter 29
1971 ~ Candlepower

The Ministry of Defence incumbent air commodore Director of Maintenance and Technical Services Policy(RAF) did not have the space on his door for the full office title. It was therefore abbreviated to D MTSPol(RAF); however, since the door was part of a listed building, reputed to pre-date Arthur Wellesley, 1st Duke of Wellington, but actually built a century later between 1898 and 1906, he was not permitted to have even the short title plate screwed to his door: it was pinned to the wall. As a Director, he was entitled to fitted floor carpet to within 6 inches of each wall skirting board. The insides of his windows were cleaned monthly, the outsides on some arbitrary periodic variant between annually and seldom. His corridor door was always locked meaning every visitor entered past his personal assistant.

Piers waited for his arrival interview. It was a ritual; probably the Normans did it, perhaps even the Romans. He could not fail to notice the flaunted civil service breasts being displayed for the benefit of the newest, and youngest, member of the Director's staff of 60. Piers had noticed that most of them, MTSPol(RAF) staff of both genders, looked to be 50 years old if they were a day. 33 years old Piers could see no advantage in flirting with this woman — she was older than he in any case — and he tried to pay attention to the boring, government framed, faded prints adorning the walls. He would learn that directors did not rate original oil paintings from the bountiful storeroom; the next rung up the ladder might be so lucky.

A buzzer rang. "The Director will see you now, Squadron Leader." Her accent was pure Gravesend. Her head cocked towards an internal door. No open the door, no introduction on first entry, just get on with it. The courtesies of military life so familiar on the windy airfields around Great Britain had long since faded in these corridors of Whitehall. She was reaching into a handbag for cigarettes before Piers's hand reached the door knob. He'd be in there 10 minutes, giving her just sufficient time for a fag.

He was greeted with a wave, towards a chair, by a fifty four years plus, grey-haired, wrinkled-faced servant of the Crown who had presumably been good at his job. He was jacketless which revealed slightly worn shirt elbows and a tie which needed pressing. He could have usefully used a barber too. Piers noticed he wore trouser braces, a male accoutrement that a gentleman never displayed in public much as a lady would conceal her brassiere shoulder straps.

"Ah... come in... err... Squadron Leader Ploughman. Welcome to MTS Pol. I see you're joining the Tech Pol 46 team... good chaps there... very effective in passing the need for efficiency and cost effective trade sense... err... this note says you come recommended by Group Captain Frobisher at Headquarters Strike Command... good man Frobisher... played hockey with RAF colours... we did our Halton apprenticeships together... err... glad to see you're a Chartered Engineer, eh? Where would we be without them... err... us, eh?... I see you're in married quarters at High Wycombe, they'll soon have you out of there... err... it's a long way to commute... look out for secondary duties while you're here, they are canvassing for a representative for badminton this week... well, I expect you'll want to get on with the job so I'll let you go. Ask Hermione for a towel and soap on your way out, she'll explain. Enjoy your tour in London... err... its very enlightening for young officers. Good Morning... err... Ploughman." No offer of a handshake, hardly any body movement behind the desk except by his head to read his welcome brief as he spoke. Piers thought he could have doubled for a ventriloquist's dummy. 'What a way to say hello...'

Through the door, which he closed gently, at the end of the outstretched arm of PA Herminone — Piers thought the name Doris would suit her better — was one folded cloth with the texture of a dish cloth, clean but off-white from repeated boiled washing and an unused bar of soap which had the moulded arrow of Government Property used during World War II. He was clearly expected to take hold of these objects which, judging by their markings, were probably 30 years or more in store before being issued. In her other hand, Herminone held a card; the odour of cigarette smoke had not yet cleared.

"Fill it in and gimme it back" It was the usual card requiring service number, rank and name, date of birth, telephone numbers (home and office), address if staying in London during the week, home address, wife's name, age and religion, retirement date. Piers glanced at it.

"Twenty nine inches."

"What?" jerked Herminone, clearly caught off her guard. "What's twenty nine inches?"

"My inside trouser leg measurement, and it's full. It's the only thing this card doesn't ask! I'll give you the card when I'm ready."

" 'ere…" she was saying as he left her office. It was the last sound that was exchanged between them during her time as PA to the Director.

*   *   *

The wide corridor floor echoed to his footstep as he made his way to the numbered room which was to be his office for the next three years. It was a six man office, constructed on a false raised floor over the never-to-be-opened Whitehall entrance to the building, styled in the civil service way as the 'The Old War Office' presumably to balance 'The Old Admiralty' across the road. Conceivably, the door was kept closed to keep out the grime of London — or possibly the riff-raff of London on Remembrance Sundays and coronations. The office view, through circular architectural feature windows, would have been fantastic, looking down into Horse Guards and with a view along Whitehall, but the windows had not been cleaned since the Luftwaffe blitz ended twenty six years previously. Not even pigeons roosted on the ledges outside these windows. Opaque was a good description of the glass which was to have special significance in Piers's second year in office.

The desks were arranged with one pair face to face and another clutch of four, two pairs both sides and face to face. A line of four tall office steel cupboards and four office filing cabinets lined the inner wall, away from the windows; each two-drawer table had a chair and a telephone and nothing else. An inner door led to the wing commander's office. The raised wooden floor echoed to every footfall; not for officers of mere squadron leader rank was the luxury of an office carpet.

The nearest face spoke. "Hi, we'll do the introductions in a moment. Leave your briefcase… oh… you haven't got one… on that desk… it's yours anyway… and go say hello to the wing co. You won't need your towel or soap in there. Honest! Then we'll have a chat. Can I get you a coffee… milk and sugar?"

Piers was in with the 'wing co', who was in charge of the group of six engineering squadron leaders, for half an hour. He would not remember a word of the interview only that he had another card to fill in with identical details to Hermione's. Piers thought it wise not to comment.

The mug on his desk, sitting on a sheet of folded paper in lieu of a coaster, had gone cold in spite of the beer coaster thoughtfully placed on top. Piers noticed the coaster advertised German beer. The nearest face began to introduce himself and the office colleagues.

"It's different here to anywhere you've served. Forget rank, say 'sir' if you fancy it, 'ma'am' if needs be and never expect anyone to remember your name. Wise tip from the oft-bitten: don't call a ma'am 'sir', you'll get rocks especially if she's got an air rank. That's your desk, don't worry about the cold 'wet', we'll throw it away in a minute and get you a hot brew. First, you're 46f, Tech Pol 46f(RAF) and that's your phone. You get a quarter use of the office electronic calculator... oh, don't worry if you've never seen one before; it adds numbers for you, honest... a good gadget."

Piers was confused and it must have showed.

Nearest face started again, "Don't sit down for a moment. Let's go round the office; standard MOD drill. You won't remember their names, but they'll remember yours."

He turned across the room encouraging Piers to follow. "Right..."

'There's that magic RAF magical incantation again...' thought Piers., 'it's the Air Force way...'

"This is:

46a Charles Sambrook." A hand was proffered across a welcoming smile.

46b Barry Cripps." He stood, shook hands and silently mouthed welcome, then sat.

46c Freddie Muldoon, he does bombs and guns." A wave because he could not reach to shake hands.

46d Paddy Halls. He leads the travelling teams." Squadron Leader Halls was going through the motions of trying to stand, thinking better of the exercise and collapsing again onto his chair.

"Hello, I'm Paddy. It gets better..." There was a nod and a grin behind his promise.

Piers did not feel reassured by this remark.

"I'm 46e Paul Dew. Long in the tooth, retired squadron leader, radars." Again a handshake from nearest face who now had a real name.

"And you are?" nearest face clearly expected an answer.

"Hi Paul, everyone. My name is Piers Ploughman — OK, let's have all the jokes about my name now — and I'm an electrical engineer, ex-cadet. I've just escaped from Headquarters Strike Command."

A remark about *the contraceptive on the penis of progress* broke the ice. The office staff gathered around Piers to make him feel welcome, aided by the *leader of the travellers'* suggestion, "The Dog and Whistle for lunch. In 15 minutes, chaps!"

The staff started to clear their desks when Paddy Halls said, "Come on, Piers, there's one more to meet, then Paul will show you where you use your towel and soap. They'll be safe enough on your desk."

In the next room sat Doris Bunn. The passage of time had not treated Doris kindly. Piers thanked heaven he had not used the name in front of Hermione *what's-her-name.* Paddy did the introduction.

"This, Doris, is Squadron Leader Piers Ploughman. He's come to be 46f. He'll make your life even worse and give you lots more to complain about. Piers, this is Miss Doris Bunn, a registry administrator of enormous experience who you cross at your peril. She is a spinster of the realm for who the Civil Service was invented when wee Samuel was a twinkle in Mrs Pepys's eye. She files, mails and does wonders with the photocopier. She is never here when we're in, except today so she can check you out, and she's always in the office when we're on the road so we can't bother her with paper. Doris has been with the Air Force Department since Laurence did Arabia and will still be here when the Brits send a cow over the moon. If you are nice to her, and bring her digestive biscuits on Leap Day, she'll make you tea and change your towel once a fortnight. Anything I've missed, Doris?"

"Yes. My hours are 6:30 to 3:30 Monday to Friday and noon on Fridays." Piers placed her accent, accurately, as just west of the Becton water treatment outfall which drains London into the Essex side of the Thames. "And I don't want no nonsense with classified mail, neither. Either I do it proper or you'll be seeing the Deputy Director pretty quick."

"Doris is a treasure, so cultivate her wisely, young man. Now we have an appointment with a frothy pint. You won't need an umbrella, it's not raining." Paddy led Piers away to collect the others.

"Come on, guys, we're wasting valuable drinking time…"

As they climbed down the three storeys' staircase, marble stairs of course with 15 feet tall oil portraits of long forgotten generals decorating the walls, Paul Dew questioned Piers, "Are you a raincoat or a brolley man?" The significance of this strange question did not become apparent to Piers until the first day it rained while he was moving between Ministry buildings — you were one or the other, but never both.

One persistent thought kept worrying Piers: Henlow cadetship hadn't adequately prepared him for the two civil service females to which he had been exposed this morning. How many more varieties were there?

*   *   *

The *Dog and Whistle* had been a watering hole for military officers perhaps since Oliver Cromwell hung up his helmet and might have been redecorated once since. However, to RAF officers doing their time in the Old War Office Building, its beer was legendary and their lunchtime snacks were exceptionally good value. Today the five stalwarts chose 'half a French stick with kidneys and bacon'. Piers made it six.

"I suggest we stick to single pints today," advised Paddy Halls. "It's Monday."

It was obvious he was not concentrating on beer; four legs mounted on Everest challenging heels had come into the bar, their surmounting skirts about the depth of a generous belt. The era of the miniskirt was with London and the menfolk of the metropolis were frequently to be seen assessing how much further up the thigh these fashion items might go.

Mature Paul Dew snapped his fingers in front of Paddy's gaze. "I say, old lad, if your jaw drops any further your beer won't go down the right hole."

"Jeez. It didn't oughta be allowed," Piers smiled at the exchange between his two new colleagues. He didn't know it then but this was the first such sighting of many to come. There would be hundreds of attractive diversions in the three years ahead, not least the 'burn the bra' campaign, but usually the proponents didn't hold a candle to the displays of lower limbs in the Whitehall pubs.

"There's no harm in looking at the menu, Paul," commented Paddy in justification. "Two to one that there'll be two more like that before we finish our pints."

"That's not very good odds, old lad."

"I'm not interested in odds. I want to know what's happened to the panty line? Do you think they're not wearing any? We need a larger statistical sample. There you are. I win…"

229

*　　　*　　　*

In the months ahead, Piers and Helen found time to purchase their first home together. It meant a longer commuting journey and a need for a second car for Piers, but their money just about stretched. Piers's job required travelling throughout the RAF's global footprint. Most of the flying stations in UK and overseas were visited on manning establishment assessments and, because he was basically an electrical engineer, he was co-opted to assist Paul Dew on his inspections of radar sites and communications facilities in the UK. Piers was grateful for the excuse to be a traveller, to escape from the Whitehall pressure of the long-lasting three-day working week, from Essex's own Doris Bunn and from the power cuts from which even Whitehall was not immune. The visits had the secondary advantage that it broadened Piers's experience of the RAF maintenance work which must surely assist with career development in due course. It was now when even Whitehall suffered power rationing that the absence of light through the windows really took effect; afternoons were shortened by at least 30 minutes and there was the spectre of office workers trying to keep their desks alive by wearing greatcoats and gloves, often working by candlelight in the office.

In very late November 1973, Paul and Piers had to visit the Maldives equatorial island of RAF Gan and then go on to Hong Kong. This was a two week excursion partly extended by the need to time their visits to the RAF's transport VC-10 schedule to allow for inclusion of facilities in Hong Kong in their review programme. Piers and Paul landed at a cold RAF Brize Norton in the middle of the night — that 02:00 arrival again. Customs formalities seemed unnecessarily protracted that night. Neither had anything to declare, but it was not until after five in the morning that they were in their separate cars pulling away from the on-station car park. Piers rued the cheap car he used, leaving the comfortable vehicle for Helen. The frost was reluctant to clear and the heater was all but ineffective.

Two hours later, "Hello, darling, I'm home. Oh, whatever is the matter? Are you sick? Is Michael OK?

"He's fine. Happy birthday, love. There are birthday cards on the mantelpiece for the day you were away. Put the kettle on for a cuppa, dearest, and make yourself a coffee. I've got some news."

"It's not your mother coming…"

"No, darling, nothing like that. This is morning sickness…"

"I told you not to eat fresh tuna…" adding a teaspoon of sugar to his coffee.

"Morning sickness is what mums-to-be have when they're going to be mums."

"Narh! It isn't possible… all those checks… adoption… it's a mistake."

"No mistake, dearest. The doctor says it is a little early to be one hundred per cent, but it seems quite likely. You're going to be a dad again."

"Blimey. Bugger the coffee. I need a brandy. It's a mistake … all those checks… adoption… it isn't possible. You're kidding!" This was an excuse for a big hug especially as he'd travelled halfway round the world.

Helen smiled at his reaction. She nodded. She had felt much the same when the doctor confirmed to her what she already suspected. She nodded at her husband, "July, mid July. Michael will be four. We can't tell Mother until we're sure, but I know. Yes, we're kidding. We're going to have a baby. Wheee!"

The kiss was a little prickly; Piers hadn't shaved since the staging stop in Bahrain yesterday afternoon.

*　　　*　　　*

The desk telephone rang at noon on Helen's birthday. Piers wanted to get home on time tonight, perhaps they could pop out to the local pub for chicken in the basket. A single Valentine's Card on a desk in the room indicated the date, the 14th February 1974. Piers was up to his eyes in statistics for a project he was doing. There were potential savings of one million pounds a year if the reorganisation of flight line trade specialisations could be made. Piers picked up his handset.

"Squadron Leader Ploughman."

The distant voice gave his name as Squadron Leader *Stoney* Rockingham, who Piers did not then know. "Could you come over to Main Building this afternoon? I really would like to see you in my office this afternoon."

This was decidedly unusual. One squadron leader simply didn't summon another squadron leader. If he wanted to talk, face to face, then he would make the journey.

231

"Look, I'm working on the concluding phase of a million pound work method study concerning efficient use of RAF engineering tradesmen in aircraft maintenance and I can ill afford the time to go anywhere at the moment." The interruption was annoying, especially as he'd sacrificed a pub lunch to make a prompt getaway.

The wing commander said he did not know what it was all about, but was disinclined to interfere. So Piers went to the next building along Whitehall, the former Air Ministry and now known as MOD Main Building, to find out. The briefing he received was to change his life.

"Do you remember, while you were in Changi, in 1967, your wing commander gave you a career advice interview during the wash up to your annual confidential report? Something along the lines of: 'We seem to think that you should state a posting preference for firstly Technical Intelligence and secondly for Signals Intelligence'."

"I guess he did. I didn't give it too much thought at the time." Piers acknowledged the accuracy of his host's surmise.

"Well he knew what he was talking about. He had completed a tour, in MOD, in Technical Intelligence. He wouldn't have talked about it because he was sworn to secrecy! So even if you had asked, you wouldn't have left with any idea of what those disciplines actually did… err… do."

"You seem to be remarkably well informed about my confidential reports…"

"You seem to have followed his advice. Good thinking, the RAF likes consistency even when it's wrong. Oh, forget I said that? I understand that for the next three years you put the same options for posting choices…"

"I'm a busy bloke, *Rocky*, say what you've got to say, then I'll clear out."

"I'd like you to have a few minutes with my colleague who will tell you the rules of this office and then we can speak rather more freely. The new baby is coming on alright, I hope. It's all in a good cause, I promise."

'Now how the hell did *Rocky* know about that? I've not even told my career desk officer at Barnwood… yet! What is all this cloak and dagger stuff about? Do I really want to know?' Piers was being escorted to the next room where the office door closed with a reassuring firmness.

Three hours later, now sworn to secrecy so that he could not tell Helen, or his wing commander, or his office colleagues, what it was about, Piers was indoctrinated into the special security that surrounded GCHQ and MOD in the field of Signals Intelligence (SIGINT) and was warned of a posting to Ayios Nikolaos near Famagusta, Cyprus in mid-May 1974. This was an activity not even hinted at during his cadetship or the intervening 15 years since.

Three months later, with the million pound project handed to others to complete, Piers with Helen now some 6 months pregnant and Michael, aged 4 years, flew out of RAF Brize Norton at 02:00 on the 14th May 1974, aboard an RAF VC-10 trooper en-route for the RAF Akrotiri, Cyprus airfield and the sun. Piers's career was going to join an Army Royal Signals regiment at the eastern end of the island.

Chapter 30
1974 ~ A Very Gentle Coup

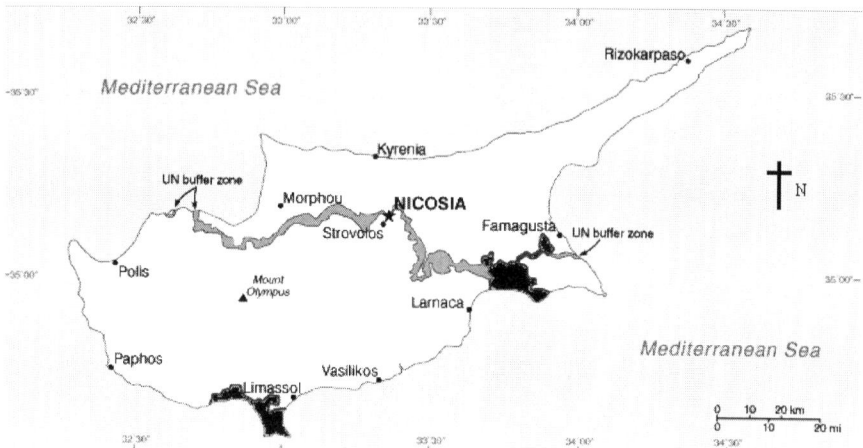

Map of Cyprus showing Western and Eastern Sovereign Base Areas and showing the UN Buffer Zone established in 1974 between the Turkish and Greek Cypriot controlled areas
(There is no political significance implied by this simple map)

Famagusta was a sleepy harbour town protected by a significant fort. In May 1974, the town was divided between two ethnic groups: the Turkish Cypriots and the Greek Cypriots who had been murderously at each others' throats since before Richard the Lionheart, in 1191, married his fiancée Berengaria close to Limassol. They had previously met only once, years before their wedding. Into the enduring Cypriot tribal divisions stepped colonial Britain with an eye to control the eastern Mediterranean and the Middle East region not least because of the Suez Canal. By 1974, the United Nations had deployed a significant buffer force to keep the warring factions apart; Cyprus was effectively governed by Greek Cypriot under the presidency of Archbishop Makarios. Famagusta had developed as a major tourist resort for the sun-seekers of Europe with multiple high-rise, beach front hotels facing directly onto the near tideless, golden sand coastline. Meanwhile, under the British Commonwealth umbrella and with one eye to NATO, a substantial British military presence was constructed addressing the soft underbelly

234

of the Russian dominated Warsaw Pact and the political instability of the region.

Within this English speaking, prime holiday resort of Famagusta, the British Army had rented several hundred properties as hirings for the families of the three armed services and a couple of hundred civil servants who worked at Ayios Nikolaos, a communication facility set some four miles inland from the coast. Piers was allocated a flat just 100 yards from the glorious beach and about one mile from the town centre where the NAFFI, banks and local shops were set. Their spacious three-bedroom, furnished flat was three storeys above street level, without a lift, and enjoyed the privations of the general community rationing of domestic water supply for three hours every third day and an unreliable electricity supply with which to pump it. Already, in May, the temperature approached 95°F by day, the upper 70s by night. It hadn't rained since March and probably wouldn't until September.

Selecting a motor car was encouraged by the multiple salesmen offering their wares. 'They probably knew about my posting before I did,' thought Piers. 'A motor cycle would save commuting costs and leave the car for Helen and Michael. I must do something about home help, too. Helen is going to have problems in this heat.'

Piers and Helen settled into regimental social life, not particularly exciting, but it was their way of greeting a 'blue job' stranger who was nicknamed 'crab' because of the colour of his winter uniform shirt. Naturally, for Piers, the summer uniform was tropical weight khaki drill, KD for short, rather than air force blue, but that made no difference. RAF KD was actually stone grey, but what was in a name anyway?

Sleeping was an issue. In the absence of air-conditioning, bedroom windows were left open. A nightly treat was the passage of the 'honey waggon' clearing sewage from the hotels because the pipes had not been connected to the disposal system. Just what happened to the 10,000 visitors' waste was something Piers never did find out.

Helen's sister, Kitty, came out to see Helen's progress at the beginning of July. Both enjoyed sightseeing, especially in the north of the island. All too soon, Kitty had to return home and the toll of the heat meant that Helen needed bed rest ahead of her delivery. So it was decided that she should go into the British Military Hospital, meaning Army run, at Dhekelia to see out her final seven days to term. The RAF Hospital was

70 miles away at RAF Akrotiri. The baby was due on Sunday 14th July. Piers had arranged leave, to look after Michael and to be at home for Helen and new baby 'Jacob' whose gender had not been determined.

But there were other events which would intervene.

*   *   *

Between 15 July and 15 August 1974, Piers maintained a diary which he intended would form the basis of letting the folks at home know the family were OK. They were sure to be worried, he thought. He had reckoned without mail censorship and, more important, the total severance of all non-military communications with UK.

Reflections on a Coup — Cyprus Monday 15 July 1974

I am sitting here on a third storey balcony in Famagusta on the day that Greek officers of the Cyprus National Guard have claimed to have deposed President Makarios in Nicosia. It is reported that the Presidential Palace in Nicosia is under siege by 10 Tanks and the coup group have nominated their own President (name Samson), a former EOKA B gunman implicated in several murders in the late 1950s.

We are closer than 100 yards from the beach and can see the Mediterranean between the 12 storey hotel blocks lining the sand. The time is dusk, 19:15 hrs, and the island is subject to curfew until dawn. There is nothing to do but listen to the news from British Forces Broadcasting Service (BFBS) and write down the events of the day.

Helen, fully 9½ months pregnant, is lodged in the maternity ward at British Military Hospital Dhekelia. The curfew prevents my going to see her if the baby comes into the world tonight. Having planned ahead, we have the fridge stocked to the icebox so at least Michael and I won't starve.

Throughout the day, Famagusta has been quietening down. At 10:00, the coup news first broke on the BBC and the town went mad — at least the traffic did. At 11:00, three explosions and some 20 seconds of automatic gunfire were heard from the town one mile away.

Since noon the town has become a ghost town. A casual holiday maker either in a car or on foot moves away from the beach without incident. In the distance, an occasional crump indicates a bomb or a short burst of gunfire may be heard. During the afternoon, three separate ambulances have passed by.

The 18:00 BBC News really gave no more details. Evidently Nicosia and Limassol are having more troubles than we are seeing at this end of the island. The News said that there had been heavy fighting in Famagusta, but they must have been using bows and arrows or swords from the visual and audible evidence available to this witness. The Turkish Armed Forces are at alert; that could be ominous for us because of Famagusta port.

Now the daylight has gone; it is reasonably quiet. The curfew seems to be effective and the only noise to be heard are the sounds of radios, alcohol fuelled hotel balcony parties or TV tuned to Beirut; and the exhaust noise from the air conditioning plants in the major Hotels. The main street in Famagusta is deserted (ie John Kennedy Street) where I can see it. There is a comfortable breeze to lessen the effects of the evening temperature of 85 degrees.

The maid has not showed up today. Michael is comfortably asleep, the effective embargo on UK personnel moving meant that we were confined to the flat since 11:00 this morning. I went out at that time to fill the car's petrol tank as a precaution against future trouble. Michael spent the afternoon with the baby bath full of water — at least it started full, but soon spilled over the balcony. I had to be especially careful that he kept his head beneath the parapet on the balcony where he was playing because there were armed militia roving the streets in commandeered taxis. Incidentally, the spillage fell two floors to where the Regiment's dentist, his blousey wife and their teenage children were becoming progressively, and noisily, more drunk.

It is now 20:10, a girl has just screamed, but that could have been something on TV. Two bursts (10 shots each) have just sounded in town. A loud speaker can be heard in the distance, possibly the civilian police announcing the curfew. It is incomprehensible to me. An exchange of automatic gunfire (distant) has been heard as I write. The situation remains confused; the

International (Nicosia) airport is closed and telephone links off island are cut. What is happening around us comes from the BBC and frankly it can only be subjective analysis of rumour since they have no means of getting their news copy off the island. We will probably have to wait for the Sunday Times insight report to find out what is happening on our own front door. This being Monday...

And now it is time for a second brandy sour, soon a shower and off to bed. It could be the first good night's sleep since we arrived: the traffic won't keep us awake tonight!

Part 2: 19 July 1974

I am lying in bed in the British Military Hospital Dhekelia with a sore right hand and a left leg in plaster; more of that in a moment. The previous part of this writing finished at 21.15 hrs on 15 July, with Michael tucked up safely in bed. I finished my second brandy and went to bed confident of a good night's sleep.

Events changed when, at 22:25 hours, Major Geoffrey Crowe, the Senior Communication Operations Officer and a colleague in the Ops Bureau of the Regiment, rang to say that the Colonel thought it would be a good idea to go in for day duty on 16 July as this would relieve the two Operations Bureau Officers (the other being Mr Peter Goodfellow). They could then cover the night shift whilst I looked after Michael. It seemed the best plan and in effect I understood that I was being recalled off leave, but that the special circumstance of Helen being in hospital was being taken into account. Only military transport was permitted, I was to use the shift bus. So far so good.

At 07:15, the convoy appeared from an unexpected direction and was obviously looking for me. Knowing it was due to stop at the pickup point 200 yards away, at 'Pop's Kiosk' on the Famagusta beach, I started to walk after it. Paused it may have, but stop it certainly did not; the leading coach of three began to move away, whilst I was still at least 100 yards away. So I started to run shouting and waving at the last vehicle which was a Landrover. I don't know exactly what happened next, but I think I missed the kerb or put my foot into some soft sand and went forward flat on my face.

I grazed my left knee, both palms of my hands, right elbow and my left leg felt about 1 inch shorter than my right leg. However, the Landrover saw me coming and waited while I picked myself up and walked the distance to the vehicle to climb into the back. It turned out that my haste was justified: the drivers were under strict instructions to maintain tight convoy and they were not to wait for anyone. I saw three civilian operators of the Regiment left behind because they did not make the necessary dash to join the convoy from where they had been waiting. I am sure there were others.

We arrived at Ayios Nikolaos at 08:05. I used the Landrover to carry me up to sick quarters to get my hands cleaned up. For the first time, I realised something was wrong with my left leg, because it would not take any weight. 10 minutes later, the doctor (Captain Tom Holliday) had diagnosed a ruptured Achilles' tendon and that I had to go to hospital at Dhekelia 14 miles away for it to be fixed.

For the record, it is worth recording that although we spent 40 minutes in convoy driving around the outskirts of Famagusta, there was no sign whatsoever of any damage to buildings or vehicles. Perhaps a dozen or so tourists were making their way to the beach in swimming costumes. Such Cypriots as were about were staying close to home. All the shops were shut. However, we did not go into Famagusta town centre or near the Turkish Cypriot port areas.

At 09:05, I was in an ambulance and, by 10:00, I was in bed in Ward 2, BMH Dhekelia being told that I was to have an operation to fix the tendon and that my leg would have to be set in plaster. The ward sister (bloody Army! did not recognise or respect rank!) decided that Helen had to be told, contrary to my vehemently expressed wish. Helen came down from Ward 8, cried a bit, worried about Michael and then went off about the baby she was carrying.

The Achilles' tendon operation started at 14:00 and I woke at 17:30 with my left leg in plaster. Naturally, I braved the pain as befits an ex-cadet. Here I have remained ever since, confined to bed and bedpans, for 10 days. As at the time of writing, 14:00 hrs 19 July, Helen still has not done her thing and 'Jacob' remains in mummy's pouch.

Map of Cyprus Eastern Sovereign Base Area, in 1974, centred on Dhekelia where the British Military Hospital was situated, showing the 14 mile umbilical road to Ayios Nikolaos and the 4 further miles to Famagusta. Piers's flat in Famagusta is located. The UN Buffer Zones were negotiated after the events recounted in this book.

(There no political significance implied by this simple map)

Chapter 31
Unto Us A Girl Is Born

Makarios escaped from Nicosia by the skin of his black cape and hightailed it to Paphos. He was airlifted to the Western Sovereign Base Area whence the RAF flew him out to Malta and then to UK. Meanwhile, there were BBC reports that Turkish Armed Forces were massing in Southern Turkey and that some element of the Turkish Navy had sailed. The BBC reported that *HMS Hermes*, with 900 commandos, and *HMS Devonshire* were sailing for the Eastern Mediterranean. A BMH nurse said that a US carrier and support vessels had anchored off Larnaca. Although Larnaca Bay was visible from his room, Piers could see no sign of the fleet.

Piers was moved, without explanation, from his officers' single room to the open ward. A rumour circulated that the Russians had put a boat in the area. Left to monitor BBC and BFBS broadcasts as his sole source of information, Piers interpreted that the UK forces were coming up to alert, in case of trouble.

'All I can do is lie here, sweat it out and wait. I find it most unsatisfactory. And now it looks as if I am going lose that nail off my writing hand. But I will grin and bear it… I want to write my diary for 'Jacob'.'

But Piers's thoughts were not confined to his plight.

'And what about my poor Helen? After that initial shock of finding me in hospital and realising that Michael is 20 miles away, Helen has settled into the business of 'Jacob'. They won't let me go to see her and she can't come down to see me. She must be frantic! Bloody doctors! Bloody Army doctors! Jacob does not want to enter this world though. Sensible chap…'

Part 3: 20 July 1974

Daily inspection and one attempt at inducement on 18 July produced nothing but a sore arm for Helen. Today, she too has to lie in bed in Ward 8 and wait. So, at 15.00 on 19 July 1974, here endeth the lesson. This reminds me that I was visited by the Regiment's Padre (Peter Plumber). He remarked that he had driven round the town of

Famagusta, even in areas where the convoys do not; there was no evidence of damage to property or vehicles, in fact the only military feature was one ancient tank which would probably be more dangerous to fire than to put on display.

On 20 July at 05:00, Turkish Forces landed at Kyrenia and Turkish aircraft flew over Nicosia. Some fighting was heard in Nicosia on the Greek/Turkish border. Cyprus radio has announced a mobilisation. Turkey has announced that the ports of Larnaca and Limassol will remain open to British shipping. Good news as the RN has ships heading this way from Malta.

At 09:00, BFBS announced the Commander British Forces Near East (CBFNE) has decided that UK families should withdraw from hirings into the Sovereign Bases for their own safety and confirmed that Turkish naval forces are anchored off Kyrenia.

11:00, I was allowed to use a wheelchair for one hour. Big deal. Not allowed to visit Ward 8. Bloody Army doctors, again!

13:00, BBC News indicates situation getting worse. Greece is mobilising her armed forces. The Russians have alerted their 7th Airborne Division and military law has been declared in coastal areas of Turkey.

13:15, It is obvious that Limassol (forty miles along the coast) is having a hard time. The (RAF?) Marine Craft Unit near the port has had to be vacated. Evacuation of British families from Limassol into the Western Sovereign Base Area (Episkopi) has begun.

16:00, One of the obstetricians looked in to say that Helen was having complications with the first stage of labour and that a caesarian delivery might be necessary. So at 16:30 it was decided to go ahead with a caesarian section. They only bothered to tell me because I had to sign the consent form.

17:35, I was told that we had a daughter and Helen and baby were doing OK. Simultaneously, BFBS went off — ie the hospital relay headphones were dead, so no more news from that source! Welcome to the madhouse Jacob(ette).

18:00, I could see the greek Cyprioy National Guard Camp at the west end of Larnaca burning (6 miles across the bay and only 2 miles from the Shell Oil refinery) and there had been the sound of distant heavy gunfire for about 90 minutes since. At about that time, an RN

Wessex flew into the adjacent hospital helipad indicating that HMS Hermes has arrived.

Piers's diary omits the vital detail that his right hand was caught in the Famagusta flat's door jam on the night of his recall to duty. The middle finger of his right hand was crushed with significant bruising to the nail. Writing his diary was not easy. Nevertheless, the diary continues:

Part 4: 21 July 1974

News is very difficult to come by as BFBS is off the hospital network. No-one has a radio.

Apparently, Nicosia is really being hammered by both sides. We hear that a major convoy of private cars has arrived at Dhekelia from Famagusta and Ayios Nikolaos and I hope that Michael is in it — no positive news as at 11:25. I have heard no news of Helen and I am reluctant to bother staff because the hospital is now accepting casualties. HMS Hermes appeared off shore about 09:30 and since then her Wessex helicopters have been ferrying things to a site near to the hospital.

News at 11:55 that Michael, with our neighbour, are somewhere in the Dhekelia Garrison so that is one worry off my mind. The Ward Nurse says I cannot go to see Helen because there are many local refugee pregnancies coming into the maternity ward and I would probably get in the way. However, at 15:30, I was allowed to see Helen and the new one; both look super though Helen looks a bit tired. So now the family are four. Shortly afterwards, I heard that Michael has been billeted at an officer's married quarter here at Dhekelia with a padre and another family with young children evacuated from Nicosia.

It is reported that a British Army convoy got through to Nicosia and evacuated 4000 British and other personnel in a convoy of 1000 cars. My news is that I have now had 3 hours in a wheelchair and can use the normal toilets and my life is beginning to return to normal. Still need painkillers for my leg though. And all this writing... right middle finger nail is now all blue... so is my language...

Part 5: 22 July 1974

The British Under Secretary of State for Air has come to Cyprus to see for himself to report back to UK. He broadcast last night to say that he was very satisfied with our forces' efforts to protect UK and other civilians during present troubles. He would say that, wouldn't he? He didn't get to Dhekelia!

10:15, The Padre, who lives in Blenheim Village, Dhekelia looked into say that Michael was OK.

Dhekelia is very crowded. The 4000 civilians from Nicosia had to spend the night on the sports field in the open air. Of course it has not rained for 6 weeks and the minimum temperature at night drops to 75°F. Daytime temperature reaches 95-100°F in the shade so they are going to be hot in the sun. There is only a very limited beach in the Sovereign Base Area and I expect the police would wish to keep the seaside clear for the Royal Navy to do their thing.

11:00, The first British casualty (of course I don't count in the total) was a 10 year old son of a signalman at the Regiment who was hit by a ricochet bullet while in a British Army coach en-route from Famagusta to Dhekelia.

14:00, CBFNE has broadcast to deny rumours that Hermes and other ships are involved in the conflict. They are only here to protect the seas. The word is that the RAF is flying 1000 civilian holiday makers per day back to UK.

My leg is not comfortable, but they give me a couple of pills every so often which makes it bearable. Boredom is the big problem plus a shortage of cigarettes.

14:15, Stella Crowe has done an excellent job of getting me some cigarettes. Major Martyn Spencer looked in to say 'Hello'.

15:45, Have spent an hour with Philippa and Helen. She is super and I can see Dad Ploughman in her facial expressions — Helen as well; looking forward to seeing Michael again.

16:00, Following dissatisfaction with the Greek handling of their affairs in Cyprus, there are reports of changes in the military government in Athens.

Part 6: 24 July 1974

The United Nations contingent had taken a hammering in Nicosia during the evening; we had some of the badly wounded Canadians in here. The feeling is that their wounds are consistent with aimed fire rather than ricochets — particularly the wounds sustained by one senior officer who was shot twice in the back. The political scene is roughly this:

(1) Greece now has civilian PM and there is a possibility that Constantine may get his throne back. The military have definitely been deposed.
(2) Kithrios as Cyprus President seems friendly to Turkish Cypriot and a moderate. It augers well for the future.
(3) Turkey is satisfied with present situation.
(4) Planned conference of relevant countries in Geneva.
(5) The evacuation of Brits from North Cyprus went without any interference from the air. The refugees are being taken to Akrotiri.

My leg is still uncomfortable especially when I have to move about; I use a wheelchair with a foot rest. This is far from satisfactory, but my gut is not operating as its usual self daily, probably because we get little fruit. The doctor has said I have to wait another two days before they'll change the first plaster for my first walking plaster. Heard that Michael is being very good. Helen is OK today, tired but mending. I could only see Philippa's head through protection glass.

Part 7: 25 July 1974

Helen is very distressed at prospects for the future. The combined worries of problems of new babe, Michael with all the problems of a 4 year old, together with no information on whether family would be together or perhaps evacuated to UK plus my leg made visiting time very tearful. I arranged for the padre, in whose house Michael is billeted, to see Helen. The situation is worse because no-one will bring Michael in to see her and the Regiment's officers' wives are ignoring her.

Part 8: 26 July 1974

My plaster was changed, but was not a high point because I am confined to bed for 24 hours for the plaster to dry.

Part 9: 27 July 1974

Much to my surprise, I was allowed out of bed and told I could return to the Regiment for duty on crutches. Further plaster work in 3 weeks and perhaps back to normal in 6 weeks. First problem: my car is in Famugusta 16 miles away, and second problem: I can't drive with my clutch foot in plaster anyway!

I scrounged a lift back to Ayios Nikolaos at midday (with a major who had come to the BMH for resupply of condoms... Army priorities! and have arranged to stay with Stella and Geoffrey Crowe. I saw Helen and Philippa before leaving hospital — she is doing fine, put on 2 ozs. Helen's stitches come out on 30 July. No news yet of future location of family with Famagusta closed.

Part 10: 5 August 1974

And now it is time to perhaps conclude this record of three eventful weeks. The last was written on 27 July and 10 days have elapsed which are worth recording. Work enveloped me in its own way. Stella and Geoffrey Crowe offered this poor cripple a bed. Rations to be strictly 'compo' (ie Army emergency) and I accept the fact that the house stairs are impossible to manage on crutches so I elected to sleep on the lounge floor. On 29th, an officer of the Regiment took me over to see Helen and the children in their various locations in Dhekelia. The children looked well if rather plump. Helen looks well and could be well enough to leave hospital tomorrow.

On 30 July, the family was reunited and we are lodged as a family unit in an officers' married quarter (one of five) at Ayios Nikolaos. We are strictly lodgers and frankly are accepted, but hardly made welcome in the difficult days before going back to the flat in Famagusta. Today a ceasefire was signed at Geneva, but it is surely tenuous and no-one sees any stability behind the signatures. The Turkish Army continue to expand their foothold around Kyrenia. The Greek Cypriot National Guard are trigger happy and they surround many Turkish Cypriot communities, including Famagusta old city, holding them in virtual siege breached only by UN patrols acting under humanitarian motives.

We returned to our flat on 1 Aug. The fridge, undisturbed for 2 weeks, and without electrical power in the 100 degrees heat, is a smell for sore noses and we settled in. Philippa is doing well and I think Michael is pleased to be home in his own environment. Mail from the UK is beginning to flow again and the news about Philippa has clearly got through. Helen looks much better and already has her figure back. I have trouble with the three storeys worth of stairs: 5 falls in 9 transits so far with my peg leg and crutches on marble tiles going all ways at once. I have to go to and from to work on the shift bus because I cannot drive the car or ride the motor scooter. Both survived the air raids unscathed. The block of flats suffered, some glass was damaged, but was generally OK. Not looted. Some of the town blocks are badly damaged from the Turkish Air Force bombs and strafing and there is considerable damage to the town centre near Famagusta hospital which suffered direct hits.

Now its 21.00 on 5 August 1974, and the last three weeks seem a bit unreal. We have a new baby and plastered leg to prove they really happened. There are some memories of happier times. We feel we could have been given a bit more help in our present situation. Perhaps it's expecting too much in the present turmoil. I'm too tired to continue except to record that the bustling August holiday crowd is literally non-existent. The British families based at Ayios Nikolaos are back in town and not 100 percent welcome by the locals either. Life outside is returning to a semblance of normality, but what does the future hold in store for us, I wonder?????

Piers's contemporaneous record finishes at that point, but his documented story had quite a way to run yet...

Before I move along from that first evacuation from Famagusta, I should record what I understand happened to Michael. On the morning of 16 July, I duly delivered him to our top floor neighbour who had her own children out from boarding school. Naturally our Michael was not keen to be left, but he was taken to the balcony to see me get on the bus. Michael saw me fall — he was four years old and realised that his father was hurt. They were to stay confined in the upstairs flat, under curfew, for 4 more days — Michael without his parents. I now know that Michael witnessed Turkish Air Force jets bomb the adjacent seaside hotels where the Greeks had set up firing points. This must have been terrifying at a distance of 500 yards. The bombs usually did not explode, one was found in a hotel bed having gone through three floors.

Dhekelia must have been equally straining, Michael was always hyper-active and longed for the fresh air. He was not taken to see his mother or new sister at any time during Helen's hospital stay — or me either. At the impressionable age of 4½ years, we are concerned that the seeds of future trouble might have been sown at that time.

When Helen left BMH, she was accommodated with the children for two days in a Dhekelia married quarter, 20 people in one house. Every quarter was the same. The news that we were to be allowed back into Famagusta was a great relief to look forward to some semblance of normal living. On 1 August, on crutches, I rendezvoused with Helen plus two in a tin storage hangar at 15:00 at Ayios Nikolaos. Sitting on wooden crates, without water or any other liquid, all the other evacuee families were there waiting transport into town. The conditions were awful, Helen trying to protect her tummy while carrying the baby, Michael finding it difficult to be good, and me on crutches. The temperature must have been over 110°F in the mid summer afternoon sunshine.

It hurt when the colonel came up to us and virtually reprimanded us for remarking on the difficult conditions, "It's the same for everybody," he said, which manifestly it was not. Only the SSAFA sister recognised Helen's plight and offered to hold Philippa while we waited for the coach to move off to Famagusta. I have no memory of how we managed to get into the flat, the awful fridge, the heat of the late afternoon. I do remember one kindness when an Army Captain, who worked for me and whose wife had already left Cyprus in anticipation of a UK posting to Northern Ireland, offered to go to the Famagusta NAFFI for essential supplies.

Thus we came to be in Famagusta when the uneasy ceasefire failed and it became obvious that the Turkish Army wanted to relieve their beleaguered colleagues in the Famagusta walled city. I was called into work, at 07:00 on Wednesday 14 Aug 1974, expecting to go home that lunchtime, or at least by 16.00 to go to the NAAFI with Helen. It was not to be.

Chapter 32
1974 ~ Family Exodus

On 14th August 1974, Piers was telephoned to be on the Regiment's first shift bus convoy circulating Famagusta accommodation at 06:15. The colonel wanted all officers in the Regiment's conference room, in Ayios Nikolaos, at 07:00. A curfew was called, Piers would not be home that night, and the British were putting themselves on alert. 'Bring spare uniform…' The only luxury permitted in the circumstances, in common with 450 other heads of family, was that he spoke briefly to Helen on the phone. He told her to pack the minimum of kit and be ready to drive out when told. The next day, the 15th, she was told to drive into Dhekelia. Helen later described the sight, all the British wives driving down a deserted road, their cars three abreast on the open tarmac. Inside the Regiment, we knew that the Gurkhas had created a '*corridor sanitair*', a ¼ mile wide ribbon along the road, and the ladies did not see anyone at all on their journey. Once again, Helen with the children came to be in someone else's married quarter, but this time expecting to be moved on to RAF Akrotiri and thence UK.

Diary continued on 17 Aug 74, written in the Regiment's compound:

By noon 15 Aug, there were two Turkish armoured divisions five miles away. Our compound was surrounded by British infantry, armed and raring to go and we were ready to destroy our Regiment's facilities (burn, break and blow up). We liked to keep what we do secret and that means not sharing it — even with NATO allies. At 14:00, there were 87 Turkish armoured vehicles parked just north of the Eastern Sovereign Base Area, ie the nearest was 3000 yards from the front door of my office and the farthest only 5 miles away. The Regiment's real estate comprises a slightly elevated plateau, say 60 feet above sea level, some 1½ by 2½ miles rectangle. To the north of the plateau lies a fertile plain 15 miles across to the Kyrenia Hills extending from Nicosia 37 miles to the west to Famagusta 3½ to the east. Our plateau is virtually barren bedrock, bleached by countless centuries of sunshine, whose flatness is only broken by the site buildings and the many radio aerials used by the Regiment.

At 14:15, probably out of bravado, a Turkish magazine of small arms was emptied into one of the Regiment's redoubts overlooking the plain to the north. Only our soldier's dignity was injured because he was not allowed to fire back. The radio traffic back into the Regiment was a bit blue and was probably heard by a passing American satellite! Sometime in the middle of the afternoon, the Turks all got agitated and pointed their guns our way (why I don't know) and simultaneously one squadron of tanks started to redeploy. Remember: it was 1½ miles away. This was after three shots, one of which missed ITV's Jonathon Dimbleby by 20 yards without casualty or damage. (The shell bounced off the bedrock typical of the area and was probably being used as a marker for the tank manoeuvres to follow.) Being the Senior Operations Officer for the Regiment, of course I knew what was going on, but we were visually blind to that side of the building.

Actually my office did not have clear windows either, but that is a detail. We had taped across all the frosted glass windows and hung a couple of blankets to protect against glass splinters

We settled, if that is the correct word, into an anxious afternoon. At one point the building maintenance staff requested that I direct all the staff who wanted to look out of their frosted glass windows, not to; the effect of opening the windows was to let fresh air into our air-conditioned areas and there was high risk that the plant would ice up. We would then have to close the site down until it thawed which would not have been popular with London or Episkopi!

In the course of our casual conversation in the Operations Bureau, we discussed how and at what point we could surrender to the Turks; we were not armed and anyway they are our allies! One useful suggestion was to wave something white, but since none of us had washed for 36 hours, or changed clothes for rather longer, the white plaster on my left leg seemed the most likely candidate.

It was my leg being in plaster (until mid-September) that made me unable to go up on the roof for myself. We had positioned an observer up there with a field telephone link into our office. At 16:00, three things happened simultaneously:

251

- Our colonel flew out of contact in a helicopter to see what was happening.
- The Colonel Signals aide to CBFNE in Episkopi (84 miles away) came on the secure radio link because his boss was talking to London and wanted to know what was happening.
- We received a signal from the Americans (Puerto Rico) that we were taking fire and were about to be invaded.

Five minutes pandemonium ensued while we informed the Americans that we knew better! Our colonel came back to say that the Turks were wheeling in preparation for a thrust into Famagusta — which was still burning from napalm, rocket and gunfire from the morning air raid. I tried to handle the secure radio, but the Colonel Signals in Episkopi wanted to use callsigns and identifiers despite the clarity and security of the link and that we both recognised each others' voice.

"Piers, you must use correct procedures, over."

I gave my handset to an Army Major of the Royal Signals Corps, to stop him looking so worried by giving him something to do, and picked the still working military, unclassified phone to dial Episkopi. I must have transposed two numbers:

Distant (female voice):   "Good afternoon.   This is Flight Lieutenant Parker. How may I help you?"

Me: "Good afternoon.   This is Squadron Leader Ploughman at Ayios Nikolaos, speaking.   You must be Flight Lieutenant Parker Woman's Royal Air Force at Episkopi.   It's quite hot today, isn't it?"

Distant: "Yes, that's right. What can I do for you, sir?"

Me: "Nothing really. I just thought that someone along there ought to know there are 88 Turkish tanks outside my back door and they are all moving towards us."

Distant: "Ooh! That does sound interesting."

Me: "Yes. I am sorry to have disturbed you; I must have dialled the wrong number. But I think I ought to tell the old man myself. It was nice talking to you."

Distant: "Yes. Well, sir, good luck."

I redialled and this time contacted the correct desk. By that time the Turkish tanks had completed their wheel and were no longer pointing our way. I was able to tell the powers that be that we were off the hook! I later learned that CBFNE was talking to Prime Minister Jim Callaghan and our verbal feed was the best information they had.

By 17:00, the Turkish force was on the outskirts of Famagusta.

I broke from duty for dinner at 19:00. This involved moving along the footpath to the Combined Mess on crutches — a distance of 250 metres. Famagusta was burning on the eastern horizon just after sunset. For the first time I saw the troops that had been allocated to guard us. There was a squadron of Scorpion tanks, which could go backwards or forwards at up to 40 mph and were doing so around our narrow camp roads. A body of Marine Commandos was in noisy evidence, noticing particularly the way that the light showed through a well endowed civilian linguist lady's see-through blouse. There were over thirty 10 ton trucks, presumably to take away what was left of us! And there were some Gurkhas, keeping themselves unto themselves. During the morning, I knew that the civilian building maintenance staff had used mechanical diggers to prepare foxholes outside our wire fence for the defending troops, but since they were digging into bedrock, without explosive, they would not have been very deep.

After dinner, I went back to the compound where it was (air-conditioned) cool. At about 22:30, before the others went off to sleep in married quarters, I went upstairs on my crutches to freshen up. The only latrine that I could get into was the female variety, so I stripped to my underpants and ablutioned. It was shift change at 23:00 and the off-going shift decided to use their facility before leaving the compound. I remember five WRAC faces staring at this RAF senior officer standing in their loo, hardly dressed for inspection, feeling rather sheepish about the incident. Another round of "Ooh sir!" and they disappeared with a lot of noise.

When I got back to my office, I organised a soldier to make up a camp bed under the telephone and I put the light out at about 02:00. I was woken at 04.00 with signals flowing in from London wanting to know what was happening, at which hour of the night was not a lot.

I was next able to go outside at about 09:00 on 16 Aug 1994. A troop of about eight Turkish tanks were back, this time on the Famagusta side of our SBA boundary, and we were able to witness visually at a distance of 800 yards these tanks obliterate an empty Greek-Cypriot National Guard camp. Watching someone else's war, at 800 yards distance across open ground, was not something a technical cadetship equipped me for! It was all over in two hours and I was able to go into the colonel's office and sleep for two more hours.

I was woken by Helen's telephone call that she was under notice to fly with the children from Dhekelia. I was transported up to the Officers' Mess where I managed to take a bath with one plastered leg wrapped in a plastic bag and propped against the side of the bath to stay dry. I found an unoccupied bed and was disturbed again when Helen rang again to say she was on her way in only 5 minutes. I didn't hear from her again although I knew she was in good, RAF, hands.

Just after Helen's RAF air transport Hercules ride from Dhekelia airstrip (Kingsfield), one of the last flights out, the Turkish army took up their ceasefire positions all along the Eastern SBA, including the 14 mile long road umbilical between Dhekelia and Ayios Nikolaos, around Pergamos and out to Nicosia. Famagusta stopped burning visibly at about 18:00. I slept like a lamb from 20:00 until 07:00 when I was able to have a decent breakfast again, in the Officers' Mess, for the first time in four days. We all remained alert for the breakdown of the ceasefire which never came.

The contact between our colonel and the local Turkish Commander seems cordial enough; fortunately we have a Turkish linguist with the Regiment. They showed us no hostility (in retrospect why should they?) and the colonel said they appeared to be friendly at his level. We hope that some of this filters down to the troops who, even as these words are being written, are looting the town and possibly our flat — not to mention my motor cycle!

With Helen and the children now safely in UK, actually in a married quarter at RAF Hornchurch, Piers settled into the life of an unaccompanied officer living in the Officers' Mess. He would stay like that until just before Christmas when the family rejoined him, in Dhekelia, where their allocated married quarter was in the shadow of the British Military Hospital.

But on the divided island of Cyprus, with Famagusta strictly out of bounds, by no measure could life be described as normal.

Chapter 33
1975 ~ Pergamos, Eastern Sovereign Base Area, Cyprus

The 14 mile umbilical road between Ayios Nikolaos and its Dhekelia dormitory was a tedious drive, frequently transited 3 times each way per day by Regimental staff. Belligerent, armed, Turkish troops were to be seen from within their dugouts, on high ground to the north of the road, following Piers's and others' transits with the sights of the weapons. There were no incidents, but something could so easily have gone wrong. Sometimes, for those confined within Dhekelia Garrison, a few minutes excuse for relaxation was very welcome.

"Come on, Piers. I am bored with eating in the familiar places in Larnaca. Quite honestly, the place has lost a lot of its charm since the troubles. Ayios Nikolaos is a bit limiting and Aya Napa is too far in the dark. Let's go somewhere a bit more exciting. I'll show you a real Turkish Cypriot *meze*; it's an experience I promise you won't regret."

Piers and one of the linguists in the regiment were chatting over the options in the Officers' Mess anteroom. Some of the Army officers insisted that, since they were unarguably east of Dover, they needed to take tiffin for mid-morning break. One of the features of Cyprus tiffin was that it had no strict Regimental definition in the multi-discipline environment and certainly not since the 'troubles'. With 4-mile distant, Turkish occupied, Famagusta off-limits and Greek Cypriot Larnaca 20 miles away to the east, relaxed regimental staff get-togethers were infrequent for the otherwise busy officers. Tea, coffee and the local overly sweet variant of a Danish pastry sufficed, for the 15 minute tiffin break. It was the officers' excuse to be out of the air-conditioned office in the compound.

Archie Repton had a flair for languages which was an asset in defusing some of the misunderstandings at the border between Turkish Army frontier troops and the relaxed British Sovereign Base authorities. They, jointly, administered the limited crossing of locally employed civilian personnel across the painted white line (the border) on the road. United Nations forces, a legacy from the 1954 EOKA troubles, who happened to be Swedish in this sector, went where they wanted whenever they wanted. The Turkish Army, occupying Turkish Cypriot Cyprus, did not always see it that way. Strong words sometimes ensued and British staff such as Archie Repton stepped in.

Piers warmed to the idea of a different outing. "Sounds a great idea, Archie. With wives of course. Helen and Beryl seem to get on, together, so well."

"Of course with wives — my life wouldn't be worth living if I didn't take Beryl. I know a roadside place on the road out to Pergamos. The Regiment is going to reopen some staff accommodation out there, in the former RAF site, to take the pressure off what we've got now. We could bring along Maurice Bates and Sheila to make it a six. Better still, a *meze* with more people the better; why we don't we make an eight? You choose."

Piers thought. What was required was a bit of fun, blended with good food and copious Cypriot wine. "How about I see if Tom Holliday (the doc) and his wife can come; Pippa hasn't been out here in Cyprus long and I haven't met her yet although Helen has called by their married quarters."

"OK, Piers. By my count that makes eight. I'll make it ten, a surprise couple, and book a table for table for twelve just in case."

"You're going to give me directions on how to find this place, aren't you? I don't like being on the wrong end of a Turkish rifle. Oh… and don't make it the colonel; I want to relax!"

"Don't worry about it, old man. There's only one road and only one taverna on the road, so even you can't miss it. You'll be fine…"

Helen liked the idea of a night out. She liked Pippa Holliday who she judged to be 7 to 10 years older than herself. There was something 'air force' about her which was different from the 'army' wives, but she couldn't put a finger on it. Perhaps Piers…?

"Who do think he'll bring as his mystery couple? I like both Archie and Beryl very much. She sings in the church choir, you know?"

"I'm not going to be put off by Archie's mystery guest. I'll get the Brownlowes to come along. They've got a good line in table talk."

Piers didn't know that Beryl Repton sang in the church choir — presumably St George's Church in Dhekelia Garrison. Anyway, he had household chores to do and there was Michael demanding to be pushed on the swing. Chatter about future social life could wait.

"Don't forget we'll need a baby sitter... What do we wear...?" but her husband had already disappeared into the garden, to pick a fresh lemon off the thriving trees in their garden.

*   *   *

Piers knew from previous duty visits to Cyprus that it was a country with a diverse culinary heritage and offering a very wide range of specialities. He and Helen had sampled some, in Famagusta, before the troubles following the anti-Makarios coup. There was no such thing as a meal in a hurry in Cyprus; conversely everything was freshly cooked. *Meze* is an abbreviation of *mezedes,* which means *little delicacies,* which the British had long ago corrupted to mean mixture. Add to the offerings of a *meze* served with a slightly chilled, semi dry, Ballapais[tm] white wine, the evening was sure to be memorable.

"The wives can drive us home," was the promise of a boozy night ahead.

The traditional Cypriot *meze* could consist of as many as 30 small plates of savoury dips and vegetables and a wide range of fish and meat dishes. It was similar to hors d'oeuvres in concept, but when eaten in the evening then it became a main meal in itself.

It took several days for Archie to organise the evening. But it was a balmy early October evening, under a clear sky, that the party assembled. The taverna was little more than a corrugated, ex RAF, shack moved for the purpose with essential male and female buckets behind decency screens to the rear. A front awning, of corrugated sheet and canvas roof sections, was supported on vertical poles scarcely footed into a sandy hardstanding-cum-carpark. A sign indicated Pergamos Taverna with the logos for Keo[tm] beer and Coca-Cola[tm] showing on rusting metal notices. There were four tables under the awning, sufficiently separated to give some privacy, the largest set for a dozen places on a clean white linen table covering held secure by washing line clips. At a second table sat three British Army squaddies, presumably from the nearby Dhekelia Garrison, smoking and chatting away the remnants of the day; a third table had three men, probably Turkish civilians, with a female who would have passed as British. The fourth table was vacant.

There was a subtle aroma of citrus leaves in the clear air. The lightest of breezes had no chill so that the ladies' bare shoulders did not yet need the cardigans they sensibly carried. The men in their slacks and long

258

sleeved shirts had no discomfort in the conditions. Soon the smell of charcoal cooking began to waft under the canopy. Piers noticed the foursome moved the seats, perhaps to escape the fumes?

Acting as host, Archie had organised the twelve diners in a seating plan around his table:

Archie and Beryl Repton
Piers and Helen Ploughman   Maurice and Sheila Bates
Tom and Pippa Holiday   Bjorn Stafrén and Sertab Yarim
Colin and Barbara Brownlowe

No sooner had they sat than twelve glasses, already dewing from being stored in a chiller, appeared with two jugs of iced water with lemons slices. Twelve pairs of eyes looked at the taverna's owner.

"Good, evening, Hasan. Ladies and gentlemen, this is Hasan Veruglu owner of this remarkable establishment and our chef for the night." Archie was still organising.

"What do you have for us tonight?"

"Ah, hello Mister Repton. The night is good for you tonight." It was not clear if this was a command to the weather god, an observation about the present climate, the fact that his catering supplies had been delivered, or just a greeting.

"Hasan. My friends here wish to enjoy one of your mezes. I know you have a menu out there so please would you bring it so the ladies can see what delicacies you are giving them. Please bring six cold Keos, with glasses of course, for the gentlemen while we sort out what the ladies would like."

Piers noticed that the 'ladies first' principle had been abandoned; this, after all, was the Middle East!

A youngster, probably no older than 12, came out with a tray of cold beers, quickly followed by the owner carrying a laminated sheet which purported to be the menu.

"You will understand that we remember our friendship with our Greek Cypriot colleagues, before the troubles, so our menu covers all the choices in a true *meze* and erected here together for your delicacy."

Turkish Cypriot Veruglu's menu, typed in English, read:

Taramosalata: Fish roe blended into a creamy pink dip of pureed potatoes with olive oil, parsley, lemon juice and finely chopped onion.
Crushed Olives: Crushed green olives with coriander, garlic and fresh lemon.
Tzantziki: Mixture of yogurt with finely cut garlic, cucumber, olive oil and a little pepper.
Tahini dip: Crushed sesame seeds with olive oil, lemon and garlic.
Loukanika: Pork sausages soaked in red wine and smoked seasoned with coriander and red pepper and spices.
Lountza: Smoked pork soaked in red wine.
Halloumi: White soft cheese, sliced and grilled, made from goat's milk, spiced with peppermint.
Sheftalia: Grilled fresh sausage made of edible leaf containing minced pork, chopped onions, bread crumbs, chopped parsley, white pepper, salt.
Afelia: Pork cubes marinated in wine and coriander.
Stiphado: Rabbit stew casseroled with wine, vinegar, onions and spices.
Koupepia: Grape leaves stuffed with minced meat and rice seasoned with mint, onions
Doner kebab: Slowly cooked thin slices of juicy compressed beef or chicken.
Rabbit stew: Casseroled with wine, vinegar, onions and spices.
Ofto kleftiko: Chunks of lamb cooked in a sealed clay oven and seasoned with pepper and bay leaves.
Fried Zucchini: Courgettes mixed with scrambled eggs and fresh parsley.
Fried Eggplants: Eggplants dipped in flour, fried and served hot.
Village Salad: Made of cabbage, lettuce, rugola, coriander, celery, spring onions, cucumbers, capers, olives, green peppers and feta cheese. Served with a dressing made of olive oil, lemon juice and salt.
Pitta bread
A selection of dry fruit and nuts

Beers: KEO pilsner
Wines: Dry white Wines: Arsinoe, Aphrodite, White Lady
Semi dry white: Ballapais, Thisbe
Red wines: Afames, Keo Claret, Ino, Othello
Brandies available: Five Kings or V.O.S.P.
Filfar: Orange liqueur
Commandaria   Cyprus port wine
Coffees.   Turkish Sketto no sugar, Metrio medium sweet or Glyko sweet.
             English Nescafe to your choice.
Table waters as required.

A camera flashed at the foursome table. The only female had moved slightly. The men were smoking.

"Do you still have some of that excellent sherry from Limassol?"

"Ah yes sir. We do not have much call for these during these days with no English ladies visiting our humble establishment."

"The ladies would like three sherries, two orange juices and a glass of white wine. Bring out two bottles of Bellapais^{tm} and one Othello^{tm}, Hasan, and we'll get started."

The camera flashed again. This time Piers noted that once again the female had moved slightly as had the cameraman. "Did we bring the camera, darling?"

Helen shook her head.

Their meal began at 19:45 and they finished at nearly 23:00. Among the conversation topics was the presence of Lebanese, particularly well heeled Lebanese, arriving by ferry and personal yacht from Beirut. The civil war in the Monte Carlo of the eastern Mediterranean Sea was generating a mass exodus of the rich into the haven of Cyprus that was only just beginning to recover from its own troubles of the previous year.

The men divided the sixty Cypriot pounds *meze* bill equally between themselves and the party separated to their various quarters.

*   *   *

Having driven the baby-sitter home, and each showered before bed, Helen wanted to discuss the evening.

"Piers? That Swedish man was nice, I thought."

"Are you asking me what I thought? Did you notice that his 'Turkish Delight' didn't say anything? She understood every word we said."

"Most of you men were talking nonsense, anyway. The wine certainly loosened all your tongues. I have to tell you that I noticed Pippa Holliday kept looking at you. I think she's got a crush…"

"No such luck. I think she recognised me from Henlow. I thought I told you I saw her at the High Wycombe Ball — the night we got news about Michael and the adoption. While we were at the Technical College, there was an incident with WRAF cadets' skirts and stockings where she had to adjudicate."

"You've got me intrigued…"

Piers was not sure he wanted go down this avenue, not this late at night. He frowned as he spoke, "The CO wanted his two girls to look as good as his men... smartwise... on parade... in our best blues. You saw when we graduated how they were integrated into everything we did ...all platonic I promise. I never heard of anyone trying to take advantage of our waafies — well only once, to be accurate, their needing to be protected and he got a cold bath for his sins. Anyway, the tailors came in for uniforms' final fittings and we each had to stand on a dining table so the old man could look at the cut of the bottom of our trousers — shape over the shoe and leg length before the crease broke, that sort of thing."

"And?"

"And greatcoat length too. All 24 greatcoats had to be the same height above the ground, to a fraction of an inch, when we were wearing them over our best uniforms. Girls too."

"And?"

"Aren't you getting bored...?"

"And?"

"When it got to skirts... well skirts stop at the knee, but knees aren't the same height above the floor, even in court shoes, so he wanted *Bumper* to have shorter skirts and *Aspirin* to have longer ones... skirts." Piers's frown indicated he really was uncomfortable having to talk about this. Helen's body language made it quite clear he'd better get on with it.

"Given that I know you are talking nicknames, what happened?"

"We males were all cleared out of the measuring room. Just the CO and Philippa Pendleton, as she then was, sorting it out. Then came the subjects of stockings, women, officers, for the use of... and Pippa — Miss Pendleton as was — had to tell the CO what was what." Piers's yawn was not convincing and rubbing his eyes resulted in no noticeable lessening in the insistence stakes.

"And?"

"She did, tell him, what... was... you know. So the girls got their uniform and all was well until it got to rifle drill."

"Go on." Helen wondered if this was what the men called drawing hens' teeth...

"Well *Aspirin* did not have any trouble with the 'shoulder arms'. The rifle fitted, if you know what I mean — left elbow close to the hip, forearm horizontal, rifle to the shoulder. *Bumper* was built differently...

up there… and the rifle and her anatomy were not wholly compatible. Someone got up a petition to 'Amazon' *Bumper*'s chest — have the offending structure removed… mounted in a glass case… in the mess… but that was not popular with the girls."

"Don't be disgusting. So?"

With a deep breath, Piers continued, "We understood that *Bumper* went off to a specialist to have a suitably strengthened undergarment constructed that could protect her where-with-all." Piers was now trying to concentrate on fastening his pyjama trousers.

"Her what?" asked Helen, incredulous at what she was hearing, for the first time, after living with this man for over fifteen years.

"Her…" Piers's hands were cupped across his chest doing a lifting movement. His mouth motioned 'where-with-all' but the words did not come out.

"Her breasts needed support?" Helen tried to clarify while becoming increasing amused by her husband's demonstration of functional control of women's bits.

"Well, yes. The left one… where the rifle goes… when you do drill." Piers's shoulders had drooped while his wife was shaking her head in disbelief.

"You're serious?"

"Absolutely! Pippa — Flight Officer Philippa Pendelton, WRAF came to *Bumper*'s rescue and saved the old man all sorts of embarrassment. She probably saved *Bumper*'s love life too." Piers's hands had now relaxed and were resting against his wife's thighs. "Talking of which — love life. I have to go down the road at 06:30 tomorrow and I need some shut eye. Now, Mrs Ploughman, I need to expunge a Swede from your thoughts…"

"Which of your waafies needed protection?"

"*Aspirin.*"

"And which honourable gentleman was trying for a slice of the action?"

"All of us…" Piers managed to duck under the first swing of the pillow, but was caught full square by the second. "No, no. I concede. It was a guy from the university cadets, so we all… the Henlow lot including the Aussies… went over and bathed the lot. They were not well pleased. Honest… Helen… come here and I'll remind you what we were protecting *Aspirin* from… Shh, you'll wake the kids…"

Chapter 34
1977 ~ "You're Going Home…"

On November 5th, 1976, Saladin Hussein sat in the shuttered room, overlooking the inner courtyard, of the East German Consulate in Nicosia. The office was nominally the Trade Delegate office; in practice it was the espionage centre for the East German Security Service, the STASI, for the whole of Cyprus with tentacles into the Lebanon, Israel, Egypt, Turkey and Greece. The name plate on the desk indicated that the desk was normally occupied by Gustav Schloër.

Nicosia, capital of Cyrus, had been a good espionage hub, with excellent air connections throughout Europe and the Middle East until the 1974 anti-Makarios coup and the consequential Turkish invasion closed the international airport. Similarly, information gathering concerning shipping through Famagusta and Larnaca had been easy to monitor and the British military presence on the island provided ready access to both their and to NATO strategies in the whole eastern Mediterranean region. It was certainly true that the 1973 war between Israel and Egypt had closed the Suez Canal, but the senior officers in East Berlin continued to press for intelligence and were unforgiving about lapses. And while the RAF continued to operate their nuclear-capable Vulcan bombers out of RAF Akrotiri, a continued monitoring of their activity was essential.

Gustav Schloër was speaking, "Let's get the lesser details out of the way before we get to the important business. What do you know about this Sertab Yarim woman?" Both men were smoking cigarettes.

Hussein replied, "She sleeps with any United Nations officer who'll pay to have her. Turkish, probably Kurdish origin, unmarried, no children, no known parents. Age about 27. Came to Turkish Cyprus with visa to work in British hotels on north coast in 1971. Speaks good English, passable Swedish when she needs to, provides distraction when necessary. Known to have association with British spies in Dhekelia, probably sexual, but she was unable to extract anything useful to us. Current associate is Swedish Major Bjorn Stafrén, an uninteresting infantry officer attached to the UN peace keeping force with no special knowledge who spends his money hotelling, whoring and drinking. He has a British woman, a soldier's wife, when he's out of the way. No evidence of association with hashish smuggling across the Green Line.

He visited Cairo and Beirut on previous tours in Cyprus. He is due to return to Stockholm before mid-December."

"Those details, with annotated photographs will be sent to Berlin."

"Thank you, Herr Schloër."

"Now, these others. They are of more interest to me. I know you have written reports… you tell me in your own words. Who are they and what is their significance?"

"They are listed in my report, Herr Schloër. They total 12 in all and 10 of them are British who have been reliably identified as:

- Major Archie Repton, Intelligence Corps and his wife Beryl; he is a linguist at the Ayios Nikolaos Regiment who we see often on the frontier crossing checkpoint to Famagusta, sometimes at Pergamos. He appears to be fluent in Greek and Turkish and may be others. He does not, himself, cross out of the Eastern Sovereign Base Area. No known vices. Three children in boarding school in UK.

- Squadron Leader Piers Ploughman and his wife Helen; he is an odd selection to be working in the Ayios Nikolaos Regiment, but he might have liaison duties with other RAF units inside the Eastern Sovereign Base Area. A technical officer who is known to visit the Troodos radar sites regularly. He probably specialises in communications and possible cryptographic protection of their communications systems. Two children, one about five years, the other — a girl born in Dhekelia on July 20, 1974.

- Major Tom Holiday, RAMC and his wife Philippa. He is the Regiment's doctor. She is a former British Women Royal Air Force officer of their Supply Branch who retired on marriage. Works as a clerk in the Ayios Nikolaos Regiment, duties unknown. No children.

- Major Colin Brownlowe, Royal Signals and his wife Barbara have few if any operational duties with the Ayios Nikolaos Regiment. He has senior officer responsibilities for the non-operational soldiers outside their Technical Compound, such as stores, transport, catering staff administration and pay. She is the Personal Assistant to the colonel of the regiment.

- Major Maurice Bates, Royal Signals and his wife Sheila have recently arrived from Northern Ireland. Little is known about the couple except that they were recently married.

- Major Bjorn Stafrén and Sertab Yarim we have already discussed."

"So far, so good. Well, Hussein, what were they talking about?

"I have no information on that, Herr Schloër. The *meze* menu seemed to excite them and it is possible that the taverna keeper, Hasan Veruglu, passed something to Repton during the evening. Repton appeared to be hosting the meal and explaining the food."

"Are you wasting my time, Hussein?" Schloër's demeanour had changed from affable to aggressive in only a few seconds. "I want information I can use not pretty pictures fit only for the files!"

"Herr Schloër, I have information. With Stafrén's departure it should be straightforward to get the girl, Yarim, into employment on the Dhekelia base. There is a vacancy in their beachside newspaper shop — they call it CESSAC — where the whole garrison comes and goes for English newspapers, magazines, ice cream, soft drinks, beach snacks, coffee…"

"And then?"

"She can wrap her legs around Brownlowe's neck. She'll make him talk and, with a wife in the colonel's office, he'll know all the Regiment's comings and goings. She may even be able to access documents too."

"Too fanciful, Hussein. A more productive target would be this Ploughman airman, or even the man fresh from Northern Ireland…" He was clicking his fingers as a memory jogger.

"Bates… Major Bates…"

"Yes, Ploughman or Bates. See to it, Hussein. Does the Regiment monitor targets for the Vulcan bombers? How often does this Ploughman person go to their airfield? Why was an officer with experience of the Northern Ireland problem brought to Cyprus? Does he show interest in trade with Libya or Syria? These are logical questions which a good agent would anticipate. I'll forward your reports and photographs to Berlin. You have to do better than this, Hussein, to merit the usual payment; I'll give you half now and keep the rest for when you give me something better. Now, get out while I get on with the real work…" The dismissal of the disappointed Hussein was made with a vigorous wave.

With Hussein's departure, department chief Helmut Mueller declared he was well satisfied with Schloër's timely reaction to the requirement and use of the money to keep Hussein on his toes. Naturally, he expected nothing less from the sections in his department; however, this time the performance was most satisfactory and would be drawn to the attention of Herr Mielke in the office of the Minister of State Security of the GDR. Mueller was sure that, when the material was passed on to the KGB with his endorsement, he would gain some high points in his deeper loyalties beyond Berlin to Moscow.

* * *

On 15th January, 1977 the snow on Moscow's Red Square lay deep. In one tall building, a thick package of papers and photographs had arrived from Berlin during the too short daylight hours reaching into the sixth floor of the Lubyanka building. Olga Brovorno sat hunched over her ever tidy desk, ready to set about her latest task. Perhaps this pack would have some good incriminating images from the decadent seasonal partying, something out of the routine, something for her tired eyes to enjoy. It would be a change from the dull material coming from London at this time of the year: lists of promotions, honours, appointments, retirements even casualties. Perhaps there would be some news about her favourites? Time would tell.

Two days later, she noticed that she was handling two familiar files, familiar because she had only just put them away and here the names were in different papers again. 'STASI sourced? Yes, there is the Maurice Bates, Royal Signals again. Photographic confirmation he's in Cyprus. That's good. The file records him departing Belfast with a promotion to major and a citation for good work in secure mobile communications. That nonsense comment about expertise in trade has no substance, but it will go in the file. Perhaps they are using the same equipment in both places? The specialist desk can work with that. Good, well spotted Olga.'

Olga opened the Ploughman folder. A black and white photographic image looked back. Aloud she greeted a favourite, "Ah, yes, Squadron Leader, I remember you. Visiting all those places in UK and overseas." She carried on thinking as she clipped the papers and photographs in the folder.

'How did you ever find time to make a baby? You kept me busy, that's for sure. That is an interesting comment from the Nicosia agent about the RAF liaison officer for the nuclear Vulcans in Ayios Nikolaos. That would be new! Vulcans need a runway not radio masts! The file shows he had previous experience with Vulcans at Waddington. It's probably the agent making it up to justify not getting a bullet in the brain. If they want it, upstairs, they'll ask for his file. Yes, I'll put a copy of the STASI report on the Saladin Hussein and Gustav Schloër folders, cross-referenced to my personnel folders, and marked '*questionable value*'. Perhaps that would help stem such material wasting my time. But wait, what's this?'

Olga checked her reading of the London-origin paper in front of her. It was a photocopy, partially cropped by masking with another sheet unrelated to Ploughman. The slip she was reading seemed to be a memorandum between staff officers concerning Ploughman's next appointment which was due in Jun/Jul 77; it requested confirmation of highest security clearance for duties related to Electronic Warfare. Was she holding a key to Ploughman's posting after Cyprus? She thought about her conclusion, closed the folder and rose to discuss the material with her supervisor.

'It looks as though you are going home, squadron leader, and we know what you'll be doing…'

Chapter 35
1977 ~ Study Electronic Warfare

"Welcome to Benson, Squadron Leader Ploughman. Sit down, make yourself comfortable. What do you know about what you've come here to do?"

"I've read the job description and the terms of reference, sir. It all seems pretty straightforward."

"Right and wrong. Good to know you can read; it helps here on the staff. The Electronic Warfare staff, EW(Studies), study electronic warfare. You know why, of course! They need information and your job is to get it. They write reports and have to answer questions, so your secondary job is to get the information they have missed out on and assist them to put it in. Our job is jammers, we don't want the nasties shooting at us. And if they do, it's your job to make sure they miss. So you can focus on nasty things that could go bump in the night!"

"I understand, sir. Threats and that sort of thing."

"Good word that, Ploughman. Threats... reds everywhere and we're going to stop them."

"I understand, sir." Piers was thinking that he would soon be away from this madman and able to talk to someone who had a vague idea of what was required.

"Your post has two other responsibilities. You are responsible for security of special material in the Command and you give lectures on electronic warfare to staff colleges and similar." The group captain's hands were rolling a pencil while he was talking.

"Yes, sir. What material and how much of the Command?"

"It's in your handover folder, in the vault. Top secret, we don't keep that sort of stuff up here. Best kept in the vault... its got a good strong green door. That's where your office is and I don't expect you to change it. You've got a good flight lieutenant; use her well. And Mrs Deakin knows her stuff, never lets anything leave the vault improperly: a really first class clerk who merits a commendation."

"That's good to hear, sir. And the lectures?"

"Straightforward stuff, to NATO and our senior warfare courses. They are good audiences because they rely increasingly on electronic warfare to stay alive. A lesson from Vietnam and the 1973 Arab-Israel turkey shoot. They've sort of got focussed — in a manner of speaking. It's why they study it." The pencil was more agitated now as if the mention of real wars stirred something internally. His uniform jacket carried a pilot's brevet and Piers noticed a gallantry medal alongside a WWII campaign medal. This chap had been around a long time.

"I'm a bit out of practice at formal lecturing, sir." Piers shifted for comfort.

"You can get some practice in 10 days time. The station is hosting the Anglo-American Wives' annual get together and the Commandant has agreed that we shall be using our presentation room for a 15 minutes lecture... on Electronic Warfare. Unclassified, of course. Not a secret in sight, OK?"

"If you say so, sir. How many... err... Anglo-American wives?

"The room can easily take 150... I expect we'll see about 100. The Americans come to see the Queen's Flight and the British wives come to find out what hubbie does all day long. They have a good day out. My wife will be there, of course. It's a good day to bring sandwiches; they eat in the mess and you'll never get served."

"Of course, sir. Will there be anything else?" The pencil had stopped.

"Not for the moment. Ploughman. Ask my PA to step inside, with some coffee on your way out. Once again, welcome to the Signals Staff. And don't forget to read the Officers' Confidential Order Book; the Commandant is very particular about that..."

"Yes, sir. Good morning." Piers saluted. The pencil now lay on his desk.

*   *   *

In the 'vault', his office for the next five years, with sealed windows, frosted double glazing with integral bars, little forced ventilation and artificial light, there were four rooms. 'Vault' was appropriate; leading off a central corridor which was normally sealed by a one inch thick steel door painted in enamel green, there were four rooms with one adapted to contain a walk-in safe protected by another steel door painted in enamel green. A meeting room had a bare table and six chairs, there were no wall decorations in that room. Two offices: one set up as a reading room, the other with two desks, two telephones, two office chairs and two filing cabinets with manifoil combination locks. The clerk's office had table, chair and telephone, but also housed the actual vault which would have done Fort Knox proud. The walls were 15 inches thick reinforced concrete and the entrance door was one inch steel plate with duplicated manifoil locks designed to remain closed if tampered with. Within the vault were seven filing cabinets, each again manifoil protected, where the EW secrets and related support intelligence was kept. Piers was assured that this strong room would take at least six hours with a thermal lance to break into.

"Hallo, Mrs Deakin, I'm Piers Ploughman and come to join you. What do I call you?"

"The gentlemen call me Florrie, after Florence the lamp lady; they say I'm the one what sheds all the light on their problems, but I don't think so, sir. Me real name is Herminone, but no-one's used that name since I was baptised." The 57 years old wrinkled face on reliable civil servant's shoulders beamed a welcoming smile.

"Ok, Mrs Deakin... err... Florrie. You can call me Piers. Now where's my office and the flight lieutenant? I suppose he's got a name."

"Ooh, sir. The flight lieutenant is out for the moment, at the drawing office. Something to do with a presentation next week, sir. And he's not a he, sir, he's a she. Flight Lieutenant Denise Mercer she is, sir. Said she knows you, too. She's got the same security clearance as you, sir. Perhaps you'll sign the Security Orders Book before we go on, sir. It keeps everything regular, sir. Then I can show you around while we're waiting for Miss Mercer to come back. She won't be long, sir. Would you like some coffee... milk and sugar? I've made a cake to welcome you, sir." She was reaching to switch on the already plugged in kettle.

"Look... err... Florrie... while we're in here, with the door closed, how about a few less sirs and such. I'm really quite a nice guy and I've got two kids to prove it. Let's have some coffee and then we'll have a proper chat about what goes on here."

"You'll have to sign the Security Orders Book first, sir..." It was the air force way.

* * *

Flight Lieutenant Denise *Aspirin* Mercer WRAF let herself into the vault. She had kept her figure through her now 39 years of age. She would be respectful of Piers's seniority in public, but in the privacy of the office they were ex-cadets together.

272

"Hello Piers. It's good to see you. I'm sorry you didn't get your wings, but then most of you didn't, did you. At least you are alive still! Anyway, you're here now and I've got the task of telling all about this job. A lot of it is routine and we can rely on Florrie to do it well. All the security clearance notifications and registering classified mail is her job and she is rigorous to the point of pain."

Florrie Deakin entered, showing her slight stature and five feet one inch height to no great effect, and placed a fresh cup of coffee, unasked, on the coaster on Denise Mercer's desk. She made to leave. Her implied, but unspoken request for instructions about whether she should close the office door drew a negative shake of the head from the flight lieutenant. Denise nodded at Piers as if to indicate that this was the way that Florrie worked: silent, efficient and mostly ahead of the game.

"Ooh, do you think the squadron leader would like a piece of my cake? I baked it special to welcome him."

Denise's eyebrows went up in query. Piers's head shook negative. "Not just now, thank you, Florrie. This afternoon perhaps?" The clerk retired through the open door to her office across the corridor. She would hear everything that was said.

"OK, Denise, save it all for later. Tell me about next Friday; tell me about this Anglo-American Wives' annual bean-feast. How the hell did we get roped in for that?"

"I've been having to give the lectures while your desk has been empty and I guess it was jobs for the girls — to mix my metaphors — to slot me into a timewaster. National security limits what we can tell NATO audiences, but the RAF and Joint Services courses need a lot of persuading that EW gives value for money. Hence my comment about *waste of time*. Directly they heard a handsome ex-Henlow cadet was posted in, booted and spurred and tanned from the Middle East sun, well you got elected from a list of one. Up to now, I have simply been reading prepared scripts; EW was not my scene. I've been concentrating on the security issues which you can see are taken pretty seriously around here."

'Typical bloody air force,' thought Piers. Something about *a bird in the hand* and *horses for courses* flashed through his mind in a mixed passage that he kept to himself. She sipped her coffee before speaking.

"This cake is good — right up to Florrie's standard. You're honoured. After Henlow, I got specialised in hospital and aircrew breathing equipment, aircraft oxygen and liquid oxygen systems until they found out that I passed Latin and Esperanto at Cheltenham. So off to the Language School at RAF North Luffenham to learn Czech and two years in the Defence Attache's office in Prague before coming here. Virtually zero engineering and lots of being a high priced clerk — as you might guess. I'm glad to see you. And what happened to you, after flying school?"

"I'll tell you later, Denise. Nothing very exciting, except Singapore and Cyprus and three wars. Later! Now let's see how far you've progressed with preparing a lecturette for post-colonial trans-Atlantic sorority. This could be hard work!"

"Piers, I'd better tell you now. I'm leaving the RAF shortly, I stayed on to wait to handover to you and then I'm out at my 38/16 year option date. I'm getting married to one of the language instructors at North Luffenham — name of Carli Petrov. It's a unit in your balliwick so I guess you haven't seen the last of me because I've applied for a civilian instructor's job up there. They haven't nominated my successor yet."

"OK. Let's get on with the priority of the day, we can chat later. Oh," whispering behind his hand, "is Florrie's cake really any good?"

"You'd better believe it, Piers. Half the headquarters staff troop in here when the word is out she's been cooking. You'll regret only getting a single slice this afternoon."

*   *   *

The wing commander said to Piers, "There's a plane going to Paris tomorrow. Be on it!"

"Where from?" The boss was not usually so imprecise; he must have something on his mind. "And timing?"

"07:45 from RAF Northolt. Report to Air Movements. You'll get by on your RAF identity card. Paris Air Show. Travel in civvies. You'll be home for supper. If you've got a few French francs its worth taking them along, but you can get by with sterling notes."

"Anything specific? Any special bit of kit?" A free ride to Paris was one thing, in an RAF Andover was OK and promised some comfort, but air shows can be pretty boring to say nothing of hard on the feet. Piers found the British Farnborough Air Shows rather trying and a swine to drive away from. And French fast food was not exactly Piers's cup of tea.

"The Russians are showing their stuff… well Concordski anyway. It's a day out and you never know who you might meet!"

The Paris air show display ground was vast. Piers recognised a couple of officers from the UK Ministry of Defence Technical Intelligence staff, but he decided it was better not to be too closely associated with them in public. The Russian stands were giving nothing away, either secrets or souvenirs. The Israelis and the South African were there, too, competing on unequal terms with American industry and, of course, the host nation. NATO was flashing all its latest hardware and, using huge TV screens, were showing how bright their ordinance explosions could be.

Some obvious defence contractors were parading their latest long-legged acquisitions; it was the year that the British mini-skirt hit France with a vengeance. There were few military uniforms about and most of those were French. A scattering of NATO officers, in twos or threes, moved between display stands of interest. Piers noticed, and he was silently amused by, two British Army staff colonels resplendent in their best uniforms, chins high under peaked caps, appearing to be wanted to be noticed rather than simply mixing with the crowd.

Piers made his way to the Russian Space Station exhibit. He thought it to be an impressive piece of hardware, externally, and there was a queue to go inside. The opportunity would never be repeated so he joined the line. The hosts were taking no special interest in any individual passing through the entrance; they were probably as bored as everyone else.

The camera flash temporarily blinded Piers. He was uncertain who had taken the photograph or where the camera was. Indeed, he thought he was probably not the intended subject since the two, Chanel perfumed, chattering starlets behind him definitely merited attention. French *Force du Frappe* uniforms close behind these catwalk starlets displayed emphasised interest in their prominent attractions.

'Anyway,' thought Piers, 'why should anyone want my photo? Maybe this is a Soviet exhibit, but why me out of a cast of thousands? There are probably a hundred spies here to choose from. I'm parched, I could do with a drink. Anyway, I'm RAF not a spy.' He had to wait for refreshment until after he had passed through the exhibit, which he found rather uninspiring.

After a long day, Piers was pleased to be home to an English instant curry from a packet.

"Did you have a nice day, darling?"

"Oh… you know… these visits are a waste of time. I don't know why industry wastes its money on these air shows. All the decisions are made before the show so they can be announced in competition with everyone else. So what? I didn't want to buy twenty jumbo jets anyway."

"I know, dear. We've got nowhere to park them. Why don't you eat your dinner and then you could have a good soak in the bath. I didn't put out any wine; I expect you had sufficient over there. Philippa has got a new tooth pushing through and Michael is playing football for his class tomorrow afternoon. I heard from Mother and we're going over there at the weekend… I can ask her if she remembers Auntie Vi's birthday for my family tree… Did you see the Eiffel Tower?"

*   *   *

Olga Brovorno had left the brightness of Moscow's August sunlight for the gloom of her sixth floor office on Lubyanka Square. The work of compiling personnel records was never done; there was always a flow of new material to be filed tidily for the customers of the KGB's First Chief Directorate (Foreign Operations) — responsible for foreign operations and intelligence. Welcoming Olga that morning, having been delivered by the overnight courier and distribution system, was a pile of photographs and a separate pile of papers from the Paris Air Show.

Brovorno sat looking at her uncharacteristically untidy desk, thinking. She was going to need help. It maybe just routine, but it needed doing before the NATO exercise season in September. There were some specialists along the corridor useful for her purpose. She would definitely need Igor Ivanovitch with his photographic memory. Some experienced filing clerks would be good too. Igor Ivanovitch would help with many of the unlabelled photographs and avoid errors and duplicates. She could not afford to file photographs or cross–references in the wrong folder.

'This is going to be a busy week,' she thought, 'with all those colleges graduating. Yes, help is desirable so that I don't get behind. The comrades on the fifth floor would not be pleased!'

So Piers's folder in the KGB system, with 2500 others, grew one or more enclosure thicker with recent comments and updated images. And when it was done, Comrade Ivanovitch spoke to Comrade Brovorno, "The staff cinema is showing the bourgeois musical *Cabaret* with Liza Minelli. It is in English, a language training film I believe, but that is no

276

matter. It shows how fortunate we are to have won the Great Patriotic War and avoided becoming decadent lackies of the American neo-colonists. Would you care to accompany me?"

"With an invitation like that, Comrade, how could I refuse?"

Olga thumbed through the file in her hands. Something, her intuition, there was something in this file — about the man whose key features and future potential were as yet inadequately defined — which suggested she was handling something important. 'I think, Mister Piers Peter Ploughman born in Wendover Buckinghamshire on 5th November 1937, that I shall be seeing rather more of you in the future. With that security clearance you are bound to attract attention. I look forward to seeing your story unfold…"

*   *   *

The wing commander said to Piers, "There's a boffin coming down from Farnborough who wants to know what emitters' recognition signatures to load on his bit of kit for the new Nimrod AEW?"

"I suppose this boffin has a name?" Piers did not hesitate although the wing commander was nodding and about to speak. "You're telling me that, unannounced, some specialist from an outfit I didn't know exists is going to breeze in and expect me to provide highly classified data about emissions from Warsaw Pact radars? And for an aircraft that looks wrong, is probably intrinsically unstable in the air and…"

"London confirms it's kosher…" The nod made it alright, then!

"Given that I can check him out security-wise, given that he has a name, what do we know about his kit, as you put it? I need a bit more than a nod, I'll need a signal to confirm his clearance."

"Nothing! The kit's secret. That's why EW(Studies) have got it. All I know is that it is slated for the new Nimrod Airborne Early Warning aircraft due in service in three years. It's probably American, so that makes it more secret… The whole of this EW world is so bloody secret you can't read some of the papers before you shred them. Look, London says give this boffin a fair wind and then let them know what happened. There will be a support requirement for the contract and it's bound to involve us in some way."

"When is he coming?"

"Tuesday, at 10:00. Give him a cup of coffee and let him talk. Arrange for him to see me before he leaves; I'll be here on Tuesday afternoon, it's already in the diary. I know, I know. You're losing Denise at the end of the month... There's no news of her replacement. You'll have to cope by yourself." He turned and left Piers to it.

With that apparently insignificant task was founded an endeavour to catalogue the world's radars, friend or foe, in a computer readable format which some years later would contribute national success in the last two wars of Piers's RAF career.

Chapter 36
1982 ~ A Distant Island in an Icy Ocean

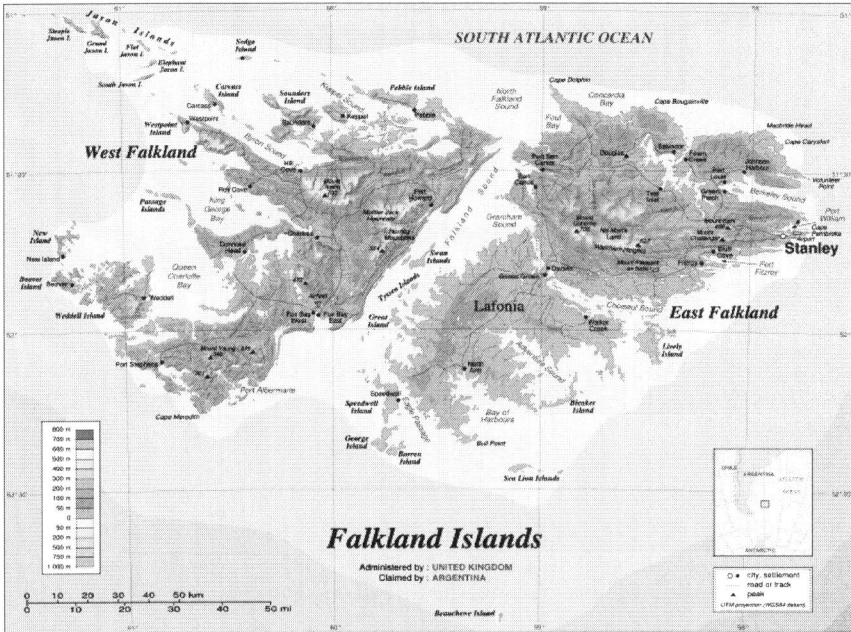

Falkland Islands

Administered by : UNITED KINGDOM
Claimed by : ARGENTINA

Piers was in the garden of his RAF Benson married quarter. Helen and the other wives of the unit were assembled in the house just letting their men get on with it. He sat under a marquee, 'borrowed' by the unit's 'Mr Fixit', with his team of specialists who had just helped win the Falkland Islands war. Long hours were behind them. Eighteen hour days had been the norm. Now was the time to recoup and regroup. Once more they should be able to concern themselves with the perceived primary threat — the Warsaw Pact.

Details of the meal's menu and the undoubted copious liquid refreshment would quickly fade in the fog of memory. On that cool, dry evening of the 18th July 1982, and relaxing in the fresh air after fifteen weeks in windowless rooms — the technical term *unfenestrated* does its unpleasantness due justice — sat forty five military men and women of the three services just letting off steam. No photographs were taken of that night of celebration. From the South Atlantic, *HMS Hermes* was home; the last Vulcan bomber was back in Lincolnshire in preparation for its deferred retirement and the breaker's yard; the airbridge to the islands, down the Atlantic, was now established. Mrs Thatcher had popped down to visit her troops and rejoice in their prowess. Soon, the temporary boost to the EW(Studies) team at Benson would return to their various home stations from which they had been extracted at very short notice.

Normality had changed. The war generals' accounts and the reporters' half-truths would be rehearsed until their version would become the only account. The horrendous film footage of gallantry, sacrifice and death would be sealed for the television end-of-year retrospect and thence to the safety of the archive; selected, politically-unwelcome, images would be consigned to the cutting room floor. Memoirs, essentially selective, would be published. Motor fuel would rise in price. The thirty five extras drafted in to support the Benson team of 10 would soon disperse. It was the nature of military service life; folk thrown together in a disciplined organisation towards a single purpose with, maybe, some lasting friendships made. They would soon scatter to the fortunes of their own careers. They would return to their loved ones never able to describe adequately what it was they had done at an airfield better known as the home of the Queen's Flight rather than the RAF centre for operational electronic warfare support.

The unremembered conversations of that celebratory garden party would slip to wait the catchup news that the media was discussing. There was the Eurovision '82, hosted by Jan Leeming, won by Germany, when the UK's entry *'One Step Further'* came 7th. There was the release of the BBC-B microcomputer retailing at £335 with its 16K of RAM. And inevitably, like so many other dads swept up in the conflict, many had missed the schools' sports day.

Piers reflected as he drained another can of cold beer, 'What were we doing? We were collating the information necessary for our electronic sensors and countermeasures to be as effective as possible. Some enemy weapons we could do nothing about — our successes may never see the light of day. But forty five men and women, this evening, know they had been part of a grand endeavour when the three armed service cooperated fully. We have come out of it the richer for the experience.'

*   *   *

"Come in Piers. Close the door… have a seat."

"You wanted to see me, sir?"

"I… we… the Group Captain… the guys in London… just want you to know that we really appreciated what your team did in the Falklands troubles."

"I had a powerful team, sir, and …"

"We know…"

" …they were hand picked. I know it caused some problems, pulling them out of the front line, but…"

" …that you pinched the cream of the EW specialists, from all three services, but it came good on the night, so's to speak, and…"

"It's good of you to say so, sir." Piers knew all this. He practically wrote the script for it, for his group captain to justify what had happened in those first few days of the conflict when apparently no-one knew the capabilities of the Argentinean forces. The EW Studies Team at Benson had a better inkling than most; the Royal Navy trained Argentinean Navy, the German Army trained their military and there were indications that the Israelis had more than a little influence on their Air Force.

Piers drummed his fingers on his knee-caps. 'What is this all about? Perhaps they want me to stay on another year…?'

The wing commander continued. His body language told Piers that this interview had a purpose and he was a busy man. "Well I thought you would like to know that your next confidential report, it's due in three weeks, will have something to say about it. I am sorry that you won't be getting a campaign gong, but the whole business here is so under wraps that we don't want it all in the open. You know…"

"I quite understand, sir. More Benson runway than Bletchley Park, sir."

"Quite. There's always a silver lining and I thought it was time to let you know what's going on."

"Have we got some new project to support? There were 24 active project support outputs from the database when the Argies stopped shooting… I don't suppose the Soviet military just sat on the terraces and watched!"

"No, it's not that." The interviewing officer waited for his junior to calm and then, "The judgement is that you need a rest — well, at least a change — a replacement has been found… you know him… you've met him at NATO conferences… he's moving into married quarters, here… across the road from you. Tomorrow!"

"Oh. Thanks for telling me… We're pretty much back to normal. We've just mailed the latest update to Stanmore for the Tornado suite, it's all the latest information. It had to go registered mail it's so red hot."

It was as though Piers had not spoken. "So you'll be pleased to know you're going overseas, in six weeks. There's acting promotion for you in it." Piers's reaction was not one of surprise; nothing could surprise him anymore. It took less than a second for the news to sink in. The knee-cap drumming stopped.

"Oh… I suppose it's no use pointing out that Christmas is only four… err… wrong… three… weeks away and everything will close down while the reindeers block the motorways? Or that they have the wrong sort of ice on the telephone wires?"

"Berlin is quite nice in the winter."

"Are you telling me that I am going to Berlin? What do the folks in London and Cheltenham say about that? I've got a security ticket that says I can't go to Berlin…"

"That's one of the reasons why I haven't been able to tell you earlier. It has taken a lot of push from the Personnel Management staff at Gloucester, and the Signals Staff in the Ministry, to get clearance. I have to tell you that some folks in RAF Germany headquarters are uncomfortable about stretching the rules for you… but… err… it seems you are the only officer available and they're going to give you acting paid rank to go. The RAF Provost Branch seems to think you need a special talking to too… err… also. So…?"

For once in his life, Piers was dumbfounded. His eyebrows went up and then settled in a thoughtful frown. As far as he knew, the RAF Provost Branch did not know what he did, or with what, and he was not about to tell them.

"Are we talking married accompanied? Berlin?"

"Certainly. It goes with the job."

"We are talking Officer Commanding 26 Signals Unit, aren't we?"

"That is what I am authorised to tell you. '*Effective in post on 16th January 1983, displaying the rank unpaid until 21st January when you've completed the handover*' is what it says on the signal message. The registry has a copy for you because you'll need the references to book travel and accommodation and rank alterations on you uniform. It also says the Air Secretary wants to see you in Gloucester, so make the appropriate arrangements with his PA and make sure we know the date."

"Blimey… Yes! I accept, not that you asked me, sir. I am fairly sure that Helen will like the idea; we haven't moved house for 18 months and we were talking 'itchy feet' last night. Is it OK to tell her? What about my team; can I tell them too? Bloody hell… it's the dream posting for all the signals engineers… 26 SU. Berlin… Wow!"

"I thought you would be pleased. Go and phone Helen with the news. You can buy me a pint, in the mess, at happy hour on Friday!" Piers began to rise and settled again in his chair.

"And this special provost interview? When do the *snowdrops* want to join the queue to get at me?"

"They say when you're out there will do. And don't call them *snowdrops* when you're in charge. It's not their fault they have white tops on their hats. It stops the pigeons' droppings…"

"I can't talk to the sno… provost folk, in Berlin, about this place."

"Then don't! Perhaps they want to talk to you about something else."

"Well, thank you, sir. What do I say?"

"Nothing!" With a shake of his head, the wing commander concluded, "Now get out and start spreading the news. You've got quite a lot of organising to do… Oh, yes, and let me know when that Tornado package arrives at the contractors at Stanmore. I'd like to go and see what they are doing with the data."

$$*\qquad*\qquad*$$

The visiting wing commander from MOD Technical Intelligence (Air) wanted to know how long Piers's organisation knew that the Stanmore package had been adrift.

"A routine progress telephone call to the company, just to be sure that the package had not been delayed in the Xmas mail, we logged that in the mail register on the 3rd December. We followed it up on the 5th, checked with Royal Mail on the 9th, they told us there had been a mail robbery on the 3rd and they thought our package was in the stolen mailbags. They confirmed it from their records on the 11th so we signalled everyone who we thought might be interested."

"Do you know what was in the package?"

"This package was so hot… classified… such that, unusually, we kept a copy on a backup magnetic tape, off the computer, in case. We can easily show the contents on a screen and print another copy if we need to. That backup copy is in the vault behind a combination lock."

"In summary, what was this hot data and what was its classification?"

"It was the highest we can… err… could send to contractors directly. It was 400 pages of *Secret UK Eyes Only* radar parameters for NATO, the Warsaw Pact and the Rest of the World in sufficient detail to programme electronic recognition sensors and countermeasures. Keys to fixed locations and mobile platforms were given for power verses range planning. The operators call it Electronic Order of Battle data, but if you know how to read the material, it discloses organisation and quantitative material orders of battle too."

"You're telling me that we've lost our understanding of what the Red forces can do?"

"No, sir, not lost. We've still got the original. It was a sizeable subset copy that was in the pack and it is that copy that has been stolen."

The wing commander was looking for a way to limit the damage. Number 10 Downing Street was gunning for blood. He was searching for a way of telling Whitehall of the monumental cockup that had occurred. He didn't find it in Piers's previous remarks or his next.

"Worse than that. The same pack includes the same data for our side too. They're red… we're blue! Radar system designers and electronic warfare planners know that both sides have to use the same radio spectrum in the same geographic space. In short they need to sort the good guys from the bad or they blow the wrong guys out of the sky… or sea. Red from blue… And sometimes, electronically, the bad guys look like the good guys and so they don't get stopped in time. It's what went wrong in the South Atlantic… Exocet and all that… Our job is to try to stop that happening."

"Holy cow! Was there any non-UK source information in there? American technical stuff?"

"Some American, a little Canadian, some NATO. It was blended with commercially sensitive stuff too; mostly military, naturally, but also some commercial and research or scientific details where we've found it in literature. We haven't done a detailed analysis of primary sources because we don't tell any customers, contractors or military, how we know. It's just that we are the authoritative data source for many UK electronic warfare contracts; how we know what we know we keep to ourselves. But yes, there was some privileged American information, in there, buried behind our more generally accessible stuff. We can go back if we need to identify the original. It would take us at least three months to unscramble it. The quantity of material is enormous."

Piers cleared his throat before continuing, "Oh, and some of the information came from your office too — at least your staff's office, sir."

"Look, Squadron Leader Ploughman, I'm here because the Secretary of State had to tell the Prime Minister and she feels honour bound to inform President Regan because of the damage in the Geoffrey Prime/GCHQ spy case earlier in the year."

"I don't think we are in that league, sir. My understanding of Prime was that he was leaking a different…"

"It's not for you to judge."

"We have nothing in common with the Prime affair, sir."

"I'll say it again, squadron leader, it's not for you to judge. I've got enough for my report for now. Don't plan on going anywhere over Christmas. It could be a busy week if SHE wants chapter and verse. We'll let you know! Print a hard copy of the material in case it is called for, I'll let you know. If it's called forward, for Christ's sake courier it by hand of commissioned officer. Now, sign me out."

The visitor's face had darkened as though he was holding his breath. Piers wondered if he would make it back to London. He had little confidence that the visitor had appreciated just how much material had gone astray. 'Blimey… it could cost me Berlin!'

All through Christmas, every time the telephone rang, Piers jumped. Packing ready to move, especially at Christmas, and for overseas too, was never going to be easy. It was a real strain. Helen could sense the extended pressure on Piers, but she had her own worries about children and clothes and packing up their leave-behind household for store. She knew she would not get a straight answer if she asked; so she let the tension ride. Perhaps one day he'd tell her.

"Mummy!" Helen looked at her daughter, Philippa, unable to cuddle her because of the Christmas cooking ingredients stuck to her hands. The afternoon TV movie had been about pilots in Korea and a memorable scene had been the formation flypast with a vacant slot — their way of having a terminal salute.

"Yes, Phillipa, what is it?" The child had the 'I want' look. It was Xmas.

"When Daddy's gone, can we have a dog?"

Helen's reply was unrecorded. She couldn't resist later telling her husband about their daughter's request and, with a kiss, suggesting the family really would like to have him around for a little bit longer. Mince pie ingredients would wash out.

Piers's reaction was to warn her that the newspaper was stating the temperature in Berlin was minus 5 degrees at noon. "You'll need your winter woollies…!"

For Piers, there was no call from London. The loss remained quiet, unannounced, out of the media: it was almost as though there had been no visitor from London. A duplicate dataset was prepared and couriered, by hand of commissioned officer with an escort, to Stanmore. Piers took minimal interest in the formalities. He was too busy preparing to handover a very special job and he had little time to do it.

Piers booked RAF transport to Heathrow for the afternoon British Airways flight to Berlin and, on Sunday the 15th of January 1983; he would fly into Tegel Airport, Berlin to take up his new appointment. The Defence Intelligence staff knew where to find him if necessary! But now there was the office Christmas party to celebrate.

*   *   *

There was a good deal of pride and self-satisfaction in the dining room of The Swan^{tm} in Goring-on-Thames on that night in 1982. The warmth of the log fire in the grate and the liqueur in his glass did not distract Piers's thoughts.

'Here I sit, in front of a glowing embers on a leather settee, with my principal staff, and I can take pleasure in surveying my creation at well earned relaxation. I regret that the USAF major, who did so much to encourage me in the early days in 1979, is not here. But here, with me, sitting quietly and no doubt reflecting with me, is a Royal Navy Fleet Warrant Officer, who recognises the tri-service cooperation we had built. He presented me with a silver bosun's call, with chain, wrapped in Falkland Island campaign medal ribbon. Where he got the ribbon I don't know; he says the bosun's call is his own so much did he respect my achievement. It will remain a treasured memento among so many.'

Such was the synergy between the two men, at ease in their loungers, that their glances exchanged as though each knew the others' thoughts. Perhaps there was shade of a smile between them, but words were neither necessary nor spoken.

Through the open door, talking with Helen, was the RAF Master Aircrew warrant officer who had been withdrawn from Nimrod flying for medical reasons. At that moment Helen was not looking at Piers. Whatever their topic, she looked content and that pleased Piers. She fully participated and supported him at these social events. She did it voluntarily and that made him grateful. The man was holding her attention.

'He had joined me in 1979. He knows exactly how I feel about what we did although no words have been spoken about it between us. It is the relationship between officer and warrant officer, between responsibility and practitioner, between members of a team with a job to do and the encouragement to get on with it no matter what the pressure. Leadership… the Piers way!'

Piers said to his navy colleague, "It's been a good evening."

"I reckon we've started something here. It…" His next words were lost in the eruption of laughter form the distant room. Lubricated jollity had erupted. It was going to be a long night.

287

'In God we trust; all others we monitor'

26 Signals Unit RAF and US Army Field Station Berlin shared (with detachments of USAF and British Royal Signals groups) a site atop the artificial mound called Teuflesberg (literally Devil's Mountain), West Berlin as photographed in 1983.

The 80 metres high mound above the Berlin plain had been constructed by the women of Berlin, known as *Trümmerfrauen* or 'rubble women' for their efforts, in 1945/46 from the city's rubble resulting from the devastation during World War II. During the Nazi period, the shell of a training Military Technology Faculty building was here. It was first occupied as a signals site by American and British troops in 1954.

Although located in the British (occupied) Zone of Berlin, following successful trials, the Americans negotiated use of the elevated site for, it is said, a one-time down payment of one box of whisky. The signature 100 metre central mast was maintained by the RAF; the 'golf ball' radomes housed American facilities.

The site would close in 1994.

Chapter 37
1983 ~ The Temperature Is -18°C

The five day handover between commanding officers of Number 26 Signals Unit RAF was completed. The professional formalities and introductions, 'excessive despite the shared occupying power status of British troops in Berlin', thought Piers, were done. The two men were standing on the steps of the Teuflesberg entrance, 350 feet above the central German plain on which Berlin is built. The two wing commanders knew each other from Henlow cadetship days although they had not been in the same entry.

"Well, Piers, it's all yours. Enjoy it while it lasts and try to avoid the politics. You've got a reputation for there being a war wherever you get posted. Here, in Berlin where east meets west in checkpoints labelled Alpha, Bravo and Charlie, there's a few of us who hope you've broken that mould!"

"I feel pretty much the same — about war — out here. It's a long walk to West Germany… 105 miles they tell me! Good luck in your new post — in London. Maybe I'll see you there when I visit."

"Yeah. At least it's the other side of the Channel from the Warsaw Pact. I never did get used to being able to hear them starting their tanks with the red star on their turret. Anyway, the RAF'll start paying you for the acting rank tomorrow; it all helps!"

"Oh?" The two men were standing on the entrance steps to the Teuflesberg complex. In the outside January air, the temperature was bitterly cold.

"I'll be driving out tonight. The car's already packed up and my boxes have gone. We'll be staying at Helmstedt overnight, and catching the two o'clock ferry tomorrow. I've got my duty-free cellar in the boot. I hope Customs at Dover doesn't get too ambitious!"

Piers shrugged. Her Majesty's Customs and Excise was not his problem, at least for the moment.

He continued, "You know the geography. Your married quarter is down there, 8 miles away, at the Gatow airfield. The closest military neighbour to RAF Gatow comprises two tank divisions of the National People's Army of East Germany. They are on the other side of the airfield, behind the section of the Berlin Wall where there is the only gap in the whole 117 miles length of the thing. As you drive along the road, or look at it from the RAF Gatow's air traffic control tower, you can see it is not in fact a wall, but a wire fence. East Germany claims that this was a 'military courtesy', but nobody at RAF Gatow believes that; it's their way of making a military invasion easier."

"That's reassuring. Especially if you're in charge! And if your married quarter is on-base."

"Yeah. I shouldn't worry about it; you won't know much about it if it happens! Your only headache here is the number of VIP visitors you get; it averages two a week. Not bad where everyone wants to know your business and you know damn well that you are not going tell them. You'll have a problem with the group captain down on the station; he wants to get in on the inside of this unit and so far I have been able to resist him. Protect your independence, old lad. If you have a problem, talk to London on the scrambler phone."

"The other side know all about what we do. Spies like Geoffrey Prime and all that." The two men were trying hard not to shiver in the cold.

"Maybe… maybe not. Our side doesn't tell you if we know what they know. In this business, the important thing is that we keep our success to ourselves and, out here, you said it… 105 miles inside the Inner German Border …we don't need to know."

"I said it is a long walk out." Piers shrugged as he reached forward with his right hand.

"Well," Piers said while shaking his friend's hand, "enjoy the pleasure of commuting into Whitehall. It's got worse in the last two years!"

"Yeah. I'll work on it." He withdrew his hand and moved towards the waiting staff car grateful to be able to pull a glove over his cold hand. At the bottom of the steps, he turned, "Oh, I nearly forgot… your first VIP is the Minister of State from Bonn — he rates Ambassador status — he's due in 45 minutes. Have a nice day…"

Piers turned and moved inside. The unit was his and 450 men and women depended on him doing the right thing… whatever that meant. Henlow cadetship had never got close at preparing him for the issues of the largest RAF unit of its role… and behind the Iron Curtain too.

*   *   *

OC 26 SU's married quarter was a robust, well insulated, detached house built on three storeys above a full width cellar of four useable rooms. The loft had a visitor's bedroom suite and the normal roof void had a concrete floor strong enough for packing crate storage: it also housed an unnecessarily complex TV aerial since the British Forces Broadcasting Service beamed a strong signal into the airfield from central Berlin. The house was heated from a nearby central boiler house which also served all the officers' single or married quarters. January's snow was lying about 10 inches deep although the main roads were being kept clear by the efficient *Berliner* authorities.

Towards the end of Piers's second week, the station commander decided to have a ground defence exercise. He gave Piers one hour's notice. Late January, central European, snow was not going to divert his intention to test his station's readiness to hold against the hordes of the Red Army streaming across his airfield and who outnumbered any resource he could muster by well-honed nine to one. That they had tanks and he had rifles was part of the challenge. Anyway, it provided a good opportunity for him to test the mettle of the newly promoted officer over whom he had little control.

Piers had a secondary site away from his headquarters on Teuflesberg, employing one third of his personnel, in a former Luftwaffe aircraft hangar located close to the runway at RAF Gatow. Its vulnerability to anything more deadly than peashooters was self-evident and one of Piers's first actions had been to review the processes for rapid destruction of classified material if the worst should happen.

In the short time available, Piers assembled and briefed his officers about the forthcoming exercise. "While we will cooperate with this exercise, there will be no let up in our operational task. I will not change the shift roster and nobody will have their leave plans altered. It's what we would have to do in the real situation — we wouldn't have time to change anyway. I'll warn the Americans that we will be playing with guns through the night, unloaded of course, but personal arms will be issued and the ammunition will be distributed, but remain boxed."

"If we're all working through the night, we'll need feeding," observed one experienced officer.

"At Teuflesberg, the American canteen facility will keep us in hot chilli beans, strong coffee and fizzy drinks. No doubt there will be donuts for breakfast. For you lucky guys at Gatow, the RAF caterers will be providing hot boxes and I shall authorise issue of war reserve rations for hot drinks — the suppliers like to turn their stocks over! Absolutely no alcohol, no matter who declares a tot for medicinal purposes."

"The temperature is forecast to drop to -15°C, with a 25 knot wind, sir. That's some chill factor." A shift officer, more used to working in shirtsleeves within the heated accommodation was making a good point. "American chilli beans at three in the morning ain't my cup of tea." Piers ignored the comment.

"Up on Teuflesberg we can expect it to get colder. With that wind chill factor, it will seem like minus 40 degrees," commented his deputy who was normally officed at Teuflesberg.

"Right," said Piers. This was all new to him; he was making it up as he went along. None of it was written down. "Local defence commanders will roster the men — and women — for no longer than 15 minutes on external guard duties. Full radio contact is to be maintained when anyone moves away from a field telephone. The girls must take their turn outside, no privileges for gender! Double protective clothes, certainly gloves, everyone outside to wear their gas masks to protect against the cold. Experience carrying personal weapons in these clothes will be useful. No smoking by the guards. Be careful to observe night vision precautions. My command room on Teuflesberg will have a landline connection with the station operations room backed up by radio."

"When Uncle Ivan has driven his one hundred tanks through our fence, will we be expected to walk to Teuflesberg to join you guys on the hill?" One of the hangar officers was asking a reasonable question.

"The only bridge across the river wouldn't survive the first five minutes, at least that's my judgement. And it's one thousand tanks not one hundred! Our Army will blow it to delay the soviet tanks driving for the Brandenburg Gate. We're not playing it that real; I would get as many out as I could ahead of the game while we were waiting for the attack. No, no-one is to try walking it. In this snow it would be too dangerous anyway. The concept of local refugees and all our families beggars belief... and the boss has fought shy of exercising that situation. Now, I want all the operational shift positions covered during the post-exercise recovery phase too. No concessions. We'll be playing lip service to the ground defence exercise situation, you know it and I know it. But, it's something different and we'll try to have the boys and girls enjoy the experience."

"Rum ration?" A young officer had heard about the rum issue at the medical officer's discretion. Someone had to ask the question and it had fallen to James Johnson to chance his arm with his new commanding officer.

"I'll repeat myself, absolutely not, James," replied Piers. "If anyone gets hurt, suffers unduly in the cold, he or she is to be moved as quickly as possible to sick quarters for the doctor's ministrations of medicinal fluids. When the exterior guards come in, the duty watch officers are to personally check that all is well. Rum? No? I don't wish to have a bunch of pissed operators on my patch. While we are having our exercise, it will be up to our guys to work out if the other side is doing anything untoward. They are bound to notice we are playing silly buggers, so…"

"I only asked," moaned James Johnson. "I am bound to be asked by a few of the hairy warrant officers."

"Well, you know my line. Now, read the Exercise Order, it's only one page, all of you and take good care of your staff AND let's not have any accidents in the cold."

*   *   *

There were no accidents. The signals unit quickly reverted to its normal routine, learning about their new commanding officer in the process. From Piers's point of view, it was different from the Regiment in Cyprus, much more immediate in tempo and scale of operations. This was an RAF unit in blue uniform. And, for local decisions, the buck stopped with him. The rate of visitors to 26 SU rose as a step function as anyone with the remotest excuse came to see the new commanding officer at work, assess how he was meeting the challenges of the biggest RAF unit of its type in one of the world's most politically and militarily sensitive environments, those visitors taking advantage of duty-free living in the process.

Helen and Piers had a consequential duty social life to follow while not neglecting RAF community of which they were an integral part.

London remained hard taskmasters, forever seeking maximum returns for the investment in equipment and manpower put into the unit. And, for the first year, there was the constant security overhead of the Geoffrey Prime spy fallout. Piers had had a privileged briefing, but that did not stop the flow of provost officers, security services' individuals and

Cabinet Ministers all seeking to be sure that there would be no repetition of a 'Prime-like' defector emerging like a phoenix from where Prime had learned his tradecraft in Berlin. So Piers had to accept the burden of repeat security clearance checks on his 450 staff, the constant tentacles of surveillance for any potential personal weakness, and the detailed intrusion into every process within the unit for potential security weakness. All the while, the unit had to meet its operational task without relaxation and with the majority of visitors having only the barest knowledge of, and less understanding of how, the job was done.

Relationships with the Americans on Teuflesberg were paramount to Piers. US Army Field Station Berlin was commanded by a full colonel and, as such, Piers deferred to him all matters concerning security and access control within the triple layers of barbed wire fence surrounding the site. Although geographically located within the British (occupied) sector of the city, within the site the place was as American as blueberry pie. Their weapons were real and loaded. Only within his own front door, manned by RAF Policemen, did his own national rules apply and it was here that he proudly displayed the triangular command pennant, appropriate to his wing commander rank, over an RAF ensign. On his patch, no weapons were on open display although his RAF Provost security personnel had ready access just in case.

The dual nationality status of the site was marked by the flying of the USA flag alongside the Union Jack; when the American needed to fly their Stars and Stripes at half mast, so also the British flag would be lowered in respect. The flags were the overt display between obvious allies. Only those knowledgeable about the inner workings of the staffs, the true operational roles of the thousand military and civilian operatives and support staffs within the site's buildings, understood the friendship and professional camaraderie yet separation between the two nations. It was governed by 'need-to-know' security principles and that was the way it had to be, from friends and family alike.

Chapter 38
1983 to 1985 ~ A Shadow Within The Wall

The sealed envelope on Saladin Hussein's desk had all the hallmarks of something serious. He could recognise the poor quality paper as meaning it had come from the East.

'Perhaps this is something more interesting than watching British squaddies or American grunts guarding a decrepit Nazi inside a treble locked cell. Even if Hess got out, how could the old man possibly get away from Spandau Gaol?'

Ten kilometres north of RAF Gatow and within the British Sector of the divided city was the district of Spandau, now well recovered from the allied aerial bombardment of three decades before. Other than its shopping opportunities, considered by many as excellent despite the continued isolation of West Berlin in 1983, Spandau's principal claim to fame was its former castle. This unimposing structure now served as prison for its sole occupant — the former *Reichsminister* Rudolf Walter Richard Hess one time deputy to Hitler until his parachute descent from a Messerschmitt 110 aircraft, after a five hour 900 mile flight to Scotland, landed him in custody. Forty years later, at Spandau, he was guarded on monthly rotation by troops of the four occupying powers. The Soviet military took this responsibility seriously; it provided the opportunity to transit the width of West Berlin and justified the presence of a permanent liaison clerk's office in the prison.

'By all the torments of Allah — it's so cold. It didn't get this cold even on the top of Mount Olympus in my beloved Cyprus.' He was rubbing his hands together in a forlorn hope of getting some warmth to his extremities. 'But in here, the filthy British keep it so cold. We let them bring enough coal in from their filthy exploitationist mines.' The view from the office window, over the exercise courtyard now 50 centimetres deep in untrammelled snow, simply emphasised the point. 'I'll have a cup of imperialist American coffee then I'll open the letter.' It was the only correspondence on the otherwise clear desk.

A double check that the door was locked and then to business. The contents were double enveloped with the inner franked 'For Saladin Hussein's eyes only'. The sticky sealing tape across every corner had not been tampered with and the date-stamp with superimposed recognisable signature was certainly intact. Security in this sanctum within the British occupied zone of West Berlin had remained intact. Warming his hands around his coffee mug, which he had placed in his protective custody while visiting a NAAFI canteen (code for 'liberated'), it was time for a double check that the windows were not being overlooked. Good. Then break the seals.

von: Office of Head of Department 17
Ministerium für Staatssicherheit
Deutsche Demokratische Republik
1983, 10 January

To: Agent FILFAR

Subject: Ploughman – Piers Peter, Squadron Leader British Royal Air Force

We have information, from known reliable unofficial sources, that the subject who is known to you is to arrive by British Airways at Tegel airfield on 1983, 15 January. You will re-establish covert surveillance of this officer and report, with photographic evidence, any contacts he makes with any Berlin contacts or other entities within the Grenzmauer 75 (Border Wall '75). The subject's travels beyond the Border Wall are the responsibility of others.

You are to take all necessary measures to ensure your operations are not compromised by the western authorities. You are not to discuss this operation with anyone outside the offices of Department 17 in East Berlin.

You are to destroy by burning and scattering the ashes of this instruction.
(signed)
Hans-Jürgen Hecht

for ***Erich Mielke***
Hauptverwaltung Aufklärung

'So the bug on the telephone has done the business again. Good for the comrades! I'll read the instructions again and then work out how I am going to avoid triggering the smoke alarm when I burn it… as those foolish French spies did last month. It is too cold to have to go outside for a simple mistake.'

*   *   *

"You have done well, Huseyin Yildirim. Twenty eight months of satisfactory surveillance has been praised by Herr Mielke himself."

"Thank you, Herr Controller."

"You record that Wing Commander Ploughman has departed Berlin through what they call Checkpoint Bravo. Our vigilant Border Police provided you with copies of his transit papers and their passports for our records."

"Yes, Herr Controller. With his family and their papers. His replacement arrived by transport aircraft, at Gatow airfield, on the Wednesday shuttle from England. There are two photographs of the officers at the greeting ceremonies and a transcript of their conversation, from our sensitive microphone on the *Grenzmauer 75* watch tower, in the folder. I have discontinued surveillance, in accordance with your written instructions and await re-assignment."

Yildirim was trying to relax, but in the presence of Controller Hussein it was unwise.

"You are ready for your new task?" It was not so much a question as a statement. In this room, the most secret room in the Office of State Security in East Berlin, the wise field agent did not question the wishes of his controller. Yildirim nodded. He would be grateful for an early excuse to get away from this room, this building.

Saladin Hussein needed a cigarette and a measure of the Scotch whisky he had become accustomed to while working in Spandau. Saladin Hussein, also known as Agent *FILFAR,* was grateful this mission was closing down; he did not relish being little more than a post boy — no more than a courier. His talents for extracting information from the NATO lackeys in the night clubs of West Berlin were much more to his taste.

"I'll be passing copies of your reports to our comrades in Moscow and Prague. The KGB has expressed great interest in that target." Hussein was touching the image of Wing Commander Ploughman on one of the photographs. "But you don't need to know any more."

"Yes, Herr Controller. I mean… no, Herr Controller." Yildirim was anxious that he was not going to have move away from the good food and easy living with the US Army in Berlin.

"You will be recruited as a vehicle maintenance mechanic by the United States Army Field Station, where you will be based at their headquarters on the artificial hill they call Teuflesberg. In there, you will cultivate contacts with knowledge about the security activities within this site. You do not need to concern yourself with United States Air Force or British activities which are taken care of by other reliable unofficial sources. Do I make myself clear? Keep clear of the British so that a link back to Spandau is not possible."

"And the French, Herr Controller?"

"There is no need to concern yourself with the French at Teuflesberg." The Controller was tapping the tips of his fingers on his clear desktop, but his eyes never ceased to engage Yildirim's.

"Do you have any particular American opportunity in mind, Herr Controller?"

"There is a warrant officer by the name of James Hall who has volunteered to cooperate. He is an army intelligence analyst. He seems to have a passion for cars, so that might be a start. Your knowledge of western automobiles will be useful. Let me know how you get on. All materials are to be passed through the usual channels."

"Yes, Herr Controller."

"And that American woman who shares your bed …" so the Controller knew about Peggy, "… she does not need to know anything." Those fingertips were busy again.

"Yes, Herr Controller."

"It is time for you to begin. You may leave, Yildirim." The open palm of dismissal indicated the interview was terminated. Turkish born, 54 years old, Huseyin Yildirim had begun on a path which would bring him to the attention of the CIA and eventually, in July 1989, to life imprisonment without parole. It would also seal the fate of Warrant Officer Hall, convicted of spying for the east.

"And next time you come through Checkpoint Charlie, be sure to bring me a fifth of Jack Daniels^{tm}."

Yildirim was through the door as quickly as possible to avoid further tasking by his controller.

Yildirim had been out of the room for 30 seconds when Erich Mielke entered without knocking. The Controller sat upright, but did not stand as the senior man settled in a chair.

"You heard, comrade?" asked Hussein. He received a silent nod. Mielke had bigger fish to fry. He was quickly seated.

His briefing was succinct. "This man, Yildirim, Agent Filfar." Mielke nodded his head at the closed door. "He is expendable. When the time is appropriate, he can be wasted to cover better sources inside Washington and Cheltenham. The same goes for Hall. But we don't have a good insight to the tactical use of the electronic data that the western agencies capture from our careless use of radio. We don't expect to get that from Hall. That is where the background information on Ploughman could take us — to the inside of western technological developments before their armed forces even know they exist."

"Do you expect Ploughman to return to Berlin?"

"It is of no consequence. We'll be his shadow wherever he goes and even when the lights go out. If we can't crack Ploughman directly, we may have success with his contacts."

"We found no opportunity to compromise the target while he was in Berlin. The RAF's security screen around him was impenetrable. Do you still have the tape?"

"Yes, comrade." Mielke's body language stated the unspoken command to play a tape cassette now. "You will recall the circumstances, comrade. The desk telephone was open and he was interviewing his deputy after being in hospital. It is a clear recording:

"Ploughman: The army docs in BMH Berlin, after I had done my back under a washing machine (don't ask!), dosed me with what the nurses called a 'happy cocktail' built out of 'mogadon^{tm}/vallium^{tm}/anti-inflamatory. The bloody concoction turns a man's gonads on alright.

Jacob Morris: Sound interesting.

Ploughman: I might add they had me on a stretch machine like a torture rack from the Tower of London.

Jacob Morris: Sounds even more interesting.

Ploughman: Happy cocktail? I'll be buggered if it was. Not being one for profanities, they were *** **** right, in spades! The nurses didn't tell me that I'd suffer withdrawal symptoms! ...probably because I chased most of them around the officers' ward in my shreddies.

Jacob Morris: Word of this has not filtered out, sir.

Ploughman: I should bloody hope not. I've not even told Helen. At the time, for Christ's sake, I had command of the largest, not to say the highest security, British formation in Berlin. As far as I know, I still do.

Jacob Morris: Very worrying, sir. My wife said you were acting rather strangely when she visited you.

Ploughman: At the worst times, I used to go into a corner of the office and crouch in the foetal position. I told the security officer that if he found me he was to get an ambulance and get me out to the room in Gatow's sick quarters where the army couldn't see me.

Jacob Morris: So we all had our troubles. I am glad to see you have made a complete recovery, sir."

Mielke waved his hand across his throat to stop the tape. He directed that a transcript was inserted in Ploughman's file.

"Yes, comrade."

"There will be other chances when he is in the west. His guard will be down and their Security Service will not be protecting him. We shall be vigilant in cracking that nut, Agent Filfar. Ploughman is potentially a very useful window into their tactical doctrine."

"That is good news, comrade."

"And you are to identify your replacement, Agent Filfar."

"Have I caused displeasure?"

"No, it is time for you to relocate from this easy life of Berlin whores and western alcohol. You will be using your English from a new base, Agent Filfar. We think it is time for you to test your skills in London."

Mielke was reaching for his briefcase and the tape. The interview was terminated.

Chapter 39
1985/86 ~ Go To Henlow, Do Not Pass Go

"The Director of Military and Scientific Intelligence tells me you are the right man for the job." The Air Commodore was in no mood for an argument. The view from his office window looked out across the familiar sports field to the RAF Henlow Officers' Mess. Piers had nor escaped from Henlow's clutches after all, no home to the RAF's signals support staffs.

"I've never met this DMSI. He certainly didn't come to Berlin while I was there."

"Sometimes we have to do what we are told! That includes you! I have been directed to release you for two weeks. Your instructions and travel papers have been retained in DMSI's office in Metropole House, London. You are to go there tomorrow, see the wise man at 14:00, and take it from there. I am advised you should take your passport — I suppose it is current, Ploughman? All I know is that you are going to the States with a civilian minder. Just let my PA know your dates... when you know them; I don't need to know where you are going... she's already got your rail warrant to London."

"What do I tell Helen? We had a caravan booked on the Isle of Man."

"If she can't take a joke, she shouldn't have joined."

'Oh Christ!' thought Piers. 'It's another cold night in the guest room!'

*　　*　　*

Cyril King hinted to Piers he was based at Aldermaston, the home of UK nuclear research. He certainly didn't glow in the dark. Credible cover stories are supposed to be convincing!

But Piers was not convinced. Something about King's manner which suggested GCHQ, and yet... Piers had seen enough of what he called 'the flat earth society' not to be persuaded with that identity either. They were not briefed that they would be visiting NSA, or any other familiar American intelligence organisation. Perhaps while they were travelling together for two weeks, this King-fellow might open up a bit.

All Piers could glean was that Cyril had read and apparently understood the Top Secret ABLATIVE folder in DMSI's private office, as had he. Well, he had read it and tried to understand the papers, but concepts such as electro-magnetic vortex fields and bending time were a bit much for a simple airman! — even if he had been especially requested, by name, by someone with clout in Washington. He had to sign a register that he'd read it. That folder was unusual too; it was WWII foolscap size when modern covers were A4. Also, it was the wrong colour, beige, for top secret which was always deep scarlet. Now, within an hour and near the witching hour on a Friday night, their RAF VC-10 transport aircraft would disgorge the pair at Washington Dulles airport — the RAF's air transport staging post and formal entry portal into continental USA.

Somehow, a minder from the Radar Research Establishment at Malvern did not adequately fit Cyril either. Farnborough? No he dressed too well to be a research scientist…

Cyril was, in Piers's opinion, a nice guy. Based on 8 hours adjacent seating in the unprivate cabin of a VC-10 on sweaty plastic seats, Piers had learned that the minder who he had first met in the Officers' Lounge of the Transit Hotel RAF Brize Norton was married. He lived, he said, in the 'the West Country' and did not trust the Yanks when they had — or might have — their own agenda. At least DMSI's aide had confirmed they both shared the exclusive ABLATIVE clearance of which Piers had never previously heard. They had been told to expect to be met, at Dulles, by a similarly cleared American individual named Doctor Roderick Chmielewski who had made the necessary hotel bookings, agency accesses and all internal travel within the States.

"If the Americans are picking up the tab for internal flights", opined Cyril, "someone sure as hell wants to talk. But what the dickens about?"

Piers thought that, 'Perhaps the Royal Aircraft Establishment at Farnborough is Cyril's heritage. Don't dismiss it on scant evidence. We'll see.'

Piers was not impressed by the American border admission process. Cyril King breezed through immigration formalities on his passport, presumably due to some covert marking on his entry visa. Unlike every other NATO country, Piers's RAF identity card — his RAF Form 1250 — was not recognised as a guarantee of his bona fides by Britain's closest ally. "British passport… join the queue, sir…at the back, sir…" After some extended wrangling, it took the intervention of an army uniformed, heavily medalled, pistol-packing official wearing full bird-colonel collar studs to let him into the land of the free and then only on production of his British passport, RAF identity card, completed immigration form, driving licence and inoculation certificate.

Thereafter, Doctor Chmielewski ("call me Roddy") was on hand through customs, taxi cab, hotel reservations at the Ramada™ Arlington, and into the hotel bar before delivering a timetable for the forthcoming series of meetings which would take the British visitors across the length and breadth of the USA. First stop would be the Pentagon — a car from the hotel reception at 07:45, Monday.

"Have two nice days! Oh, don't go to Georgetown with those accents..." and he was gone.

Piers was thinking about the day's events as he stood in the shower with his body already complaining about the five hours time zone change. 'Strange how Dr Roddy Chmielewski had no difficulty about my name. The Americans in Berlin never got the hang of it.'

*　　　*　　　*

Monday morning, inside the massive Pentagon building, three storeys up, two corridors in, double sound-proofed doors from an outer office into a darkened conference room with chairs sufficient for fifty. Piers noticed how it differed from secure rooms in Cheltenham and London — or his own in Berlin. Here it was padded with leather walls, windowless, soundless. Two men stood waiting as Roddy escorted Piers and Cyril to chairs.

"Let's introduce ourselves," opened Roddy Chmielewski. "This meeting is Top Secret ABLATIVE US/UK Eyes Only. No notes, no papers, no recordings, no images."

"Right. I'm Julius Knapp, better known as "Jules" to my friends and, I suspect, to the reds as well. I'm a grade 16 out of Special Projects Office, Department of Homeland Security." The speaker was grey haired, mature and well dressed.

The next speaker raised his hand. He sported a very short haircut and had the bearing of a military man. His uniform carried three rows of medal ribbons. "Hi. I'm Jodell Lee Grant, Colonel, US Army Intelligence Corps. For today's purpose, my qualification for being here is that I served with the 1574th SPSG at Snodland, Kent, England until April 1944 and was then assigned to follow up on German SS General Hans Kammler until he disappeared in May '45."

The host was short, close cropped and noticeably upright. His bearing exuded confidence and his practice at public speaking was evident from the outset. "My name is Roddy Chmielewski. I majored in sub-atomic physics at MIT, Boston and sometimes flaunt the Doctor when it will buy me a beer. I'm hosting this exercise because, in 1943/44, I was US Army Air Corps Lieutenant Colonel Operations Officer and Senior Intelligence Officer, No 1574th Special Projects Support Group flying modified P-38M out of RAF West Malling. My commanding officer was one Colonel Makepiece Ploughman who died about seven years ago. Our headquarters was at RAF Snodland, as Jodell said."

'Ah! The explanation of the ease with the Ploughman name,' thought Piers with a nod.

"My name is Cyril King, reader in advanced propulsion systems at Cranfield University College, Emeritus Lecturer at the Military Academy at Shrivenham, sometime specialist adviser to the Joint Intelligence Committee on subatomic physics. I am fluent in German, Russian and most Slavic languages."

"And I am Wing Commander Piers Ploughman. My speciality is in the field of reconnaissance, predominantly electronic, although I have some knowledge of the technology and limitations of imagery from space and air-breathing platforms. I should say that I have no knowledge of the American officer whose name is similar to mine; indeed I had never heard of him before reading the ABLATIVE file in London."

"Thank you, gentlemen." Chmielewski wanted to get on with the business at hand. Their first plane departure would leave Washington National Airport at noon. "Julius, would you please take the lead." With a hand gesture by the host, all attention switched to Julius Knapp.

"We are gathered because we have KEYHOLE satellite imagery to suggest that the Russians may be reopening the Wenceslas Mine facility in Silesia, Poland that was of Presidential concern way back in '43. Back then, we had the word that Hitler was researching a weapon credited with knocking the spots off the atomic bomb which at that date no-one had yet tested. So the President sent the 1574th to go and find out. Roddy will bring in for each of us a copy of 1574th final flight mission report in March 1944, together with the follow up analysis done by the working party extracted from the MANHATTAN bomb project to advise the President. Some of our conclusions were not released to the British —

not even to Churchill. And we were pleased that Joe Stalin took no interest in the place when he was going for Berlin. I can tell you this CHRONOS weapon sure scared the pants off some White House butts. You must commit the details to memory, gentlemen; nothing leaves this room except to go back in the safe in the outer office."

"Are you… er… we…. sure the Germans actually tested the device?" queried Cyril. "I mean… where?... when?... There'd be a pretty big hole if it went off!"

"Something happened when Colonel Ploughman overflew the site in March '44. There is photographic and electronic recording of the event backed up with communications intelligence transcribed by Jodell here. The original material is still available, but I don't think we'll be able to get more details out of the films; the technology was not very good compared with today's capability."

"That's correct, gentlemen. Also, we have reason to believe that simultaneously with the release of enormous levels of energy, the Germans launched a substantial aircraft possibly with the assistance of altered gravity — the so-called 'zero point' prediction made by Einstein." Jodell Grant was reflecting nearly forty years of accumulated frustration at the lack of closure of the whole Wenceslas Mine affair. "We don't want the Russians to have this technology. And we know that President Reagan wants to share this knowledge with Prime Minister Thatcher."

"Gentlemen," interrupted Chmielewski with opening his palm towards the assembly, "time presses. We should refresh our memories and then we have to travel some. We can talk about the niceties later. We have an appointment with the Assistant Chief on Friday week and he goes to brief the President that day at 14:00. By the time our British visitors have crossed the Atlantic, Ronnie will have chatted to Maggie and they will be working out what to say to NATO."

*   *   *

Eleven days later and the two British investigators were sitting in a quiet corner of the Dulles airport departures lounge waiting for the call forward to the RAF VC-10 return flight to UK.

"If they had asked me I'd have told them that they — the Russians — would have needed an awful lot of dc current to get the CHRONOS bell device to go critical. When, or by whoever, it was destroyed with its nearby power station, they took away the basic ingredient to power the whole thing. The birdcage, henge or whatever it is, would need megawatts of shock to make it resonate and, even then, it would probably fry any reasonable power cables the Germans could have installed. The reinforcing rods in the concrete, too, I shouldn't wonder."

"So you are saying," summarised Piers, "that we should tell DMSI that our considered view is that the Russians are wasting their time if they are going after CHRONOS. Without oodles of energy there's no hope. Our interpretation of the imagery is that they may be reactivating the worked out silver mines, or trying to. They might find some unusual isotopes when they do their metallic analyses, but that is part of the fun in doing geology. If they find a few skeletons, Moscow'll write them off to enthusiastic slave masters during the war."

"Well, there is always the secondary matter of the flying vehicle…"

"Go on. We know that Colonel Ploughman photographed something launched vertically, possibly from the birdcage. The German voice exchange later confirmed as much."

"There has been no trace of the vehicle… err… aircraft… whatever it was… but, heading north, would take it over lots of ocean or icy wilderness even if it didn't burn up with aerodynamic heating. There are all sorts of metallurgy problems above Mach 3.5," Cyril was frowning with thought. "It really is not surprising that we've never found it. Perhaps it's the way that Kammler got out of Germany. Who knows? But unless the Germans invented the secret of eternal youth, our General Hans Kammler would be in his mid-eighties, maybe nineties, and probably long time dead."

"You don't think this whole thing is a Yank coverup, do you? What if Kammler was a PAPERCLIP lift like von Braun leading to the Apollo mission to the Moon? Kammler could have been given a new identity to give the Americans a technology edge. Maybe a new face and, God knows, he needed it! Photogenic he wasn't! Persuading us that the Wenceslas Mine story had really been closed down, taking all its secrets to oblivion, would suit the American black projects' paymasters rather nicely. Putting one over the Brits is not beyond them."

"They've done it before, Piers. Look what they did to the jet engine!"

"That was a long time ago. We're on the same side now." Then, a little more tentatively, "Aren't we? Anyway the Yanks didn't close Wenceslas, the Krauts did!"

"They certainly seemed genuine enough, those Americans that is. I think they were a bit long in the tooth to be acting out some drama to fool a couple of Brits." Cyril King was shaking his head as if he was not altogether convinced. "I think we should tell it as we found it, over here, and let the high priced help in Whitehall work out who to believe."

Suddenly Cyril's face creased with a grin, "Hey, Piers. We're missing out on good drinking time. It's a pity the RAF hasn't found out that passengers fly better when they're half sozzled. Just think, we've haven't touched our temporary duty allowances yet. I'll buy the first round."

"Just one thing, why did they ask for me? I had never heard of that Makepiece Ploughman guy. Surely it was not anything to do with the Falkland Islands and their idea of revenge for my asking for their help. That would be taking it a bit too far, wouldn't it?"

The two men rose from their chairs, and after checking the departure board, moved directly towards the nearest bar.

"Tell you what, Cyril, we could drop the idea that someone is looking for a new skiing centre and the project hasn't been cleared with Nike^{tm}. Mine's a brandy and coke…"

Chapter 40
1986 ~ Tea at Chequers

The message waiting at RAF Brize Norton was to the effect that both were expected to take lunch at The George Hotel in Wendover the next day, a Sunday. An RAF staff car would convey them to Chequers where the Prime Minister would receive them at 3 o'clock.

"Those Yanks certainly did have a bee in their bonnets," commented Cyril.

"I expect DMSI will be there. Who else, I wonder?"

So it was agreed that Piers would take the lead in explaining to Mrs Thatcher what it was that had so energised the American President and his staff. They also agreed that it was best to assume that 'she' would want an overview and would ask for technical detail if she thought it necessary.

At the appointed time, the three men stood waiting for the 'enter' command. The Director of Military and Scientific Intelligence shook hands with Piers and Cyril King and he advised that the Prime Minister would set up the interview so that she had an unobstructed view of the visiting guests. They were in the Stone Hall and were to be ushered into the Hawtry Room which, much to Piers's surprise, was furnished as a drawing room rather than a conference or presentation suite. Chequers's Hawtry Room is a splendid lounge of the Prime Minister's official residence, in the foothills of the Chiltern Hills, since the house was gifted to the nation in 1921. A major oil landscape adorned the wall above the fireplace, but it scarcely competed with the real view from the near full height leaded glass window. The visitors were invited to make themselves comfortable, but not offered refreshment.

"We know why we are here, so let's get on with it, gentlemen."

"Ma'am," opened Piers, "the site of interest is on the Czech/Polish border at about 4500 feet. It is rated as good skiing country. In World War 2, the Americans identified advanced weapons research at the site, thought to be of the highest priority, because Himmler had assigned an unique security classification to the project. In short, they called it *Critical to the War Effort — The War Winner —* and of greater significance than their work on the atomic bomb or fuel-air bomb technologies."

Mrs Thatcher was all attention. She enjoyed having a professional serviceman share advanced engineering — such an interesting diversion from the trivialities of the European Union. Her body language encouraged the young officer to continue.

"It seems the Germans had latched on to some pre-war Czech research about an Einstein mathematical prediction of unimaginable energy stored in the atom. Find the key to that store and the maths showed you could bend time itself."

She sat with her hands clasped in her lap and her eyes never straying from the speaker's face. Cyril noticed that her visage was just off the smile and that she swallowed with a slight movement of her lower jaw. He was not sure if the lady believed what she was being told with such confidence; she had graduated from Oxford University with a science degree.

"The Germans probably destroyed their underground, I mean, mined or caved facilities and removed the plant from the nearby power station ahead of the Red Army advance into Eastern Poland in late 1944. It is believed that Himmler, or his principal engineer General Hans Kammler, had all the knowledgeable scientists shot before their knowledge could be passed on to the Allies. But, on the site, the Germans had constructed a very strong, reinforced concrete, structure rather like a twelve pillar 'Stonehenge' which has remained largely unweathered by time and is clearly visible from space. The purpose of this henge is disputed."

The Prime Minister nodded her understanding of what she was being told. She hoped this young man would get on with it. Ronnie Reagan must have had some reason to ring her. Piers tried to gauge if he was pitching his story at the right depth.

"Well, Ma'am, American satellites noticed some obviously military manoeuvres in progress about four weeks ago. The visible and infrared signatures were obvious and served to associate activity at the henge with a nearby cave entrance. But we could not identify any construction or assembly work of telltale structures necessary for a high power electricity generating plant. No fuel store, additional cooling plant, that sort of thing. No on-site accommodation or specific security fences. It was possible that any such work was underground, but there was no sign of heavy truck movement on the nearby forest roads or access tracks. In short, Ma'am, we concluded that the Soviets are not reactivating the henge as a high powered weapon research facility."

"If that is so, then what were they doing... and are they still doing it?"

"I... we... believe they may be testing the site for its radio interference qualities — a sort of long range communications jammer. Alternatively, it is a long way from any built-up area, so it could be useful as a radio monitoring facility or even something to do with their space programme. As you know, Ma'am, in telecommunications, in the lower atmosphere there is a phenomenon in which radio signals are guided or ducted so as to follow the curvature of the Earth, and at the same time experience less attenuation in these ducts than they would if the ducts were not present. The duct acts as an atmospheric waveguide and limits the spread of the wavefront to only the horizontal dimension. We know that in over-the-horizon radar, ducting causes part of the radiated and target-reflection energy of a radar system to be guided over distances far greater than the normal radar range. It also causes long distance propagation of radio signals in bands that would normally be limited to line of sight."

Mrs Thatcher nodded. She offered, "The sort of thing we were doing at Orfordness?"

"I believe so, Ma'am. The Soviets are very strong on over-the-horizon radar with lots of consequential interference problems experienced in Canada as they monitor ICBM test launches from the US mid-west. But I don't think that is what they are doing here. The henge limbs are not tall enough to be good HF antennae, for frequencies 3 to 30 MHz. But above that frequency band, say in Army land-mobile frequencies up to those used by aircraft and microwave point-to-point links, reduced refractive index due to lower densities at the higher altitudes in the Earth's atmosphere bends the signals back toward the Earth. It's a bit like a mirror at altitude. In some situations and weather conditions, atmospheric density changes so rapidly that radio waves are guided around the curvature of the earth at constant altitude. What that means is that signals thought to be line-of-sight may now be interceptable over hundreds — maybe thousands — of miles. But we could not identify any VHF antennae either."

Piers hesitated then cleared his throat. "Forgive me, Ma'am, am I being too technical?"

The *Iron Lady* shook her head, "Go on, Wing Commander, you're doing just fine."

"A third option we considered, Prime Minister," interjected Cyril King, "was the possible use of the henge as a transmitter aerial associated with a killer beam in their version of anti-satellite 'star wars'. But there was the absence of power plant and… how could they steer their beam? The henge definitely is immobile."

"You've told me what it isn't, so what is the site used for?" Piers noticed the characteristic lowering of the pitch of the Prime Minister's voice and the slight adjustment of her body position.

"Ma'am, we don't now believe it is used for anything other than recreation — skiing for those with transport to get away from it all. The sort of place where the military of the Warsaw Pact might exercise. Much the same as our Marines exercise in Norway!"

"Are you telling me that the Americans dragged you over there, at their cost, to watch a bunch of Red Army infantry playing snowballs?"

"It seems so, Ma'am. It cost me a holiday on the Isle of Man!"

"Is this what your American colleagues are telling the White House?"

"Of course we can't be sure… but…"

"Go on."

"They won't want to lose face. So they'll probably dream up some worrying interpretation and send an innocent TV crew in looking for the lesser-crested snow bats as an excuse to get into the Wenceslas mines and caves."

The Prime Minister was not impressed. She glanced out of the window as though she wished she was in the fresh air. "Tell me, Wing Commander, who was this Kammler?" Someone had been briefing the Prime Minister in some detail. She still had her penetrating gaze fixed on the RAF officer. Was this the onset of a proverbial handbagging? Piers was telling her how he saw the matter at hand.

"General Hans Friedrich Karl Franz Kammler was born in 1901 in Stettin, Poland. He was an engineer and high-ranking officer of the SS. He oversaw SS construction projects and, towards the end of World War II, was put in charge of the V-2 missile programme. He is credited with the destruction of the Warsaw ghetto, the development of the Jewish extermination camps and many advanced weapon projects. The exact circumstances of his death are unknown, but he is thought either to have been killed in the fighting around Prague, possibly shot on his own orders by his adjutant or maybe escaped in a heavy lift transport aircraft to South America. One fanciful rumour is that he did a deal with Patton or even bought his own skin with the Russians. There is no proof of any of these stories."

His comment was received with a frown. The great lady did not like unanswered issues.

"May I add one other thing, Prime Minister?" Receiving no indication that a further comment might be unwelcome, Piers continued, "Well, ma'am. Wenceslas Mine is a long way inside the Inner German Border which is already copiously equipped with radio monitoring sites. I have heard a figure of more than 50,000 men are listening to NATO activity from East Germany and most of them along the Iron Curtain. I don't think they would split their resources to a site so deep behind their front line unless there was something exceptional about the geographic location and isolation of the site. We simply don't know."

"Thank you." It was her clear instruction to 'shutup'! "Do you have any comment, on behalf of Cranfield, Mr King?"

"I have nothing to add to what has already been said, Prime Minister. I'll ask my contact at GCHQ to have them double check with their NSA liaison group when I return to college, and let DMSI have the details."

"Thank you." Turning to DMSI, the Prime Minister issued the one word question, "Director?"

DMSI, having sat patiently through this wasted Sunday afternoon, suggested, "We need to keep in the American's good books. I suggest that when you call the President back, you tell him that we are really concerned that the Russians may be using former German installations to monitor what NATO manoeuvres and exercises we are planning. He can rely on our support, for anything he can do, to find out what's going on at the Wenceslas site. Perhaps one of the American Defence Attaché folk in Prague could take a skiing holiday in the Silesian Mountains?"

"That sounds a good way forward." The Prime Minister stood and offered her hand. "Thank you Director, gentlemen. Let's get on with what's left of a Sunday afternoon. It's a shame to be indoors. Director, would you give me a minute?" The other two left, closing the door behind them.

Out the hearing of the others, Mrs Thatcher said, "Did I detect that there was something else to this story? You looked a little tense."

"Prime Minister. There really is no conclusive evidence about what the Soviet bloc is up to there — if anything. I checked with MI-6 and GCHQ and neither can offer anything. I suspect nothing sinister is going on, but the Americans are really agitated. I have got no basis to surmise anything at any level of security. I fancy that war games or leisure pursuits are the most likely. However, one tool which we have not tried is satellite active radar surveillance which would not be fooled by infrared masking camouflage or bad weather. The technique is being developed to survey the outer planets as part of our contribution to the European space programme. Some of Farnborough's early test results, using orbital passes over Norfolk, have produced images as good as any in visible light. I'll get the team at Farnborough to do a couple of test runs over West Poland and have my folks at the Joint Air Reconnaissance Interpretation Centre evaluate the images without specific prompting. That way we will avoid any possible bias and maybe steal a march on the Pentagon."

"Is there something you have not told me, Director?"

"Well, yes Prime Minister. The American Keyhole satellites circulate the globe in fairly fixed orbit. In short, their time overhead in known with considerable precision. We assume the Russians know this. So they can hide or even stop what they are doing when a satellite is due and therefore keep their secrets undetected by that source. However, our radar satellite is horizon to horizon, visibility independent, and, being a research tool, unclassified except in its ultimate processing power which uses state of the art computers in ground-based laboratories. We have no reason to believe the Russian are paying it any attention. In short, Prime Minister, if there's something to see then we ought to be able to see it."

"Thank you for that, Director. Make it happen and let me know what you find, if anything. Goodbye and good luck."

After a 20 minutes drive away from the Elizabethan façade of Chequers, as Piers climbed into his own car parked in Wendover, he reflected that he still had not learned where Cyril King really came from or what he did. Cranfield aeronautical lecturer, maybe, but there was more to the guy than that. 'And what did the *Iron Lady* say to DMSI? Has my career taken another turning down the pan?'

*   *   *

"How did you get on at Chequers, Piers?"

"Not even a bloody cup of coffee. You would have thought that after criss-crossing across America on a hair brained, wild goose chase, she'd have offered a cuppa. Well I hope I didn't screw it!"

"What? Screw what, dear?"

"It! Research into how the Warsaw Pact trains its alpine skiers to, err… ski."

"That doesn't sound a good reason to stop your holiday in the Isle of Man, my love."

"Right."

"I thought you were a telecommunications engineer, not a sports coach. Alpine skiers sounds more like their line of work."

"Right." Piers shrugged. "What's for tea, Love? I had lunch in Wendover while I was waiting. I'd love an egg and bacon sandwich. Filling the travel claim form for the last two weeks is going to require a lot of creative accounting. Why do I stay in this madhouse called the RAF?"

Helen shrugged. "Because you love it, my dear… game, set and match!"

"But I did get to hear about a Colonel Makepiece Ploughman, who flew from Snodland during the war. Perhaps we could take a weekend off and do some detective work. It would make a change…"

Chapter 41
1988 ~ Back On The Heritage Trail

Piers had timed their journey to Maidstone so as to avoid the London ring road, the recently completed M25, during the morning rush hour. But he had planned without the road delays resulting from work on the new high speed rail link between London Waterloo and the Channel Tunnel. Arriving nearly two hours later than planned, they were lucky to find somewhere to park in the Maidstone railway station car park which happened to be within walking distance of the Kent County Archive.

Piers was tired before he started to search old documents and had to work hard to contain his patience as yet another identity security check and stowing their bags in a lockable locker cleared their way into the big room.

With sets of readers' tables beneath windows along one wall and rows of bookcases along another, the room looked falsely busy with a library's dry atmosphere. On the distant wall there were two doors: one closed while the other appearing to usher into a darkened room with an unknown number of film and fiche readers. Even at eleven o'clock, on the main floor, there were six readers with papers spread over their tables including one middle aged fellow in a lawyer's suit poring over an old parchment map that was bigger than the table top. Everyone seemed to be writing furiously with pencil into notebook. None looked up as the Ploughman couple entered the room, the double doors closing silently behind them.

The centre of the room was occupied, dominated, by a counter service containing two women and one man, all apparently beavering away at material on individual busy desks with computer screens flickering with white texts on green. They did not move as Piers and Helen approached. At the same time, a grey-haired lady appeared from through the open internal doorway clutching three boxes of microfilm cassette. She put the cartons on the counter, without stopping, said, "Thank you," and made for the exit. This activity caused a middle aged lady, probably aged the wrong side of forty five, to stir.

"Oh, I didn't see you." Piers thought it was all too obvious that she was either blind or just plain rude. However, he was hoping to have his mind changed with helpful service beyond their wildest expectations.

"How may I help you? May I see your readers' tickets please? I know it's a bore, but …"

She didn't finish her sentence. She was glancing at the tickets. "Ploughman? Mister and Misses, is it? Now there's a coincidence. What a pity. Betty Ploughman was in here, a week ago last Tuesday, doing some research for her latest book. She got a PhD for her family history studies, you know. Spinster. Lives by herself near Crawley. Wheels all her papers in a shopping trolley. She draws her family tree on rolled up wallpaper."

Helen could sense that Piers was approaching the bursting point. She answered, "Yes, we're Mr and Mrs Ploughman. We've driven down from Buckinghamshire this morning. We're researching my husband's family, from Kent. We thought there might be something useful here. We are not sure where to start. Perhaps you could help?"

"Well, as far as I know, Betty is looking for roots associated with the Dorset family, beyond Wimbourne Minister and westwards. She had her tree laid out on that table last week. There seems to be a link with tradesmen in the East End of London and fishermen working in the Thames Estuary. We're mainly Kent here, you understand; our files are concentrated mainly here with an overflow into the Strood archive for the estuary locations. But it so happens that, last week, we had out of the vault some old papers which the Ploughman family obviously treasured. It's got some folios going back to 1600. I could get that out; it'll take about 10 minutes." Her arms were beginning to point to various features in the room. "While I'm gone, why don't you settle at a table and see what the library shelves have got to offer? There's an index in the tray box over there, and the shelves are organised by parishes in alphabetical order. You'll get the hang of it very quickly. There's a canteen upstairs, no food or drink allowed in here, of course, and the Ladies and Gents are out there too. My name, by the way, is Millie Wilde, Misses Millicent Wilde. Please call me Millie."

"Thank you, Millie." Piers was grateful something was to happen. "We'll have a look round while you get the papers…"

*　　　*　　　*

Piers carefully opened the brown paper binding, neatly tied with durable ribbon, and found two stiffening boards protecting some very ancient parchments. Millie had returned with three pairs of white cotton gloves.

"You need to protect the documents from the natural oils in your hands," she explained.

"Here, Helen, this is something special; we're touching something that was written three and a half centuries ago."

"It will be alright to touch these pages, won't it?" Helen asked Millie Wilde. "Aren't you excited to be handling stuff that is 300 — no 370 — years old?"

"It's not new to me," responded Millie. "I was here when Colonel Ploughman came over from the United States in the '60s and, of course, when Betty had it open. Some of the writing is not easy to decipher, is it? Someone had a go at the really ancient scripts. You'll soon see. I'll leave you to it. Just come and find me if you need help. I suggest you start here with Susannah Ploughman's original letter; it sort of makes sense — gives a framework — for what you'll find later." Mrs Wilde moved away.

"There, Helen. That's the second reference I had in recent months to an American with the name Ploughman. Strange coincidence…"

"Oh phooey," dismissed Helen. "He's the reason we came to Kent. Look, Piers, there's the more recent version here — easier on the eyes. You read it, Piers, I'm too excited."

'Madam

Forgive this formal salutation for I know not of your family name, nor your given name but I hold dear the knowledge that you are born from, or wedded into, good family stock. This casket records our heritage. The deerskin scroll in my own hand shows we hold our line from John of Gaunt in 1200 or thereabouts. The signet ring was my beloved husband William's, bearing the seal that his great Uncle William earned from the Privy Council in 1463, displayed in the firebreast at the Hall and as set in brass in the memorial at All Saints Church Snodland. You are on trust to provide documentary details of the family for the generations of your time, sealed with those who went before, the record for passing to our descendents. Once sealed, never reopen the casket but bequeath it on to the most likely matriarch of the Ploughman heritage. Remember the family revolves about the home you provide. Be true to your husband, be receptive for your children, be a friend to your family.

Susannah Ploughman (born Catterall)

317

Sealed Fifth Day of November, year of our Lord One Thousand Six Hundred and Fifteen King James reigning.'

"Isn't this wonderful? I wonder what happened to that signet ring? And the casket? Look Piers, inside the back cover there is a single sheet of typescript within an unsealed envelope. Go on, you read it; I just can't bear the excitement. What date did you say? The Fifth of November? That's your birthday. 1615... Well, I'll be... After all, this is has got to be your family, somehow, although we might have a problem proving it."

11ᵗʰ March 1945

Cleeve Lyon Cottage, Near Maidstone, Kent, England

To the Reader. Greetings.

Grandmother Susannah Ploughman's family heritage volume has been safeguarded through the centuries within the County Archives. Its longevity is as assured as it can be. It should be a matter of record that two photo film copies of the texts were made during 1943. Colonel Makepiece Frisby Ploughman (American national born 5 November 1900 stationed in Kent on American Air Corps war business) visited the County Archives seeking information about his family. We found this material which had been handed to the Archive, when it was founded in 1933, by a legal firm of Maidstone. Colonel Ploughman had the facilities to make copies and I accidentally mislaid the pack while I researching my second novel: 'Warranted Traveller'.

While it is locked away in a stuffy vault, Susannah's message to her family progeny is denied transmission to the next generations. The mystique of the casket has been lost but its theme lives on through the set of duplicates. One copy is here in your hands. The second went with the American colonel whose personal fate, and the fate of the copy I do not know. I hold, as did Susannah, that a woman's support to her man in no way diminishes her ability gladly to give her love, share her intelligence, and donate her comfort. Treasure your family, be there in your children's time of need, and bear witness to our common heritage for the future wellbeing of your family and Grandmother Susannah's trust.

Aynette (born Cleeve Lyon)(widowed) Bates

Archivist Assistant, Kent County Archives, Maidstone.

A second handwritten sheet was folded into the envelope. Piers carefully unfolded the single sheet, its wartime quality was beginning to show in the initial discolouring of the paper, and read the text. It was what Aynette Bates had written as what she called her confession. Piers read the text in a whisper, savouring every clearly scribed word as if Aynette was there, listening to the words in her script.

Revelation of a Ploughman's Lover

I loved a fighting man, a married man, who I could never have to be my own exclusive man. He was a pilot, a senior commander of a very secret USAAC group with unimaginable burdens he kept unto himself. I could not share the burden of his mission. Mine was the role to provide but a short-lived bolthole from the pains of war, release from the pressure of command, succour from the absence of dear ones and the loss of friends. I took Makepiece Frisby Ploughman to my heart and body as I took no one before or since. I was keeping him for his family across the ocean. They do not need to feel jealousy or contempt for me or my Ploughman man. It was war, total war, when none knew if this day was to be the last. We both knew that our closeness must end. There was never a suggestion of commitment, either way, beyond the immediate needs of the moment. This I affirm with all my being, confident that heaven knows we both lived only for our time together, not as sinners, but as seekers of peace of mind and body.
Out of our love came a boy who I christened Bernard Makepiece Bates. Makepiece Frisby Ploughman did not know his boy was conceived when his war took him away from me. Perhaps, one day, the ocean will divide to bring my son to meet his father. For the record, Bernard Makepiece Bates was born at Maidstone, Kent, England on 5th November 1944.
Aynette Bates

There was silence. Helen eyes had begun to flood and it was clear that Piers was reading with a lump in his throat. She had never witnessed such a reaction in her strong husband just from reading a simple handwritten page. She tried to communicate sympathy, touching his arm, but somehow that did not seem to be possible in this extraordinary moment. Piers would not let her make eye contact; this was a moment in the Ploughman history. She reached out with an open hand and took Aynette's once private confession so that she could re-read it and then reached for the other document.

Helen went over to the central counter and asked if she might have a copy of the two documents in her hand. She had no inkling that the reference to a very secret US Army Air Corps group was confirmation of a link back to Piers being sent to Washington DC.

"We have to make a charge for copying, Mrs Ploughman. It's the rules. There a number of other documents which summarise the whole family and you might wish to copy those too. Why not make a job lot of it; we could mail you the copies and we do take credit cards."

"That'll be OK. Whatever. Give me the two letters and I'll put them back with the pack. I'll be over there with my husband."

"Is he alright, Mrs Ploughman? He looks poorly."

"Oh I think so. It wasn't an easy drive down this morning. He's a strong fellow. We used to have a saying about *someone walking over your grave* and I think the skeleton in his closet has just woken up! He just wants to be quiet for a moment. Did you say there is somewhere we can get a coffee?"

"There is a staff canteen which you are welcome to use. It serves hot snacks between twelve and two. There are facilities for… ladies… you know… just through that door on the right. The 'Men's' is next door to the 'Ladies'."

"Thank you. We'll be fine." Helen returned, her footfall echoing in the otherwise absolute silence, to sit next to Piers. He had not moved and did not react when she took his hand. She squeezed Piers's hand.

He slowly turned his head to look at her. He tried to smile at her support, but there was an internal anguish he could not control. He was fighting back tears, tears he could not explain, tears that a grown man needed to shed. Then he whispered, "Ask the staff to put the papers to one side for a while, Helen. Tell them we'll be back when I've had a breath of fresh air."

*   *   *

"Have you decided which folios you want copied?"

Helen shammed a mournful look with a smile for her husband. She loved this man very much and was pleased that whatever had happened this morning had now been overcome. "I don't suppose they'd let us have a copy of the whole thing?"

"I don't suppose they'd let us have a copy of the whole thing," repeated Piers. "You just ask them for what you want and let them tell you what they'll do about it. Have you got your credit card ready?"

A few minutes later and the couple were sitting in the deserted corridor outside the canteen collecting their thoughts.

Helen said, "Of course you were right, 'they didn't suppose they could let us have a copy of the whole thing'. But all the folios I had labelled, with those sticky thingees, they would do for us and mail it and for a very reasonable price, too. Millie said that we could always come back and refer to the folder again, for anything we wanted to check. She might even be able to answer straightforward queries on the telephone or by fax. She was very nice."

"While you were doing that I was looking at a random selection of the books on their shelves. I found that, in 1547, Jillyngham Dockyard — which is what we now call Gillingham — was established as a royal navy fleet base. That would be (singing) *Henry the Eighth, I am I am*. I did part of World War II there — under the blitz!"

"Well I never…"

"And in 1584, hops were introduced to Kent so we could all drink a better drop of bitter…"

"Aren't you a clever husband? All those useless facts…"

"And, wait for it, in 1586, Chatham Naval Dockyard opened."

"Glory be, just in time for Elizabeth One to declare she'd got the body of a woman, etc…"

"More to the point, and accounting for why the Ploughmans of East Kent stopped making children, on the 4 October 1624, oodles of boats were wrecked in terrible storms and the whole area was littered with wrecks and dead bodies."

"And you are saving the best to last, I hope…"

Piers looked cock-a-hoop with the findings of his quick fire research. "On 12 March 1635, bubonic plague raged through Sandwich, catching 180 persons in 78 houses. They were burying them at a rate of 10 bodies each week in one parish right through to October. I'll bet there were some Ploughmans among them."

"Enough my love! I can take no more. Let's call it a day. I need to collect my thoughts before we hit the road. Look at the time; it's the rush hour out there. The traffic will be awful. Let's go and find somewhere to sit and work out what we're going to do."

Piers cuddled his wife. "That's a good plan. The canteen will be empty. Let's go and see if they've left the vending machine switched on. Have you got any coins?"

"Do you think you'll like doing the family history stuff, my love?"

"I couldn't rightly say, ma'am. But on this evidence there does seem to be merit in writing it down, posterity-wise."

*   *   *

"Helen, do we have to rush home? Couldn't we leave it until the morning?"

"What about Philippa? She's only 15 you know. With Michael away…?"

"Let's ask her. Say it's an adventure. She can listen to her music all night if she wants to. Or watch TV. There's no-one to complain and she could always knock on the Yates' door, next door, if she's worried about anything. She's old enough…"

"I suppose we could give her our phone number… you're suggesting we stay in a hotel, down here?"

"Yes, Helen, that's right. Let's splurge for once. I could buy a razor from reception and we don't need nightclothes in a hotel. Come on, what do you say?"

"You would have to check with the Yateses… and we'd need a toothbrush… Well all right, I suppose. We'd eat, properly, at the hotel?"

"I promise."

"And you'd drive straight home tomorrow, no excuses."

Piers pecked his wife's cheek before whispering, "I promise."

"It's all that family stuff… it's got to your hormones."

"Men don't have hormones… well not that sort… and it would be just a little bit romantic."

"And no hankie-pankie for at least an hour after we've finished dinner."

"I promise, cross my heart."

"Well… just this once… I don't suppose it can do any harm… and Philippa is a very sensible girl."

"And my Helen is a very sympathetic Ploughman wife who understands just where her responsibility lies according to G G G … Grandmother Susannah's bequest."

Helen replied, gently pushing her husband away so that she could see his face, "I don't recall Grandmother Susannah requiring any laying. She wrote something about *a woman's support to her man to give her love, share her intelligence, and donate her comfort*."

"Well, I promise… Comfort…?"

"You've got her mixed up with Aynette and her *immediate needs of the moment and*… and …*not as sinners, but as seekers of peace of mind and body*."

"I promise you can sin just as much as you wish. Now, Mistress Ploughman mine, are we going to drive for two and half hours or are we going to do the other thing?"

"Some of the other is just fine…"

Chapter 42
1989 ~ Sixteen Young Officers and Several Hairy Warrants

The engineering staff inspection of RAF Aldergrove, in Northern Ireland, had gone well. Although it was only a small station with its runway shared with civilian flights for Belfast, Piers found the communication facilities in good order and the maintenance records correctly completed.

The inspecting team from group headquarters were invited, unusually, to visit the Sergeants' Mess where there were a number of 'old hairies' departing for the mainland and their necessary launch celebration beckoned; it promised to be a good way to wrap the inspection 'well and truly' up. The courtesy check with the station commander established his agreement that visiting commissioned officers might attend the Sergeants' Mess and, with some trepidation led by Piers, the officers made their way to what might turn out to be an alcoholicly painful evening. Civilian clothes were appropriate.

The party had thinned by the time that Piers recognised a warrant officer policeman leaning on the bar, alone. Piers approached him. "Aren't you Warrant Officer Jack Frost of the provost fraternity?" The pleasantries completed, Piers asked the warrant officer, who would be retiring from the RAF shortly after landing in UK, if he had done anything particularly interesting in his long career. Piers was in for a surprise.

It appeared that there had been a Royal Mail train robbery of registered mail and a highly classified RAF package had been stolen. According to the warrant officer, on 17 December 1982, a damage assessment was being prepared by the Defence Intelligence Staff for a report to the Prime Minister (Margaret Thatcher). She, in turn, needed to discuss the situation with President Reagan before Xmas because some of the information was of USA origin. The loss was especially significant at the time because the UK had suffered two intelligence setbacks that year: the Geoffrey Prime affair at GCHQ and the damaging 7 servicemen in Cyprus charged with passing classified material to a foreign country.

Jack Frost commented, "The material was potentially extremely damaging although its release to the Tornado contractor had been properly sponsored by the Ministry of Defence."

Warrant Officer Frost was beginning to cheer up with the retelling of this tale, but he refused to permit an officer to spend money in his bar. "Officers don't buy warrant officers drinks in their own mess — it's not the air force way." He continued his tale, "Four months later, in March 1983, I was ordered to meet with the Metropolitan Police at a site on the Grand Union Canal near Paddington. It was brass monkey weather! It was a Sunday morning and the police were breaking the ice and dragging the canal. Evidently, the police were quite impressed that someone pretty important had authorised Sunday working for the team working in the cold underwater. It seems they had caught some thieves with property identified as having been in the registered mail consignment that had been stolen during the previous December."

Warrant Officer Frost sipped his drink, his experienced eye noticing that Piers was becoming very interested in his story.

"As I watched, the divers were recovering watches, a couple of bikes and jewellery, but they were obviously looking for something else. Not finding what they were looking for, the warrant officer was invited to question the thieves concerning the loss of some classified documents and who were reported to have admitted to 'being thieves but not spies!' Well, they had indeed found the envelope, more like a package actually, which contained 450 pages of computer listing each marked Secret." This was being stated in a matter of fact way, a tumbler of Irish whiskey in one hand, a partially smoked cigarette in Frost's other. "They had taken it to Karl Marx's grave in Hampstead cemetery and burned it."

"Really?" questioned Piers. "How very odd!" This was the first time Piers had heard this story. He pinched his nostrils while he thought about what to say next. His brandy and cola remained safely on the bar while he watched the warrant officer's face for a trace reaction to delivering this tale to a receptive audience. Could this be a fitting end to that ruined Xmas six years ago?

"So I had to get a sample of the same computer paper and it was incinerated in same location for forensic proof of the tale," Frost continued. "Apparently the samples matched others previously taken and the thieves' story was accepted. There had been no security compromise of that material." A sip of Irish whiskey filled the pause; was this a moment when the policeman knew he had baited a line and waited for a reaction?

"I'll earn my drink by finishing your story," said Piers. "That stolen package was mine — well I originated it. All through that Xmas holiday I waited for the summons to Chequers, where I knew Mrs Thatcher was celebrating the holiday. The summons didn't come. Between Xmas and the New Year, I spoke with an RAF Provost wing commander who knew of the problem, but had no news. I heard no more of it until now — at least they didn't cancel my posting to Berlin."

The glasses at the Aldergrove bar chinked in salute, two RAF professionals exchanging closure.

"There now," continued Piers. "It would be nice to know that the loop was closed with Mrs Thatcher and that the relationship with America had not been put at risk by the material having been passed into hostile hands. I suspect the great lady was too busy to be bothered with such details despite turning out the Met on a Sunday morning".

The warrant officer grumbled, "And on double pay, too. That's more than I got."

* * *

It was Piers's departure interview from group headquarters on posting to a ministry appointment in London. Across a busy desk, the group captain who had been a year's technical cadet entry after Piers at Henlow, looked at his posted staff officer with the coldness of 'yet another chore to be done' look on his face — another assessment to write.

The group captain said, "How did the funeral go?"

"Pretty good, as such occasions go. We saw him off as he would have wished."

"You knew him well?

"I think so. He was one of the team I cobbled together for the Falklands Islands electronic warfare support… at Benson. He should have got a BEM for that but he already had one, for flying, and you can only get a second one for gallantry. He was one of the good guys in the service."

The group captain shrugged. There was no benefit in trying to buck the system. He did not know that second medals are only awarded for gallantry.

"Yes." Piers thought for a moment, then continued with his description, "A military funeral, even for a Master Aircrew, is not a happy place, but the chapel for his cremation, designed for 20 mourners, had 80 of his colleagues adorned of every uniform pattern. Some of my civilian contractors were there too. The assembly on this occasion was spontaneous with many returning from long distances for this strange reunion. He really packed us in."

Piers looked out of the window before going on. A slight smile creased across his cheeks. Military discipline and culture makes apparent light work of such sad situations. "There was a surprised look on the face of the officiating vicar who, I reckon, did not normally have to direct the prayers of so large an impromptu congregation. I had the feeling that Ron was there, in that chapel with us, nodding his approval that we were seeing him off in the way he would have wished."

There was a lump in Piers's throat as he went on, trying not to display emotion in this interview situation, "There was a wake in the Sergeants' Mess at RAF Wyton. His widow sought me out to thank me for the comradeship, pleasure and pride I had brought into her husband's life. She said I had turned around his world from a pointless ground job into a rewarding and responsible mission. Gosh that was a moment, I can tell you. Even as I tell this story, a shiver runs down my spine at the memory of that occasion, somehow not sad more a fitting farewell to a great guy..."

"Yes." The group captain was anxious to get on. "And now it's farewell to you, Piers. Thanks for all you've done in your two years here. Any highlights...?"

Piers thought the interviewing group captain would not recognise a highlight unless it merited promotion, preferably his.

"I do try to leave the world a better place for my having been here. My 2½ years..." Piers could not resist the correction, "...on the staff at Upavon allowed me to improve the ground communications standards at 16 front line stations... to say nothing of the crew along our headquarters's corridor here. I regret not getting out to Belize, I was crooked with my back and couldn't fly... I'd had the jabs too. In my second tour, I was at Honington as a junior officer responsible for ground communications, we used to look on group headquarters's guidance epistles from on high as our Moses's tablets to be ignored at our peril. That which I had so painfully learned in my career I was able to pass many lessons on to the next generation of young officers entering the RAF. Most accepted willingly the bias, cajoling or discipline that I injected in their engineering activities. The young officers, correctly assisted by good warrant officers on the bigger stations, are all good guys, not forgetting one female who holds her own in this challenging world."

"You make it sound as if you had to learn the hard way and taught the same."

"In a manner of speaking, yes. It came home to me when a cheeky young officer, male, poked his head round a door and greeted me with, 'It is you — the guy that taught me all I know!' Very satisfying! It cost him a pint in the mess! And in no small measure that was due to the experience drummed into me by a predecessor RAF Group Staff Officer, doing this same job then at RAF Mildenhall, in 1963/65, who did his inspections and made sure that 'his' stations did things the correct way. His way…"

For the group captain, this would soon be over.

"In those days it was the V-force and nukes and fifteen minute alerts and no compromise. Now it's computers and economies and insufficient staff or time with no compromise. It's the same, but different…"

The farewell handshake was unremarkable. Piers's new challenge was to sort out the Ministry of Defence — a somewhat more significant undertaking than the role he was just finishing.

Chapter 43
1990 ~ Invitation to the Cabinet Office

It was the prime function of the Ministry of Defence signals staff appointment, which was the latest in Piers's career, to keep the old systems working. The desk telephone disturbed Piers's thought process. His need for an additional desk officer, familiar with the engineering of hard-wired telecommunications, was pressing. Along the corridor, colleagues were working on high capacity digital technology which could see the end of copper wires for telephones and teleprinters. The anticipated demand for communications — connectivity in the new jargon — was diverting attention from the need to maintain the present facilities until the new network was working reliably. Piers guessed this would be at least five years, even with British Telecom and their mammoth research base backing the venture for the commercial world. The need was to keep the old systems staffed and working and the Treasury was already looking for its manpower saving well ahead of deployment of the more efficient, less manpower required, equipment.

The desk telephone insisted attention. "Hello, Piers. Long time no talk!"

"You've got me. The voice is familiar but…"

"David Johnson — Cyprus — we last met in '76. You were my…"

"Colonel David? What can I do for you?"

"I'd like to buy you a coffee. It'll have to be in my office, but we do a great job on Kenya beans. What are you doing on Tuesday at 10:30?"

"I'm a bit busy, Colonel. The Royal Air Force is moving from old to new and…"

"I know, I know. We have the same problem over here in Whitehall. We need to chat — it's David by the way; I dropped the Colonel handle some years ago after the knee operation. Your Director says you are the right man for the job."

"I can make Tuesday, err… David. Where in Whitehall? Do I need to bring anything?" Piers thought that when the Director put it that way then who was he to argue?

"Come to the Cabinet Office entrance in Whitehall, just by the Downing Street gates opposite the Cenotaph. They'll be expecting you and your pass will get you in. Someone there will bring you up. Good to talk to you. We have a date. Don't bother with a briefcase, they'll make you leave it at the gate. See you Tuesday. My best to Helen…" The phone connection clicked into silence.

*   *   *

On the appointed day, Piers approached the entrance to the Cabinet Office building facing onto Whitehall. It was quite easy to miss, up a couple of steps in a blank stretch of walls. His Ministry of Defence pass was insufficient 'identification' as a visitor on such hallowed ground and he needed his RAF identity card before being invited in. Carrying it was routine, old habits die hard, especially when they were ingrained at Henlow 35 years ago.

His escort had just turned the corner, for a staircase, when a tall, smart-suited man approached. "All right. I'll escort the wing commander from here." He waved his identity badge suspended form a blue ribbon around his neck in front of the uniformed escort's face.

"He's going to meet Mr Johnson. Needs personal escorting…"

"Cyril! Cyril King! Fancy meeting you here." Piers was delighted their paths were crossing again.

"I'm going that way. I'll take him. I promise he won't get away…"

Piers shrugged, but was unable to contain a grin. Officials in all government buildings had to earn their keep. It was more easygoing in his building across London in high Holborn. But Cyril overcame the escort's reluctance to release his charge.

As they descended a flight of marble stairs, beneath heavily framed portraits which Piers did not recognise, Cyril said, "I saw your name on today's visitors' list. I thought you'd like to know the closure on that Wenceslas Mine affair."

"Do you work in here? You might have said."

"Look, once round the cloisters and then back up stairs to meet your man. Wenceslas! What a cockup! About the time our man got there, CNN had got a reporter and two camera crews researching disused silver mines and miscellaneous werewolf legends. Then someone 'accidentally' trips over a mass grave which has to be hushed up and it got confused with real Neanderthals' and mammoths' skeletons. Our man said there was no sign of the Russians while this was going on, but strangely there were a couple of North Koreans and more East German STASI secret policemen than you'd need to run a Monty Python Policeman's Ball."

330

"So?"

"It turns out the silver had been mined out, the Neanderthals and mammoths had died out from causes not known, the Koreans walked out because no one would interview them, and the STASI called time-out and left."

"So it turned out that there really was nothing going on and the shrine that was Kammler's monument to history remains henge-like and intact." Piers frowned at the waste of time for everyone involved.

"Did someone think of asking Einstein what he thought about it?" asked Piers.

"Selfish old chap has popped his clogs and wasn't answering the phone. The hot line to eternity was out of order..." Cyril King's face indicated pleasure in his version of closure.

"Oh, so we have to wait for the next generation to cause a stir."

" 'fraid so, old man. I know it a bit unsatisfactory, but it's the only closure we're ever going to get. Now we've got to climb those stairs for your meeting; we're just in time."

*   *   *

At the appointed time, Piers was issued through a door into a big, square room furnished with the biggest polished mahogany square table he had ever seen. This was surrounded by 10 chairs on each side. The table was clear of all papers except for one corner. The matching red leather chairs, with an inlaid gold crest on the backrest, were widely separated along the sides of the table. The flocked wallpaper was reminiscent of stately homes and there were many ancient portraits hung on the three walls not hosting a window overlooking an interior courtyard.

The familiar figure of David Johnson was already moving to greet Piers; the walking stick appeared to offer little relief from pain. He just nodded a silent acknowledgment to Cyril King, as if they met frequently, who departed closing the door behind Piers. A second man was rising from the table to greet the visitor.

"Good to see you, Piers. I don't think you've met Bartholomew Barnes. He's better know as Boris — a good name for a spook, eh? He's your equivalent in the Security Service — last ditch, post nuclear communications on behalf of the Home Office and all that. We don't call it MI-5 in here. Help yourself to coffee and we'll get started."

"This is a big room for a small gathering, David."

"Don't worry about it, old lad. We're not going to be disturbed here. Mrs T knows there's something hot going on in here and she'll steer everyone away from our door. Of course, you've met her…" Piers did not know how to react to the revelation that his o-so-secret meeting with *The Iron Lady* was so well known.

"Now, let's be seated and we'll talk. We're all cleared Top Secret and the room is OK for that level. You need not take notes, nothing leaves this room. I'll send you a minute through channels outlining the issues."

For an hour the three specialists poured over charts and tables of wartime telecommunications designed to survive the worst the Luftwaffe could throw at the United Kingdom. Affectionately known as the Last Ditch Communications Network — or LDCN — it was buried deep underground, its manual telephone exchanges and linking copper wires protected from bomb and natural damage. The design was intrinsically nuclear weapon proof short of a direct hit above the deep exchanges. The network, installed and maintained by the General Post Office, forty five years before that public utility was privatised into British Telecom[tm] in 1984, was showing its age. Annual testing was identifying absence of spares, failures of cable insulation and lack of engineering experience in fault finding and remedy. Until BT's new resilient digital network came on stream, duplicated where necessary by the emerging military system, the Government's 'last ditch', post catastrophe infrastructure for managing the country was in an extremely precarious condition.

David Johnson asked, "At the highest level, and given the Cabinet does not want to spend any money unnecessarily, what services do we need to have in a minimalist LDCN? Today, I want to draft a list so we can go back to our specialists and flesh out the necessities, with costings, to present to the Cabinet Crisis Management Committee. The PM views this as a high priority."

"How long do we have? I mean, you have brought this out the blue." Piers's concern was shared by Boris the spook. "I presume you'll be calling in the Army and Navy… Police and others?

"Eight weeks. I'll grease any wheels to get you the support you might need, but we have to give the great lady a shopping list in eight weeks or we'll all get a handbagging — not a pretty experience I can assure you."

Boris Barnes volunteered, "Challenges are OK, wars are difficult, but the impossible takes a little longer. Then there's the handbag…"

"Not an option, Boris. Look, I'll give you a steer. What would the LDCN requirement for the Navy be? First guess answer: the deterrent; submarine control communications from wherever the Prime Minister happens to be with her briefcase, perhaps a bit of port management along the Channel coast? Same for the Army? Answer: cross channel links to the NATO headquarters and our troops in Germany plus access to motor fuel controls. RAF? Answer: UK air defence? … or transport? … or both? And of course fuel. You tell me!"

Boris offered, "Obviously the Regional Seats of Government and the strategic stocks of fuel and food. The met office… I get the idea. We mustn't forget the Port Authorities."

"What about GCHQ and the other intelligence facilities? And the Royal Mail?" asked Piers. "Is there an American dimension to all this?"

"Buckingham Palace?" added Boris. Then, after a moment, "The privatised utilities?"

David replied, "I'll be having separate meeting with each of them and, separately, the broadcasting and telecommunications companies. Of course we don't want to paint too gloomy a picture so our approach is to break the problem into manageable pieces with the advantage of limiting need to know."

Silence descended. The magnitude of the task was beginning to sink in.

David closed the meeting, "Gentlemen, doing nothing is not an option. We don't yet know how the fall of the Berlin Wall is going to affect global politics, but I don't think we should plan on the world being a safer place. There's always the Middle East to say nothing of home grown troubles in Northern Ireland. It was not christened Last Ditch Communications Network for no reason."

*   *   *

Piers and Boris walked out into the August sunshine glare. The usual breeze was blowing along the wide road preventing an uncomfortable assembly of diesel fumes from the many buses and taxis moving sightseers and office workers about the Whitehall tourist trap.

Boris said, "I don't think there will be much hurry with David's task. The Cabinet will have other fish to fry tomorrow."

Piers responded, "When a guy in your profession comes out with something as deep as that, the world usually falters on its axis."

Boris shrugged. "Of course it's just a guess. It might be worth listening to the news tonight. I think that Saddam Hussein has got a wanderlust — again. There are going to be lots of lights burning in Whitehall tonight."

"Oh."

Bartholomew *Boris* Barnes was waving at a black London taxi. "I'll keep in touch. I've got your number and office location from the MOD Directory. I wasn't planning to go on holiday this month, anyway." With no delay, he was away.

Across the road, standing with his back to the five storey Ministry of Defence, a photographer finished taking pictures of the Cabinet Office and the Cenotaph. His images would record the couple of city-suited gentlemen who had just come down the steps from the main building. One man he recognised — Ploughman was the reason he was there, but Control would be interested in the other fellow. The photographer climbed into a heavily used mini-cab, which turned to follow the black cab. Piers had no reason to notice the movement on the opposite pavement.

He glanced at his calendar wrist watch. It was just short of noon and the date was the first of August, 1990. Some 3000 miles away, the Iraqi Army commanders were opening their sealed orders ahead of their pre-emptive push south across the Kuwait border at midnight.

Chapter 44
1990 ~ This Is My Eighth War

The Deputy-Director was not impressed by Piers's report on the morning's meeting in the Cabinet Office. If it was a high status planning meeting then he should have been there not one of his desk officers. However, his personal agenda was to succeed in installing the digital highway of new communication infrastructure. The RAF would naturally be taking the lead in maintaining and controlling the network on behalf of the three services. 'We put it in, we will look after it. Simple.' Pottering around with old fashioned telephone stuff, which should have been retired with Noah, was not what his staff should be doing. He would check with the Director. Until then, Ploughman was to follow the office priorities which he had minuted to all his staff wing commanders.

"Don't allow yourself to be diverted from the main objective, Piers. Keep the appointment in Stevenage next Tuesday and hold their noses to the grindstone. We need the replacement message servers and an adequate supply of desktop terminals. Is that clear?"

"Yes, sir."

There was a yellow *'While you were out'* message slip centre desk in his office. It was a request to call a Graham Yates on a civilian number. This was a name he did not recognise. But, before he opened the day's files he might as well clear away this problem. Like everyone else in the Ministry at the moment, the caller probably wanted something which the system could not provide unless he had a budget to charge it to. And the cryptic aside by Boris Barnes a few hours ago was still nagging.

"Hello, my name is Piers Ploughman. You called earlier. How may I help?"

The distant voice, sounding very well spoken, after the 'Eton' dialect, invited himself to Piers's office tomorrow morning. "Say 9:15. No, there's no need to prepare anything. I'll tell you about our little problem when we are face to face. It's better not to talk on open telephones, I'm sure you understand. It's a tad urgent, old lad. I have a Ministry entry pass. Until tomorrow then. Goodbye."

*   *   *

The news from Kuwait broke too late for the early editions of the newspapers, but the radio news and, of course, all the later editions of the national newspapers were dominated by the Iraqi invasion of their smaller southern neighbour. The UK had a defence treaty with Kuwait so inevitably British troops would be involved. Piers followed his early morning arrival routine: along the corridor to let the registry staff know he was in and pick up any mail from his box, bid 'good morning' to his five staff, open the combination lock on his filing cabinet and switch on his computer.

The officers in the directorate wanted to talk of nothing else, but Piers had seen it all before. 'Wait to be told what to do and be ready for long hours!' The axiom had seen him in good stead up to now and he had a 9:15 appointment. 'Oh, God, does the Deputy-Director know about this Graham Yates chappie at 09:15? He didn't say which department he is coming from.'

More conflict of priorities looked imminent. Piers took a deep breath and let it out with a silent sigh.

'This will be my eighth war if you include the Cold War.' Having heard the news on his car radio, Piers had done the calculation on the commuting train into Kings Cross this morning. 'Never knowingly shot at though! Let's hope it stays that way.'

Graham Yates turned out to be the wrong side of 45. His ministry pass even allowed to him wander this Turnstile House building, a converted wartime hotel, without the normal escort. He held his head with a slight stoop which did not prevent his eyes searching every nuance in the others' face. His speech was indeed clear, positive, to the point. Unfashionably, his pinstriped suit sported a kerchief at the breast pocket. In this man's presence, you were left in no doubt that what he had to say was important.

"Do you mind if I close the door, Piers? You don't mind if I call you Piers, do you? I find it sort of breaks the ice. Please call me Graham. Here's my business card." The visitor handed over a visitor's calling card which had just the name Graham Yates and the telephone number Piers had already used. No post nominal letter, no office symbol. Just his name and phone number.

"Have you got some form of identity card? You said you had a Ministry pass. Where exactly do you fit in?" An MOD photocard was flashed from the visitor's wallet, but not released for Piers to inspect closely.

"We look on ourselves as being… well… sort of policemen. Not exactly Scotland Yard, more like country cousins. Let me just say that Bartholomew Barnes and I dine at the same club."

"Are you Home Office, then? Part of the Security Services?"

"That's not quite right. Let's skip that part and get down to the important matter." The visitor was satisfying himself that he could not hear what was being said in adjacent offices and that the single office window was not overlooked.

"I say", he said, "that's a fine collection of calling cards on your wall."

"300 — give or take."

""Some pretty interesting attributes being offered, what?" Piers had a good collection of the call-girls advertising cards liberally distributed around London's telephone kiosks. The menace was cleared four times daily by a BT squad assigned to the task so Piers had no qualms about liberating the more salacious examples for his collection. The ladies of the office registry did not complain and they provided a talking point for visitors.

Piers asked, "Has this anything to do with Kuwait? Your visit?"

"Oh no. It's much closer to home than that. Actually it's about you, old lad."

"Go on. I've a war to catch up on so it had better be good."

"Right." He was reaching into an interior jacket packet and withdrew a photographic wallet. "You did service in Singapore, Cyprus and Berlin, I believe."

Piers nodded.

"Pretty sensitive work?"

Piers nodded. 'Where is this going?' he thought.

"And Electronic Warfare planning — all the latest gizmos? Ivan would not have liked that — nor the Argentineans either if they had known."

"We tried to make sure they didn't know what we were up to. Most of the Brits hadn't got a clue either! Does this have a point? You above all will know that you are edging on the 'no talk' topics." Piers face was screwed into a questioning visage which was completely pointless to the other man.

"Plus a little bit on the nuclear delivery safety side? Kept up good relations with the American brethren, have we? Personal briefings of the PM?" His manner was almost condescending, but just short of irritating.

"You've read my CV or my service records. I don't deny you're right on all counts, so far. Am I in trouble, spoken out of line, whatever?"

"Let me show you some photographs." The photo wallet opened and three black and white photographs fell on to the desk. "Do you recognise this man?"

Piers picked up each sheet in turn. They were obviously photographs taken at long distance surveillance, but clearly centred on one individual. Having quickly scanned the images, Piers returns the photographs to the desk.

"This was taken in Cyprus, in 1975. Near the Pergamos enclave by Dhekelia. This second was taken in Washington while you were visiting the Pentagon on EW matters. This last was taken in '84 at the foot of Teuflesberg while you had an appointment there. You'll notice that 'Chummy'," he was pointing at a man in the photograph, "has a camera slung over his shoulder. The back of the head, in the Pergamos picture, by the way, is you — you had more hair then!"

Piers thoughtfully chewed the inside of his cheek. 'How do I respond to this?'

"Does Chummy have a name? Given the coincidence that I may... I say again, may... have been around when you got these snaps, what does this have to do with me. I do not recall ever having met the man let alone spoken to him."

"He was taking your photo, yesterday, while you were chatting with our friend Boris Barnes."

"I thought Boris left rather abruptly. You don't seem to have a snap of Boris and me with Chummy. Boris didn't say anything..."

"He wouldn't. It happens that we have been watching Chummy — real name Saladin Hussein — for quite a while. He travels on a Turkish passport, and probably others, but seems to know a lot about North Korea, Pakistan and the former German Democratic Republic. We don't think he is a relative of Saddam but... you never know... Hussein is sort of their version of Smith on the family-name front. Now, it seems that there is a target list that the Iraqi heavies have inherited from the former Soviet nasties, along with certain bits of hardware, and your name is on it.

And with this list comes a KGB register of agents most likely to recognise their target in a crowd. We think Chummy is preparing for a hit and we think his masters would like it if you were not cooperating with the Yanks or NATO or anyone else including the good guys in Whitehall."

He had experience of being told he was on a target list while in Berlin so he was able to remain outwardly calm.

"You're serious." Piers tried to see deeper into his visitor's eyes with no success.

"Never more so, old chum." The hand close to the photographs on Piers's desk rolled slightly, almost dismissively. "Especially now, with the Kuwaitis and their Royal air Force chums being uncooperative with the Saddam crowd; you understand."

"There was a similar situation in Berlin — I was number 14 on a hit list of 175. My SIS liaison in the British General's Headquarters would not confirm there was a list or who drafted it. My own provost officer seemed to know — he was probably tipped off by the Yanks, but no British hotshot mentioned it directly to me."

"We know. It sort of gives us confidence that our story is valid."

"What do the flat-earth guys at GCHQ have to say about all this?" Piers was floundering. It was not every day that you were told that you were the wrong end of someone's target practice. "I was kind-of working for them a lot of the time."

"They leave these things to us. Very sensible, really. Anyway, you're not one of them now — in a manner of speaking. You've gone native — spherical-earth you might say!"

Piers frowned of this dismissal of 15 years of loyal support and close working relations with the lads and lassies in the farm — as he derogatorily described GCHQ — when flat earth society was inappropriate..

"We don't think Chummy is the trigger man; they'd use a professional for the dirty work. But we'd really like to stop him filling your file just because the folk in the sort of agencies with which you used to cooperate are not on Baghdad's Xmas card list."

"Who else knows?" Piers was looking for a way out of this mess. 'Christ! I can't tell Helen about this!' Trying to remain outwardly calm,

"My wife didn't know about the Berlin list. Does anyone else in the directorate know?"

"I'm afraid not, old lad. You must not tell them either. We can't afford a leak — now of all times; it makes for such difficult press. Boris knows. Stopped short of adding David Johnson to the approved list, that's why I didn't see you yesterday."

"Has this some tie in to Cyril King?"

"Cyril likes to keep himself to himself. He would not like me anymore if I answered your question. What I can tell you is that my boss says you are one of the good guys and we want you to keep the Great in Britain. You've got friends in high places."

"That's terribly reassuring. She wears blue, too. So what happens now?"

"The word is that you are setting up an urgent meeting at Stevenage — all the more urgent because of this Middle East fracas. You just do the mystical engineering wonders for all us British peace-loving folk and come back with a done deal. Simple really; you just do what the Queen pays for you to do. We shall be just behind you, all the way from now on, and we'll make sure you come to no harm. The ministers in Number Ten would not have it any other way. Just check your car before you drive it; car bombs make such a mess and we don't know if there is an Irish dimension to all this."

*   *   *

"A good lunch, was it?" The deputy-director's acid greeting to a later-than-scheduled return from the Stevenage morning meeting foretold more displeasure to come.

"It wasn't my fault. I've got some news and some bad news. Which do you want first?" This group captain was from a Henlow cadet entry two years behind Piers. But Piers had to tell him why he was late back.

"There was a bit of a do at Stevenage railway station. It seems some woman started to deliver while the train was standing in the station. That sort of caused everyone to get off because it — the fast to Kings Cross that I was getting on — wasn't going anywhere until they got an ambulance. So there was a bit of a push on to the opposite platform just as the non-stopper from York went through… doing 100 mph plus I reckon! Some guy fell under it… or something. Lots of blood and gore and splattering as you can imagine. So along comes the cops and does a body count — if you'll forgive the pun. They collected the names and addresses for their database and allowed us on our way when the next train came in. But the line into London was closed so we had to use the pretty route through Hertford and now I'm here."

"That's some excuse, I suppose. It happens somewhere on the network once a week — someone under the train wheels. And the news?"

"They say you can have your first server and desktops quite quickly, subject to contract. They've been testing the software and it's up and running on their laboratory benches. But the Army has first call over the production line. It seems the Royal Signals Corps are intending to stop Saddam by filling the Gulf States with new electronics and the RAF specification fits the bill."

Seated, Piers shrugged with the inevitability of all good plans going astray.

"You've heard it all before. But because there's a war on, the brown jobs get priority. It could put our delivery back six months on the quantities that the pongos are talking about and that's before the logistics and movers and tank corps have their say. I'd say that that will push your project back a year and then the war will have to be paid for so there will be another Defence Review and you'll have to rebid and that could slip the whole thing another two years minimum."

"And the bad news?" The sarcasm was now very pronounced.

"Conservative! I think our best guess about the delay is conservative. That is because Margaret Thatcher is coming under increasing pressure from her men with knives and I'll lay odds there will be a coup. Lady Macbeth had it easier! If a new government with the peace dividend Defence Budget cuts takes over, your project could become an 'efficiency saving'."

"Write up your meeting and have it on my desk by 09:15 in the morning. I'm seeing the Director at 10 o'clock and we'll see what he has to say about it."

"Right. There will be no point in hurrying to Kings Cross to catch my regular train. The service will be shambles because of the idiot who could not wait for the train to stop. I'll call Helen and tell her to feed my dinner to the cat."

"09:15! Sharp! Two copies!"

"Right!"

Piers rose from his chair and returned to his office. He'd be working into the evening. There was a yellow '*While you were out*' message slip centre desk in his office. It would have to wait its turn in the grand order of things. He opened the combination lock on his filing cabinet and switched on his computer.

Chapter 45
1990/1 ~ A Short Distance To Drop

The Gulf War was a month old, except that it wasn't a shooting war yet. The Americans were reinforcing their presence in Saudi Arabia; the British were sending boats and fighters... and computers; both nations were seeking the active cooperation of all oil consuming countries for a great coalition to protect the small guy against the marauder from the north. So the war to be, couched in veiled threats along the lines of 'withdraw or face the consequences', was christened Operation Desert Storm.

Piers's role was to ensure the UK forces' garrisons, airfields, headquarters and the Ministry could communicate securely in voice and telegraphed text. The deputy director's grand design for a digital highway with every RAF desk in the UK and Germany having an interconnected personal computer went, as they say, on to the back burner. Piers's eighth war was to be fought, at least as far as he was concerned, from a London desk. Until, that is, his Friday afternoon was interrupted by a phone call. He recognised the voice from common time as Henlow cadets — he had been an entry before Piers's.

"Director here." The unwarranted assumption that a mere wing commander in his directorate — and only one of fourteen wing commanders at that — only spoke to one director, him, reflected a basic misunderstanding of how the Ministry of Defence functioned. On this occasion, Piers was quick on the uptake — voice recognition-wise.

"Yes, sir. What can I do for you?"

"You know about protected war headquarters, right?" Protected war headquarters was military shorthand for buried office blocks protected by yards thickness of concrete and a metal shield designed to keep out the nasty effects of nuclear, bacteriological and chemical weapons and with protected communications to ensure that our troops could fight back if attacked assuming there were any who survived. It was also the principal item in the terms of reference for Piers's post.

"High Wycombe is doing fine, sir. I checked this morning. No complaints, they say. Communication with the Gulf is AOK. The Alternate Headquarters will be on-stream in six days, sir. Operation Desert Storm communications are in good order."

"That's what I've heard. We've got a problem. I can't find your deputy director at the ..."

"He's in with the Procurement Executive trying to find slack in the budget for the LDCN project..."

"...moment so I want you to find him and both be in Historic Room 25 in the Ministry of Defence Main Building at 3 o'clock this afternoon. I can't say anymore now, just be there. They'll tell you what it's all about."

"Yes, sir." The phone was already dead.

The deputy director insisted on walking from Holborn to Whitehall; this was usually 25 minutes' walk at keen pace. Piers and his immediate superior did the distance in 21 minutes and arrived with three minutes to spare. Their passes cleared them through the formalities at the security control. Three more minutes were required to climb three storeys, rather than wait for a lift, and to walk the internal corridors to find the conference room known as Historic Room 25. It was christened as such due to the inappropriate oil portraits of last centuries' generals and admirals. An oval table already had 20 people conferring with an obvious chairman sitting at the centre of one long side. 'Obvious,' thought Piers, 'because under thick grey hair, and bushy eyebrows to match, he looked the part.' He had a notetaker sitting on his left. All eyes were focussed on him until the new arrivals entered, looking hot and bothered if not exactly lost, and he was obviously used to having his way.

"Yes?" the chairman asked of the latest arrivals.

The deputy director, being of Group Captain rank, not used to an impolite greeting and least of all from what was obviously a civilian in this most military of buildings, introduced himself and Piers. The chairman looked at his notetaker, who referred to a paper and nodded. The chairman wordlessly waved to two vacant chairs and continued as though nothing had happened. A heavily overweight attendee, wearing an unbuttoned blazer over an open neck shirt more in keeping with a Hawaiian beach than a London conference, leaned back in his chair relishing the manner that the Brits ran their meetings. As Piers adjusted his clothes to ease some of the overheating due to their swift transit, he looked at his watch. It showed one minute past three o'clock on the ninth of September, 1990. It was a date that would register over the next eight years of his professional life.

"For the benefit of the newcomers," a clearing of the throat, "the Prime Minister has promised President Ronald Reagan our full cooperation in modernising accommodation, communications and certain other facilities associated with intelligence of shipping in the eastern Atlantic. Certain decisions have to be made today in order to have the facility operational by August 1995."

'Here we go,' thought Piers. 'Another competing priority and this time there is no doubt there is an American dimension close to hand. Who is this guy? And why are Yank heavies sitting in? And, for God's sake, we're fighting a war …'

"Colleagues in the US Navy have completed a one year survey of all the British coastal sites fronting onto the Atlantic and have concluded the only suitable location is RAF St Mawgan, Cornwall. You gentlemen… being Royal Air Force," looking at the deputy-director, "…are charged with making it happen. A budget of £100 million has been identified as our contribution, although we recognise the American investment in technology and manpower is on a rather grander scale. Nevertheless, I am sure the Prime Minister Thatcher would wish everyone present to understand that this project has the highest priority in Anglo-American cooperation in ensuring we jointly retain control over this vital water route to our mutual survival."

Nonplussed, the deputy-director asked, "Would you please identify yourself, Mister Chairman, and perhaps the others present would be so kind to do likewise. Also, are we to be copied with the minutes of this meeting and the appropriate budget line references for buildings, communication, travel and staff which I hasten to point out will be competing with our interests in the Gulf?"

"I am Gwilliam Moncrieff, Assistant Secretary of State for Defence. For the time being, certain gentlemen in this room have requested that their identity be reserved until everyone present here and later, that is everyone involved in the project knowing its real purpose, has been suitably security accredited." It was obvious he was referring to at least two individuals who were wearing the casual attire of American civilians contrasting with the formal suits of the British. However, there was no point in arguing. The Civil Service grade of Assistant Secretary put the chairman in the very highest echelon of authority in the Ministry — a very powerful servant of the Crown.

Secretary Moncrieff continued, "No papers leave this room except through my secretary here. Absolutely none. Those who have to retain working papers in their offices will have accredited storage facilities provided and appropriate authorities for custody of the classified material will be issued by the relevant staff."

Piers asked, "Would I be correct to assume that we are intending to build a protected facility at RAF St Mawgan to British standards, but compatible with American requirements?" He hoped his sigh of frustration with yet another problem was not too apparent in this high-priced help.

The chairperson replied, "To American standards satisfying the minimum British security and survivability standards — and, of course, safety — standards for occupation on British soil."

Piers nodded he understood. There would be a lot of horse trading between the two nations. How would they handle the American 110 volt mains problem when all British fittings were designed for 240 volts? So many questions meant a busy staff desk when there were so many other demands already. 'Had someone warned Saddam?' Piers wondered.

"We shall meet fortnightly, on Fridays, so that I may brief the Prime Minister on the following Tuesday. She will be taking a personal interest in the progress of this project. Meanwhile, I emphasise that this project is Top Secret. Are there any questions? Round the room… identify yourself for the secretary if you are able…"

Eventually it was Piers's turn. "We shall need a cover story to account for building a big hole in Cornwall and to explain our setting up unforeseen long distance communication and power supplies along the spine of Cornwall. There has to be an explanation; site construction is bound to draw attention of the locals and the media."

"Well? Do you have any suggestion, Wing Commander?" Moncrieff's face revealed that the issue of public awareness and the need for a reasonable explanation had not occurred to him. 'He's probably never seen a hole in the ground big enough to bury an aircraft hangar. He may never have seen a hole in the ground big enough to bury him!'

Piers responded to the invitation from the chair, "Someone will need to tell the station commander at RAF St Mawgan that contractors were going to dig up half his airfield. Does Headquarters Strike Command know what you want to do with one of their principal airfields?"

'This wiper-snapper wing commander is talking himself into the job!' thoughts could not be concealed from Moncrieff's face.

"Since I shall have to sponsor a lot of the specialist engineering through the Ministry procedures, it might just as well be called a communications facility." Piers was making it up as he continued, "Since there will be a joint navy and air force presence, I suggest 'Coastal Communications Headquarters' or, to better recognise the American presence until it becomes obvious they are the prime movers, 'Coastal Communications Facility' or 'CCF' for short."

"I shall think about it and record my decision in the minutes. Now the hour is late and some of you have a real war to prosecute. Thank you for your time. Good afternoon."

As they manoeuvred for the door, the deputy-director told Piers to make his way back to Holborn while he went and briefed the director. There was no indication that, even at his level, there had been an inkling of this project in wider defence planning and yet an American survey had been in progress for a year. How on earth did they get access to all those military stretches of coastline which were apparently so important to their project? In Cornwall, they were specifically talking about Duchy of Cornwall real estate and coastline.

Piers made his way towards the building entrance and was surprised to see the familiar face of Graham Yates studying an interior newsstand close to the rotating doors. He still looked as dapper as previously.

"Hallo, old lad. Glad to see you looking so fit."

"Would I be wrong to assume you just happen to be there waiting for a bus?"

"Oh, we don't have buses indoors, old lad. Nor trains, come to think of it. I read somewhere that you were witness to a terrible accident at Stevenage railway station last month. I hope you didn't find it too distressing."

"I was quite a distance away from the worst of it. I didn't really see what... Did that have something to do with you and... err... Chummy?"

"I really couldn't say that it did, but then I really couldn't say that it didn't." With raised eyebrows, "Not much of a drop off the platform, either."

"Oh my God!" beginning to shudder.

"Boris seems to think that you should breathe more easily, in the circumstances."

"That was Chummy…?" the shudder calmed.

"It saves all that tedious paperwork needed to get the little squirt deported. It would have had to have been a trumped up charge… false passport probably… something like that. So much cleaner this way, don't you think? It sort of helps when you have to leave your kids at boarding school, doesn't it? Knowing he's gone to his share of the virgins in paradise."

"Oh my… I hadn't thought about that. Surely those bastards wouldn't stoop that low. Not the kids…" Graham Yates' silent shrug insisted that those 'bastards' indeed probably would have gone to any lengths to achieve whatever their mission was.

"I must pop along now. I have to see a man about a dog, as they say. Enjoy your trip to Washington; take a scarf and gloves." His shuffling stance emphasised his wish to move on. "DC in December can be very cold, but it is good for Christmas toys. Byeee." He had turned and disappeared into the labyrinthine corridors before Piers could register a farewell.

'What was he on about, '*Washington in December*'? Blimey, does he know about what we've been talking about this afternoon? Perhaps I would rather have him protecting my *six o'clock* after all.'

*   *   *

Washington DC, or more precisely a three day technical conference in its suburb of Crystal City, came and went. New Year was uneventful for the Ploughman family except for the need to visit his widowed mother who refused to leave her home. Conflict in the Gulf States seemed ever more inevitable with the Prime Minister, now John Major, flying every which way to give the coalition an impetus. It was early on Sunday morning, the 24 February 1991, when the US VII Corps launched an armoured attack into Iraq just to the west of Kuwait, taking Iraqi forces by surprise. Within hours the world's media were showing images of Iraqi troops retreating out of Kuwait, setting fire to Kuwaiti oil fields. One hundred hours after the ground campaign started, the newly in-office President Bush declared a cease-fire, stating that Kuwait had been liberated. Five days later and Iraq bowed to the inevitable by formally accepting the cease-fire. Piers's eighth war was over.

But even before British troops had engaged their enemy in the Middle East desert, the Treasury was demanding a ten percent reduction in defence expenditure, rising to 25 percent in three years. Plans for a headcount reduction, bases' closure, air squadrons' disbandment and withdrawal from Germany continued with no attention to the real fighting world which needed so much support. Planning to keep the RAF communicating while these changes were being implemented made more work for Piers's office staff. The new technology of the replacement digital highway was still years away although the plans survived the arrival of a replacement deputy-director who needed briefing on every detail of what was going on.

Morale in Piers's team was sinking under the strain.

A routine six monthly meeting, hosted in April by the residual rump of the former Post Office within the umbrella of the new British Telecom, brought together representatives of the three services, GCHQ, the Home Office, the Cabinet Office and British Telecom. The meeting was held in the rotating former restaurant of the Post Office Tower which remained closed to the public because of continuing Irish terrorist threat after the bomb explosion in 1971. The pre-meeting conversation ignored the spectacular view over London's rooftops; the topic today was how would the Kuwaiti oil fires and the massive black cloud and oil slicks be brought under control?

Eventually, the meeting settled, under the rotational chairmanship of the navy specialist. Routine matters, handling base closure telecommunications so as to keep those remaining online and similar issues were discussed and the principles for a way ahead were agreed. The need to get clearance at tri-service director level was the formality to sealing the way ahead.

Then the Cabinet Office representative spoke. "Gentlemen, you will be sad to learn that David Johnson died last evening. He was in hospital suffering with arthritic cancer. He left me his briefing notes to the effect that the Emergency Planning Committee has decided that we no longer need to retain the LDCN hubs and interconnections. In effect, BT may close the facilities, recover whatever they wish for reuse or recycling and scrap the remainder. The old network saw us proud for 50 years, but now technology has moved on. David would have wished to tell you of this decision himself. I'm afraid that was not possible. The Cabinet has decided that we are not going to be nuked!"

'That should help morale…' thought Piers. 'I wonder what their source was?'

Beyond the windows, the panoramic view to 30 miles distance, seemed to reflect the mood of the meeting. Over an excellent alcohol-free sandwich lunch provided by their BT host, who had just lost a million pound per year contract, the discussion was about the way the world was changing, driven by new financial imperatives and pressing technologies. Could anyone predict the future any more?

The 30 second sinking feeling in the high speed lift from 500 feet above the London pavements seemed to Piers to herald the need for some alternative to RAF life. It was not in his nature to close facilities down. He would have to retire from the RAF, on age grounds, within 3½ years anyway. Perhaps now was the time to consider jumping into civvy street before being pushed.

'Thinking of being pushed, it's amazing how unsteady I am on my pins now I'm down on terra firma. We must have been shaking about somewhat up that tower.' With some care he moved towards the nearby bus stop.

Chapter 46
1991 ~ Seven Years and One Deep Hole

Piers held a particular affection for RAF St Mawgan although he was never been posted there. He had undertaken several visits to the station since 1964 and retained his link with the station in his time as Project Executive for Systems Installation Design Authority for a new facility of which more later.

The affection for the place had it origins when, as a child, the family often took their summer holidays in North Cornwall. In the austere years after World War II, a caravan or rented flat was what the Ploughman parents could afford. Helen and Piers, then engaged to be married, had a holiday in the region in the summer of 1960, the year that Piers needed to forget about a career in military flying. In later years, his association with the station had more to do with RAF St Mawgan as a flying airfield with strong maritime attachment. But first, there was the V-force attachment.

The two Victor bomber squadrons, at RAF Honington in 1963/65, had RAF St Mawgan as one of their dispersal options. The idea was that the Soviet Air Force could not destroy all the dispersed aircraft before some of them were airborne and therefore safe to deliver their counter-strike nuclear weapons. Theoretically, four armed V-aircraft could move to a prepared dispersal airfield where they would find accommodation, pre-stocked food and communications and some essential ground support equipment to keep them self sustained for up to 30 days. All the sites were built to the same (type-design) pattern with four aircraft servicing hardstandings and four Quick Reaction Alert strips at the runway's end. All that is except RAF St Mawgan. For some reason, the bomber dispersal and the accommodation secco huts and sleeping caravans were laid out in mirror image to the normal pattern. The rumoured explanation was that when the Clerk of Works was laying out the site for construction, he spread the blueprint across the bonnet of his staff car. It is reported that it started to rain and, to protect his valuable drawing, the blueprint was turned upside down. However it rained so hard that the print became transparent and when the work recommenced no one noticed the error.

By the time the first practice dispersal took place it was far too late — the place was built. As it happened, building reversal did not affect the functionality of the site. Piers first flew into St Mawgan as a passenger in an Anson from Honington in March 1964 on a commissioning check of the communications systems. Thereafter, he was required to undertake a six-monthly check of the systems. The air journey took 2 hours each way, depending on the wind; the road journey was a 1½ day journey each way. Helen travelled twice on such visits.

Piers had to visit RAF St Mawgan twice more; in 1973, while serving in the Ministry of Defence; and later, in 1989, as part of a review of the HF ship-to-shore radio networks. Then, out of the blue, and while he was heavily involved in UK support to the British contribution to the build-up of forces and their communications ahead of the 1991 Gulf War, he had been summoned to Whitehall to learn of a highly security sensitive project which was to involve him with St Mawgan, in different capacities, for at least another six years.

*   *   *

In 1988, US President Reagan and Prime Minister Thatcher had initialled an Agreement that the UK would host a component of the planned upgrade of the US Navy Integrated Underwater Surveillance System (IUSS). Under the most secret conditions, the Department of Defense was considering a US$2 billion project whose purpose was to give tactical advantage to US and UK submarines in their Eastern Atlantic and other operating areas. In mid-1989, under chairmanship of an Assistant Secretary of State of Defence reporting directly to 10 Downing Street, a UK working group convened to form the host nation component of a Joint US/UK project. Its purpose was to specify, build and man a facility at a chosen Cornwall site by August 1995.

By spring, 1991, the UK had agreed to provide the protected buried building, other domestic facilities and the telecommunications within the UK. It fell to Piers's desk to sponsor the engineering work through the various Ministry of Defence procurement and budgetary management desks. In return, the US were to train 50% of the planned 400 overall operating and support staff to be drawn from RAF and RN sources and provide the recognised underwater picture to Northwood where the UK Naval and Air Force Maritime staffs operated. The project had the impetus to survive the end of the Cold War. Specifically, a Joint Project Office comprising the MOD sponsor working with the Property Services Agency, the construction company, the user command (Strike Command) project officer and a contracted Installation Design Authority were charged to design, build, dress and transfer a buried building bigger than any hotel in nearby Newquay in just 4 years.

Flying operations at RAF St Mawgan were not to be interrupted by the project.

The electricity mains power grid along the spine of Cornwall was to be upgraded to meet the expected new energy load. The RAF's mature war-survivable telecommunications network programme had to be revisited by Ministers to provide the UK communications into agreed American hubs, including redeployment of assets to dress the facility with internal and external voice and data comms. Kernel to the communication plans was to be the employment of a proven capable organisation replicating that just completing its contract at NATO's new Primary War Headquarters at RAF High Wycombe. The company won a competition to supply additional contracted design staff capability, initially from its High Wycombe office, later largely (but not completely) to migrate to RAF St Mawgan.

In April 1995, after the publication of the following press release, Piers was able to tell Helen what he had been up to.

"In the event of war, a major threat would be posed to allied resupply and military reinforcement shipping by enemy submarines. Such submarines could also inflict damage on UK mainland and other allied territory. A US Navy programme, to which the UK has access, is devoted to the detection and identification of the submarines and forms the Integrated Undersea Surveillance System (IUSS). The mission of the IUSS is to support anti-submarine warfare command and tactical forces by detecting, classifying, tracking and providing timely reporting information concerning submarines. It has an additional function to gather long term oceanographic and underwater geological information. The Joint Maritime Facility (JMF), when it was transferred to the US Navy on 4 October 1994, is an anti-submarine warfare centre jointly operated by US and UK personnel and is part of IUSS. The construction of the facility was completed on time after a 3-year building programme by UK contractors and will be operational, when fitted with its electronic systems by US contractors, in August 1995."

Helen was not overly interested. Her life now centred on her village life in Buckinghamshire. What the RAF got up to, and what part Piers had to do with it, was pretty much academic. She was not impressed that after seven years hard work, and just 90 minutes earlier than originally planned, the already operating Joint Maritime Facility at RAF St Mawgan was formally declared operational by the appointment of its first USN officer commanding. The project had been returned on time and within budget. It fully satisfied its specification.

In 1998, following an Open University TV programme, the true nature of the facility at St Mawgan was released into the public domain. By now there were few Soviet submarines in the Atlantic — one RN officer said that the only traffic their sonar heard was NATO boats and the mating calls of the whales. Piers had helped design and construct, once known as the Coastal Communication Facility, then the Joint Maritime Communications Facility and finally renamed Joint Maritime Facility, a buried building which will be there for many decades if not centuries!

Chapter 47
1991 ~ Let's Talk Numbers…

"Yes, Piers. I agree. You must do what you want to do. You have been so tired with the commuting and work. It's wearing you out. Those doctors told you last year that you have to look after yourself. We want you around."

"I'm not planning to go anywhere yet, Helen. Look, if I stop on 31 July I'll have accumulated 32 years commissioned service so they only dock a little of my retirement pay — my RAF pension if you want to call it that. I can commute a little of it to pay for Philippa to finish in boarding school; we can remortgage the house if we need to, so we'd be alright financially. Anyway, I would not jump until I got a firm job offer in my hand. They're not going to promote me to group captain with only three years to serve — not even acting rank. My career has peaked and the only places they can send me is another job here in London or back to High Wycombe."

"Where would we like to live? I mean, you want to be by the sea and I can't stand the noise of waves at night. The country is out because of your hay fever and I can't abide the traffic in towns. We would want to stay in England for the children and, anyway, you can't stand foreigners or their food."

"Right. It's easy then. Find a job, find a house, move and make a home."

Helen looked at her husband earnestly. "Don't be hasty. It will work out OK."

"Somehow you don't sound convinced. Let's face it, we've moved so many times that the boxes pack themselves. I know you didn't fancy living in Preston — it's hardly an inspiring place on a Sunday morning in the rain and I am truly glad that the position at BAE Warton didn't materialise — but there is a possible opportunity at St Mawgan digging holes for the Ministry."

Helen replied, "We do like Cornwall although I wouldn't choose to shop in Newquay; but there are other places." Her voice perked up. "Cream teas too! We don't have to live on the coast. Perhaps we could go down there while Philippa is at school and have a proper look around. Michael will manage."

"Now that sounds like a good plan. And a cream tea, too — for two — in Looe... for you... coo! I'll set it up from the office during the week. If I make it a staff visit I can claim the miles and hotel — well at least the miles because they'll say I could have stayed in the Officers' Mess. And now, I suppose I've got to cut the blasted grass. It never seems to stop growing nowadays." He was reluctant to rise.

"Yes, dear." Helen began to move to make herself a cup of tea. Things always seemed better with a cup of tea. 'What was that Mother used to say? *Tea's too wet without a biscuit.* Yes, today I'll have biscuit.'

"There's a film on BBC2 TV if you'd rather, Piers. The grass looks too wet to cut. It's got David Niven in it; something about flying, or something... and a moving staircase... and he crashes into the sea."

*   *   *

"I am just phoning to say I am pleased you won the St Mawgan contract. It was nothing to do with me, mind you. The MOD PE contracts people do all the adjudicating." Piers sipped his coffee while he listened for the delayed reply. "All I had to do was to write the specification of work."

"We got your letter, Piers." The female voice on the telephone was its typical calm self. "My MD says I can talk with you about the job possibilities in Cornwall although there would need to be some special paperwork to get clearance to employ you. You have been pretty close to the protected headquarters' contracts and the civil service insists on being sure that no-one is going to call foul — no inside knowledge and all that. Look, in 10 days there will have to be a contract meeting to agree the final fee and payment procedures for the St Mawgan thing. You won't be at that session — not while they are talking money. Our contract folks will want to take the MOD contracts people out to lunch, but I could cry off that and perhaps I could take you out for a bite?"

"Carole, I'd like that. I haven't been taken out to lunch since this Gulf thing started. Oh, apart from a snack up the British Telecoms Tower as they now call it and that doesn't count. It was only sandwiches."

"You're on."

"Will you pick me up from the office when you've done your finance business?"

"About 12:15. I'll be seeing you."

*   *   *

Carole Whiting, Business Manager for the Special Projects Division of her company, was precisely on time. Piers was still clearing his desk into the manifoil protected filing cabinet as she knocked on the door. Her tailored business suit over court shoes was set off by a frilly lace choker blouse and visible cuffs. As always, her greying hair was worn tight to her head and immaculately groomed. If she wore makeup it was undetectable. She entered confidently. Trained at Bristol University in Electrical Engineering, she was one of the first women to attain the prized status of Fellow of the Institute of Electrical Engineers, Piers was just a member grade of the same institution.

The door to Piers's office was ajar. Perhaps eight years older than Piers, Carole eased her way casually glancing at Piers's collection of phone cards rescued (as he put it) from London's telephone kiosks. The sometimes lurid advertisements offered female services to the males of the species and were considered by many to be an affront to the London scene. Undeniably, these cards had a culture of their own, were reputed to be cleared away four times per day and were replaced within twenty minutes. Piers's collection amounted to over 200 cards, too many to count, none repeated, all displayed in the style of a fan on an otherwise blank wall.

"Are you hungry, wing commander?" She adjusted her thin file folder under the other arm, appearing not to notice the display by the door.

"Travelling light, Miss Whiting?" They were on Christian name terms and would probably have described their relationship as close working colleagues rather than friends.

"The contract's men can do the heavy work. All I need is a calculator and a shorthand pad to help me memorise the detail."

"Are the details OK — about St Mawgan? I will have to say something about it at the Friday project meeting. It's the last hurdle before they open the meetings out to monthly, which is still too often. John Major is more relaxed about the project than was Margaret T."

"Worry not, Piers. Your man will be up to see you with a copy of the signed contract. We are ready to go when we have recruited the staff. Now, lunch beckons. We'll walk, it helps the appetite and prevents the conversation getting too serious."

'I wonder what Chummy the stalker would have made of this,' wondered Piers and they turned into the top end of St Martins Lane.

Carole Whiting was a shade older than Piers and wore her age well. There was a ring on her left hand, but it did not look like gold. 'This is a business lunch; don't blot your copy book today, Piers.'

Carole steered Piers into a narrow-fronted Italian restaurant where a discreet table for two was set back from the window.

"Ah, Miss Whiting. Your table is waiting for you. May I take your jacket? … Non? Your bag? … Non … Sir? … Non? Would you care for an aperitif?" There was the familiar shuffling of chairs and spreading of linen serviettes.

An hour later, after four delicious, and expensive, courses served with an excellent wine chased by liqueurs and coffee, following a lull in the conversation, Carole came out with, "Shall we talk numbers?"

"I'm sorry, I don't quite follow."

"Numbers. Pay. That sort of thing. What do you want?"

"Oh, well, I … err…"

"I told you we had received your letter. We don't think the St Mawgan post is right for you. In fact we thought you might like to pick the man for that job yourself. Don't look so disappointed. No, we have something a bit more senior in mind for you — if you're interested, that is."

"Really? Well, I …err…"

"You seem reluctant. Would you like a brandy?" The opening of her right hand above the cleared table was the waiter's cue to approach.

"Piers? I'd like a Remy^{tm}, please, Benito. Piers?"

"The same, please,"

"Make that two, Benito. Doubles I think. It's a special day. Please tell the cook the meal was excellent, as usual. And a jug of tap water please, two glasses, with ice, no lemon. Now, Piers?"

"Look, Carole, I never been in this position before. I've worn Royal Air Force uniform since I left school and we did not negotiate … err… numbers, as you put it. Other things, yes but… Numbers goes into the bank and Helen takes them out. What do you have in mind for me to merit numbers? You tell me what you want done then I can tell you if I think I fit the job specification. And the numbers…"

"That's not quite how it works, Piers. I'll tell what we want doing, we decide if you could do it, then we agree a rate for the job, then Human Resources employs you."

"Oh!"

"Oh, right. Now we need someone who understands war headquarters, protected buildings, military procedures and security, be familiar with national and NATO rules, is familiar with the American ways of doing things, can travel, has a security clearance (although that would have to be refreshed), is a team worker, is contract savvy, can use a photocopier and won't kick the office cat when things go wrong. Our judgement is that you could fill the bill. The bonus for us is that you know about telecommunications and the CESG security overheads too. So you could go in at the deep end without armbands. And the final question is: will you work for... with... me?"

"You give me a number."

"28"

"Per?"

"28000 per year, payable monthly, company car, company pension scheme. We'll assist relocation expenses if we have to. Free medical insurance according to your grade. We'll be calling you a 'Project Executive' so we don't expect you to go on sickies. 5 weeks paid holiday, rising to six after four years."

"Interesting numbers, Carole. How long do I have to decide? I would like to talk to Helen. Where would I be based?"

"Say 10 o'clock on Monday morning. That gives you the weekend. Tell me where you would like to be based, bearing in mind this register of sites," she reached for a folded slip of paper in her jacket pocket, "you'll be familiar with most of them — but don't pick St Mawgan. I'd want you nearer the centre of gravity, within one hour's travelling from Whitehall. I'm sure you understand. Now, if you'd like to shake hands on the offer, without commitment..."

Carole reached out her right hand, her eyes watching his face for some reaction.

She continued over the hand clasp, "Your phone call by Monday 10 o'clock will be good enough and I would trigger a written offer very quickly."

Carole was searching about the legs of her chair when she said, "Oh, there is one thing."

"Yes."

"We don't think it would be appropriate for a Project Executive of the company, likely to host senior military officers and female employees, to have a display of the available totty on his office wall."

"That won't be a problem…"

"I didn't think it would be."

*   *   *

The formalities of exiting RAF service were rather less drawn out compared with getting in. Piers's interview with Carole Whiting had been in mid-March. A letter of job offer had been received, with conditions of employment, details of the company car, pay and pension arrangements very much as Carole had described. Accordingly Piers wrote his letter requesting premature retirement, and received his letter of approval with 48 hours. The countdown to working in civilian life had begun.

Piers and Helen agreed that they should live in Buckinghamshire; they both liked the Chiltern Hills and it was central to Piers's principal work centres. The company agreed to relocate Piers and his household, including removal and legal costs which amounted to over £5000.

By early July, a final date had been agreed, a handover of his ministry duties to a replacement wing commander was planned and all that was necessary was for Piers to pass the exit medical and enjoy being dined out of the RAF in time-honoured fashion. It was the air force way.

Chapter 49
1994 to 1999 ~ Through the Millennium Bug

Kelly Millington waved through the separating glass wall into Piers's office. She wanted him to pick up his telephone handset. She could equally have used the secretarial 'call boss' facility, it just didn't suit her that day. Piers accepted that Kelly did things differently, but she was an efficient PA, a reliable administrator and her coffee with Chocolate Hobnobs[tm] biscuits was invariably quickly served to visitors so they brought more business. She had the knack of knowing when boss Piers wanted to be protected from calls; she equally knew when it was expedient to interrupt. When Carole Whiting called from head office, interruption was expedient.

Speaking while his telephone was still moving to his ear, Piers looked at his PA as he spoke, "Yes, Kelly? I'm doing the monthly accounts and travelling expenses."

"It's Carol Whiting. She says she wants you. It must be nice to be wanted…"

"Very well, put her through…" He pulled a mocking frown at his impertinent PA. "Hallo, Carole, long time, no talk. I was just assembling the monthly timesheets and accounts to catch the mail…"

"I want you to be in my office at half past eight tomorrow. We're seeing the Managing Director at nine and he has a video conference call with Seattle at two."

"That sounds important. What's going on?" There was a click on the line as Kelly put her handset on its cradle. It was obvious to her from the expression on Piers's face that coffee and biscuits would be appreciated.

Carole replied, "Read up on Year 2000 Conformity. You'll also get some information if you look for Y2K in the technical literature — it's the abbreviation that the software guys are giving to Year 2000. The computer industry freebie magazines are full of it."

"Oh," breathed Piers.

"Simon Walker from Corporate Computing will be there and so will Ian from Contracts. Seems the MD homed in on me as the Business Manager for his Special Projects Division, saying that Y2K was right up our street."

"I'd not paid it too much attention. Is that about to change?"

Carole ignored Piers's comment. "8:30 prompt. They're digging up the M25 again so give yourself an extra half hour. You'll be able to park if you get here before 7:45. Bring the timesheets and travel claims with you; it'll save the postage."

*   *   *

By the autumn of 1994, Piers had been with the company for just about three years. Life in civvy street was a great deal less dynamic than working in air force blue, but it had its own challenges and priorities. For the first time, Piers had the commercial worry about making a profit and working within the dictates of a contract. He had survived RAF life using lateral thinking to achieve his ends. One grounded pilot, in the Ministry of Defence and known as 'penguin flying a mahogany cockpit', had described some of Piers's more risky methods as 'pushing the envelope' meaning taking his processes beyond safe limits.

Carole had aged appreciably in the three years since the St Martin's Lane recruiting lunch. The British electronic industry was generally going through a bad patch and it was largely thanks to the profitability of her Special Projects Division that the company kept its financial head above water. There was management pressure to exploit any business opportunity that arose. Carole, invariably, was opportune to advance her team with a quick response when needed.

The usual pleasantries about 'a good journey', 'lousy traffic especially at the M25 road works', 'did you find a parking space?', 'the timesheets and claims forms?' occupied the first 90 seconds then down to business.

"OK, Piers. Let's have it? Remember, our MD is not a computer geek — I'm not sure he can even type — so you'll have to explain it to him in small words, with one or two good sentences, so he can demonstrate that he has a grip to the Americans. They are fielding the Vice President International Operations at their end of the video link and they are hoping to display global prowess in this Y2K business so that they can sell their skill set to the White House."

"Right, Carole. I get the picture. The Year 2000 problem, or the 'Millennium Bug', is really about making a computer clock recognise the calendar. This is not a new phenomenon, and was known about in the 1970s, but it has only recently received widespread recognition. Because of the high cost of data storage in the early computer systems, the two extra bytes to store the full four digits of the year rather than just two was not thought cost-effective."

Carole was astute enough to recognise that Piers was settling down to his theme. Now was the time to let her man describe the issue his way and then to channel him into 'boardroom mode' before going live in front of the MD.

"The Year 2000 problem comes about because of the way electronic digital clocks store a date. So if they are set to use year-year, month-month, day-day they do not know that year 2000 stored as '00' comes after 1999 stored as '99'. This means that all the sums are wrong. All the bank accounts and interest calculations are out, any automatic functions trigger at the wrong date. There is an added confusion about the status of year 2000 as a leap year."

Carole breathed deeply. She knew this was going to become detailed. How much more...?

"Normally every four years is a leap year except for a century year. However, every four hundred years the century year is a leap year again and this was overlooked or not understood by many software teams. Many software systems do not handle the 29 February 2000 correctly, including some widely used applications in desktop computers and company accounting networks."

"So you are saying that all the world's computers are going to get the days wrong?"

"At the moment, Carole, that is what the computer industry believes. Worse, the bigger the company, so the magnitude of the problem and the greater the opportunity for intense embarrassment. At midnight 31st December 1999, PC clocks could behave in a number of ways ranging from correctly handling the time and date to setting the year to '1900' or to some other figure such as '1980'. Systems that rely on being manually reset to '2000' and may thereafter function correctly, but then doubt arises about the leap day. Every date calculation is at risk; all financial; periodic maintenance, pay, tax, scheduling, the whole caboodle could come crashing round our ears. Financial interest, calculated on a per-day basis, are the most vulnerable; the risks are enormous. The only systems that will stay up are those fitted with the very latest chip set and software. Everything else is worse than scrap. Worldwide! That's why the Americans are up in arms. The Germans and French haven't caught on yet. We don't know about the Russians, the Japs, or the Indians, or the folks down-under.

"You're talking about billions to put it right?"

Piers replied, "Make it trillions if it is allowed to go wrong — maybe a couple of hundred million to replace the kit before collapse happens. Just imagine the problem for the City of London — or any other market." He was nodding, confident that he had made his point strongly.

"So what's the fix?" Carole, basically trained as an electrical engineer, understood Piers's message. "Have we got to survey every electronic device and check its chipset and software... worldwide?

"Not quite, just every machine which uses electronic timing of date setting for any mission critical purpose."

"We're talking virtually all equipment or product, including any embedded control logic, that conceivably may fail completely, malfunction or cause data to be corrupted. That's all commercial, industrial, governmental, defence, home, office... you name it; you're telling me they all need fixing! Worldwide...! Medical kit? Some vehicle computers." Her hands were spreading wide as though to encompass the global issue.

"It's a tall order," Piers acknowledged with the mildest of shrugs.

"Yes, and we've only got five years to identify the problems and install remedial solutions. I'd call that challenging, planet-wise. I hope someone in the Ministry of Defence has got its finger on this particular pulse. But I don't have much confidence that they will have been that far in their forward thinking." Piers hoped he had not exaggerated the issue beyond belief.

Shaking his head negatively, Piers said, "No single company could possibly undertake the task. It would need something on the scale of the United Nations to make sure all cross border systems are coordinated, all international communications links remain synchronised, you name it and there is a potential problem."

Piers thought a moment, rubbing his clean shaven chin for effect, then suggested, "Obviously we have get our house in order and maintain it. Perhaps we might set up a training school — maybe a consultancy — in the field and earn a host of dollars that way."

"I like the approach," beamed Carole. "We ought to be moving downstairs. The MD does not like to be kept waiting."

Piers chuckled as he rose from his chair, "I wonder if that new car of his is fitted with computer-based maintenance scheduler? Tell the MD that his car is likely to stop at midnight on Millennium night and see what his reaction is to that."

*   *   *

The Vice President International Operations, Bernard Makepiece Bates, sat centre desk for the video conference. He was a big man, confident, self–assured and exactly the character that Piers would describe as having a presence so that you knew he was there. Thin, closely cut grey hair and a formal suit rounded off a visual impression that this was the leader of the pack in Seattle. Piers judged him to be an active 50 years old, the type of individual who used a gymnasium frequently. He sat behind a desk label simply annotated VP. If you didn't know what VP stood for, you had no right in this room.

"Do I see, from your personnel register of attendees, a Mr Ploughman?" The accent had an American twang but there were definite hints of New England and perhaps old England too.

Piers identified himself while being careful not to show he was making an association with his knowledge of archived letters in a Maidstone vault.

"We must meet up when I visit. I have some blood relatives with that name, out on the East Coast, although I don't use it myself."

"I shall look forward to that, Mr Bates."

"Now… the business today is what we are going to do about those misfits in Silicone Valley that have rendered the computer industry with their testicles round their necks. What's this bull about millennium bugs?"

Speaking from the UK, being fully familiar with the colourful language employed in the headquarters in Washington State, the MD replied, "We see a business opportunity with global reach here." There was a glimmer of interest across the video link — were the Brits going to steal the show again?

The MD in UK continued, "Our analysis is that few data logic processors anywhere in the world will escape the Y2K conformity issue and there is a business opportunity, under your leadership, to put this whole sorry situation out to roost."

"Go on. You have my attention. What's Y2K?

"Year 2000. When the calendar clicks over from 1999 to 2000, we believe all hell will be let loose. Just imagine, in the USA alone, there are five time zones and each will experience its own problem. The power grid is sure to shut down — nationwide — nuke stations too!"

"I heard a rumour…" shrugged VP Bates as though the matter was over-rated.

"We don't think any one company, not even the Microsoft^{tm}s of the world, could resource a survey of the globally distributed embedded logic devices and then commission putting right the wrongs. Just imagine all the bank systems — not to mention aircraft. I hate to think how many devices there are in the typical hospital. But while our company can obviously put our house in order, we could develop the international standard and training courses to help other self-help… so to speak."

"You're suggesting we help them get themselves off the hook and charge them for being trained."

"Right. And… if they get their fixes wrong, or do unnecessary work, then they take the stick not us."

"Now this has got regular promise." Enthusiasm flowed from his body language.

"Minimum risk and maximum revenue, Mister Vice President."

"Have you done any numbers, over there in the old country?"

"Very loose, first order of magnitude, we think the global Y2K fix could be US$1billion for hardware and, with survey and consultancy, the same again. Globalwise. First estimate. The training slice could be 15% so there's an opportunity of US$150 million to US$300 million across the next five years. I must emphasise that these are very preliminary estimates."

"Gimme a margin of error."

The MD was not expecting that question. His hand rolled as he tried to conceive something logical to answer. He came out with a hesitant, "An order of magnitude — either way." He instantly regretted what he had said.

"Are you telling me that you folks don't know the difference between US$15 million and US$3 billion? That's a generous tolerance by any measure."

"Mr Bates. My staff have prepared a short resume of the Y2K problem and a draft of a possible international standard to put it right.

The corporation would have much better prospects of having the standard accepted, and getting the credit for it, if it appeared to originate in your offices. I'll put it in the fax, if you wish, so that you can study it at your leisure."

"Holy saints! Do you Brits think we have time for leisure when there's US$300 million up for grabs? No wonder you don't make movies no more." Bates was making to thump the table, but he knew he'd ruin the sound if he disturbed the microphone.

"Mr Vice President, we're about to go timeout on our video link. It was nice to talk with you all. Our suggestion will be on the fax."

"Gudday… and have a nice day, doing your leisure…"

The video link went blank. The UK group leaned back in their chairs. A coffee would be welcome.

"Let me see that draft, Carole. I'd better get it away quickly."

*   *   *

Carole set up a small team to assist Y2K compliance in any organisation that would contract their assistance. Piers's offices were compliant anyway; he'd been ahead of the game before the issue was well known. This was one problem he could step back from. Around the world, hundreds of million of dollars were spent in avoiding the foreseen problems and there were no serious failures of critical systems when the midnight chimes heralded in the new millennium.

Meanwhile, with the completion of Carole's defence projects and the government seeking its peace dividend, redundancy loomed for Piers with a second retirement (and small company pension) before the new century celebrated its first birthday.

Chapter 50
2002 ~ In Search of Heritage

Piers and Helen were in the Genealogical Society's building in London, specifically in the rest area in the basement. After two hours using microfiche readers, both were grateful for the excuse to rest their eyes. It had not been a particularly productive morning; Helen was content to carry on with her search for references to Ploughman or Blythe births, marriages and deaths, but Piers thought there might be easier sources in the thousands of books in the society's library. The only things that put him off spending all his time there was the inevitable dusty nature of old books and papers and the claustrophobic atmosphere of closely stacked shelves.

Two further hours and the couple agreed to call it a day. Their notebooks were brimming with material for further study. As they made their way towards the Barbican Underground station, Piers suggested that they should again visit the Medway valley, this time to look at Snodland where there seemed to be church records of Ploughmans who had emigrated and, having telephoned bookings for readers' tables, to explore the Kent County Archive at Maidstone.

The noise of the tube train delayed further discussion of the plan. A glance at the Marylebone departures board, a rush for their train, and Piers and Helen settled into a first class compartment, its windows labelled 'No Smoking'. Departure was on time; nevertheless, in a tunnel, their train stopped after 90 seconds while a train rumbled past going towards the station. The blackness of the walls of the tunnel reminded Piers of the soot and grime in the days of the old steam trains. Then, accelerating through three flashes of daylight where the tunnel breathed fresh air and the train pulled out into open. Their compartment was comfortable and quiet, they could talk. The train was non-stopping to High Wycombe so they were not interrupted.

"Did you find anything useful?" Piers asked his wife who was already looking through her notes.

"Heaps... I found G.G.G. Grandfather William Blythe marrying Mary Reed in Gadshill in 1790 and from them came..."

"I thought we were looking for Ploughmans."

"There's lots of them too. The International Genealogical Index puts a whole clutch of them at Snodland, that's just up the Medway from where your folks lived in Chatham. Some of the dates are in the 1600s."

"I went to Snodland as a boy, during the war. I seem to remember something about a prisoner of war camp there, seeing them behind the wire. Perhaps I've got the wrong place. It's not my favourite place with factories and a cement works. The best thing about Snodland is the railway through it and that was pretty awful. Still, that was nearly sixty years ago. Perhaps we should go there again."

"Did you find anything in the library?" she asked.

Piers smiled; she guessed that there was something he was dying to tell her and was relishing the tension.

"Come on, don't keep it a secret. Tell me..."

"They went to America... well... some of them went to America, as colonists, in the 1600s. These are probably the same family as you are talking about. It seems they thrived because lots more of them went over later according to the shipping passengers' register. There were too many to count, but I have made a note of the dates and register entries so I could go back and check." His wife was chuckling at his discovery.

"I tried to find a coat of arms," he said shaking his head, "but perhaps they were not entitled."

He shrugged; there was something in the way she was looking happy with herself. "I have the feeling that you've got something new."

"Well," she said, trying to look serious as she checked her notes. Her subterfuge did not fool her husband for one moment. "Well, it seems that... you remember that vicar at St Mary's Chatham... warning us about spelling and legibility and such... well..."

"Get on with it!" There was just an edge to Piers's comment because he was more interested in eating a sandwich.

"I found Ploughman as we spell it, and Plowman with a 'w', and Ploman without the 'w' or the 'ugh', and even a Plotman. Some of these were obviously the same person because of the village where they were recorded. It will take ages to unscramble who is who. There are transcriptions going back to 1560 for some churches..."

"OK. I found that there is a records office in Strood, just across the river from Rochester. We could combine a visit there with a day in the county archives and work out what to do next. We may find out more about the relationship with the dockyard and, God forbid, the Navy. The thought of having sailors in the family makes me shudder. Did you enjoy your day, Helen? You look pleased with yourself."

"It was fun. Lots more information to put on the family tree. Yes, I did enjoy my day and to celebrate, you are going to buy us fish and chips for supper and we will settle in front of the telly and watch *Eastenders*."

"Oh… I thought we might start to plan a trip to Maryland… the weather should be nice in May…"

*　　　*　　　*

Wolfgang Schwanitz, released from a Polish gaol having served a 10 year sentence on narcotics charges, boarded a train for a journey through Berlin and Hamburg to enter England at Harwich. There were passport formalities, but they were cursory. Schwanitz's motive was to set up a base to avenge the killing (as he judged it to be) by the British authorities of his friend and co-agent Saladin Hussein.

It was November 3rd, 2002. There was £15000 pounds in the account he had shared with Saladin, so money was not a problem. That was more than enough to set up a lucrative cash flow in west London. Colleague Pierre Golland had disappeared; the word in the boxing club was that Golland had been lifted by the Americans as part of their post 9/11 recovery programme. First a new name, legitimate work permit, maybe small business close to Heathrow as cover, and the real work could begin.

And while he was doing that, he had to find the Ploughman target that had been Saladin's and he could then work out the execution. There was no hurry…

*　　　*　　　*

Helen called Piers to come and see the television programme. The usual repeat season was showing of an antiques valuation programme, from the series 'The Collectables and Jewellery Show' made five years ago, in the grounds of an English stately home in Cambridgeshire. The television cameras were gathered around a male specialist interviewing a mature lady. She had just one item, apparently jewellery wrapped in tissue, to be valued for the programme. The expert was Tobias Grant, resplendent in showy London suit with lacy shirt cuffs displayed and wearing an out-of-place cravat, was well known to regular viewers.

Tobias was speaking, "And what do you have for us today?" He was pointing to the small tissue wrapped bundle. Piers guessed that this was

370

not the first time the expert had seen the ring although, of course, he was supposed to suggest that it was.

"Why don't you undo it?" offered Tobias, pointing at the tissue folds on the table.

Piers said, "He's fishing for clues…"

"Shsh! I saw this bit in a trailer. I think you are going to be very interested. I've set the video tape recorder going…"

On screen, the lady did as she was bid. "It's a ring," she offered knowledgably, "a bit ancient, really. I thought you might help me find out what it is — or rather who it might have belonged to."

"Yes, it's not got a hallmark to help us date it, but…" said Tobias turning the ring for the camera to see the embossed crest. "…I would say that it's gold. It weighs heavy and if I run a finger nail along this edge you can see that it's just soft enough to mark without removing any material."

"I thought it might have been a 15th century earl's ring, or something like that?"

"I think the camera ought to be able to see the crest," Tobias burbled obviously in reaction to the director's prompt. "But I don't recognise it. I don't think it was from a nobility or top-echelon chap. It could have been one of those rings which embossed a pattern in sealing wax for correspondence, rather like a stamp today."

The TV image cut away from the ring to the lady's face. She was obviously forcing a look of interest; Piers guessed that all she wanted was a valuation.

Tobias tried to sound persuasive and in control. "Perhaps it was used by a local big-wig, a mayor or sheriff. Tell me, how did you come by it? I am pretty sure it's quite old, late medieval — Henry Seven has the right flavour."

"I bought it at a car boot sale. An American family was going home from the local air base; they were selling off their bits and pieces at a Sunday market. She said something about there not being an understanding about yard sales in this country, not like Missouri, she said. I saw this ring and I thought my Bob would like it as a surprise Christmas present. Paid five pounds for it, but he did not like it, too heavy for him while he drove his truck. So it went into my jewellery box until I saw the notice about your show on the church notice board."

"That's very interesting," said the unimpressed expert. "Have you asked anyone… to value the ring — for insurance purposes?"

"Oh yes", came the reply.

"And what was the result?"

Piers interpreted Tobias's body language as considering the ring to be an insignificant item. His attitude changed abruptly when the woman spoke.

"Ten thousand at auction, maybe thirty thousand at a specialist international affair… with provenance."

"Dollars?"

"Pounds."

Tobias had dropped the ring, but fortunately it rolled towards its owner who deftly caught it. The camera managed to track the movement. A second camera cut to Tobias's surprised face.

"That's very interesting. Did he say what grounds he had for placing that value on the ring?"

"I told him what the American airman told me."

Tobias was now quite interested; he reached for the ring, but the lady was reluctant to let him have it. "Oh?" he queried.

She said, "Seems there was a guy with a metal detector, perhaps his dad, sweeping the area around of an American battlefield called North Point just outside Baltimore, Maryland. He found the ring which led someone else to come along and do a bit of digging where they unearthed the remains of a British marine."

Tobias, the specialist, interrupted. "Yes, that's right." A second expert had appeared on camera.

"After they burned Washington's White House, the British under Robert Ross sailed up to Baltimore intent on stopping the US Navy from interfering with our ships. Unfortunately, Ross got caught in teenage crossfire and died. So our Admiral Cockburn thought that enough was enough and withdrew."

The recently arrived expert calmly added, "So your American trader suggested the ring had been it the ground since 12 September 1814."

"That's right." The camera was now on the lady, "He said, that's the American airman said, the ground there seemed to favour polished bronze with a low tin content. I let him bang on because I could tell it were gold and he didn't know what he was talking about. You know what a car boot sale is like." Her face spoke volumes for her opinion of Tobias Grant.

"A British marine is unlikely to have been wearing a ring like this when going into battle."

" 's right. He weren't wearing it. It were in his pocket, or something, because they found it next to his thigh bone, or something or where his thigh bone would have been, but it weren't. My man what valued it said it was an English ring because it assayed that way and only the Spanish had got anywhere near the same type of gold and it weren't one of theirs."

The latest arrival asked, "Did your valuer put a date on the ring? That would greatly affect its value."

"Oh yeah! He said 1563 to'69. 'Couldn't be more precise', he said. 'Something to do with the shape of the horse's hoofs — in the crest,' he said. He said, this valuer, '…he thought it was probably made somewhere near the Guildhall in the City of London, perhaps one of the alleys near St Mary's Bothaw Church what got burned out in the Great Fire.' Said it had the looks like the work of Rupert Plant who made signet rings for the gentry. That's why I kept it, because we've got the same name…"

Tobias had rendered silent; only his colleague sustained his interest in the artefact.

"Mrs Plant… er… was your man able to identify the crest? Although the ring is in very good condition — buried gold usually is — the embossing on the upper surface is a little worn." The camera men had moved back from close-up; Ethel had not yet stood to leave the table, but her handbag was visibly closed.

"Well this valuer chap said he had done a university masters in 13th century churches along the Pilgrim's Way." Mrs Plant was fiddling with the clasp on her handbag. "He said there was a similar crest, not identical but close, in the floor of All Saints, Snodland by the River Medway. 'Very worn it was', he said and he suggested I contact the rector and make an appointment to see inside the church. They keep these old churches locked these days…"

Helen pressed the 'mute' button on the TV remote control.

"It's Snodland and Maryland again. The connection seems to be very strong. You don't think that this could be G. G. G. Grandfather

William's signet ring, out of Susannah's chest, do you? I wonder where Mrs Plant and her treasure trove are now?"

The programme's credits began to roll. The closing screen dwelled on:

© *1998 London & Cambridge TV*

Piers said, "Nearly five years ago… there's precious little chance of following up on that lead."

Chapter 51
2004 ~ Around the World in Eighty Stops

Wolfgang Schwanitz had changed his name. Johannes Black gave an explanation for his accent which would pass as Durban-based from South Africa even though his English was to native speaker level matching his Polish and German dialects. With time on his hands, a good public library giving unlimited access to the internet, it was only a matter of time before an electoral roll identified the P P Ploughman family residence. The same source gave confirmation of an RAF commission, a telephone number (number discontinued), a street map and estate agents's photographs of adjacent properties on their sales registers.

It was straightforward for Johannes Black to purchase his false identity, to obtain all the false papers including passport and driving licence, credit cards, car hire discount cards and the like, so that he could easily switch when Schwanitz had completed his task. Black became a popular member of the local self-defence club — how sensible to be aware of the threat if you intended to travel as a successful business man. He was even working up his credit score.

His new identity gave him access to temporary airport work on the airline reception desks. His company password unlocked the bookings for Mr and Mrs Ploughman on their pre-paid year long journey. As a bonus, staff membership also gave Black discounted single airline seats through to and within Australia, New Zealand and Fiji where, he explained, he would decide which route he would follow to return home.

*   *   *

"Well, what was the best bit?" Neither Piers nor Helen were watching the airliner's seatback TV on their final leg to UK.

"I would say… after a great deal of thought, mark you… that the best bit was…"

"The beach in Fiji? Or maybe my birthday party in West Australia?"

"If you've made up your mind, why are you asking me?" Piers was not being intentionally brusque, but it was very early in the morning on their body clocks, still operating at American East Coast Time.

"We've taken eleven months to go round the world. There must have been a best bit."

"That's woman's logic. It was all good, especially panning for gold in New Zealand… or digging up sapphires in Queensland… If you wait a minute, I'll tell you the best bit."

With a nod Piers offered, "Fossicking. Digging up precious stones in Australia is called fossicking."

"I know that. I know you enjoyed looking at ancient volcanic lava flows and walking in the lava flow tubes and the open air DIY breakfast after sleeping in a converted railway carriage with that 21 year old Swedish model doing her stretching exercises."

"Not when there were flies about. That place with the monastery …" His head shook with disgust.

"New Nocia nunnery."

"…monastery, called New Nocia, Spanish Benedictine; they had it right with their sign: 'a million flies can't be wrong'. I didn't enjoy that place. It sounded like *nausea* spelled the sick way; it would have been sufficient description for me. We didn't even see any ghosts; I felt somehow denied."

"Sydney Harbour?" Piers knew the answer before it was given.

"No. That's strictly for the birds. And neither Russell Crowe nor Nicole Kidman came out to give us a wave as we cruised by their homes; they might have made the effort! I liked the quiet places, the desert places, silence and stars you couldn't count there were so many." For the first time for ages, Helen moved her head to see Piers's face and to gauge the reaction to their exchange. He was more interested in the stewardess's legs approaching in the aisle.

But Helen was still remembering, "Even the quiet of the Rabbit Proof Fence was acceptable, despite the heat. The road train trailer lorry went by very quickly."

"And eating barbecue near Ayres Rock to the sound of a didgeridoo. Now that was great."

Memories of eleven months and one day were flooding back. They had been away from home continuously and were not too sure they wanted their holiday to end. Of course, there were the children; Philippa and Michael with Olivia and their grandson Quentin.

"It will be nice to get home, to see Quentin. He's nearly four now. Your name will live on — your Ploughman heritage is assured!"

"That's grandma speaking. It will be nice not to be wished 'have a nice day' even when it's raining. And to drive on the proper side of the road."

"They drive the same side as us in Australia and New Zealand."

"Sometimes! Fiji, too, when they bother about such detail."

"You shouldn't be so fussy." Philippa's stern remark put a pause in the conversation which was broken when the stewardess turned towards them with a tray of fruit juice in paper cups.

After a long pause, Helen said, "I'm glad you kept a diary." She had declined the fruit juice offer.

Piers did not know what to say so he said nothing... until, "I do know my most unfavourite bit. That was the baggage check at LAX while we were going through to Vancouver and missed our flight connection and nearly lost the hotel room."

"What was that all about, Piers? They seemed to want to know about your cameras." She turned her head to look at Piers leaving her shoulders firmly against the seat. "It was a good job there was no film in the still camera or we'd have lost our pictures. They had the contents of all four of our cases unpacked, dirty undies and all. And they didn't do the straps up properly so it all got spilled on the apron under the aircraft at Vancouver in the middle of the night. We lost a suitcase because..."

With a frown, Helen let her head settle again against the seat cushion.

"I must make an insurance claim about that. I think their sensor sniffed the sulphur from the New Zealand geysers and assumed it was gunpowder residue. Bloody idiots only had to look to see they were real cameras. I haven't fired a gun since I worked at High Wycombe."

"We'll know where we went because of your diary."

"I know where we went! Do you realise that last night was our eightieth stop in the whole trip and that's not counting the 32 days/nights in the motorcaravan in New Zealand."

"You don't sleep well on a new bed." To Piers this was patently obvious; to Helen it was one of the hazards of married life for which there was only one — disagreeable — cure. Don't travel...

"Yes. I don't. There's another one tonight, too. We have to look forward to another new bed at Michael's."

It had always been a matter of some concern to Piers that he was not always able to keep up with his wife's mental agility; 'grasshopper brain' he called it. So it was not really a surprise when she said, "Your diary will help you label all those photos on your computer."

"2010 at the last count."

"You must throw away the ones that are rubbish. There's no point in keeping them."

"I like the way you say that I have the chore of labelling the photos... not we!"

"Do you think they are safe? On the computer?"

"The photos are OK. I backed them up on CD. Eight CD to be precise." This time it was Piers's turn to look at Helen's face. She looked tired. The bustle of Washington Dulles Airport, preparing for the night flight was telling for, especially for, the seasoned traveller.

"It was good to see all the Blythe family in Australia. I didn't realise just how many nieces and nephews I've got." She smiled with the memory.

"I will get my old age pension this year. That will be useful." If she could jump subjects then why shouldn't he?

"The tax man will take his share. We must check our wills when we get home."

"Only two and half hours to Heathrow. Michael said he'd be there to meet us."

Helen switched back to heritage, "It was good to talk family history to those Ploughmans you found in the telephone directories. Wasn't it strange to be talking about Betty Ploughman in New Zealand? We first heard about her at the County Archives in Maidstone back in 1988 and she'd been out there to met the same folks. They weren't my best moments though. My best was my birthday party in the wine tasting place..."

"The vineyard..." suggested Piers helpfully.

"...with the family and friends. There you are... I've decided my best moment. Not the The Pinnacles, or the helicopter ride in Fiji, or visiting Albany, the train ride through the Canadian Rockies, nor meeting the Ploughmans in Maryland. No. Having my family and friends around me for a huge family picnic... Oz style."

"Yes."

"You can take me to do that again, if you like. We won't stay away for so long, next time.

"No."

"Well, give it a couple of years. Perhaps Philippa will find someone…"

"Yes."

"I am pleased we did it. But it's so good to be going home." Helen's hand had reached to settle on Piers's, on the seat's arm rest. They didn't need to look; actually Piers's eyes were closed. They were there for each other, just as they had been 45 years ago on their honeymoon flight, whatever the future might bring.

Chapter 52
2006 ~ Where Did Fifty Years Go?

Piers looked at his collectables in amazement. It was the space they occupied — every time the family changed house, the collectables had to be boxed, labelled, moved of course, safely stowed in a new location (cupboard, shelf, under the stairs) awaiting the next addition.

'We all do it,' Piers reflected, 'collect too much.' Now the children were making their own nests, he had a spare bedroom to call his own 'Study'. Even Helen knocked on the door or phoned him on the internal connection before venturing on to his hallowed carpet. 'For some it's sea-shells, some beer mats, others stamps, guns, flat irons, or cars, even women. I, too, collect: plastic, functional, ball point, pens. Ideally the collectable example will still write (not essential), be attractively designed (desirable), cost little or — better — be a free swap. Very occasionally, one gets liberated...'

Piers smiled. "Of course, I'm not averse to 'winning' a sample. Restaurants and banks were — still are for that matter — fair game; sleight of hand has become well practised. Worldwide! There was a certain frisson in the act — perhaps a little dishonest, but... it's advertising anyway!'

Turning half-a-dozen pens over in a desk drawer, he thought, 'Of course, any new pen should be different from the other 3500 in the collection. Duplicates are only of value for swaps. Yes, it's nice if they compliment a type; for example, souvenir or public relations styles generally follow genre patterns. Any logo should legible with the best examples being unblemished. Nationality or language is unimportant, size does not matter and it is immaterial if it is retractable or capped so long as the closing mechanism, if any, is available.

'It must be pocket friendly, ie it must not leak.'

Piers did not know of anyone who had a collection of pens to rival his. Quick searches of collectors' magazines on the newsstands had never given a clue and he was too mean to actually buy a specialist magazine off the stand. There seemed to be no-one in the world who shared his hobby.

'Everyone knows about pens, well at least the Biro[tm] ball point, the felt-tip and the fibre gel tip. These days, few, except the old fogies, use wet ink. I have to admit I like signing important letters, or condolence letters if I have to, in real ink; it makes them sort of 'proper'. Gone is Bob Cratchett scratching in real ink with a sharpened swan's qwill. Only calligraphers, practising their art, would use a nib. In this disposable age, if it stops writing — bin it. If the retractable spring malfunctions, bin it: lose the top, bin it. But if I see you binning it, I'll pick it up.'

Helen tolerated his hobby and sometimes even suggested a suitable, paid for, addition to his collection. He thanked her for her concern and usually followed through her suggestion. She didn't complain — one way or other.

Piers handled a few items of his collection. 'Going round the world was a fantastic opportunity. I came home with more then three hundred more for my collection.'

He leant back in his office chair and just admired the open boxes.

'There's pens and pens, some big ones, some small ones, some as big as your hand. There are coloured quill pens no swan would be seen dead in; there's ecologically protected forest log pens in wood and there's bank pens on chains. There's small capless pens at the lottery . There's a stationery pen from the office cupboard and there are charity pens through the post. There are resort souvenirs at five times the normal price for places you'll never visit again — that makes them doubly collectable in my book. And there are those pens with moving ships, falling lady's swimsuit, forest animals or coloured fish. There is delight in the surgery, or the chemist, seeing a medicine suppliers' attractive example.'

The small selection in Piers's desk was being stowed tidily until the number grew when it would be worthwhile unsealing the large transit box to add the latest items.

'It's global, making pens. The multinationals give them away promoting their products. Every major hotel bedroom has a logo embossed gratis pen. Smaller companies give a pen as an *aide-memoire*, incentive, or just plain gift. You've only got to Google[tm] the topic. No matter the language, *Remember me when my ink marks your paper.*'

One of Piers's pleasures was exchanging pens with reception counter staff. They didn't believe anyone would collect pens. "Can't give it away, sir ... Oh, does that one write? ... Well, alright, but don't tell the supervisor!" It was almost as good as using the receptionist's pen and forgetting to give it back. 'Not her Parker[tm], that would be theft. But, forgetting that I had absent-mindedly put a plastic trademarked cheap example in my pocket is fair game.'

Piers considered, as he pushed his desk drawer shut, that there were fewer pens about now. The opportunities for acquiring good examples were diminishing. Piers put it down to the bankers' cards with their chip and pin mentality; what with texting by phone, hole-in-the-wall, emailing, and such, the public has forgotten how to write. Witness a National Trust[tm] shop, the pen jar is tightly full. There was less call for a dispenser of jellified ink.

'Those 3500 loners, collected from around the world, will sit in their storage boxes, protected against direct heat (minimise runny ink), out of direct sunlight (lessen solar fading) and scratch-free in their uncirculated mint condition. The air hostess niece will bring some rarity from Peru or the Caribbean; a son will persuade an Estonian waitress in Denmark to part with her treasure. I'll just have to make do. I don't know what the world is coming to.'

He shrugged and heaved a sigh.

'They should be out where I can see them. But how? 3506 pens is quite a lot. I don't want to part with my hard won pension for something that's going to sit in a box, unloved, undisplayed, and passive. Just like the stamp collection sealed for the past 37 years, 125 matchbox collection unattended for ten years, 230 individual size packets of sugar in a tight box, the pen collection will continue to occupy shelf space until the great ink cartridge in the sky runs dry. By then, perhaps, I will be collecting printer cartridges! I'll have to give it some thought.'

He finished tidying his desk. It was a habit of fifty years.

'Is that all I have to leave the kids? A few old papers and a couple of pens? It hardly seems worthwhile, does it? So many questions! Gosh, I nearly forgot about the 4500 postcards, some dating to the 1890s... they must be worth a fortune... just sitting in a box in the garage. I think I'll start all over again... deciding on what I have to get rid of.'

The screensaver image on his desk top monitor caught his eye.

'But I think I'd still collect my Helen. Perhaps one day I'll remember to tell her...'

The telephone rang and Piers answered the call on his study handset.

"Hello, Piers. Long time, no speak. It's Graham Yates here. Have you got a moment for a chat for old times?

"Hey, Graham. Long time, no speak indeed. It's good to hear from you. Are you writing your memoirs and needing a few hints?"

"Not exactly, old man. Look, could we meet? There's something I'd like to talk about with you. It's not the *at home* sort of chat, you understand. Why don't you walk to the end of the road and we could take a drive… perhaps to a local pub? They say the King Billy does a good glass of real ale."

"Err… I'm not sure…"

"Say, in five minutes, old man. I'm just around the corner. It really is quite important. You'll know it's me. I've borrowed one of the office's blue Jaguars^{tm}. You won't need a hat, it's quite warm out."

An excuse about needing some envelopes, six elapsed minutes and a handshake later, Piers was being whisked along a country lane towards a local section of high speed dual carriageway. "I presume you will explain what this cloak and dagger stuff is about. I retired from all that stuff ages ago and…"

"You remember a nasty piece of work called Filfar? You seemed to want to rename him Chummy. His real name was Saladin Hussein who seemed anxious to prevent you drawing your pension."

"You resolved my remuneration package with 250 tons of steel hurtling through commuter belt at one hundred miles per hour."

Graham Yates frowned with quickest of glances at his passenger. "I suppose it was a bit of a blunt instrument, but effective in the circumstances. Anyway, Saladin Hussein had a brother, actually not a blood brother — more of a family brother in the Mafia style. You know: you hurt my brother and I'll take care of you and your wife and your kids and your…"

"I get the picture," said Piers. The traffic was slight, the ride very comfortable. "I assume this car has been swept for bugs?"

Graham Yates with a nod and another quick glance of reassurance to Piers, "Yes this car is clean to talk. Now it happens that the cousins in the CIA had an interest in Saladin Hussein and his brothers…"

"Brothers? There was more than one? They say while you are waiting for one, two more come along as well." The car was slowing for a roundabout.

"Quite. Two more brothers, actually. So while Saladin the Filfar was planning evil deeds in Stevenage, it happened that brother number one was being renditioned to an American holiday camp called Guantanamo, and brother number two was walking into a narcotics sting setup by our Special Branch on behalf of a European Arrest Warrant for Interpol."

The car went round the roundabout and began to travel back the way it had come. No other vehicle followed this manoeuvre. Piers now felt more comfortable in paying attention to Graham Yates's facial and body language while he spoke.

"What's all this got to do with me?"

"You'll not be too sad to learn that Chummy no 2 — that's brother number one — was bitten by a cerebral malaria mosquito — it doesn't matter where — and died of his wounds. Cremated, *finito*, absolute closure. But Chummy no 3 did his time, and took umbrage at the hurt done to his family, blaming all things British in general and a certain RAF officer targeted by Saladin Hussein in particular. I am reliably informed that, during his time while incarcerated, Chummy no 3 majored in the offensive use of hunting and most other varieties of knives."

"Did you say '*did his time*'? He's out? You didn't tell me? Holy Mother…"

"Calm down, old man. I've not finished yet. Now we couldn't let Chummy loose on the Ploughman family; we couldn't afford the bad press and Tony Blair might have been asked questions in Parliament. So we let you do your thing and we did ours and kept the cousins in the CIA informed. And when you decided to fly the world, we had a good exercise in interdepartmental cooperation and data exchange."

Now Yates seemed noticeably more relaxed as he was confident they were not being followed.

"Chummy no 3 knew what you were up to, world trip wise, because your mailbag kept on supplying brochures and tickets and receipts and other giveaways and much of it went into the recycle garbage bin in your road. He actually flew out to Perth and was in the vinery garden while you were celebrating Helen's birthday. So were we — at least some Australian heavy mob on our behalf — was there in case things got hot. But we in our offices, watching the ducks in a row on the Thames, were relaxed about everything. And you did your part in doing everything as though you didn't know that Chummy was biding his time. We knew that Chummy no 3 was waiting until you got to Fiji because, he'd worked out, the local police there would not give him the hassle that the Aussies or the Kiwis might — even to protect a Brit's hide. Very true, actually, because he could only get a transit visa in both those countries because of his criminal record to say nothing of travelling under an assumed name on a false passport."

The Jaguar^{tm} swept pass the turning back to Piers's village. Evidently this tale had some distance to run.

"To cap it all, a knife would be easier to get in Fiji so he did not need to carry a firearm through airport security checks."

"At the risk of repeating myself, what's all this got to do with me?"

"We'll turn at the next exit and run back to your village. Then I'll buy you that pint and you can get whatever it was you told Helen you were popping out for."

During the vehicle manoeuvre, the men remained quiet. Piers's thoughts were racing, trying to remember anything untoward on Fiji, but nothing came to mind. It had been so restful after 32 days in the motorcaravan in New Zealand. The Jaguar^{tm} settled again to dual carriageway driving and Yates resumed talking.

"We asked the NZ Secret Intelligence Service to look after you when you reached North Island — to make sure you got on the right plane for Fiji, that sort of thing. I am not surprised that the engineer in you dragged you to the Rotorua geothermal generation plant — not much there for Helen. When you've seen one boiling mud pool, you've seen them all. And those geysers do pong. They didn't christen it 'Hell's Gate' for nothing. Not a good place to go swimming; your brain would boil in about ten seconds and your complexion, well… We identified him by his prison dental records, but we didn't think we ought to own up to an interest to the local Kiwi constabulary; there wasn't much else left so the inquest declared the body unidentified and a John Doe was cremated"

"He just happened to fall into a geyser?"

"Piers, old man, accidents do happen. The cousins were quite impressed with the closure. So now Mr and Mrs Ploughman are off the hook… as they say. I'm sorry that your STASI record remains in their archive, but it won't have had anything added to it since April 1990. It would draw too much attention if we tried to extricate the file and, with your career, there must be many cross-references on other folders."

The Jaguar^{tm} slowed, cruised into the car park of the King William public house and the engine was switched off. Piers was lost for words.

Graham turned to look at his passenger, trying to draw a reaction from one who was sucking the inside of his cheeks. What could he possibly say?

Piers's head began to nod. "You know, I used to say that there were some experiences in my career that the Henlow Cadetship did not prepare me for: multiple handbagging for a start, cuddling a live hydrogen bomb for another. But that story gets fairly close to the top of the list. Now you owe me a beer for putting me through listening to it. No-one is going to believe me."

"Then don't tell it, old man. In the words of the sage, '*Silence is golden*'."

Chapter 53
2009 ~ Closures

"What are you going to do now it is finished?" Helen was leaning against his desk, looking at Piers with an elbow on his twenty sixth writing competition entry.

"Teach." Piers was a little concerned that his wife had interrupted his train of thought. This computer game was proving irksome. Solitaire was a good name…

"Darling man."

"And finish a piece I started writing for the Millennium Time Capsule."

"So it's goodbye from him and it's goodbye from her. You mailed the Millennium Capsule stuff eight years ago." Piers looked away from his screen. He still adored his wife although he rarely admitted it to her.

"Did I? You have such a remarkable memory, my dear. Not really goodbye more *auf wiedersehen*. You've got the Women's Institute and I've got the University of the Third Age Writers' Group. And we'll meet over your excellent pastry fruit pies. Eight years? Did I?"

"Oh. Flattery will get you everywhere. Yes you did; we wondered if it was a hoax. We never did find out how many had responded to the time capsule thing. I'm glad you like my pastry; you've been eating it for forty-eight years. I'll make some next time we buy some cooking apples."

Piers avoided looking loving. "Promises, promises." He continued, "The challenge is to remember what to do when I get there. The trouble is that the Women's Institute women always look surprised when I walk in — like something the cat brought in. And the writers' group complain that I use big words and put the commas in the wrong place. I remember mailing it to the capsule people — I've probably still got the Post Office receipt somewhere in my desk; it was oversize so had to go special delivery." Licking his lips with a smile, "Will they be double apple?"

"You'd better switch off the computer while I switch on the kettle. A cup of tea will do us both a world of good. I'll call you when the news is on the telly… We'll try to invite Philippa for lunch."

*   *   *

"Are you going to the reunion? It's the 50th anniversary of your being commissioned. There's bound to be a lot of your old fogies there."

"A whole load of them are dead, so they won't be there — it's the air force way! Reunions are funny; you remember the good times, and the dead ones, but never let on about anything that anyone wants to hear. A bit of scandal, that everyone knows, is repeated about those that haven't showed up. By one in the morning, you're half cut so you won't remember what it was that you promised faithfully to tell your wife. And when the whole show is over, you depart in gratitude that you don't have to put up with them until next year."

"I don't know why you bother."

"I don't know why I bother. I posted my form and cheque yesterday. At least with cheques you don't have to remember if you've paid."

"Only if you've remembered to fill in the stub, darling man." Helen picked up his empty tea mug off his desk.

"I've been meaning to speak with you about this 'darling man' thing you've latched on to. The trouble is… I can't remember what it was I wanted to say about it…"

"Well then, I shouldn't bother. You can tell me when you remember."

"Yes, I shall…" was wasted as Helen strolled out to the kitchen for another cup of tea.

*   *   *

"Well, did you enjoy it?"

"Yes, as a matter of fact I did. Especially the breakfast."

"Who was there? Is there any news? You went there for the dinner."

"Yes, there is news. I'll give you this list to read. We managed to account for all twenty four of us. I've indicated who we think didn't stay married. I wrote it before the waiters cleared for pudding… so I wouldn't forget. Of course, there were some who couldn't make it, too far away was their excuse. But, hey, I got all twenty four names; the only entry to survive without anyone being chopped — all through the hell of Henlow without one of us being kicked out. One or two got close…"

"A certain Technical Cadet Piers Ploughman?"

"Don't be so unkind, woman mine. Going out-of-bounds every Sunday to see you was my only choppable thing. I just didn't get caught. Others did much more heinous crimes."

"Such as?"

"Now that's for me to know and for you to guess. Torture won't make me talk! I'll show you last night's list; here… sorry about the gravy stain. Piers passed Helen last night's dinner menu with the entry register reasonably legibly inscribed:

Lionel Banks	*Shylock*	wings, made air commodore, ret 1994, there
Allen Davies	*Shark*	killed flying accident 1984
Robert Dewhurst	*Bunk*	wings, retired 1994, 2nd career 2000, absent
Bartlet Dunmow	*Nurse*	killed yachting accident Tasmania, 2001
Peter Fischer	*Simon*	Late wings, mainly training, ret 1993, there
Julius Henson	*Pimple*	at GCHQ to 1997, nothing since, absent
Ian J. King RAAF	*LMN*	known married 1982 in Australia, absent
Oliver Knight	*Ollie*	still Ivy, 4 kids, ret 2001 from AWRE, there
Basil Leitch	*U*	career in American film industry, there
Denise Mercer	*Aspirin*	Prague, divorced, ? Aus? FCO? absent
Richard Petts	*Rick*	ret 1994, SA with Pamela, hotelier, absent
Julius Shepherd	*Ba*	still with Ursula, career in intelligence, there
Martin Caine	*Abel*	ground comms, sqn ldr, ret 1994, absent
Osma Drake	*Imam*	divorced, Burma, nothing from 1973, absent
John Dawtry	*Ganglion*	changed branch to Navigator in 1964, absent
Paul Ellis	*Crab*	still sideways, accident investigation, there
Derek Hedley	*Uncle*	no news since 1978, unmarried, absent
Theo Kaggel	*Neutron*	died cancer 1994
Kirk Knight	*MacKay*	2nd wife, four children, there
Claudette Leigh	*Bumper*	ret ?1980, never married, Canada? absent
Joe MacLion	*Southpaw*	wings, still consultancy aero-engines, there
P P Ploughman	*Peetot*	there
B.P. Thackray	*Derv*	still with Aspen, ret from MOD 1994, there
Drew Wilde RAAF	*Fu*	Australian civil aviation, alive 2008, absent."

"You've never before showed me the list of nicknames." Helen was scanning the list unwillingly given by Piers. "Are you going to tell how they got them? Yours? *Peetot*? What does that mean?"

"I left the power on to a pitot tube heater and it burned out. *Peetot* is a corruption of pitot. An aeroplane needs a pitot tube to measure airspeed." The reluctance to admit a stupid mistake 52 years after the event was apparent in Piers's reply. He knew his wife would persist. The next few minutes could be hell unless he took control. Could he escape needing to explain the urinal altitude record… the pee... on that course visit?

"And *Asprin*?" Helen had jumped in the list, whew! "Denise Mercer was a lovely girl when we met at Benson. Shame she had to marry into the Army, though. *Asprin*?" Actually, Helen already knew the derivation, but it did no harm to her cause of pursuing the others.

"She wasn't there. Rumoured to plead a headache when asked…"

"You told me that there was no hanky-panky at Henlow."

"There wasn't… as far as I know. I'm pretty sure … there wasn't. Anyway, there wouldn't have been enough privacy to… It was a rumour… pills for a headache. And I don't recall her husband being Army; I thought he was a civilian linguist instructor at the RAF Language School…"

"And what about…?"

"Look, I've got to go to the supermarket for some petrol for the car." A deep breath might aid his escape. "We can talk about it later. I just thought you'd be interested." Piers was heading for the door.

"So, how many of you showed up, then?" She was getting close to placing a restraining hand on his arm while Piers was gradually withdrawing.

"Well, counting me: nine plus me makes ten of us were there; three are known dead, two Aussies and Denise Mercer in Australia and *Bumper* Leigh in Canada plus seven not known make a grand total of twenty four."

"Why *Bumper* Leigh?"

"You'd know if you saw her. No," waving his hands quickly across his chest and then to suppress more questions, "I'm off to get petrol before it closes."

"But it's Satur…" Piers had already escaped more questions, at least for the time being.

*   *   *

"Piers, darling man."

Piers sensed that what was coming could be difficult, or expensive, or both.

"Yes, my dear. I did find the Christmas card list on the computer. I printed a copy for you to correct."

"That's not what I wanted to talk to you about. Do you think I should talk to Philippa about the clock?"

"She wears a watch, my dear. And I expect she can hear Big Ben from where she works. And we gave her a clock radio for her bedside table the Christmas before last. And her cellphone has the time…"

"I don't mean a time clock. I mean her biological clock. I mean, she was born in 1974…"

"I remember. You were there at the time." Helen shook her head in frustration.

"Tcch. I'm serious. She's getting on and it's much more difficult if you are older than if you are young." Piers was sensitive to his wife's anxiety; she was rolling her fingertips in her lap. This had all the portents of being women's business.

"I have the same problem with a certain…"

"If she's going to have a family, she ought to be seeing a man — on a regular basis — to get…"

"Sorted out? It's more general than the air force way."

"There's no need to be disgusting. I mean, we left it rather late… well I was her age when I had her… and it wasn't easy…"

"She was a bit unexpected — after all that fuss about Michael. The Turkish Army and the British Military Hospital might share some of the troubles you had."

"A mother has certain wishes for her daughter."

"Your daughter has her head screwed on. She is a successful career civil servant, whatever it is she does, and I know she's comfortably off, financially. OK, she does travel a lot and we sometimes worry about her because we don't hear anything for weeks. But then she pops out of the woodwork expecting apple pie and custard just as though she'd just come home from school."

"I am talking… trying to discuss… babies. She ought to be having babies before it's too late."

"It's no good talking to me about that sort of thing. That's women's business. Perhaps she can't have babies."

"She'd have said something… to me… about it."

"Well, I don't suppose she'd have said anything to me about it. She knows I'm squeamish about all that stuff. I mean, I can't watch the nature programmes on TV without coming over faint. I don't know how snakes manage…"

"I think I need a day's shopping, in town, with her. I'll let her buy me lunch and then I'll talk to her."

"You must be very careful, Helen. I mean, she might leap off Waterloo Bridge, or worse, marry an ex-colonial. Oh no, God forbid she marries an Australian! Worse… an Aus soldier! Your daughter is a clever and resourceful woman. I wish we knew a little more about what she does. She's been doing it for nigh on eight years and we still don't know. I hope she'll tell us when she's ready."

"She did say something about a chap she met in her office, Graham Yates I think she called him, who wanted to pass on his regards to you. He wasn't one of your lot at Henlow, was he?"

To be continued

Now you have enjoyed the story of *Piers's Cadetship*, you will wish to learn what happened next to the Ploughman and Plowman *Warranted Land* families of Maryland and of the Medway valley of Kent.

The following sample chapter of the *Warranted Land Saga* is taken from the saga's seventh novel *Philippa's Licence* due to be published in 2014. The novel primarily concerns the only daughter of the Piers and Helen Ploughman of the *Piers's Cadetship* novel. She enters a police career to exploit her Spanish and Farsi language skills. With the Cold War is now assigned to history, the world faces the emergence of extreme terrorism as a political weapon. Searching out the control and disposal of narcotics derived funds, measured on a scale of billions of US dollars annually, has become a significant concern to the British Government and its American ally. Such is the danger to world peace, Philippa's intelligence licence removes her from her chosen career to a much more specialised aspect of national security which will eventually take her across the globe. Is there an association between narcotics and the quest for an Islamic nuclear weapon?

See http://www.warrantedland.co.uk for further information on publication details.

Sample Chapter of *Philippa's Licence*

Chapter 1
2001 ~ 'Subject to Satisfactory Medical…'

The letter, a quite thick brown paper package, arrived by courier. It contained a short and to the point letter, the details being confined to attachments:

Secretary to the Minister   *Telephone: 0101 298 0000*
Chancellery House
High Holborn
London   WC1V 9ZZ

4/Licence.43   *30ᵗʰ January, 2001*

Madam,

1.   I am directed by the First Lord of the Treasury's office to inform you have been selected for me to offer you a post in the First Lord of the Treasury's Office at the equivalent to Civil Service General Service Grade 8. The appointment has been accepted for the 'Fast Stream' posts scheme and, subject to satisfactory performance assessment, you may expect to be promoted to Senior Civil Servant grade 7 level after 12 months' service. The full conditions of service, remuneration scale, allowances and pension entitlement is summarised in the enclosed leaflet.
2.   Subject to satisfying appropriate medical checks at a clinic of our choice (in Harley Street, London) and your confirmation of willingness to undergo certain training described in the attached memorandum, this letter includes the offer commencement of service on 1ˢᵗ March, 2001.
3.   If you wish to accept this offer, please return a signed and dated copy acknowledging receipt of this offer. I enclose an envelope and second copy of this letter for the purpose. Please also enclose a short letter of acceptance and state your agreement to undertake the training described. Our reply letter will advise you of the date for your medical appointment. Your initial place of reporting to your new appointment will be notified by couriered correspondence in due course.
5.   If you do wish not to accept this opportunity, please write a short letter advising me of your rejection of this offer.
I have the honour to remain,
     Yours truly

Arthur N. O. Nonsuch

*   *   *

The door off High Holborn was unremarkable. Three steps up off the pavement, escape from London's busy road network and into a reception hall where, along a ribbon of marble tiles, she was guided to where sat a uniformed reception clerk within a glass panelled cubicle. Philippa had elected to wear her two piece 'London suit' as a confidence booster. Now, she really did not know what to expect of an office which chose not to declare its existence at the entrance.

Along the echoing featureless hall, a nervous Philippa approached the forbidding official who looked disinterested at the arrival as he placed his daily *The Sun* newspaper on the counter. 'Is this really a government office? It looks so rundown.'

"Yes, Miss? Can I help you?"

The latest letter had given Philippa a time to arrive, the address of course, and the essential identification documentation required — her passport and the offer letter. But it still had given her no indication of what her duties might entail — some extension of her former police duties perhaps? In here? Using her linguistic skills?'

The clerk looked at a list withdrawn from under his counter. From what little Philippa could see there were few visitors planned, at least on this daily sheet.

"Yes, Miss. I see you are expected. Could I see your ID, Miss? It's just routine. Would you please fill in the visitors' pass? You'll need it until they give you one of your own. Miss Brown will be down to escort you... we wouldn't want you getting lost in here, Miss. I'll telephone her..."

Opening her passport at the photo page, the clerk turned away from Philippa, as if his conversation was private and must not be overheard by this newcomer. But all seemed to be in order. 'Good thing too,' thought Philippa, 'the CCTV camera over the reception desk would have recorded the situation if it wasn't.'

Now once again looking at Philippa, "Yes, miss. Miss Brown is coming down directly, miss. I'll just stamp your visitor's pass... make it official like..." For a moment nothing happened except that Philippa had a chance to look along the entrance passage she had just crossed; yes, there high on the wall clear of the sunlight was another CCTV camera imaging all who entered off the street. Surely there was a better wall colour than 'burned earth' brown for a reception?

Miss Brown appeared out of a far from silent lift. She was wearing a dress that looked as if it had been recycled from a Red Cross shop during WWII. Her shoulders were wrapped in a woollen cardigan with her arms outside the sleeves. The fingers of her right hand were nicotine stained and when she spoke it was with a rasp. She did not offer a handshake.

'And I wore my best suit...'

"Have you got your pass, Miss Ploughman? Good. Could I see your passport? Just a formality."

Miss Brown inspected every page, all 16 pages, including the micro-chipped back page, compared the photograph and handed it back to Philippa. "That's fine, come along; we'll ride the lift. Did you bring your letter of offer? Did you enjoy your visit to southern Cyprus?"

"Northern Cyrus, actually. Just along from Kyrenia... on the panhandle."

"Quite."

The lift had clearly seen better days. It wheezed its way directly to the top floor. Philippa wondered who occupied the other four floors, but she would wait to find out. In the confines of the lift, Philippa could smell the nicotine on her escort's clothes. When the lift doors opened, there was another uniformed reception clerk within a glass panelled cubicle. Philippa noticed that his glass seemed thicker; the aperture to visitors was much smaller and that all the doors leading away from the cubicle were metal faced and closed.

Miss Brown spoke. "This is Miss Ploughman, James. She's coming to join us."

"Right Miss Brown. Miss Ploughman you say. I'll just check my list..."

A list was recovered from some hidden crevice, a detailed examination of the single entry of this copy, and, "Could I see your ID and your pass, miss?"

Miss Brown stood by, impatiently, as the whole exanimation process was repeated.

"And your letter of offer, miss?"

Philippa extracted the tightly folded letter from a jacket packet. James seemed satisfied that all was in order. Then he asked an unexpected question.

"How does you spells your second given name, miss?" Sniff. It was so unexpected and Philippa did not recall ever having been asked to supply it after the initial application forms to join the Civil Service. "Just for my records, miss."

A momentary pause then Philippa responded, "P E T R A, pronounced Petra."

"Yes miss. 's unusual name, like. Right Miss Brown. Miss Ploughman is all yours. I have been instructed to instruct you as to that Miss Ploughman here, is to be escorted into the office of the deputy director forthwith. 'ere, Miss Ploughman, you leave your door pass 'ere along with your 'andbag if you was carryin' one, which you weren't, and you collected it, your pass, on your way out otherwise you won't get out, like. You wears this clip pass while you're inside, like. You can have your letter back. Like." Sniff.

"Thank you, James. I'll take Miss Ploughman to see the DD."

A buzzer sounded, a metal door slipped off its catch and Miss Philippa Ploughman took her first steps into the weird world of counter-counter espionage otherwise known as MI-4.

"What was that rubbish about Cyprus?"

"A simple check, Miss Ploughman. You'll get used to it."

"And my middle name?"

"We've got to make sure we've got the right man… or in your case… woman… err… you know. We take identity issues rather seriously in here."

End of sample chapter

Author's Notes
Historical Footnotes
Royal Air Force Technical College, Henlow, Bedfordshire.
Extract from the Air Estimates, 1956–57 delivered by Secretary of State for Air (Mr. Nigel Birch):

There was a time when it was possible to hope that with advancing science some things might become simpler, and that hope has not been altogether in vain. But, considering all developments as a whole, things are getting more complicated all the time — for instance, bombsights for bombing from great heights or in cloud and darkness, new navigational devices, new airborne interception devices, and, most recently, the most difficult problem of the lot, the problem of the guided missile.

The most obvious consequence of this increase in complexity is the need for very highly trained technical officers. A number of things have been done in respect of it. The first is the Technical Cadet Scheme, open to young men with the General Certificate of Education at the advanced level in physics and pure and applied mathematics. Those cadets start by spending a year at the Royal Air Force Technical College at Henlow. Then the scheme splits into two, some of the cadets remain at Henlow and receive permanent commissions at the end of their course while others go on to a university as officers.

The first group of cadets to complete their three-year course at Henlow finished last year, and the results are extremely satisfactory. Nearly all of them obtained the Higher National Diploma in engineering. Officers training through the universities are still reading for their degrees. There are fifty-one officers at the universities, thirty-six of them at Cambridge, reading for the mechanical sciences tripos, and others at Oxford, Bristol, Glasgow, London and Southampton.

In addition to the technical cadet scheme, a number of serving officers take post-graduate training as technical officers. In particular, there is a post-graduate course in guided weapons which has been running for

some time. A number of officers who have been through this course are now serving in the research and development branches of the Ministry of Supply.

Hansard 5 March 1956 → Commons Sitting → SUPPLY

Signals Officers. As used by the RAF, 'Signals' as a term spanned different disciplines at different times. At the end of WWII, it comprised radio communications (air and ground), radio aids to navigation, radio as an airborne bombing or interception aid, airborne and ground radars (both those used for weapons' aiming, fighter control and for air traffic management with their processing computers), beacons and telemetry, communications and electronic intelligence, electronic warfare (both active and passive), management of cryptographic material, plus teleprinter, telegraph and telephone services including facsimile, both by landline or radio. Latterly, it extended into information technology and data services together with remote control, unintentional radiation (Tempest), communications using satellites and fibre optics. This list is not exhaustive. It spanned both the operation of these services, both in the air and on the ground, and the maintenance of the equipment used. In some circumstances it included the design and installation of this equipment, including the assembly of aerial masts and antennae.

RAF Technical College, RAF Henlow — Historical Overview

01 Apr 1924	The Officers' Engineering School moved from Farnborough.
01 Jun 1936	Under the Expansion Scheme, No. 1 Wing trained Fitters 1 and machine tool operators, and No. 2 and No. 3 Wings trained Flight Riggers and Flight Mechanics. New accommodation at RAF Henlow was built.
01 Apr 1938	The training roles had superseded the original repair functions. In anticipation of the war, two thirds of the Training Wing moved to RAF St Athan, and No. 2 Mobilisation Pool was formed with a view to returning to the repair role.
01 Dec 1938	The increase in vehicles required to operate the additional country services by Birch Brothers Bus Company meant that a further depot was needed and this was opened in London Road, Henlow Camp, near the RAF base.

01 Dec 1938	RAF Henlow, Bedfordshire became School of Aeronautical Engineering.
01 Apr 1939	No 1 Wing moved to RAF Halton adjacent to RAF aeronautical apprentice training.
31 Mar 1940	Decision announced to form the RAF's Technical Branch from the former (commissioned) General Duties branch specialists in Engineer, Signals and Armament disciplines and, in future, from airmen commissioned for technical duties.
15 Aug 47	The School of Aeronautical Engineering became The RAF Technical College Henlow
01 Apr 1949	The Empire Radio School at RAF Debden became the Signals Division of the RAF Technical College, but did not move to Henlow until April 60.
02 Feb 1951	The Armament Division of the RAF Technical College moved to Henlow from RAF Lindholme in February, and was renamed Engineering and Armament Division.
01 Apr 1951	The RAF Technical College offered courses in guided missile technology.
01 Oct 1952	The first Technical Cadet entry admitted to the RAF Technical College.
01 Jun 1953	The RAF Technical College Henlow raised to Group status consisting of a HQ plus 5 wings: Basic Studies, Mechanical Engineering, Electrical Weapons Systems, Engineering, and Cadet Wing.
02 Oct 1956	No 5 Technical Cadet (Henlow) entry began to assemble in Cadet Wing. All male, two RNZAF cadets joined the nine terms, thirty three months course. All twenty four cadets of the entry academically graduated and were commissioned on 30 July 1959. Twelve cadets undertook a nominal 120 hours basic flying training, at Henlow airfield, in Chipmunk aircraft.
08 Apr 1960	The RAF Technical College Signals Division moved from RAF Debden to Henlow.
01 Jan 1962	The Shefford to Hitchin railway was closed completely in the post-Beeching cuts.
31 Dec 1965	The RAF Technical College merged into the RAF College Cranwell. Relocation of the RAF Technical College from RAF Henlow to the RAF College was completed on 3 January 1966.

01 Jan 1966	RAF Technical College, Henlow closed and became Engineering Wing, RAFC Cranwell.
10 Jan 1966	Non-cadetship training for direct entry graduates or airmen being commissioned from airmen service at the RAF Officer Cadet Training Unit moved to RAF Henlow from RAF Feltwell.
01 Apr 1967	RAF Technical Officers were renamed as RAF Engineering Officers.
14 Oct 1968	The Birch Bros Bus depot at Henlow Camp closed.

RAF Station Broadcasting. Post WWII, a popular hobby, particularly on the bigger airfields, both in UK and overseas, was the RAF stations' own broadcasting networks usually dependent on Rediffusion^{tm} technology of landline distribution. A notable exception to wired systems was at RAF Gan, Maldive Islands on the Equator where the service was broadcast by radio and the signal acted as a navigation beacon for incoming aircraft up to 200 miles away. Other wireless stations existed but none with so powerful a transmitter as RAF Gan. Funding, volunteer staffing, audience support all governed how big the station became. Much more local than the London-based British Forces Broadcasting Service, Changi Broadcasting Service (CBS) was without doubt one of the biggest of its type. Being set up to broadcast commercial advertising, often with professionally produced audio tapes, and using some broadcast quality BBC transcription long playing gramophone disks, the station was self sufficient, employing a local civilian to manage the output between 0800 and 17:00 daily and volunteers at other times. It broadcast on two channels throughout 24 hours everyday, often relaying the BBC World Service which was sometimes difficult to receive on private radios in Singapore due to atmospheric interference. CBS had a music record library exceeding 10,000 titles plus, on disc, BBC programme transcriptions of their major popular comedy series, thrillers and serials totalling another 1000 discs. The CBS 'Wives Club' programmes on Monday to Friday mornings were always popular. There were two air-conditioned, sound-proofed studios which comfort, no doubt, added to the attraction of the facility for the station's unpaid production staff.

James Hall III and Huseyin Yildirim. James W. Hall, III, was an US Army warrant officer and intelligence analyst in Germany who sold eavesdropping and code secrets to East Germany and the Soviet Union from 1983 to 1988. On 20 July 1989, Hall was convicted of espionage, fined $50,000, given a dishonourable discharge and a 40-year sentence at Fort Leavenworth, Kansas. The case against Hall began with a tip from a CIA source who defected from the East German Government. Hall sometimes spent up to two hours of his workday reproducing classified documents to provide to the Soviets and East Germans. Between 1982 to 1985, Hall was assigned to the US Army Field Station Berlin, Teufelsberg on a site shared with the RAF No 26 Signals Unit, making it one of the premier listening posts of the Cold War, and he spied for both East Germany and the Soviet Union. Hall betrayed hundreds of military secrets, including a worldwide electronic network with the ability to pinpoint armoured vehicles, missiles and aircraft by recording their signal emissions during wartime.

After his arrest, on 21 December 1988, Hall's activities were assessed to have inflicted grave damage to US signals intelligence and he is considered the 'perpetrator of one of the most costly and damaging breaches of security of the long Cold War'.

The FBI also arrested Huseyin Yildirim, a Turk, who served as a conduit between Hall and East German intelligence officers. Hall had received over $100,000 in payments.

Jeffrey Carney. A second spy with interfaces to RAF No 26 Signals Unit was a former US Air Force intelligence specialist convicted of spying for East German State Security. Enlisting in 1980, from April 1982 to April 1984 Jeffrey Carney was assigned to the 6912th Electronic Security Group, Electronic Security Command at Tempelhof Central Airport in Berlin as a linguist and intelligence specialist, with his duty station at the 6912th ESG Marienfelde Field Site. The 6912th ESG worked for the National Security Agency and eavesdropped on communications of Eastern Bloc countries. In the mid-1980s, Carney defected from the USAF and travelled to East Berlin via the East German embassy in Mexico City, Rio de Janeiro, Havana and Prague. There he continued to work for the East German State Security by intercepting and translating non-secure telephone communications of US military commanders and the East German telephone lines dedicated to the US embassy in East Berlin. In April 1991, Carney was apprehended, returned to the USA to plead guilty to charges of espionage, conspiracy and desertion and was sentenced, before an empty courtroom in December 1991, to 38 years in prison.

Fictional Footnotes
Closure on the original 24 cadets of 1956 Technical Cadets (Henlow)?

Real name	Nick Name	Career ex Cadet
Lionel Banks	*Shylock*	Nothing known from 1994 onwards when he was thought to be in servicing development.
Martin Caine	*Abel*	Career retired from RAF in 1994, thought to be in technical communications.
Allen Davies	*Shark*	Killed in flying accident 1984.
John Dawtry	*Ganglion*	Changed RAF branch to permanent flying duties in transport fleet. Last news 1964.
Robert Dewhurst	*Bunk*	Career in Operational Requirements and Flight Safety. Last news 2000.
Osma Drake	*Imam*	Married, two children, left RAF before mid-career break, rumoured to have settled in Burma (Myamar). Last news 1973.
Bartlet Dunmow	*Nurse*	Married, killed in yachting accident off Tasmania in 2001.
Paul Ellis	*Crab*	Aircraft serving until 1983, then air accident investigation and into civilian career.
Peter Fischer	*Simon*	Career in training. Retired in 1993, tutoring at Cambridge.
Derek Hedley	*Uncle*	Development work then intelligence duties in UK and exchange posts in USA.
Julius Henson	*Pimple*	Ground communication, employed by GCHQ until 1997. Nothing heard since.
Theo Kaggel	*Neutron*	Died 1994 victim of prostrate cancer.
Kirk Knight	*MacKay*	Married with four children. Second career in business software
Ian J. King	*LMN*	Australian, known to be married in 1982.
Oliver Knight	*Ollie*	Armament, retired into Atomic Energy Authority from which retired 2001.

Claudette Leigh	*Bumper*	Never married. Retired from RAF approximately 1980 for job in Canada.
Basil Leitch	*U*	Career in the film industry.
Joe MacLion	*Southpaw*	Maintenance policy on aero engines. Settled in Derbyshire.
Denise Mercer	*Asprin*	After Prague 1979, rumoured to have emigrated then returned to UK in FCO. Seen in London in 2007
Richard Petts	*Rick*	Specialised in maritime surveillance aircraft development, retired to South Africa 1994.
Piers Peter Ploughman	*PeeTot*	Settled to authorship. Engineering consultancy. Still married to Helen in 2009. Two married children.
Julius Shepherd	*Ba*	Career in intelligence. Rumoured to be burser at a girls' college. No contact since 2003
B.P. Thackray	*Derv*	Retired from MOD in 1994 after career in flying training and flight safety.
Drew Wilde	*Fu*	Australia, eventual career in civil aviation, known to be alive 2008.

On New Year's Eve, 1999 Piers Ploughman realised there really should be a record of way life was like at the turn of the millennium. With an opportunity to safeguard the material in a safe environment, Piers settled to construct his letter for the future:

	Begun on	December 31st, 1999
And	Finished on	February 18th, 2001

Dear Descendant
Millennium Time Capsule — to be opened in year 2201

Were we a happy family? The truth is not always, but we were more fortunate than most. We lacked nothing that anyone of our generation would have considered really important, we had enough money to do what we wanted, when we wanted, subject to the limits imposed by a military life. Married life sapped the energy and opportunity for our childhood sport, although I continued to sprint (100 metres in 11.0 seconds) and play rugby football (Captain of the station 2nd XV) until 1965. We bought our first new car (a pale blue Sunbeam Alpine two-seat convertible) in May 1964 and this was the first and only time we drove at 100 miles per hour (150 kph). We were happiest while away on holiday, just relaxing and doing what we liked best which was looking around stately homes. We ate well and fortunately Helen was an excellent cook (me noticeably less so!). I adopted the ideal of wanting to leave my mark on the world — to leave it a better place for my having been here — possibly inherited from my maternal grandfather who built private and public buildings in the Medway towns of Kent between 1900 and 1930. I contributed to the peace of the country and there are military facilities which will survive to your time most notable the underground headquarters at Naphill High Wycombe and at St Mawgan Cornwall. Helen became increasingly involved in church parish life and leaves a legacy of an enlarged church in the parish. I am still working at the age of nearly 63 years in part to keep the brain active although a period at home following redundancy made me feel that I was invading her space in our home. The high points, at least for me, were that delicious blend of happiness and excitement:

- Holding father's hand as we chased the waves on Birchington beach in 1944.
- My first solo glider flight, from RAF Hornchurch, Essex airfield in April 1953.
- Winning Hampton Grammar school representative swimming colours in 1954.
- My first real kiss, New Year's Day 1955 with Helen Blythe later to be my wife.
- My first solo powered flight in a Chipmunk from RAF Henlow in 1957.
- The commissioning parade then Officers' Mess Ball, on 30 July 1959.
- An open car ride in Wales's mountains Lake Vyrnwy, in snow, in Feb 1960.

- A solo night navigation flight (1 hour) over Shropshire in April 1960.
- Our wedding at All Saints Parish Church, Hampton, Middx on 10 June 1961.
- The first day — a Sunday — of our honeymoon in Dublin, Eire.
- Our first new car (after 4 second hand ones) at Thetford, Norfolk in May 1964.
- My first par 3 golf hole at Mount Fraser, Malaya in 1967.
- Helen's first pregnancy (we knew for 3 days), then recovery in March 1968.
- Oxfordshire social services letter that Michael was available June 1970.
- Shopping for Michael in Aylesbury in just one day in June 1970.
- Collecting Michael from foster carers in South Stoke, Oxfordshire in June 1970.
- Queuing for, then buying our first new house at Sendmarsh in August 1972.
- Learning that Helen was pregnant with Philippa in November 1973.
- Philippa's birth in British Military Hospital, Dhekelia, Cyprus on 20 July 1974.
- Homemade wine from Oxfordshire hedgerows at Xmas 1981.
- The tri-service Christmas party after support to Falklands Isles War Dec 1982.
- Promotion and posting to command a Signals Unit, Berlin in January 1983.
- Summer holiday in northern Germany on way home from Berlin in July 1985.
- Running experiential specialist courses for young RAF officers 1988.
- Recruitment lunch in St Martins Lane for civilian job in London in Feb 1991.
- Initiating through to occupation in May 1995 the buried facility at St Mawgan.
- Buying our 3rd home (not new) in Buckinghamshire in June 1991.
- Collecting my Open University BSc degree diploma in Birmingham in May 1993.

- Driving my 2nd (new) company car from Harlow Essex to home in Aug 1996.
- Holiday in Perth, West Australia with Helen's niece October 1997.
- Reaching North Cape, Norway for midnight on Midsummer Night 1999.
- Michael's wedding in Sweden in June 1999.
- Completing this Millennium Time Capsule in February 2001.

When you open this Time Capsule, dear descendant, you will be sharing the time capsule experience with many others who have chosen to participate in the Millennium Time Capsule project. At the time of writing 200 years ago, the concept has proved to be popular both for businesses and individuals. Therefore, Helen and I have tried to choose items to include in the capsule which are either unique to the Ploughman family or are unlikely to have been stored by others since they have little intrinsic value. The Family Tree is there, as are the recorded voices of some of the family. I have put in the device on which the voice were recorded and which would play back the tapes if you can find the correct electric power source — as a guide I have packed some example chemical batteries which I hope survive.

Technology change and particularly video data storage has proved to be problem in how to handle this timecapsule project. The rate of change in electronics is too fast to keep up with, and I have my doubts that any of the video tapes that are stored in this or any other capsule will be readable. Nevertheless, I have decided to store a copy of the tape which records our family visit, in the summer of 1999, to Norway and Michael's wedding in Sweden. At the end of the tape there is a trip around our house. If some museum or archive somewhere has a playback device or (better) a conversion to whatever you do with video images in your era, you may find it interesting if rather long at 3 hours play time. The mechanical wristwatch with original purchase receipt contrasts nicely with the digital mechanisms widely used from the mid-1980s.

The Highway Code as a book is self explanatory when you get inside the seal in which it was purchased. The illustrations show far better than I could describe what travelling on the road was like in the year 2000. (I wonder if you still use surface transport.) There are some bright coins minted in the year 2000 — you may not use coins in the year 2201. It would be interesting to know if global warming did happen and what resulted. And what about the global population predicted to peak at 7300 million in 2050, then to decline?

Last, but not least, there is a solar powered calculator. This is included because it shows the state of the electronic art in the year 2000; it should work in normal room lighting. But also it represents the first portable computer available to my generation. Calculating devices (with negligible electronic memory) first became available in the early 1960s. The age of popular computing had arrived. They added, subtracted, multiplied and divided and that was all. They need batteries bigger than the keyboard. Although 40 years on, this device is certainly not the smallest of its genre it is quite representative. Now every child learns how to use a calculator at an early age and carries one into every exam he or she takes.

A final point, we wonder if any or all these millennium predictions really came about:

- Global temperature rise by 1.5^0 to 5.0^0C with sea level rise of 10 to 20 metres.
- Human colony on the Moon and Mars.
- Human landing on Titan — a moon of planet Saturn.
- Implanted communications chip with powerful processors of information.
- Method of diverting a comet or asteroid from Earth impact.
- Human genetic engineering for intelligence and personality characteristics.
- Tele-transportation.
- Abandoning the Monarchy in the United Kingdom.
- The creation of the United States of Europe.
- Worldwide peace with equality of opportunity, tolerance and consumption.

- Identifying extra-terrestrial life within the Solar System or out in the stars.
- Defeat of gravity as a limiting force to our freedom to move about.
- Replacement energy source away from hydro-carbon based sources — oil, etc.

We hope you find both pleasure and interest in the contents of the box and that you may be able to share this enjoyment of our joint heritage with other members of the Ploughman family (dare we say dynasty?) however scattered it has become.

Good fortune to you all, we wish we could be there to see your reaction as you read this. Perhaps, just perhaps, in a supernatural way we may be, but somehow I doubt it. (Hold your right hand at shoulder height, palm away from your face; if you feel a tingle in your arm it could me.) To prove we are real people I have attached a couple of recent photographs.

Spare us a thought sometimes,
Yours sincerely and with love that passes through the ages,

Piers Peter Ploughman   Helen Blythe
(born 5 November 1937)   (born 12 February 1937)
Son of Arthur & Marjorie Ploughman   Daughter of Leslie C & Annie Blythe

Footnote:
This letter was prepared in February 2001 on a personal desktop computer, IBM-PC compatible, having 32 Mbyte RAM, 2.1 Gbyte rotating disc backing store, operating at 166 MHZ on 586 (Pentium II) processor — considered to be state-of-the-art technology when purchased in April 1997 for £1100. The attached printer was a Hewlett Packard 1150c inkjet colour model. The software used was WordPerfect version 6.1 with the letter's stored file size being 173 Kbytes plus 850 Kbytes for the logo graphic bit map plus another 3500 Kbytes for the images.

About the Author - J N Cleeve

This page introduces J N Cleeve, the creator of the fictional Ploughman family, whose story is told in the *Warranted Land* saga's novels.

J N Cleeve served a full career in the Royal Air Force, graduating from officer cadetship at the RAF Technical College in July 1959, as a ground engineering officer, eventually specialising in electronic communications. This was followed in related defence consultancy until, taking a holiday in Virginia and Maryland, he asked the question, "Why did those colonists come here?" There proved to be no single or simple answer. So were born the first six novels in the *Warranted Land* saga.

Author carrying a RAF Technical College crest adopted by the Minerva Society

Having a 40 year interest in family genealogy in southern England, and specifically Kent, the germ of a research study was sown. From that seed sprang an idea about the rationale for emigration to the Americas, its cause and effect, loyalty and love, the consequences for the families separated by the Atlantic Ocean. How would the two independent nations work together when having to face a common foe? For the 21st century family historian, how do you confirm a link between an emigrant and the stay behind? For the last eleven years, the archives of England, around the Chesapeake Bay and Australia have disclosed hidden stories — related ideas spanning centuries and oceans. Six sequential novels, essentially fiction inspired by historical events, sought, but did not get a 21st century closure.

By design, a common thread of family runs through all the novels; it matters not in which order they are published or read. Just as in real life family history study, heritage explanations are discovered disclosing why something happened, or why a character acted the way he or she did. The saga is a voyage of discovery — you will want to know more... Beyond this sixth novel, *Piers's Cadetship*, the UK Ploughman generations sustained in Chatham... and the daughter of the family, Philippa, looks to be set on a trail of intrigue and adventure.

Piers's Cadetship has to be a work of fiction, governed by the need, even now, to protect our secrets and the honourable personnel involved. Here I repeat only what has already slipped into the public domain no matter how obscurely or in what medium. An author's dictat is to write about what he knows. There really was a programme of RAF Technical Cadets, for 13 years all male, at Henlow followed by fewer years at Cranwell and elsewhere. All who graduated entered challenging careers as engineering officers. The Minerva Society was formed by former technical cadets. This author completed a ten academic terms technical cadetship in December 1959, and went on to serve his last 17 years as a signals officer. But, this is not an autobiography — it is much more an assembly of inspired disconnected real events spun together by a web of calculated misstatement. It is historical fiction. None of the fictional characters, which includes all named cadets, are real or representative of any living or dead person. Historical events have been observed, but some liberty has been taken with both geography and time in the interests of literary pace.

"Throughout my construction of the *Warranted Land* saga, I have found it enthralling to write about how close history came, so often, to being nudged along completely different tracks. I have not reinvented history, even if I have taken a few liberties with the fictitious cadets and imaginary officers, and with certain geographical settings, to keep the plot moving. The players in my tale interface with actual characters who did their bit for what they thought was right.

I hope you have enjoyed reading the *Warranted Land* saga. To all those readers who have let me know how much they wanted more of the evolving saga, I pass my thanks for your support. I am fairly sure that Piers's daughter, Philippa, by entering that unprepossessing government building described in the sample chapter of her tale to be told in *Philippa's Licence*, has sought a rewarding career change and, in this dangerous world, there will be some opposing forces keen to make her life difficult. For just a moment, though, it is time to put down my metaphorical quill and relax.

Why the pseudonym? When I started this saga in 2002, I lived in a village called Bishops Cleeve, in a cottage called Juniper. J N Cleeve stuck and I saw no reason to change it."

J N Cleeve
29 March 2013

The *Warranted Land* saga tells of the proud heritage sustaining the family and its continuity, through 3 previous and 13 subsequent generations, in England, America, the East Indies and on the high seas. The full saga has evolved into seven novels, each designed to be free-standing. Any novel in the saga could be read individually, or the whole sequence could be taken in any order, although there is a chronological structure to the seven titles:

Warranted Land	broadly 1605 to 1662
Bernard's Law	broadly 1662 to 1730
Rosetta's Rocks	broadly 1752 to 1799
Ada's Troth	broadly 1770 to 1840
Makepiece's Mission	broadly 1943 to 1997
Piers's Cadetship	broadly 1938 to 2009
Philippa's Licence	broadly 1974 to 2015.

A prequel to the saga is a possibility, again to be written as a free-standing novel which might be read out of sequence. The novel has the working title:

Susannah's Petticoat   broadly 1550 to 1615.

The significance of the title, and hence the garment, will be familiar to those who have read *Warranted Land* (1605 to 1662). In a manner of speaking, indeed as Makepiece Ploughman described it during a visit to the Maidstone archive, it was 'how the whole caboodle began'. Of course, there is a tale to be told about how the scarlet garment became Susannah's... and how her husband William Ploughman's signet ring came to be placed in an elm casket...

Piers's Cadetship